FELIFAX

FELIFAX

by
Paul Féval *fils*

translated, annotated and introduced by
Brian Stableford

A Black Coat Press Book

Acknowledgements: We are indebted to Marc Madouraud, and to David McDonnell for proofreading the typescript.

English adaptation, introduction and afterword Copyright © 2007 by Brian Stableford.
Cover illustration and illustration p. 328 Copyright © 2007 by Hank Mayo.

Visit our website at www.blackcoatpress.com

ISBN 978-1-932983-88-3. First Printing. March 2007. Published by Black Coat Press, an imprint of Hollywood Comics.com, LLC, P.O. Box 17270, Encino, CA 91416. All rights reserved.
Printed in the United States of America.

Introduction

In the latter part of the 19th century, there was a boom in new English-language periodicals that extended the reach of popular fiction to a further maximum. In England, the boom lasted for little more than a decade, but in the USA, it continued for a further 30 years. Such booms were not unprecedented; similar phenomena tend to follow the advent of near-universal functional literacy in any country, and France had attained that goal some time before Britain and America. In France, a vast proliferation of *feuilleton* fiction had taken place between the 1840s and the 1870s, setting many precedents that were followed by British and American writers in their turn.

To some extent, the French *feuilletonistes* suffered the fate of all pioneers, in that the foundations they provided were overlaid by more successful work done by other hands. French writers invented both popular adventure fiction and popular crime fiction, and put in all the early developmental labor on both fledgling genres, but it was later arrivals on the scene who took them to their extremes of extravagance and elegance. It was in Britain and America that the most influential archetypes of both genres were created.

These archetypes included two of most significant literary hero-myths of all time. In the 1890s, the British invention of Sherlock Holmes provided the detective story sub-genre of crime fiction with its key exemplar, and in the 1910s, the American invention of Tarzan provided a paradigm for a uniquely extreme sub-genre of adventure fiction. These two characters formed a sort of complementary pair, Sherlock Holmes being the embodiment of the modern intellectual virtues, while Tarzan was the very model of physical cultivation; one was the brain of his era, the other the brawn.

Both these characters had significant precedents in French popular fiction of the 19th century. The first significant fictitious professional detective, Gregory Temple of Scotland Yard, was featured in Paul Féval's *Jean Diable* (1862).[1] Féval's then-secretary, Emile Gaboriau–who presumably acted as an *amanuensis* when *Jean Diable* was dictated and who later collaborated with his employer on a pioneering crime fiction periodical of the same title–went on to establish the key conventions of the *roman policier* shortly thereafter by creating the character of Sûreté detective Monsieur Lecoq.

French crime fiction, however, always had a tendency to focus on criminals rather than detectives: Féval's most successful series chronicled the exploits of a sinister criminal conspiracy known as the *Habits Noirs* (1863-75).[2] Féval's chief rival as a Second Empire *feuilletoniste*, Pierre-Alexis Ponson du Terrail, chronicled the adventures of the heroic outlaw Rocambole.[3] The tradition was continued into the 20th century by the likes of Maurice Leblanc's Arsène Lupin and Marcel Allain and Pierre Souvestre's Fantomâs.[4]

Despite the fact that Edgar Allan Poe–who provided a conspicuous precedent for detective fiction in his three short stories featuring C. Auguste Dupin–was more successful in France than in his native America, 19th-century French writers were sparing in their use of amateur detectives–Henry Cauvain's Maximillien Heller (1871) being a remarkable exception–and made no attempt to refine or further exaggerate Poe's model. It was, therefore, left to Arthur Conan Doyle to take up where Poe had left off, in crafting Sherlock Holmes as a free-lance "consulting detective" who can work with the police but is free of their routine obligations. Holmes' reputation became awesome even on the continent, where he spawned various grudgingly respectful imitations, including Gaston Leroux's Rouletabille. Leblanc took care to have Arsène Lupin come out on top when he pitted his anti-hero against the borrowed detective, but not everyone was convinced.

A similar pattern is evident in the development of generic adventure fiction, although that had much more ancient

---

[1] (See Notes p. 335)

historical roots, extending back to the origins of literary endeavor. Adventure fiction had been adapted to the format of the novel from its inception, most successfully by Daniel Defoe's *Adventures of Robinson Crusoe*–another work that was more influential in France than in its homeland–and had been adopted into French fiction long before the first leading lights of *feuilleton* fiction, Alexandre Dumas and Eugène Sue, began to draw upon it and adapt it to their particular medium. French fiction already had philosophical groundwork prepared for the development of the exotic sub-genre of adventure fiction that was ultimately to produce Tarzan, because the idea of the "noble savage" as a human ideal had been widely popularized in the wake of Jean-Jacques Rousseau's diatribes regarding the stultifying effects of civilization.

The first significant *roman feuilleton* in which a human becomes a king of the jungle and ruler of an animal empire, Léon Gozlan's *Les émotions de Polydore Marasquin or trois mois dans le royaume des singes* (1856; variously tr. as *The Emotions of Polydore Marasquin, A Man Among the Monkeys* and *Monkey Island*), is a satirical Robinsonade in which the castaway achieves his temporary dominion by deceit after adapting the skin of a giant gorilla as a costume. It was, however, lavishly illustrated, and its illustrators included Gustave Doré, then at the beginning of his illustrious career. It was probably this circumstance that attracted the attention of another ambitious illustrator, Albert Robida, whose first venture into serial fiction was *Voyages très extraordinaires de Saturnin Farandoul dans les 5 ou 6 parties du monde et dans tous les pays connus et même inconnus de M. Jules Verne* [*The Very Extraordinary Voyages of Saturnin Farandoul in the World's five or six Continents, and in all the Countries known–and even unknown–to Monsieur Jules Verne*] (1879).

Robida's episodic novel was a humorous homage to Jules Verne's status as the most popular and most progressive contemporary French writer of adventure fiction. The first element of the story sequence, "*Le roi des singes*," [5] explains how Saturnin Farandoul's upbringing by a family of monkeys, after being cast away as an infant, transformed him into a man of exceptional vigor and strength, as well as innate nobility of character–a free spirit of a blithely Rousseauesque variety.

Further partial anticipations of the character of Tarzan in French serial fiction included Jules Lermina's *To Ho le tueur d'or* [*To Ho the Gold-Killer*] (1905), which made the significant move of attempting to treat the notion more earnestly, but again, it was left to an English-language writer to produce the definitive noble savage in the infant castaway John Clayton, heir to the title of Lord Greystoke, whose education by apes equips him with the new identity of Tarzan. It was not just Edgar Rice Burroughs' ability to treat this essentially preposterous notion in a determinedly earnest manner that gave his version the edge but his blunt denial of certain notions that Robida had taken for granted.

Because Saturnin Farandoul lacked a prehensile tail, he could never be more than a mediocre monkey, although the other skills he developed helped to make him a more successful human being; Tarzan, by contrast, overcomes his apparent physical limitations to become a champion ape as well as overcoming his educational shortcomings to become a superior human being. Farandoul exiles himself from his monkey-ruled island when he comes of age, and never entertains the notion of going back, even before he discovers human civilization; Tarzan, on the other hand, always returns to his impossibly-hospitable jungle after his various excursions to civilization, and can never be happy anywhere else. In Burroughs' work, the power of daydream wish-fulfillment invariably triumphs over the reality principle.

Given that Doyle and Burroughs both built partly on French foundations, it is not surprising that several 20th-century French writers felt perfectly entitled to borrow the archetypes of the great detective and the noble savage, and to make every attempt to recast their own avatars in a distinctively Gallic mould. There is a certain propriety in the fact that one of those borrowers was Paul Féval *fils*, the son of the creator of Gregory Temple. There is also a certain propriety in the fact that the younger Féval took on the eccentric, and perhaps impossible, task of trying to bring the two archetypes together, in a novel that would bring a clone of Sherlock Holmes into confrontation with a clone of Tarzan, in the hope of generating a peculiar literary synergy. That novel was *Félifax*, which was first published in book form in two volumes in 1929-30, although it might have appeared as a magazine serial first.

Paul Augustin Jean Nicolas Féval was born on January 25, 1860. He was the third of eight children and the eldest son of Paul Henri Corentin Féval, who was then 42 years old and at the height of his success. The elder Féval had published his most successful work, the historical swashbuckler *Le Bossu* [*The Hunchback*], in 1857, and went from strength to strength thereafter, becoming a *Chevalier de la Légion d'Honneur* in 1865, the same year in which he was elected president of the *Société des Gens de Lettres*. In 1868, he was commissioned to write the section on the novel for a *Rapport sur le progrès de lettres* [*Report on the Progress of Literature*] commissioned by the French Ministry of Education.

Five years later, in 1873, the elder Féval's streak of good fortune began to peter out. He was a candidate for the *Académie Française* in that year, considering himself the key representative of what he had long tried ardently to promote as the *métier de l'homme de lettres*–which is to say, the trade or profession of writing. Alas, the Academy was not yet ready to recognize the respectability of literature practiced as a trade rather than a vocation, and Féval's candidature drew a hostile response. He diplomatically withdrew in favor of the popular playwright, Alexandre Dumas *fils*. Paul Féval *fils* was 13 at that time, and must have been keenly aware of his father's disappointment. Much worse was to follow, though; in the last months of 1875 and the early months of 1876, the elder Féval lost his fortune gambling on the Bourse and plunged the family into bankruptcy.

The elder Féval reacted to this disaster by recommitting himself to the ideals of the Catholic faith, loudly repenting all the sins for which God might have been punishing him. We can only speculate as to what effect all this had on his teenage son, but it must have been profound, and it certainly blighted what had previously been exceedingly bright prospects of a handsome inheritance. The elder Féval still had his literary capital to draw on, and almost managed to recover his solvency, but he suffered a second financial disaster in 1882 when the official in charge of his funds absconded with them—a blow compounded by a paralyzing stroke, which prevented him from writing anything more.

Paul Féval *fils*, who had come of age by then, had no alternative but to earn his own living—which he set out to do just as his father had done, in *le métier de l'homme de lettres*. He eventually became a writer of such thoroughgoing tradesmanship that he became a conspicuous example of the literary hack: a casual mass-producer of what would eventually become known as "pulp fiction."

Félifax, published in 1929, was written near the end of the younger Féval's career, when he was in his late 60s; it was by no means his last book, because he continued publishing until his death and left several more volumes behind for posthumous publication. The Baudinière edition includes a list of previous works that features 64 novels, although several of those were multi-volume works that might be reckoned as series; his eventual total was in the region of 80 novels, plus two volumes of poetry, one of short fiction, several plays and a volume of dramatic monologues; he also wrote unpublished scripts for the fledgling movie industry.

The Baudinière list is annotated with the observation that the four-volume *D'Artagnan contre Cyrano de Bergerac* [*D'Artaganan versus Cyrano de Bergerac*] written in collaboration with M. Lassez (1925; tr. into English as *The Mysterious Cavalier, Martyr to the Queen, The Secret of the Bastille* and *The Heir of Buckingham*) had sold 300,000 copies by 1930. Its sequel, the three-volume *D'Artagnan et Cyrano ré-*

10

concilié [*D'Artagnan and Cyrano Reconciled*] (1928; tr. into English as *Comrades at Arms* and *Salute to Cyrano*), had sold 100,000. Baudinière's estimates of sales figures were, however, limited to books he had published, and it seems likely that some of Féval *fils'* earlier works had achieved sales figures of similar or greater magnitude, and that his most popular books continued to expand their sales considerably for some years after 1930.

Féval *fils* first began publishing in book form in 1890, when a collection of his *Nouvelles* appeared alongside two novels, *La trombe de fer* [*The Rain of Iron*] and *Le dernier Laird* [*The Last Laird*]. In *Le livre jaune* [*The Yellow Book*] (1891), he attempted to combine melodrama with thematic elements borrowed from the Decadent Movement. *Maria-Lauria*, published the same year, also attempted to respond to contemporary fashions, but with equally modest success. He never stopped trying to do distinctive and original work, but he had little success in establishing a literary career that extended much further than the blurred edges of his father's shadow.

Féval *fils'* commercial breakthrough came with an epic account of the adventures of *Le fils de Lagardère* [*The Son of Lagardère*], written in collaboration with Albert d'Orsay and published in 1893. Lagardère is the hero of *Le Bossu*, and Féval *fils* went on to add several more novels to the expanding series on which he was now collaborating with his late parent. *Les jumeaux de Nevers* [*The Nevers Twins*], also written with d'Orsay, followed in 1895 and both *Les chevauchées de Lagardère* [*Lagardère's Rides*] and *Cocardasse et Passepoil* in 1909, while *Mariquita* (1923), *Mademoiselle de Largardère* (1929) and *La petite-fille du Bossu* [*The Hunchback's Granddaughter*] (1931) were added towards the end of his career and *La jeunesse du Bossu* [*The Hunchback's Childhood*] (1934) was added posthumously. His father had successfully adapted *Le Bossu* for the stage, and the younger Féval had his biggest hit in that medium with a five-act dramatization of *Le fils de Lagardère*.

11

Féval *fils* followed up his most explicit early attempt to walk in his father's footsteps with various other emulatory moves. His early work for the stage included an adaptation of his father's *Le loup blanc* [*The White Wolf*]. Like his father, he dabbled in eccentric supernatural fiction in *Histoire d'outre-tombe* [*Story of the Afterlife*] (1903-04). *Les bandits de Londres* [*The Bandits of London*] (1905) was clearly modeled on, although it was not an explicit sequel to, his father's *Les mystères de Londres*.[6] Although he wrote several *romans de cape et d'épée* of his own—most notably *Mam'zelle Flamberge* (1911)—his derivative works sold far better.

It must have seemed a natural expansion of this activity to begin plundering other *feuilletonistes*, and the younger Féval was by no means the first writer to produce a sequel to Alexandre Dumas' most famous work, *Les trois mousquetaires* (1844; tr. as *The Three Musketeers*). He published *Le fils de d'Artagnan* in 1914, some years before bringing Dumas' hero together with Cyrano de Bergerac—whose personality had been extravagantly celebrated in Edmond Rostand's play of 1897. Féval *fils* also wrote a further sequel to Dumas' novel in *La vieillesse d'Athos* [*Athos' Old Age*] (1930). The actual d'Artagnan was presumably acquainted with the actual Cyrano de Bergerac, as both men had fought at the siege of Arras in 1640, but the younger Féval's literary versions of the two heroes, and his fanciful account of their changing relationship, owed far more to the exemplars provided by Dumas and Rostand than to history. His posthumous works included a further two volumes detailing *Les exploits de Cyrano* [*Cyrano's Exploits*].

All of the younger Féval's accounts of the further adventures of Lagardère, d'Artagnan and Cyrano, and their various hypothetical offspring, are still easy to obtain in French reprint editions, but almost all of his other works—including *Félifax*—are hard to find. The younger Féval thus became his father's literary heir in more ways than one, similarly becoming a prodigiously prolific writer whose work was mostly doomed to be utterly forgotten. This oblivion, while not entirely undeserved, has served to bury some interesting works.

Féval *fils* never gave up trying to apply his skills to work of a more immediately fashionable nature, and his pursuit of new fictional trends led him to produce a five-volume sequence of short novels hybridizing occult fiction with science fiction, *Les mystères de demain* [*The Mysteries of Tomorrow*] in collaboration with "H.-J. Magog" (Henri-Georges Jeanne) in 1922-23. *Félifax* was a further exercise in much the same vein, attempting a similar hybridization of related but not-entirely-compatible genres, with a science-fictional element.

The younger Féval not only made conspicuous efforts to draw further dividends from the elder Féval's literary capital, but did so by mimicking his father's literary method. As a prolific writer of newspaper serials, the elder Féval had had little alternative to making his plots up as he went along, and his son also became a very obvious make-it-up-as-you-go writer. The elder writer had been forced by the pressure circumstance to write very quickly, probably being one of the first writers to develop the habit of dictating his work rather than actually writing it. It is not clear whether the younger Féval also dictated his work, but he certainly produced it in a tearing hurry, and was not in the least inclined to revise his first thoughts.

The inevitable result of this method of production is a tendency for plots to wander, often straying so far from the original plan that their endings are not at all what their beginnings seemed to imply, and the continual insertion into the stories of improvisations designed to excuse errors and follies committed in haste. In his earlier works, the younger Féval was usually capable of keeping his plots more-or-less on course, and his improvisations were executed with a reasonable degree of craftsmanship. He was never as inventive or fluent as his father, and rarely attained the remarkable pitch of melodramatic intensity that was the elder Féval's chief stock-in-trade, but he was a thoroughly competent craftsman for the greater part of his career. By the time he was in his '60s, however, he had become noticeably less careful in such matters; *Félifax* makes little effort to hold steady in its narrative direction, and its improvisations pile up in a markedly awkward fashion.

Although these tendencies are certainly faults, they do not rob the novel of its interest. There is a sense in which they serve to illuminate and expose the fundamental contradictions of the exercise, questioning the clichés of popular pulp fiction by presenting them as a kind of crazy collage. The fact that the elder Féval is still worth reading is largely due to the bizarre comic element built into his works by his inability to take the clichés he was deploying entirely seriously; Féval *père* was the first writer to demonstrate that there was a good deal of narrative energy to be drawn from the chimerical juxtaposition of the comic and the melodramatic. His son was less expert in that strategy, too, but could not help but use it when he got carried away, as he did in the latter half of *Félifax*, which takes on a high-pitched note of bizarre black comedy.

Unlike the vast majority of Tarzan-clones, the younger Féval's noble savage is not a feral child but the result of a biological experiment. This element of the plot is particularly interesting, because it forges a thematic link with the comic book superheroes who emerged in a medium spun off from American pulp fiction. Although he is very obviously second-hand in his capacity as a blurred carbon copy of Tarzan, Felifax (I shall use the version of the name used in my translation from here on) is brand new as a significant anticipation of the Incredible Hulk.

Felifax differs from other Tarzan-clones raised by big cats, such as the heroes of Otis Adelbert Kline's *Tam, Son of the Tiger* (1931), C. T. Stoneham's *The Lion's Way* (1931) and F. A. M. Webster's *Lord of the Leopards* (1935)–all of whom he predates–in that his tiger-like qualities are physical stigmata. whose emergence when he is aroused threaten to undermine the controlling influence of his innate nobility. His most significant precursor in this regard was the anti-heroine of Edward Heron-Allen's calculatedly-pornographic *The Cheetah Girl* (1923), but that story was privately printed in a very small edition and it is highly unlikely that Féval *fils* knew of its existence. (Had he done so he would have disapproved of it wholeheartedly.)

Félifax starts with the apparent intention of being a conventional melodrama, reproducing the straight-faced tone that had made *Tarzan* so successful in spite of his blatant absurdity. By the time Part Two begins, however, the author has no alternative but to dabble in macabre comedy as his improvisations become increasingly desperate, thus moving his action-sequences into the strange hinterlands of comedy melodrama. There they take on a quality of naïve surrealism that was eventually to become a significant element of the artistry of the comic book medium, and *Félifax* resembles many pulp novels in being an obvious precursor of comic book fiction.

There is a certain propriety in this, in that the elder Paul Féval had invented certain key devices of comic book melodrama long before they would be required–most notably the secret identity motif–and his son had been dutifully carrying them forward for 30 years before penning *Félifax*. Had he not died in 1933, the younger Féval would doubtless have been fascinated to observe the evolution of the comic book medium, especially in its French *bande dessinée* form.

I shall leave extrapolation of some issues relating to the novel's narrative method to an afterword, where their discussion will not be handicapped by the need to protect the reader's experience of *Félifax* by not giving away too much of the plot in advance, but there are a few more observations that might to be made here in defense of the book's eccentric merits. There is admittedly a sense in which *Félifax* is a bad book, replete with the characteristic awkwardness of pulp fiction–but there is a sense, too, in which it acquires a certain charm by means of its extreme pulpiness. Although it is primarily of historical interest as a peculiar addition to the prolific subgenre of Tarzan-clone fiction, it is also remarkable for the sheer stubbornness with which the author soldiers on having long ago exposed the errors of his own assumptions and the folly of his initial prospectus.

Most of the anachronisms featured in the story are probably accidental, but that does not prevent them being consumed with wry pleasure by readers familiar with the calculated anachronisms of steampunk fiction. The absurdity of the names and nicknames given to many the English characters, on the other hand, is almost certainly deliberate. Féval *fils'* understanding of English usage is unsteady, to say the least, but he knows perfectly well what the words mean and what effect they will have when used as names. There is an inevitable spirit of spiteful caricature in his representation of all things English, whose particular grotesquerie has a distinctively piquant flavor. It is, of course, designed to appeal to French prejudices regarding the English rather than to the English themselves, but there is no reason why English-speaking readers should not savor it too, even in England.

Félifax is replete with echoes of the elder Paul Féval's work, many of which will be obvious to readers familiar with my other Black Coat Press translations. It also echoes more widespread fascinations of 19th-century French fiction, especially its peculiarly reverent attitude to "the Orient." The Benares in whose vicinity the first part of the story is set bears far more resemblance to the magical and symbolic Benares invoked in Jean Lorrain's classic analysis of splenetic desperation, *Monsieur de Phocas* (1900), than to the historical city that became the modern Varanasi. In the same ways, Féval *fils'* depiction of Indian religion–whose blissful unawareness of the distinctions and tensions between Hinduism, Sikhism and Islam are bound to seem odd to a modern reader– is a fantastic construct reflecting blurred 19th-century ideas of the exoticism of the Orient. Such imagery was just as obsolete in 1929-30 as the pseudo-biological ideas on which the account of Felifax's origin are based, but it is typical of the stubbornness with which the misconceptions of popular fiction of that period outlasted their use-by dates, and provides modern readers with an insight into the vast strides that such fiction made in the latter part of the 20th century.

If all this makes the text sound more like a specimen for detached consideration than an exciting reader experience, so be it–that may well be the best way to read it nowadays–but for all its faults, the story is certainly not dull. It moves in bizarre ways, but it does move.

Although I was able to work from the Baudinière edition of *Londres en folie*, the second volume of the novel, I was only able to obtain a 1964 Arthème Fayard paperback reprint of the first volume, *L'homme-tigre*. The latter economized drastically on the number of pages; although I do not think that the main text has been abridged, the Fayard edition has no chapter titles, and might well have omitted them to save space. I resisted the temptation to make up my own chapter titles in order to conserve the symmetry of the two parts.

The translation posed a few other problems, most notably with reference to Féval *fils*' use of words that are not French. His Indian terms can usually be straightforwardly substituted with similar terms that are to be found in English, while the rest are explained–where possible–in footnotes, but his use of English is a different matter. I have left many of his English interpolations untouched, and mostly unidentified, but I have felt free to modify some to make them more plausible; I have included footnotes to explain the changes I have made whenever such changes were more than minimal.

I left most of the names as they are in the original, including many of those that are implausible in he extreme, but I did change "Mecfull" to "Macfull" and I took the liberty of giving the Police Commissioner a Christian name. Féval *fils* persistently refers to him as "Sir Nimbly", just as he often refers to his hero as "Sir Palmer," but English cannot tolerate that usage; it was easy enough in the latter instance to substitute "Sir Eric"–which is mostly what I did–but I had to invent a Christian name in order to make similar adjustments in Nimbly's case. Nothing else has been added or left out, although my choice of substitute terms and phrases is sometimes a trifle adventurous, in the interests of helping the story read better in English.

Brian Stableford

FELIFAX

3.5

L'HOMM
TIGR

par

PAUL
FÉVAL fils

Part One: The Tiger-Man

I

"So my father isn't here, John?"

"No, Miss Grace. The doctor was called away by telephone. He should be back soon, although he's already been gone for two hours. The matter must be important, that's for sure."

The young woman gave a slight shrug of the shoulders, signifying her annoyance at the thought that her father, summoned by the Metropolitan Police, might miss the little party she had organized that day in honor of her birthday and her return from France.

Grace Palmer had, in fact, turned 18 that very morning. If her delicate and divinely pretty face gave scant evidence of that age, her robust, supple and well-proportioned figure, practiced in many sports, was suggestive of three years more. She had come home after spending two years in France, studying at medical school–an opportunity opened up for her by her father's name.

Sir Eric Palmer had a worldwide reputation, not only because his abilities as a doctor had advertised themselves in marvelous cures, but because numerous complicated police cases owed their elucidation to him. Much like Doctor Watson, the friend of the great Sherlock Holmes, he had begun by collaborating with two or three notable detectives. Then, his own methods being in flagrant contradiction to those of the police, he had undertaken to interest himself personally, working alone on several mysterious cases in which he had succeeded where others had failed.

Thanks to the light cast by this profound psychologist and savant, the most surprising results had been obtained. Doctor Palmer had solved the so-called Mystery of the Tower of London, the Theft of the Royal Necklace, the Assault on the Bank of England, the Case of the Hyde Park Strangler and many others. He was held in great esteem at Scotland Yard. Nevertheless, as he did not draw a salary from the Metropolitan Police and did not wish to do any disservice to professional detectives, he was only called upon when situations became desperate. Tall, and of Herculean build, he fixed his square jaw in a purposeful manner–a fine specimen of the Anglo-Saxon type. When his steely blue eyes searched the inmost depths of the most hardened criminal, the latter, unable to resist, usually ended up yielding to that persuasive and implacable force.

However, despite his proven passion for the solution of mysteries, Sir Eric often manifested a desire for retreat. Barely 50 years old, he was already dreaming of a little house in a forgotten corner of Cornwall. He harbored a nostalgic desire to retire with his beloved collections, forgetting all about crimes and criminals. He would take care of his garden, fish, and–above all–devote himself to the happiness of his daughter, his dear little Grace. It could not be long before she got married and had adorable children, which he would take care to fashion in his own honest and loyal image. From time to time, his older son, a lieutenant in the Bengal Lancers, would come to stay with him for a few months, then return to the colony where he intended to build a career.

The doctor had confided his intention to several of his friends. In a letter that was already written, he had even announced his decision to the Metropolitan Police, although that letter was still in his drawer when the telephone call from Scotland Yard summoned him urgently, with news of a sensational affair. He had forgotten his retirement plans immediately. Less than a quarter of an hour afterwards, he was seated in a large armchair listening attentively to Sir Harold Nimbly, the Police Commissioner.

The honorable functionary read him some singular cablegrams from the Indian government. They called attention to disconcerting and mysterious events in Benares, the holy city of Bengal. The local police declared themselves utterly incapable of getting to the bottom of them and asked, with all possible urgency, for the assistance of the Metropolitan Police. The question must have been exceedingly interesting because, two hours later, Doctor Palmer was still sitting in the same armchair, listening attentively to his interlocutor–who was giving him elaborate instruction on the subjects of Indian religion and fanaticism.

In point of fact, Nimbly's words were unnecessary, for the obliging detective had no need of this information. Having spent many years in the country in question, he had more confidence in his own personal observations–but Palmer's custom was to avoid contradicting people, and although he said very little he was thinking hard.

Grace had invited a few friends to lunch to celebrate her birthday. She had been out all morning, as usual, and was now, with John's aid, setting the table where the most uninhibited gaiety would soon reign. The slamming of the house door informed her that her father had returned. His worried expression immediately informed her that he had something serious on his mind. She accompanied him into his office, leaning affectionately on his arm. There she charged the doctor's favorite pipe and held it out to him, along with a match.

To her great surprise, the distinguished voluntary colleague of the Home Office refused the pipe and the match. Then, sitting his daughter down on his knee, he said with a certain sadness: "My dear Grace, you'll have to leave this evening to go stay with your Aunt Molly in Plymouth. I have to undertake an important mission abroad, and I'll be taking John with me."

The young woman started slightly. Putting her arms around her father's neck and her head on his shoulder, she adopted a coaxing tone. "This business must be very important," she suggested, "if my dear father has already forgotten the conversation he had with his dear daughter yesterday evening." When the doctor made no reply, she added, with a delightful pout: "Doctor Palmer decided to sever his ties with all lawyers, coroners, sheriffs and so on, to forget the way to Scotland Yard forever, and to take the train to Cornwall with his dear Grace!"

"That was indeed my plan, my dear child," he said. "I have here, in this drawer, a letter to the Metropolitan Police, telling them of my decision to..."

"To remain at their disposal permanently! Oh, Dad, your decision not to get involved in further police matters is somewhat reminiscent of a drunkard's promises, which are incapable of holding up in confrontation with a glass of vintage wine or a pint of regal stout."

"My dear Grace, it's a matter that is so very extraordinary..."

"I'm not blaming you, Papa. On the contrary—I only want to you remember the promise you made yesterday evening not to leave me again."

"But..."

"There is no but! Doctor Palmer is as good as his word. If you're leaving, I'm leaving."

"That's impossible!"

"You've taught me to regard that word as devoid of meaning, and unworthy of an Englishman. Besides, you've acknowledged my flair for police work several times over, adding—not without a certain pride—that I was born to be a detective. Let's see, father—what's this about?"

The doctor ended up smiling. Grace had an answer for everything. He took some sheets of paper from his pocket and gave them to his daughter. "These are copies of cablegrams received by the India Office, the Lord Chancellor and Scotland Yard. I wouldn't be displeased to know what you think of them."

The young woman, suddenly becoming serious, read the documents attentively twice over. During this time, Sir Eric Palmer finally lit his pipe and lost himself in contemplation, drawing sensuously upon the ancient companion of his hours of perplexity.

"There's no other solution," she said, abruptly. "We'll have to go out there. Such a sequence of events is genuinely worrying in a land of fanaticism, especially in the holy city of Benares. Are the occurrences the work of Hindu agitators, or are they the result of dangerous doctrines spread by the agents of a revolutionary power dreaming of nothing but murder and pillage? In either case, the science and psychology of Eric Palmer are needed. When do we leave?"

"This very day, my child."

"It's understood, then that I'm going with you?" Grace did not wait for her father's reply; she threw her arms around his neck and hugged him ardently. Then, becoming suddenly serious, she declared: "I'll send my friends away as soon as they arrive. I'll tell them we're going to India."

"Detectives don't do that, girl. No one must suspect our important mission. In order not to attract attention, welcome all the charming young ladies. I'll lunch with you. So far as anyone knows, we're going to Cornwall. In reality, we must get to Croydon aerodrome at five, so that we can fly to Paris in time to take the 10:30 train to Marseilles. There, we'll embark for Colombo. A plane will take us to Calcutta, and we'll go from there to Benares by train. We'll be there in a fortnight or thereabouts."

"Shall we see Edward in Calcutta?"

"No, we shan't see your brother. My presence in India must remain secret until I'm told otherwise."

"Very well, father, I'll get everything ready. Do you need John?"

"Yes, send him to me. I've a few instructions to give him."

A minute later, John joined his master. The gentleman detective announced to him coolly, without going into detail, that he would be leaving for a long journey. Palmer did not even tell the servant where he would be taking him. That information was of little importance to the brave fellow, who was ever ready to follow his master, even into Hell.

John was a fine "lad" of some 25 years. His father had been Doctor Palmer's foster-brother; the doctor had shown such benevolence to the latter's numerous family when it was suddenly deprived of its head that any of them would have cheerfully given his life for their benefactor. John was the most faithful of servants; highly intelligent, as cunning as a monkey and endowed with a strong sense of purpose, he had rendered sterling service to the amateur detective. He listened religiously to all the doctor's orders, and left to execute them without saying a word.

Having lit his pipe again, the doctor began making preparations for his journey, all the while keeping an eye on the cablegrams. One sentence, in particular, intrigued him:

A supernatural individual supposedly brought up in the temple of Kali could be dangerous if exploited by fanatics.

His knowledge of Indian affairs inclined him to believe that the incidents would not be isolated.

Meanwhile, a few thousand miles away, the events that had awakened disquiet in Scotland Yard were unfolding. When it is midday in London, 10 p.m. is sounding in Benares. That evening, the festival of the goddess Kali was being celebrated.

In Benares, the holy city, every religious festival takes on enormous significance, most of all the *Durga-puja*,[7] the festival of Kali the Black, whose respect is proportional to the dread that she evokes. Is she not the goddess of the inferno, the destructive force of the Brahamanic pantheon?

The delirious crowd was stampeding along the banks of the sacred Ganges. Myriads of torches and lanterns illuminated the diverse and agitated population, as well as various river-craft in emblematic guise. Suddenly, rockets, skybursts and serpentine fireworks sprang forth from every direction, while the fires of Bengal animated the strange panorama with their bloody glare, Everything was on fire: the city, the people, the waves and the sky itself.

In the midst of that radiance, *bayaderes* [8] performed their most skillful dances on great biremes, in front of the herd of spectators. On others, young children possessed by the goddess or drunk on *arak* [9] howled holy rhapsodies. Further away, skillfully made-up actors underwent inexplicable contortions. More distant still, bizarre orchestras led a diabolical racket while smoking altars dispersed an odor of melted butter. Brahmans performed their rites in diverse chapels, droning litanies. The entire populace was singing or wandering around in an intoxication of prayer and joy.

Suddenly, cries were heard. There was a new intoxication of terror. Men, women and children were running, jostling one another. Some were falling to the ground, as if overwhelmed and dying of fright. Others, howling and wild-eyed, were trampling them underfoot.

A tall and supremely handsome man–a demigod, rather–was walking through the crowd, laughing at the alarm that he produced. His legs moved freely beneath loose-hanging linen, gathered at the waist and tied in front, but the upper part of his athletic body was naked. One strange detail: his back was marked with light brown stripes, somewhat reminiscent of those on a tiger's skin.

The man was not the cause of the terror; it was generated by the distressing sight of his animal companions, two regal tigers in all their splendor, in the prime of their savage beauty. The strange individual drew them along, holding them securely by the scruff of the neck, and the terrible carnivores made not the slightest attempt to flee. They went with their bizarre conductor in a docile fashion as he walked along the bank of the Ganges toward the jungle.

This terrifying apparition, in the bloody glare of the fires of Bengal, amid the frightened cries of the prosternated crowd, already resigned to await death as a punishment for their sins, was accompanied by these words, repeated in an extended murmur:

"Rudra the man-eater!"

"Durgane the crusher!"

"It's him... *him*! *The son of Kali*!"

English patrols were running around, exchanging information. The man and his ferocious companions had disappeared, and none of the natives could–or would–tell them anything about him.

II

Sourina, the chief Brahman of the temple of Kali, was performing his ritual ablutions on the shore of the Ganges. The amber and rose of the tropical morning tinted the mists beneath the iris-blue sky. The buttressed bank of the sacred river displayed an accumulation of palaces, towers, sanctuaries, spires and minarets. Innumerable stairways descended to the water in chaotic and menacing disorder, the lowest steps sunk in the water. In Benares, the closer a sanctuary is to the divine river, the holier it is.

The Brahman Sourina was performing his ritual ablutions beneath an esparto shield which served as a parasol. Lost among a multitude of similar shields, like a forest of monstrous mushrooms, it sheltered his meditation. A few paces away, hunched within his rags, a beggar seemed to be asleep; a thick beard covered more than half his bronzed face. Between the eyelids of this tatterdemalion, the gleam of his pupils was just discernible. Strangely for this region, his eyes seemed to be steely blue instead of dark. During his meditation, the profound and luminous black eyes of the Brahman were fixed upon the sacred waters; by contrast, the half-closed eyes of the beggar were fixed upon the high priest, and did not miss a single one of his movements.

It was the hour of fabulous religious life and grandiose prayer. Benares suddenly poured out all of its inhabitants. All of its flowers and all of its birds and beasts flocked in the direction of the river. The men rushed forth, cheerful and serious, draped in pink, yellow or rainbow-hued cashmeres; the women went down in white processions, veiled as of old in muslin.

Beneath his esparto shield, the Brahman Sourina continued his meditation. Likewise, under countless other shields, thousand of other Brahmans were meditating in the same way. The beggar had still made no movement, but his eyes were

29

watchful between his eyelids and his ears pricked up as soon as a follower approached the chief Brahman.

Followers were, in fact, flocking all around them, filling the steps like an immense amphitheater in ceaseless motion. Each of them wanted to offer garlands to the river, as if those thrown in previous days, still floating there, were insufficient. Naked children arrived in joyous troops, holding hands. Yogis and fakirs were going down slowly. Inoffensive sacred cows were going down, to which passage was respectfully ceded by everyone, honored by the offer of fresh bunches of reeds or flowers. Sheep and goats were going down, as well as eager dogs and monkeys.

On the numerous rafts and the lower steps, Brahma's people were putting down their garlands and water-jugs and beginning to get undressed. The white or rose robes and the cashmeres of every color were thrown down randomly, and handsome naked bodies appeared, dark or light bronze in color.

The men–svelte and athletic, with eyes of flame–went into the holy water to waist-depth. The women–less completely unclothed, retaining muslin about their throats and their hips–only dipped their perfect legs and their bracelet-circled arms into the Ganges; then they knelt down and leaned over to dip their long, dangling hair into the river several times over. The water streamed over their breasts and shoulders then, flattening the thin revealing cloth upon their flesh. No carnal thoughts seemed to be evoked by the admixture and brushing together of superb naked bodies, so exclusive was the religious sentiment. They did not see one another; the only saw the river, the Sun, the splendor of the light and the morning.

The Brahman Sourina had not noticed the immobile beggar who was watching him unremittingly. That poor man was perhaps the only one not to have made his ablutions, but no one paid any attention to that. Suddenly, he broke out of his immobility, lifted himself up with seeming difficulty, and drew away, limping. Doubtless coincidentally, Sourina completed his ritual ablutions and climbed back up the *ghat* [10] with supple strides.

Strangely enough, the beggar's infirmity did not hinder the rapidity of his progress. He slipped through the long processions of women who were resuming their modesty, carrying the holy water away in copper jars to serve its sacred functions in the home.

Sourina went back to his temple through the swarming crowd of worshippers crammed into the labyrinthine streets of Benares. He soon arrived at the Temple of Kali, and went in. At that moment, a young Englishwoman, blonde-haired and very pretty, wearing the uniform of a Red Cross nurse, passed close by him. Utterly preoccupied, Sourina did not even notice her.

This young nurse did not glance at Sourina as he opened and closed the exterior door of the temple; she had just perceived the old beggar, and hastened toward him. As she did so, the tatterdemalion resumed his halting gait; he staggered, perhaps from the effect of the Sun, which was already burning fiercely. She went swiftly to his aid. Having sat him down on a stone, she appeared to question him kindly. What astonishment would have overtaken the Brahman had he been able to hear the miserable wretch ask, in a plaintive whisper: "Have you any news, Grace?"

His astonishment would have been redoubled by the nurse's reply: "Yes, father. Something must have happened in the Temple of Kali. For more than an hour, there has been a great stir inside. Baber has arrived, and has gone in with the benevolent followers who come every day to tend to the sacred animals. That Hindu appears to be very intelligent and entirely devoted to the English cause."

"Yes–the worthy Sir Ralph Napper,[11] the chief of police, answers for that. It's a personal matter of revenge, it seems. Where's John?"

"John's busy getting things ready at the bungalow put at our disposal. He'll meet us in due course at the chief of police's house."

No passer-by in close proximity to the nurse and the tat-terdemalion would have been able to suspect the importance of this conversation. It was common enough to see a Red Cross lady come to the aid of an indigent who had lost every-thing. There was no cause for alarm there. The old beggar, after bowing down humbly before the pretty nurse, went to prostrate himself at the entrance to the temple, paying homage to the terrible Kali. All those who were passing by did like-wise, but the poor devil was doubtless more fearful than the rest, for he prolonged his adoration and seemed to be reciting mantras at great length.

Sir Eric Palmer, having arrived the previous evening, had already begun his inquiries.

III

The temple of Kali in Benares is an absolute marvel. Her worshippers wanted to prove to the infernal goddess the respect in which they hold her. It is a square edifice, gilded from the base to the roof, assiduously maintained, surmounted by a central cupola flanked by four neat crenellated turrets. In the cloister girdling the edifice are numerous statues of the goddess, each one enclosed in a chapel with a gilded gate: black Kalis with white eyes, brandishing severed heads at the ends of their four arms, with necklaces of skulls around their necks. Further to augment the dread generated by these frightful effigies, several enormous cages with gilded bars contain tigers and tigresses: magnificent specimens of Bengali fauna in its wild state. Behind the temple an immense tract of land, similarly enclosed by walls, is reserved for the sacred elephants. In India, where everything is symbolic, elephants represent strength and tigers ferocity and cruelty.

Sourina went directly into the temple to prostrate himself and intone a few mantras before the great statue of Durga. At the moment when he knelt down, he started slightly as he noticed the fearful attitude of the Brahmans, who seemed desirous of avoiding his questions.

"He came last night, didn't he?" he asked, in a voice tremulous with anger and anxiety.

The priests appeared to become doubly attentive to their prayers, as if they had not heard the question. There were 20 of them there, of various ages, trembling and distressed. He repeated the question more imperatively. This time, one of them came forward, mumbling in an unsteady voice: "Revered master, your anger may extend to all your servants, all your faithful Brahmans. None of them, however, is at fault. Felifax came, yes–but he went away again, laughing at our efforts. The souls of two of our brothers have departed for Vishnu's heaven."

A cry of wild rage burst forth from the chief Brahman's breast, echoing in the temple. He moved forward, his fists elevated, towards the man who had come to reply to his question, shook him violently and howled brokenly; "You lie, dog! You're all in league with him. Take care–my punishment will be pitiless."

"Alas, master, we swear to you by Kali, our respected goddess, that we have stayed awake all night–as you did yourself, with some of our brothers–watching over the temple of Durga, to which Felifax had already made several successive visits. We were positioned at all the entrances and watching from the walls. He suddenly appeared before our eyes and called out threats, saying that if Djina were not freed within two days, he would first release the sacred tigers in Benares and then set fire to the temple of Kali–as he has done to the college of Brahmans, the meeting place of your disciples and the stronghold of our cult..."

"Could you not leap upon him while he was speaking and render him incapable of doing harm? First, how was he able to get in here?"

"Master, Felifax was in the tiger cage, and they surrounded him. We saw him there, but could not determine by what means he had arrived. We wanted to detain him at any cost; he understood that. Then, with a burst of demoniac laughter, after having had the charity to warn us, he released Durgane upon us–the most ferocious of animals."

"And you fled, cowards!"

"As you would have commanded us to do yourself, revered master. The tigress seemed to be out of control. Rina and Seoul, two animal-tamers, paid for her re-entry into her cage with their lives. When we returned, Felifax had vanished again–and yet I can swear to you that he did not go across the courtyard. Since then, the animals no longer seem to be the same. Just listen to the tigers roaring! They are clamoring for their friend–their half-brother, who dared to go to sleep between their redoubtable claws, and whom they obey like dogs. Listen to the trumpeting of the elephants, happy to have seen him again–the one who brought them freshly-cut reeds every morning."

Sourina was unable to take things so philosophically. His face was utterly distraught with rage and his fists were clenched. In an exhalation of wild anger, he muttered: "Where can he come from? I know all the secret entrances to the temple; my Brahmans were watching them. It's incomprehensible." Suddenly, an idea having sprung into his tortured brain, he cried: "Have Djina brought to me, and bring animals too, for a great sacrifice."

An immeasurable anxiety took root in every visage. Why had the master asked for Djina? Everyone knew that he was capable of the most terrible actions in his efforts to recover control of Felifax, whom he called the god-child and the new Rama. Would he go so far as human sacrifice to summon the goddess to render up his idol?

An old *dubash* [12]–which is to say, an interpreter–came forward and said, tremulously: "Revered master, Djina was not mentioned without reason. She has been imprisoned in the dungeon since the day when Felifax fled the temple. Please don't attempt to harm her, or your formidable pupil's threats will be executed immediately. The thought of his vengeance terrifies all of us."

"Enough! Kali speaks through me. Go find Djina for me."

In the face of such an injunction, there was no further hesitation. A Brahman left very hurriedly and returned a few minutes later bringing a girl of about 13, already on the brink of womanhood and divinely graceful. Trembling in every limb, she prostrated herself at the feet of the wrathful servant of Kali.

The latter drew her up, rather brutally. Plunging his incendiary gaze into the girl's large black eyes, he demanded in a ferocious voice: "I want to know what passage Felifax uses to get into the temple! If your perfidious tongue does not tell the truth, you shall feel my wrath!"

"I don't know, master," she replied, half-dead with fright. "I haven't seen him since the evening when he left me to go, as usual, to sleep with the sacred tigers–because I've been imprisoned in a secret dungeon, on your orders."

"That is not an issue. For nine years, you have been close companions, hiding nothing from one another. You must, therefore, know the route by which he fled and by which he has come back several times to taunt me. I want to know that secret, you hear? I demand to know it. If necessary, I shall go so far as to sacrifice you to Kali. Think on that!"

In response to a sign from him, *palomen* [13] led forward two zebus, four she-goats and six kids: innocent victims dedicated to the bloodthirsty goddess, who requires blood before granting the prayers of her devotees. A great sacrifice was going to take place.

Sourina had entrusted the girl to one of his disciples. The latter, following his superior's orders, forced her to watch the repulsive spectacle that was about to get underway.

A half-naked sacrificial priest, his body girdled solely by a Brahman's white loincloth–the emblem of the twice-born–set the garlanded head of a zebu on a block in the form of a fork placed at Kali's feet. Another poured the sacred water of the Ganges on the victim's muzzle, and the knife fell with a muffled noise.

Djina fainted in the arms of her torturer. Despite her continual presence in the temple, she had never been witness to such a spectacle, *gopis* [14] not being admitted to sacrifices. The young girl lived among the temple women: wives of the Brahmans, sacred dancers and servants of the goddess. Her pure and innocent mind could not conceive of such horror. Although she had heard talk of sacrifices, she knew nothing of their cruelty, so happy had life seemed to her in the company of the one for whose disappearance and bravado she was paying so painfully.

She did, however, know the secret demanded by Sourina. Being Felifax's only confidante, she knew that he had fled into the jungle, intoxicated by freedom and a spirit of adventure, finally leaving the gilded prison in which they had tried to hold him–in order to make him a god–because he wanted to experience the life that had been hidden from him. Djina knew, too, that there was a passage which opened directly into the middle of the great tiger cage. Felifax, only being able to work by night, had devoted nearly two years to digging that tunnel. The passage, slipping under the cloister walls, came out in an abandoned building.

The young man had already made two or three nocturnal sorties before his definitive flight. No one dared look for the secret in the midst of its ferocious guardians. By this means, Felifax could vanish and reappear like a genie, before the stupefied eyes of those who wished to capture him. The young girl knew all this, but not a single word would escape her lips, even though Sourina might carry out the terrible threat of sacrificing her to Kali. Felifax had asked her to remain silent; she would guard his secret jealously.

The expiatory work continued. Kali wished to be surrounded by death.

Insensible, as if in ecstasy, not taking the least precaution to avoid the blood that periodically stained his white robe with purple, Sourina murmured his most ardent mantras, prostrate before the wrathful and fearsome goddess. Eventually, his voice was raised to pronounce a sort of invocation:

"O Kali the Black, Kali the exterminatrix, Kali, wife of Shiva! You who destroyed the famous demon Durg, deliver Felifax to me. You know, O Kali, what monstrous crime presided over his birth; you know that he was born under your sign and is dedicated to your cult; you also know how much human blood he must shed for the liberation of our land and for glory.

"Deliver Felifax to me, O Kali, you who, in the centuries of legend, consented to incarnate yourself as Hanuman, king of the monkeys, to assist Rama to vanquish Ravana, the giant of Sri Lanka! Deliver Felifax to me, O Kali, you who take the form of a tigress to remind men that they belong to you! O Kali, may the blood of these sacrifices cause you to answer the mantras of your humble servant. Deliver Felifax to him; deliver to him the child whom he claims to be your son; deliver to him the one who is his entire life, the hope of India enslaved!"

The goddess seemed to roll her white eyes in her black face, prey to fervent wrath. A Brahman took Djina away, still in a faint, intending to put her back in female hands before she was returned to her dungeon.

The Brahman responsible for such matters was looking to replace the two animal-keepers who had fallen victim on the previous night to the ferocity of the tigress released by the indomitable Felifax. He was taking his pick from the faithful volunteers who had presented themselves, as they did every day, to care for the sacred beasts. As usual, the hopeful volunteers were numerous—because, in recompense for their servitude to the goddess, they would earn her eternal protection.

At the announcement that two of them would definitely be admitted to the temple in the capacity of animal-keepers, they all pressed forward. The Brahman examiner wanted to choose wisely, but it was difficult. Two of them appeared particularly suitable to fulfill the duty, and he had them extracted from the group.

The first was a man of about 40, with a slim and wiry figure. His chin was ornamented by a black beard, cut short in the Sikh style, and his jet-black eyes shone with intelligence.

"What is your name?" the Brahman demanded.

"Baber. And you know, master that Baber means the tiger. In consequences, my place among my four-footed brothers is entirely appropriate."

"You are but an infinitesimal dust-mote beside the beasts consecrated to our goddess. Here, you will lose the habit of speaking, and you will learn that the work is the most dangerous of all. It is a great honor to be an animal-keeper in the temple of Kali, and to ascend to Vishnu's heaven, struck by the spouse of Shiva. You seem to me to be intelligent; I shall ask Sourina, our high priest, to accept my choice. Now, get on with your work."

The Brahman examiner did not see the gleam of savage joy that lit up in the new animal-keeper's eye just then. Prudently, however, Baber shut his eyes and went to prostrate himself at the feet of the goddess, beside the chief Brahman, for the morning mantras.

Outside the temple, the old beggar had abandoned his adoration in front of the door and was heading for the European district, his rags trailing on the ground.

For her part, the young English nurse was wandering through the pilgrims' quarter with a nonchalant air. With great interest, she studied the narrow streets in which half-naked tailors, sweetmeat-sellers, money-changers and open-air cooks crouched beneath a profusion of oil lamps, whose lighted wicks flickered without providing any illumination.

Suddenly, having looked at the time on her wristwatch, the young nurse abandoned her nonchalant stroll and, in her turn, strode purposefully in the direction of the European district.

IV

The brave James O'Connor, an Irishman from Kildare, an agent of the Indian Police Service, would need a very long time to recover from his surprise. The poor lad was on orderly duty in front of the Benares Police Station at about 8:30 a.m., thinking of his beloved Ireland, with his eyes more-or-less unfocused, when he was jolted so violently that he lost his balance and fell over.

Abruptly returned to reality, he was astonished by the sight of the author of his misfortune. It was a Hindu tatterdemalion, bowed down by the years, who did not even excuse himself for his carelessness.

James O'Connor, a good-humored fellow, contented himself with muttering a few impolite words on the subject of clumsiness. The delinquent, instead of seeming contrite at having knocked down an agent of His August Majesty the King of England and Emperor of India, made a grimace and let loose a stinging insult. Showing a remarkable even-temperedness, the Irishman did not take offense, limiting himself to recommending that the indigent show a little more deference and politeness.

Then, in a truly unsociable fashion, the indigent launched a jet of saliva upon the agent's astonishingly well-polished boots—an extremely incongruous manifestation of his immeasurable scorn. James O'Connor finally felt the ardent blood of green Erin's children boil in his veins; he seized the exceedingly insolent tatterdemalion, not brutally but with a firm hand, without observing any attempt at resistance, and forced him from the outside of the post to the inside.

Scarcely was the door closed behind him, when the Hindu, who had been hunched over until that moment, suddenly stood upright. Revealing the metallic gleam of two steely blue eyes, he said: "Perfect, my lad. You've played your role with the superb distinction of a Drury Lane actor. You've wrapped up a coarse vagabond with a masterly hand, and because of that I shan't be suspect. Take me to your commander." [15]

James O'Connor, flabbergasted this time, did not appear to understand–but his superior came in at the exact moment when the arrested man was repeating his demand and the Irishman almost sat down in a daze. Ralph Napper, a very highly-placed person, hastened to shake the miserable Hindu's hand, saying to him in an affable tone: "I only recognized you by your voice, sir. 'Pon my word, it's prodigious! Would you like to come into my office?"

Almost at the same time, a pretty young English nurse arrived at the Police Station. She entered without hesitation and asked for the commander. A slave to standing orders, the scrupulous O'Connor accompanied her to the office to announce her–but then thought he must have lost his mind, for the wretch was installed in the best armchair, with his legs crossed and a pipe in his mouth. What was more, the nurse ran to embrace him, saying: "Hello, father–I'm not late, am I?" She also extended her hand to the commander, with an exquisite smile.

That was too much; the brave O'Connor, refusing to see any more, had closed the door again.

Sir Eric Palmer, however, in response to questions put to him by the chief of police, said in a grave voice: "I observed your Sourina throughout his ritual ablutions, neither speaking not exchanging gestures with the other indigents. What's his part in this?"

"He passes in high places for a friend of England. Until recently, I shared that opinion. Since the events that have motivated your coming here, though, I'm not so sure. The enigma's very puzzling."

"When I arrived yesterday evening, you scarcely had time to fill me in on these events. You simply directed me to a person who is suspect in your eyes–Sourina, the high priest of the temple of Kali–mentioning a possible conspiracy against our country. Now that I've observed the man, I'd like to know more factual details."

"So be it. About two months ago, in the middle of the night, a fire broke out in a college of young Brahmans, which has a special link to the temple of Kali. Fires are frequent, quite ordinary, events, you say? This one was supernatural! Firstly, there's only one fireplace there–but when the firemen arrived, as soon as they brought their hoses into play, flames sprung forth everywhere under the influence of the water. Moreover, numerous witnesses affirmed that a tall young man, as handsome as a god, was running through the burning building, making gestures like a sower of seeds. When the water fell, after he had gone by, new fires started."

"Incendiary devices, very probably?"

"Yes, based on sodium and potassium. Since then, a significant theft of such devices from the Benares arsenal has been discovered. Nothing remains of that college, of which Sourina was the former master. On the following night, the man was seen again in the smoking ruins, and the next morning, an inscription in the Bengali language was found. It translates thus: *All the children of India must be free to choose their lives. First warning to Sourina.*"

"Was this inscription, as you understood it, a call to rebellion?"

"It could be so interpreted. A fortnight later, a new fire was manifest in a beautiful house, also belonging to Sourina. The house served as a meeting-place for his disciples. It was there, it appears, that he preached complete obedience to the orders of Kali, the bloody goddess, and received gifts for the sacrifices. Well, as at the college, on this occasion too the mysterious person was seen sewing his incendiary capsules."

"Twice over!"

"You couldn't have put it better. In the remains of the second disaster, the following inscription was found, in Bengali: *Sacrifices are cruel. Even beasts are free to seek their destiny. Second warning to Sourina.*"

"There's no call to insurrection in those words either."

"A few days later, a third fire broke out–again, by a strange coincidence, in one of Sourina's properties. The chief Brahman, feared by everyone, had created a workhouse for his cult; there he imprisoned, for various lengths of time, those who appeared to deserve punishment for infractions against the worship of the goddess Kali. The inmates were subject to dire penances: fasting, flagellation, hair-shirts, manifestations of fakirism and so forth. Many penitents perished under the strain. We could no nothing about it; our orders, which are very specific in regard to religion, left us no option. Well, a fire was set in the workhouse by the same individual and–as in the two previous instances–this fateful inscription was found there: *Brahma alone may order punishments, not his disciples. Third warning to Sourina.*

"During this last occurrence, one of our agents was on the point of capturing the author of the misdeeds, and even got hold of him. He's a young man, seemingly endowed with Herculean strength, for he twisted the wrist of the agent who had apprehended him without the least effort, and disengaged himself easily without doing him any further harm. Our man was able to get a good look at him. He goes about nearly naked, and his back is marked with stripes like a tiger's. His eyes display a particularity that's even more incredible. They're a greenish yellow, with pupils like a cat's. The agent also claims to have detected the odor of wild beasts in his presence; he's presumably impregnated with that characteristic jungle odor."

"All in all," Sir Eric said, "there doesn't appear to me to be any danger to the Indian Empire in this–the threats seem to be addressed solely to Sourina. It's the latter, in particular, that must be watched, and apprehended if need be."

"In my opinion, that would be an unpardonable folly. Sourina is one of the most powerful religious leaders. His arrest would set the 25,000 Brahmans contained in Benares against us. Moreover, the indigenous population is blindly obedient. The movement would spread throughout India."

"In these circumstances, the persecution directed against Sourina should be cause for celebration. The mysterious man appears to be one of his most relentless enemies, determined to break his power."

"Can one ever be sure with these natives? In any case, that might make him all the more dangerous. We must discover his exact intentions, for he's enormously important in the eyes of the crowd; already they take him for a god.

"At exactly 18:00, on the evening of the festival of Kali, he showed himself in the midst of the popular celebrations on the banks of the Ganges. That apparition struck terror and admiration into the delirious multitude, and many of our people. He walked unhurriedly, exceedingly handsome and genuinely powerful. He was framed by two tigers, magnificent jungle specimens replete with ferocity. He gripped them playfully by the scruff of the neck, in the manner of mastiffs restrained from fighting. The beasts, incredibly, obeyed him meekly."

"Might this not have been a collective hallucination, augmented by native superstition?"

"No! I saw it with my own eyes! I immediately issued an order to have him followed by patrols. Alas, the patrols could not obtain any information–the Hindus have been unanimous in maintaining silence. I was only able to ascertain that the two enormous cats had been stolen, a few minutes before, from the temple of Kali."

"How exciting, my dear colleague. This is one of the police missions I like best, their mystery being redoubled by scientific interest, In the cablegrams received by Scotland Yard there was mention of a child brought up in the temple of Kali–could this be that child?"

"Sir Eric, here's Baber, the most devoted of our native agents. He can give you all the available information on that subject himself."

The Hindu who had been engaged as a animal-keeper in the temple of Kali an hour or so before had just entered Napper's office, after having knocked discreetly. The police chief offered him his hand. "Hello, Baber–have you any news?"

"Some, sir. I have been taken on at the temple of Kali to look after the sacred tigers. Some time last night the man got

44

into the temple, without anyone being able to determine how–for they're always on the lookout to surprise him. He fled, releasing a tigress named Durgane against the Brahmans who ran after him. Result: two animal-keepers dead on the pavement. He has demanded that Sourina release Djina, a young *bayadere* the chief Brahman has imprisoned. If Sourina does not comply within two days, he will release all the temple beasts into the city."

"The Devil he will! This business becomes more and more exciting. Your demigod seems to me to be an extraordinary fellow, whom Sir Eric Palmer can't help but applaud. Go on, Baber."

"Sourina wanted to talk to young Djina in order to discover the passage used by the mysterious man. Having been brought up with him, the girl must be the confidante of his secrets. To persuade her to talk, the chief Brahman forced her to watch a great sacrifice, and the poor child fainted at the sight of the blood. After an hour of mantras, Sourina, initially downcast, regained his strength. He appears to have accepted his adversary's challenge. He will, therefore, set out to search his jungle domain. He has organized a hunt for dawn tomorrow, with the temple elephants, and claims to be certain hat he will find himself in the presence of *Felifax*..."

"*Felifax*? Whose name is that?"

"The mysterious adversary's."

"It's a bizarre name, to be sure. It doesn't sound Indian at all! Baber, my friend, tell me everything you know about Felifax."

"I can't tell you very much about him, Sahib. He was brought up in the temple by Sourina with great care and in rigorous secrecy. The Brahmans themselves do not know his origin–for a very good reason, I think. I am certain that origin had something to do with the death of my brother."

"Your brother was attached to the temple, then?"

"Yes, Sahib, my poor brother Rao was a Brahman. We have that right by birth. We are, in fact, descendants of the great Baber the conqueror,[16] although our family was ruined by the various competitions over his succession. My elder brother was not yet 16 at the time of his mysterious death–his murder."

"Mysterious death, you say–murder? But a Brahman is sacred."

"Certainly, Sahib–to kill a Brahman is the most heinous of crimes; but one such might be condemned to death, even so, for some frightful offense. That is why it has been impossible, until now, for me to avenge my brother. Rao, I swear, was done away with by Sourina. Faithful to his religion, to the cult he embraced, my brother never talked about the temple. However, as he adored my mother, she was able to obtain a few scraps of confession–among others, that Sourina, in association with a doctor in the Indian Army, had carried out mysterious and terrible deeds in the temple of Kali. My brother was mixed up in these actions, along with a young and very beautiful *devadasi* named Sita.[17]

"One morning, my poor Rao was found dead, of some strange disease. We did not have time to determine what it was, because his body had been incinerated on the Burning *ghat* on the bank of the Ganges, on the instructions of some other Brahmans. My conviction was already formed, though, and was merely reinforced when Sita, the priestess of the sacred tigers, disappeared in her turn less than two days afterwards. No witness now remains to the mysteries of Sourina and his accomplice, unless it is this child, who cannot know anything and upon whom no lay person laid eyes before his escape from the temple.

"This is why I have placed myself in the service of the police. I have no doubt that Sourina, despite his apparent amity towards England, detests her with all his heart and is conspiring against her. My ambition is to bring him down, to lead him to the gallows, and to reveal myself at that moment as the author of his ruin, telling him who I am–for he has killed my brother, I tell you, with the complicity of that accursed surgeon."

"Do you know this doctor's name?"

"Yes, Sahib; it is engraved on my memory. My brother Rao is not his only victim. He is called Sir Edmund Sexton."

An indefinable smile came to Palmer's lips. He was quite familiar with the former surgeon in the Indian Army. Bitten by the human grafting bug,[18] Sexton believed that he had found in India a limitless field for his semi-demented experiments. He had been forced to go further afield when the government had been ordered to send him back to England. There was no need to speak of that in front of Baber, nor even in front of the police chief. Already, though. Palmer believed that he could see a tiny glimmer of light in the obscurity of the mystery.

Ralph Napper's voice drew him out of his meditation, saying: "If you would like to follow the hunt, my dear doctor, I would be able to ask Sourina for..."

"Useless and dangerous, sir; I would find out nothing. However, I think it would be useful if you organized your own company of beaters, and sent them out tonight, before the chief Brahman's–and arranged that the two parties should encounter one another. It will be necessary to maneuver in such a fashion that they continue to beat together, but I shall absent myself."

"Really, doctor, I don't quite understand why..."

"Why I'm asking you to do this? Simply because it is absolutely necessary to show that the Benares police take an anxious interest in the misdeeds of this enigmatic man. If you leave Sourina to regulate his affairs by himself, it will seem suspicious and put him on his guard–exactly what must be avoided."

"Should our hunt be a grand affair?"

"Grand enough not to seem laughable, but not too grand. It needs to be kept well in hand, made up of trustworthy men, voluntarily incompetent. It's unnecessary for Felifax to be caught."

"Bah! Why not? It will be the best way to lay this business to rest."

"If you want to–and if you can–by all means capture him. Wound him if necessary, but slightly. Will you even see him? It's doubtful. In your opinion, Baber, will Sourina capture this young chap?"

"No, Sahib. According to what I've heard from the Brahmans in charge of the beasts, Felifax will escape every trap. He'll be captured only when he wants to be."

"Will you go on the hunt with Sourina, Baber?"

"If Your Excellency wishes, I will make a deal with one of the men responsible for the elephants, invoking if necessary my expert knowledge of the jungle."

"Perfect, my lad. If, by chance, you see Felifax–especially if he escapes–do your best to ascertain the exact spot in the jungle where you encounter him."

As there were no further orders to be given to the Hindu, the latter left the room. He could not remain too long absent from the temple of Kali. As soon as he was outside, the doctor observed: "This brave Baber will be suspected by his coreligionists if they see him hanging about this place too often."

"They won't see him. Baber knows how to make himself invisible. He's a truly precious fellow."

"Especially on the day when you have to rid yourself of Sourina. The matter's already rather complicated, but there's now the certain involvement of Sir Edmund Sexton. Hopefully, what we learn might rouse the indignation of the entire world some day. In the case of a madman or a genius, one must be ready for anything, mustn't one?"

During this conversation, John had arrived at the Police Station carrying a small suitcase. On being informed of the fact, the doctor went into a neighboring office. He emerged a few minutes later, once again the impeccable gentleman–in whom James O'Connor, the orderly, certainly would not have recognized the incongruous old Hindu beggar.

O'Connor saw him pass by, though, with the young nurse hanging affectionately from his arm, saying with a kind of ecstasy: "Oh, father! It's so exciting!"

V

The elephants from the temple of Kali, tall and broad, were marching in Indian file under the guidance of *kimki*.[19] Sourina was studying the jungle from the carbuncle-encrusted, saddlecloth-mounted *howdah* of the lead elephant, which was called Manaor.

Atop the second elephant, two implacable black eyes glittering with hatred were fixed upon the Brahman; Baber had evidently contrived to join the hunt. Could there be any question of hatred and vengeance amid such splendor and perpetual intoxication? Yes, for the Hindu soul forgets nothing. In the vermilion morning, however, there was only joy. All of nature magnified the intoxication, stretching out her innumerable arms, brandishing her flowers, distending her fruits and titanic vegetables. All the trees seemed to be launching an assault upon the sky, in a contest to determine which could climb highest towards the nourishing light.

Manaor made a sudden movement. The superlative hearing of the enormous animal had apprehended a sound, just as its marvelous sense of smell had scented something unusual. Sourina sat up straight. Was that the object of his search already?

No, the sound was growing louder. What could it be? Horses were whinnying; English faces came into view. It was obviously a hunt organized in honor of some British person of note. They would let it pass by. Manaor's reaction was soon explained: an elephant had appeared at the junction of a lateral trail. It was, indeed, equipped for a hunt–and in the *howdah* that it carried, the astonished Sourina recognized the chief of police. He could not suppress a start of annoyance. What could this encounter signify?

But Sir Ralph Napper was already addressing him. "Were you drawn to the jungle by the same desire as ourselves? Are you searching for that singular being who seems to have declared war on you, if one can believe the inscriptions left in the ashes of the fires lit by his hand? No complaint has been laid against him, it's true; nevertheless, I intend to find out who this man is."

At this declaration, Sourina had difficulty masking his anxiety and resentment. He knew how tenacious the conquerors could be, and dreaded now that he might see some injury done to the person for whom he was searching. He feared the possibility of capture even more; they might find out exactly who Felifax was.

In a tremulous voice, he asked: "What do you want with this man, Mr. Napper?"

"'Pon my word, I don't really know! To make his acquaintance, and to teach him–if he does not know it–the respect due to the property of others."

"Will you imprison him?"

"Perhaps not, if he promises us to put a stop to his foolishness in future. There is however, the matter of the theft of incendiary capsules from the Benares arsenal..."

Sourina interrupted him brusquely. An idea had just sprung to mind as he listened to the police chief's tentative plans. If, with the means at his disposal, the latter were to find Felifax, he might hand the youth over. Then, his adoptive son would be less inclined to blame him for the loss of the liberty that seemed so dear to him, for he would not hold him responsible for his capture.

In a persuasive voice, he ventured to say: "All in all, this man has committed no serious offense against anyone but me, and I have not brought a complaint, for my religious duty obliges me to set hatred aside. If you capture him, return him to my care. He is said to be a very young man, so he is still capable of being corrected–a matter for which I shall gladly take responsibility."

The functionary remained impassive, and limited himself to replying, good-humoredly: "'Pon my word, that might be a solution that would be satisfactory from several viewpoints. To put the man in an English prison might upset your fellow

50

Hindus, while confiding him to your care would be proof of our mildness. Between ourselves, the youth would gain nothing by the exchange–quite the opposite. One doesn't challenge the chief Brahman of the temple of Kali with impunity!"

This time, Sourina's habitual deceptiveness had met its match in one who was well-accustomed to such games. Not for a moment did he think Ralph Napper capable of playing a role. An indefinable smile played upon his lips.

At that moment, the police chief exclaimed, with a touch of irony: "Hold on! Perhaps we're trying to sell the bearskin before we've killed the bear. In fact, my men and I have been beating the jungle for hours with no other result than flushing out an assortment of wild beasts that could well finish up making us sorry. Your mysterious man is retaining his mystery. Doubtless, we shan't catch sight of him."

Sourina was now fully in accord with the Englishman. He was no longer anxious about his curiosity. He lost sight of everything but the one objective that hypnotized him: to get hold of Felifax. By the same evening, the latter would have disappeared, imprisoned in one of those monasteries from which there is no escape. That way, no one would be able to see him or to interrogate him, and he could offer the conquerors the excuse of the prisoner's unexpected flight.

Desire gave rise to imprudence. With no thought that he might be betraying himself, he replied with a venomous smile: "If you wish to join me, gentlemen, I believe I can assure you that we shall see the mystery man. I have brought bait capable of drawing him out of hiding. In the name of Brahma, though, do not kill him–entrust him to me as soon as his capture is accomplished. He shall be kept in my *howdah*. It would do no good to show him to the people of Benares, you know, for they are too inclined to believe in miracles."

Ralph Napper pretended to accept cheerfully. What would happen when the prey was taken was settled. In the meantime, he believed that he had the upper hand over the Brahman, just as the Brahman believed that he had the upper hand over him. So the Englishmen joined Sourina's men. The police were a dozen strong, chosen by their chief from among his best men, and he knew that he could count on them.

For a further hour, the two companies went deeper into the jungle, which became ever denser. They made headway with difficulty through an inextricable tangle of roots, lianas and rhizomes [20] which interlaced, coiled and twisted around one another; it was as if monstrous rooted serpents were engaged in some protracted mortal struggle.

The tangled, tortuous and mysterious jungle, deploying its troubling charms and exotic grace in the shadows, was wild and menacing in its strange and captivating beauty. Sourina told himself that Felifax might believe himself safe from all pursuit in this jungle, full of bizarre flowers, acrid perfumes and dangerous denizens–but he would drive him out of it, if Kali wanted him to be found.

He issued a command in Bengali in a peremptory tone. Then, as if in response, a cry of atrocious anguish was heard, released by a child's voice. In a small palanquin on the third elephant, poor Djina was in the hands of a Brahman torturer–a veritable monster of bestial appearance. Sourina had chosen him intentionally, because Felifax had detested him for his cruelty and ferocity in the days when he was in the temple. The Brahman reciprocated that hatred, for both the child and his female companion; he was, therefore, the ideal man to bring forth the complaints of his little victim.

From now on, the march continued amid Djina's cries and moans. The Englishmen felt ill at ease, understanding now the significance of the chief Brahman's words: *I have brought bait capable of drawing him out of hiding.* Although their civilized souls disapproved of this means, they dared not intervene. To put an end to the torture, they wanted to see Felifax appear as soon as possible. Every eye was fixed on some shadowed gap or tiny hiding-place.

No one thought of looking upwards, except Baber–and sometimes, the latter's eyes took on a bizarre gleam.

Suddenly, the elephants stopped abruptly. Manaor was bracing himself on his huge callused feet. His nearest companion had drawn himself up to his full height. The third–the one that carried the palanquin in which Djina was still moaning–placed itself between them. The other pachyderms formed a solid mass; sensing danger, all their eyes probed the bushes. The pachyderms' trunks were raised up, as if to signify joy.

Then, a demon leapt out of the forest canopy. With vertiginous dexterity, he fell upon Manaor's curved trunk, and moved on to the beast in the center–the one on which the torturer was still martyrizing the girl. The man whom they were searching on the ground confronted the tormentor, having arrived by the aerial route. A sacrificial dagger shone in his hand.

With a howl of savage glee, the torturer reached out, but the gleam of the sacred dagger passed before his eyes. He collapsed, releasing a torrent of blood.

It is easy enough to imagine the confusion of cries, shouts and English oaths caused by this apparition. Sourina, drunk with wrath and joy, was calling to everyone, issuing orders. But the jostling was in vain, the hope chimerical; more rapid than a lightning-flash, Felifax had lifted Djina in his arms and, making the same use of the elephant's trunk, already resumed his aerial flight.

Despite the *mahouts*' best efforts, the elephants would not obey. They had recognized their former companion from the temple–the one who had brought them a meal of freshly-cut reeds every morning. Their animal intelligence seemed to perceive that all these people wanted to harm their friend, and they set about preventing them from doing so.

Alone among all the *mahouts*, Baber seemed not at all disturbed. On the contrary, he assisted the flight of the mysterious climber. Forgetting the instruction their chief had given them that Felifax was not to be killed, the English, excited by the adventure, were bringing their rifles to their shoulders. Suddenly, guided by Baber, Manaor appeared to go mad–as if he had been stung–and launched himself into the midst of the horses, which were already alarmed, their ears laid back as if

53

they had sensed the approach of a tiger. A few badly-directed shots were fired.

A burst of juvenile laughter replied to the noise of the shots. Then two elephants trumpeted in pain, having been slightly wounded by bullets that had not been intended for them. A stampede ensued; the horses took flight, their riders terrified by the madness of the elephants, which could only be calmed with the greatest of difficulty.

Further hope was futile; Felifax, having been on his guard, had taken what he wanted—and knew how to defend her with all his might.

Sourina swallowed his rage; he ordered the retreat. The chagrin of the Englishmen was not feigned; as spirited sportsmen, they felt cheated by this outcome. Sir Ralph Napper grumbled at the fulfillment of the prediction made by that devil of a doctor that no capture would be achieved. He had been keen to have the honor of bringing Felifax in without the help of the great detective summoned from the metropolis, who believed that he understood the complex soul of India.

That evening, Baber came to make his report. He spoke of the blind wrath of Sourina, who had wanted the *mahouts* guilty of not being able to master their elephants to be put to death. Although he had ended up giving way to the pleas of the other Brahmans, no one in the temple was any less fearful of him.

The Hindu agent could not specify the exact spot where Djina's abduction had taken place. Despite that, his information was quite valuable, for he explained how he had been able to keep track of Felifax's silent march for a long time, without giving any indication to him.

Later that same evening, Sir Eric Palmer informed the chief of police that he would be going into the jungle the following day. He had to go in search of one of his friends: an engineer responsible for the exploitation of a silver mine on behalf of the Maharajah of Benares, at a place called Silver-Hole, deep in the forest. He would use the mine as a base, from which he could go in any direction to make detailed explorations. John would accompany him–and so would Miss Grace, an intrepid horsewoman to whom her father could refuse nothing.

Somewhat resentful of this decision, taken against his advice, Ralph Napper wished him good luck, secretly hoping that the detective would fail.

VI

Felifax showed Djina around his domain. He had established his lair in the heart of the jungle, in an ancient temple of Shiva abandoned for centuries, from which Hindu angels and lyre-playing *apsaras* [21] sprouted in profusion. The forest had invaded it: it was encrusted with a hardy mass of roots and brambles, cracking the mortar and cleaving the stones. Over the centuries, the construction–which might once have been highly important–had crumbled away, respected now by none but the spirits of nature.

Tenderly holding hands, the two young people wandered around the temple, and what Felifax called his wild garden. Djina's joy was further increased on seeing that there was a large pool in which the weary sunlight faded away, where the temple was reflected in attenuated colors, and in whose waters fish were darting hither and yon.

All of this was new to Djina. Like Felifax, the girl had been a prisoner in the temple of Kali, and knew nothing of nature. He had told her that she was perfectly safe in this ancient temple, and that no one would dare to come looking for her here. He knew, in any case, how to defend her, with the aid of his redoubtable friends, who slept by day in the humid thickets and waited for nightfall before going hunting.

His "fort" was abundantly stocked with provisions, which he shared with her: a bird killed the previous day, cooked in the Hindu manner, followed by delicious fruits, of which there were immeasurable reserves in the immense verdure of the jungle. He sat her down on a bed of dry leaves while he prepared it all, and Djina could not help admiring the man from whom she had been separated since his flight from the temple.

Felifax was 18 years old. It was impossible to find a human specimen more handsome or more poised. As on his appearance in Benares on the night of the festival of Kali, he

56

wore no garments other than an animal pelt carefully wound around his waist, reaching as far as his navel. This pelt formed a sort of loose *lamba* [22] in which his graceful limbs could move freely, for he detested the constraints of clothing. His pale bronze body was gilded by the rays of the ardent sun.

People claimed that his body was marked by a tiger's stripes. Although not false, the affirmation could not always be sustained, for the stripes were only clearly manifest when Felifax was very angry. By an extraordinary peculiarity, the young man had a tiger's scent, to a perfect degree–which might be the explanation of his power over wild beasts. This odor was of scant importance to Djina, who had long grown used to living alongside him in exceedingly close proximity to the temple carnivores.

Until he turned 18, Felifax had never left the house of Kali. All the marvels he had encountered during his initial journey to freedom he recapitulated with his little companion.

When one has only been able to admire the sky within the narrow horizons of courtyards enclosed by high walls, and when one has known no trees but the centuries-old banyans of the sacred enclosure, no animals but sacred ones, it is permissible to faint with emotion on seeing the gilded immensity of the celestial vault, finding oneself in the midst of the tropical forest redolent with powerful and intoxicating perfumes.

Felifax was already a learned young man, thanks to Sourina, who had explained the mysteries of nature at length, and Djina had also had the benefit of these lessons. Now, though, she was all a-quiver, just as he had been two months before, confronted with the richness of that nature which nourished the frightful pullulation of beautiful plants.

Felifax has already experienced that sensation; he experienced it again today. It all seemed new to him. He ran through the jungle, with his arm around Djina's waist, almost carrying her. In those woods full of unknown dangers they seemed like two schoolchildren on holiday, intrigued by all the sounds they had never heard before, the myriad insects whose existence they had never suspected.

They were so happy to be reunited that they ran like madmen. The tiger-man, the terror of Benares, who made the Indian government so anxious that they had summoned the most famous detective in London, was nothing but an overgrown boy. His laughter rang out clearly, like a joyful trumpet, and Djina's was pure crystal. Unknown animals fled in fright at their approach; they were astonished by that, for they had wanted to caress them, as they had caressed the tigers, elephants and cows consecrated to Kali the Black.

The young woman was amazed by the regal supremacy that her friend had over the creatures that frequented the unexplored jungle by day. She did not know that a Machiavellian intervention had endowed him with a terrifying badge of identity for all those that were weak and went in fear of a redoubtable enemy: the scent of a tiger.

All afternoon they ran together, tasting a thousand delicious fruits at the dictates of their whim—the inexhaustible wealth of their domain—and discovering fresh crystal-clear springs beneath the trees, in which they might quench their thirst.

Eventually, they saw the Sun setting little by little and the twilight dying in an orgy of greens and mauves, on the infinitely calm surface of a stream.[23] Exhausted, they threw themselves down on a bed of moss and giant ferns next to an enormous fig-tree growing in the old Shivaite temple—a fig-tree whose lower branches replaced the roof that had fallen in centuries before.

Night had fallen completely. The sky, an authentic sky of dreams, was powdered with gold, so bright and star-laden that the two friends were rendered dumbstruck for several seconds. It was a spectacle of splendor. The jungle around them was silhouetted in blue-tinted shadow. Everything was blue: the great catalpas, the vast euphorbias, the slender bamboos, the angels and the *apsaras* of sculpted stone.

Although they lay down, they could not go to sleep. The experienced a strange sensation of pleasure in hearing the song of the jungle raised towards the limpid gold-studded sky. The

Moon, very high in the sky, overhung the jungle, whose lakes resembled sheets of polished silver. Night having arrived in full measure, the population of the forest was wide awake. The animals were commencing their nocturnal wanderings through the thickets, and the savage hymn that they dedicated to the benevolent darkness burst out on every side.

Lying in one another's arms, on their bed of ferns and mosses, they listened. Felifax, vibrant with a formidable gaiety, welcomed the voice of that strange choir joyfully, but Djina's heart was a trifle constricted in spite of everything, by the discovery of the unknown and the mystery of the darkness.

Suddenly, the slow and heavy footfalls of a company of creatures drew near. A bellowing sound–a sort of raucous snoring–grew by the minute. Djina realized that she did not yet know these denizens of the forest. They were obviously moving unhurriedly, stopping to browse young shoots, then setting off again, pausing again, indulging their ponderous idleness in the moist obscurity of the forest. They seemed to be going around the place chosen by the children.

Felifax got to his feet, sensing danger; his hand gripped the sacrificial dagger, the only weapon he had brought from the temple.

Djina, disquieted by her companion's attitude, directed her eyes at the wall of opaque darkness formed by the trees in front of them. A monster appeared before her. The child realized almost immediately what sort of creatures they were; their vague resemblance to the sacred cows in the temple informed her that they were wild cattle. Sourina had often spoken to them of the strength of these animals, of their ferocity and their combative instinct. They stood their ground fearlessly even against a tiger, which they sometimes vanquished. Djina understood Felifax's defensiveness then.

The zebu that had just appeared was a powerful beast. The moonlight gave its hide a dark red tint, almost black. It came forward tentatively, and stopped by one of the small ponds near the large pool, inflating its capacious muzzle to sniff the air

59

It took two or three more steps and grunted coarsely. It was a summons to the herd, which came out of the undergrowth to rejoin it, making the ground tremble. There were 28 massive males and a dozen slimmer females, slightly less wild. They went together to the pond and drank slowly, wallowing delightedly in the shallows.

The largest male did not participate in these games. He seemed to have detected something unusual. After a long bellow, he suddenly shook his head, showering flecks of foam all around him. As he directed his ferocious forehead toward the young couple's retreat, Felifax took firmer hold of the large blade with which the Brahman sacrificers cut off the heads of their expiatory victims, almost with a single blow. The beast let out another long bellow of fury. At that signal, the herd fled. The big male remained, poised for a charge.

Expecting the attack, Felifax pushed Djina into the shelter of the stub of a column and drew away from her. He was just in time. With an impulsive forward leap, the zebu rushed at him with its horns lowered. In a spray of water and mud, it plunged through the shallow pond and hurled itself upon the stranger, the intruder in the wild beasts' domain.

Felifax saw it coming. Fear was unable to grip his young and well-tempered heart. An innate reflex allowed him to make a nimble sidestep to avoid the impact; at the same time, his robust arm was extended, armed with the razor-sharp knife. He rolled on the ground, knocked over by the buffalo's shoulder–but the latter, abruptly arrested in its dash, collapsed in a heap, its enormous body touching the one that should have been its victim.

Felifax had just accomplished a fantastic feat. He owed it to the education provided by Sourina, who had taught his protégé how expiatory murders were carried out. The ferocious buffalo had had its throat cut as if by the hand of the most skillful of sacrificers.

The trembling Djina was now in her friend's arms. His hearty laugh rang out. It as impossible, however, to remain in that corner; the monster's blood had inundated the bed of vegetation.

Fortunately, there was no lack of retreats in the old house of Shivaism, and they were soon stretched out in the shelter of another fig-tree every bit as bushy as the first. Overcome by fatigue and emotion, Djina fell asleep in Felifax's arms. The latter, his eyes wide open, remained awake like a big brother.

No carnal thought came into his mind, although the darkness was the accomplice of such thoughts, with the intoxicating odors of the perfumes that surrounded him, There was another powerful charm too; the warmth of the supple and defenseless body of the young Hindu girl–but that was Djina, his childhood companion, the little sister of his gilded captivity.

In that healthy and handsome body, however, emergent from its youth, desires were mounting in muted fashion, especially since his flight from the temple. Many times, during his solitary existence, he had prowled around villages and along the banks of the many streams and streams letting out into the sacred Ganges; he had seen beautiful girls making their ritual ablutions, and had wanted to embrace them. And Felifax was holding in his arms the most exquisite of creatures. Djina was 13. Out there, a girl is already a woman at that tender age. Djina's body was a delicious Tanagra of pale bronze;[24] her warm lips would have been tendered with pleasure to those of her great friend. She would undoubtedly have given herself with all the ardor of her young love–but the "son of Kali" was a noble soul.

The child could rest in peace; her fleshy mouth, adorably outlined, could offer itself, as if for a kiss, without any carnal thought emerging to trouble the harmony of their affection. Djina was a beloved sister.

VII

For a month, Sir Eric Palmer explored the forest carefully–not as a huntsman, which would have put his quarry on guard, but in the fashion of a botanist and geologist. He was accompanied by John and two Hindus provided by his friend the engineer, who were very familiar with the great forest.

The doctor detective, one need have no doubt, was not much interested in stones and plants. He was looking for Felifax. He was looking for the boy–for whom he had developed a considerable sympathy–not so much as a policeman but as a man of science. He was desirous of success in the mission entrusted to him, and of casting light on an absolutely extraordinary mystery. He had, moreover, begun to perceive the hostility of the Chief of the Benares Police, and had taken note of his sarcastic attitude towards the negative results so far obtained. By virtue of these facts, his self-respect was definitely at stake, and he wanted to teach the other a lesson.

This Felifax was no common criminal, so his capture by the English authorities would be primarily a matter of satisfaction. In fact, he would be charged with a few peccadilloes, nothing more. His punishment would not be very serious. The rebel had made further nocturnal incursions into Benares, but without sowing terror everywhere. Thanks to the reports made by Baber, who was still an animal-keeper in the temple of Kali, the doctor was kept up to date. These reports were mostly conveyed to Sir Eric Palmer by Grace, who had returned to the city less than a week after her departure for the jungle–a move virtually forced by the flagrant ill-will of Ralph Napper's subordinates. The young woman was staying with friends, and had a bungalow on the bank of the Ganges at her disposal. This residence was in the quarter reserved for Europeans, and she received a visit from Baber every day.

With his great intelligence and marvelous instinct, the Hindu had recognized in Doctor Palmer qualities far above those of the professional police, overinfatuated with routine. In this imperturbable man with steely eyes, he had immediately seen someone who might aid him in the completion of his vengeance, without any fanfare but also without any weakness. He had, therefore, not been in the least astonished when he had been approached in the native city by a young Red Cross nurse seeking some unimportant item of information. It was, of course, a matter of not awakening suspicion in other Hindus.

Baber, having recognized the young woman instantly, had replied in a vague fashion–but the brief exchange had allowed Grace to slip him the address at which he could find her, and apprise him of the urgency of her visit. The place chosen for his daughter's residence in Benares had been skillfully elected by the doctor. Its owner, Reverend Douglas, was a former pastor, well-known and well-respected even by the Brahmans of the holy city, and one of his best friends.

It is a common thing for a Hindu to visit a pastor–an everyday matter. The animal-keeper was not running any risk by so doing. That is why, less than an hour after the encounter with Miss Grace, he learned from her, without any surprise, that the doctor was not being kept fully up to date with the most interesting developments.

Indeed, Sir Eric knew nothing about one further visit paid by Felifax to the temple of Kali. In the course of that incursion, the visitor had stolen textbooks and works of Hindu literature from Sourina. He had also carried off clothing in Djina's size and a *sarangi*, the abbreviated mandolin that *bayaderes* use to accompany their songs.[25] This time, the Brahmanic minister had not manifested any anger–to the extent that one might have thought him delighted by the theft of his books. Baber had heard him murmur, in one of his prayers to the goddess:

"Kali be praised, Felifax still loves the beauty and the glory of our land. He wants to continue studying its history. One must not lose hope; he will return to us stronger than ever, seasoned by the hard jungle life, and my dream may yet be realized."

What was that dream? Baber still did not know. He did not despair of finding out some day.

The animal-keeper made Grace a formal promise to come and tell her every time something happened that might interest the doctor, whether it occurred in the temple or in the city. The next day, a long letter from the young woman was dispatched with the provisions for the mine, and informed the doctor of his colleagues' bad faith.

Since then, Felifax had made two further incursions into the temple of Kali. The young man had committed similar larcenies on each occasion, stealing books and clothing.

For his part, Sourina had regarded them with the same satisfaction. Indeed, the young man had carried off books set out with that intention. The surprising thing–and this explains everything–was that these writings were calls to revolt: vehement accusations regarding the misdeeds of the conquerors, or poems glorifying the defenders of India.

If Baber had been put in possession of this particularity, it would have been further proof of Sourina's hatred for England, for it was by this means that he was trying to instill that hatred in the soul of the tiger-man.

In truth, Felifax had recovered a fervent desire to educate himself. His avid brain demanded food for thought. Since his earliest years he had studied with a kind of frenzied passion everything that Sourina had condescended to teach him. He spoke most of the Indian dialects fluently, especially Bengali, Hindustani, Maharashtri and Tamil.[26] He wrote Sanskrit marvelously, and all the other characters in use in the peninsula.

To the best of his ability, he repeated the lessons to Djina. A faithful pupil, the girl attempted to show herself worthy of her companion. She had been four years old when she had been taken in by Sourina following the death of her parents–primarily to serve as company for Felifax, who was then nine years old. The Brahman wanted to spare his singular child ill-advised solitude, and the two children had adored one another from the first.

A profound obscurity must, indeed, have enveloped the birth of the young boy, in view of the respect in which he was surrounded, in spite of the fits of anger that frequently took hold of him. What redoubtable atavism must have weighed upon him at that time, suffering the gilded captivity in which he was held while he dreamed of the jungle and of liberty? When these fits occurred, he became intractable, sowing terror among his entourage, appearing to manifest the ferocity of a young ocelot.

Sourina only allowed one form of correction to be inflicted on the person who, in his eyes, was destined for great things, but he designed a most original punishment for his chastisement: Djina would receive the whippings merited by her companion. This fustigation, however, sent the young boy into mad rages. One might have taken him for a demon!

So these two creatures intoxicated by liberty were in want of books. After the hectic activity of the day had nourished their muscles, they had need in the evenings to nourish their minds. Djina was also in need of clothing. The light veils she had worn on the day of her abduction had not lasted long. Muslin cannot resist the scratches of thorns and branches. By the second day, the girl was almost nude.

As dexterous as a fairy, she had rapidly put together a sort of garment made of tree-bark, woven lianas and the hide of an animal killed by her companion. This costume was useful enough for running through the jungle, but Felifax hated to see his little sister dressed so grotesquely in their hours of repose–hours during which they resumed their former life.

Felifax had been seen by the *bayaderes*, in the midst of whom Djina had lived. None of them, however, had raised the alarm–was he not a good and gentle friend to all the weak? On the contrary, when they found out that it was a matter of finding garments for Djina, they had become ingenious in facilitating his searches, adding little gifts thereto.

Meanwhile, Sir Eric Palmer continued his methodical search. Only he and John were armed, with repeating rifles; one of his two Hindu companions carried the doctor's botanical specimens, the other the provisions for the journey. They had no idea what the *sahib* was looking for. They believed their mission to be botanical and geological.

Every evening, the herbarium was overflowing with plants and stones; the doctor did not want to give rise to any suspicion regarding his occupation. Besides which, the flora of the jungle is always interesting to a learned man, by virtue of its immeasurable variety.

His perseverance was eventually crowned with a partial success. One afternoon, after having been on the march for hours on end, the doctor looked at his watch and saw that it was nearly 6 p.m. He was about to turn back when he thought he heard a woman singing, accompanied by the chords of a *sarangi* plucked by agile fingers. As he had just located the ruins of a temple, a sudden intuition cried out to him that he had reached his goal. Prudently, he slid through the profuse vegetation surrounding the ruins and was dumbstruck by emotion and surprise. Beneath his very eyes, the diffuse light illuminated a touching tableau.

Leaning against a bed of ferns and mosses, on which a young native of extreme beauty was stretched out, a Hindu girl was softly intoning a refrain by Kalidasa, the famous Indian poet.[27] She was accompanying herself on the *sarangi*.

Crouching behind a fallen cornice,[28] Sir Eric Palmer was able to contemplate this spectacle at his leisure, and to study the man for whom he had been searching. There was no possible doubt on his part: the person before his eyes was certainly Felifax, the incendiary, the inaccessible Bengali capable of causing alarm in the Indian government and stirring Scotland Yard to action–the man whom the people were already beginning to call the *son of Kali*.

He could not help smiling. The man advertised by the chief of police as a bloodthirsty demon appeared to him as the most gentle of creatures, in love with the bucolic. He had to arrest him despite that, with the help of John and the two Hindus.

Felifax was an athlete of the highest class; the play of the muscles beneath his bronzed skin was visible at the least movement. He was quiet strength and perfect courage personified–but Sir Eric too could pass for a redoubtable man, his faithful John had fine achievements to his credit, and the Hindus had been chosen from the most robust. Felifax would be subdued in a few seconds!

The die was cast. The doctor was getting ready to go in search of his men when an unexpected occurrence took the legs from under him, giving him pause. Brushing aside the vegetation, an enormous wild beast with a striped coat came out of the ruins and came to lie down beside the young man, emitting a vast yawn. Almost immediately, a second tiger did likewise.

The doctor's soul knew no fear, and his rifle-shot was infallible. Two bullets could rid him of the carnivores–but the advantage of surprise would be lost.

Felifax was not a man to let himself be taken. If he would not risk a fight, where would one look for him in this vast forest that he knew so marvelously well? Besides, there might be other wild beasts in the vicinity.

At that moment, one of the monstrous cats scented an unusual presence and let loose an disquieting roar. The doctor saw his two Hindus then, taking to their heels at full speed, while John, not yet inured to the surprises of India, showed distinct signs of anxiety.

At the cat's roar, Felifax had leapt to his feet. His only weapon, the deadly dagger, was in his hand. Sir Eric judged it imprudent to risk the venture. He beat the retreat, not without being tripped several times by lianas and brambles. He now knew the phenomenal being's retreat, and would return in force–accompanied, this time, by Europeans proven against the emotions caused by the rebel's redoubtable companions.

The young man had resumed his place on the bed of mosses and ferns, and Djina continued her song. Felifax was anxious, though; the tiger's roar stuck in his mind. Why had it made that sound, usually made by wild beasts at the approach of danger? He did not delay in getting up again. It was impossible for him to remain tranquil when he was thus preoccupied. Should he be afraid of some new manifestation of Sourina and the conquerors with whom the Brahman had allied himself?

In two or three bounds, he was outside the ruins examining the surrounding jungle. Suddenly, his perspicacious gaze spotted something on the ground.

As Sir Eric Palmer had turned around, he had been snagged by a thorny liana. By an unfortunate mischance, one of the leather buttons on his waistcoat had come away, without his even being aware of it

Felifax picked it up; the break was fresh. Moreover, he saw fragments of tobacco in the same place. An addicted smoker, the doctor always had residues of the nicotinic herb in his pockets; involuntarily, his hand had caused a few to fall out.

The young man immediately foresaw danger. A man had definitely been there–a European, as indicated by the button. Besides, there were still traces in the soil left by hobnailed boots.

Why had the man not attacked? He knew the hiding place of the person for whom they were still searching–as one of the *bayaderes* in the temple of Kali had told him during his last incursion. His capture would please the conquerors. Must he flee again? Yes, they must leave the ruins, where they had fared so well. He hurried back to the ancient temple of Shivaism and told Djina about the imminent danger.

He knew where to go because he lad located several retreats appropriate for a long encampment, in anticipation of this circumstance. They would have to undertake a long march, though. It was important to move to another region of the jungle. When they found the cage empty, the pursuers would not hesitate to search for the birds that had flown.

As he rapidly bundled up all that they possessed, Felifax advised Djina to change out of her muslins into her jungle costume. They were soon en route. A prudent "bushman," Felifax went along a stream that fed the large pool in order to leave no trace of his passage. It became their road; they walked close to the bank in order to avoid water-snakes and caymans. Everything that they could not carry with them they had hidden in the trees. If they needed anything therefrom, he would come to fetch it by the aerial route, in order to escape the attention of any lookouts placed around the ruins.

For the greater part of the night they marched, partly through the undergrowth and partly along the banks of the stream–which meandered elaborately through the jungle before letting out into the hospitable Ganges.[29]

They finally arrived at a little clearing surrounded by brambles so inextricable that it was necessary to slither under the branches covering the water in order to get into it. It was a safe retreat, in which they would not be easily found. They slumped down on their bundles of clothing, overcome by fatigue, and fell deeply asleep. Even the sunrise did not awaken them.

Although he got back to the mine very late, Sir Eric Palmer was nevertheless up at dawn. Accompanied by a dozen trustworthy and well-armed men, he departed on horseback for the Shivaite temple. Precise instructions had been issued. The man they were tracking was not to be killed under any circumstances; although he could not be considered a great criminal, his capture was a matter of urgent necessity.

Heading the column with his friend the engineer, Sir Eric Palmer retraced his steps. After three hours of marching, they arrived at their goal and took the necessary precautions for a surprise attack. Disappointment awaited them, alas; they found that the ruined temple was empty, and all the indications testified to a recent decampment.

Who had warned Felifax that his hiding-place had been discovered? Certainly not one of the Hindu porters; the unfortunates were still trembling over the roars heard at such close range on the previous day. In any case, they would hardly have dared to go into the jungle by night to warn their coreligionist of the threat hanging over him, even if they had not been ignorant of what was afoot.

Evidently, Felifax had had an intuition that he was not safe, and had put himself out of range.

The detective had the solution to the enigma soon enough. Above the bed of mosses and ferns, pinned to the trunk of the fig-tree by means of a stout thorn, he saw a sheet of paper torn from a Hindu book. On this sheet, traced in pencil in a neat and not at all shaky hand, in perfectly correct English, were lines that he read and reread:

Felifax has done nothing to justify his pursuit, and asks only to live in peace. Welcomed and nurtured by the fiercest lords of the dark expanses, he is the true master of the jungle and is able to call upon his friends for support. Take note and farewell!

The button the doctor had lost the day before was attached to the piece of paper, providing the explanation he had sought. Having thought about it, he smiled, and said: "That's a detective, my dear Palmer! I like this Felifax, definitely–and I'm glad to say, as my dear little Grace would: how exciting it is!"

VIII

For three days, Grace had been with her father. She had come to give him an account, in an emphatic manner, of things she had observed, especially regarding the persistent sarcasm of Ralph Napper. An indiscretion had been committed in respect of the failed capture, and the jealous functionary was exercising no restraint in his gibes against the famous detective who was supposed to be better than Sherlock Holmes.

The doctor's placidity was undisturbed. He permitted himself to laugh, and made every effort to calm his daughter. Grace could not take the animosity so philosophically, however. Her annoyance was caused primarily by her pride in her father's science.

"Let them talk, dear," Sir Eric repeated. "The yapping of these dogs doesn't worry me. I don't know whether I'll capture this Felifax, who seems to me to be an excellent fellow, at bottom. If chance grants me the satisfaction and permits me to bring him to Benares, I think I'd be capable of going in person to open the doors of his prison, to put him out of reach of the claws of these incompetent hounds."

"Why do you want to capture him, then?"

"It's purely a matter of satisfying my pride as a policeman. Afterwards, the boy wouldn't have any more enthusiastic defender than me. There are undercurrents in this business, it seems to me, that are not to the credit of England or of civilization."

He had told his daughter about the scene he had witnessed in the ruins of the ancient temple of Shiva, and described the charming couple formed by the unassailable person and his companion. Now the lovely Grace experienced an ardent desire to meet this fabulous youth about whom everyone was talking, and who was becoming a heroic figure in her eyes. He surely would not do her any harm–and what a fan-

71

tastic adventure to recount to all her friends in England when she returned there, after her father's latest triumph!

An intrepid horsewoman, educated by the doctor to be fearless, the young girl thought nothing of going out into the jungle alone and ranging far beyond any possible assistance. Mounted on a small but spirited and lively horse, wearing a comfortable riding-habit with trousers and boots, she had a repeating rifle in a leather sheath attached to her saddle, and her hand would certainly not have trembled in firing a shot.

On the first day, she had followed her father, but his slow manner of progress, examining every bush and every hidey-hole, was not in the least suited to a Miss Quicksilver like her. The following day, therefore, having declared that she was going out, she set out on her own in a different direction.

Sir Eric Palmer merely laughed; knowing that his daughter's decisions were beyond appeal, he did not try to put up any resistance. He contented himself with advising her to be careful.

The young woman continued these excursions for five days, taking a different direction every time. She trusted to the sagacity of her horse to find the way back to their lodgings when the time came to retrace her steps.

It was about 3 p.m. in the afternoon on the fifth day. Grace had dined frugally next to a spring, on a few provisions carried in her saddlebags. This young woman, intrepid and full of life, was quite unused to taking the siesta that is so dear to English residents of India, but it was necessary not to move about too much while the Sun was at its hottest. Obedient to paternal instructions, she had remained seated in the shade for two hours, reading the last popular novel she had brought from Benares.

The Sun having become milder, she was preparing to resume her journey when her mount suddenly began to show signs of nervousness and froze, with its legs shivering and its ears laid back–definite indications of serious alarm.

Grace put her hand on her repeating rifle, but she had not yet been able to draw the weapon when the horse broke into a mad gallop despite its rider's restraining efforts.

The young woman's cry of alarm brought a response from someone else. Djina having remained behind in the hut they had constructed in the fortress of lianas and brambles, Felifax was out gathering the nourishment necessary to sustain them. He was making his way through the forest canopy, as happy as ever in his liberty.

For several days, the young Hindu girl had seemed very sad, and had refused to tell her big brother the reason for her sadness. He too felt that he was prey to strange disturbances. What was the provenance of this state of affairs? A batch of books recently stolen from Sourina included the *Bhagavatapurana*, which described the loves of Krishna, and similar texts by the best Hindu authors. The young man had been aroused by reading them, and felt an ardent virility increasing within him, creating a desire for unfamiliar embraces. Despite this, he had not perceived Djina's love. When he went out adventuring, he dreamed of meeting a princess as beautiful as the day, at whose feet he might fall down. This was the state of mind he was in when he heard a cry of terror emitted by a female voice.

Passing before his eyes, he saw a horse galloping furiously through the jungle. A young European woman was trying in vain to rein it in. A second scream escaped from her throat. He understood the danger immediately. Without any doubt, the unfortunate woman would break her head on the trunk of a tree or a low branch, or would be strangled by some treacherous liana playing the role of a noose or lasso.

He acted reflexively. Letting go of the game and fruits he was carrying, he leapt down. He ran with unimaginable rapidity, like a bullet, leaping over obstacles. With the aid of his steely leg-muscles, he felt capable of matching the speed of the maddened animal and thus prevent a catastrophe. The European woman would then be able tell the people pursuing him about his presence in the vicinity–she might be an enemy herself–and he had to be careful, but she was in danger. That was the only thing that mattered to the noble and generous soul of Felifax the outcast, Felifax the hunted.

Suddenly, that which he had foreseen occurred. The horsewoman was brutally thrown to the ground by an encounter with the elevated root of a banyan, and the horse continued on its way riderless.

In three prodigious strides, Felifax was beside the young woman, who was stretched out unconscious. Her helmet had slipped to the ground at the beginning of the run. Her short-cropped hair had provided no protection and there was a rather large cut on her forehead, from which blood was running abundantly over her frightfully pale face.

How could he bring her help?

Fortunately, Felifax was not very far from the hut he had built to shelter him and Djina. He lifted the young woman in one arm. Carefully protecting her head, he resumed his course, no less rapidly than before. He soon began to experience a vague sensation of well-being as he held that curvaceous body, whose warmth was tangible through thin khaki cloth, tightly against his own. The delicate face was equally seductive: young, ideally beautiful and replete with a new charm.

Squatting in front of the hut, Djina was preparing the evening meal in vessels brought back by Felifax from one of his trips to Benares. On seeing her cherished companion arrive carrying a young white woman, with his naked torso covered in blood from her wound, she released an exclamation of astonishment.

Felifax deposited his burden on a bed of leaves. The Hindu girl hurried to the young woman's side. Under her diligent care, Grace recovered her senses. The violence of the blow, however, had caused a severe concussion, rendering her delirious.

The chief Brahman's science had instructed the young couple in the innumerable resources the jungle contains for the healing of wounds and many diseases. Felifax departed again, going in search of beneficial plants. He left the Englishwoman in Djina's care.

The young man's absence extended to nearly an hour. This was because he had thought about the wounded woman's horse, exposed to danger from predators. He succeeded in locating it, caught in some lianas and unable to extract itself. The animal's fright was redoubled by Felifax's approach. The feline emanation that his body gave off terrified the poor beast, and its legs were trembling as he led it back to the clearing. There, he shut it in the little hut where he kept his provisions, sheltered from wild animals avid for such windfalls.

When he went back into the cabin with the plants he had gathered, the two young people were able to give the wounded girl the necessary treatment. While Felifax crushed the herbs to make a poultice to put on the wound, Djina set some leaves and cinchona bark on the fire to boil, with the aim of producing a febrifuge beverage.[30]

While they worked, they exchanged their impressions of the stranger, wondering where she might have come from. English misses did not have the habits of venturing alone into the depths of the jungle.

When the stew was ready and the first dressing had been put on the wound, Sourina's learned pupil brought a sovereign ease to the wounded woman by means of some antispasmodic and refreshing massage. Peaceful sleep replace the delirium almost immediately.

Meanwhile, Sir Eric Palmer had already returned to the Silver-Hole mine, and his daughter's lateness was making him anxious. Grace usually returned at the same time as he finished work, to make the cocktails that no self-respecting English person neglects, whatever the latitude. On this occasion, the cocktails had to be made by the engineer, and drunk without any pleasure. The doctor's understandable apprehension was shared by his friends.

Dinner time arrived too quickly that evening, even though it had been put back considerably in the hope that the latecomer might arrive. The daylight was fading rapidly. Her absence became disturbing.

What could have happened to the young woman? Might she have encountered a predatory beast? Had she had a fall? Or had she stopped in one of the jungle villages comprised by the workmen and their families? There were so many awkward questions that it was impossible even to place the answers in order of likelihood.

Mad with worry, the doctor could not remain inactive. He begged his friends to go out and search for his unfortunate daughter–but what could they accomplish by night in such a hostile environment, animated by wild beasts out hunting? The engineer had to get angry with him, amicably, to prevent him from going out alone to look for her. He did not want to leave the detective alone, promising that they would send out patrols in every direction at first light, even if it was necessary to suspend work in the mine.

Nothing could calm the poor father. These disquieting regions were even more dangerous by night for a young woman on her own. Sir Eric Palmer's desperation became so great that the mining engineer brought all his men together. He was easily able to obtain volunteers for an immediate search, carried out with the aid of torches by a company numerous enough to scare away the denizens for the forest. For several hours, the indefatigable patrols wandered through the immense jungle surrounding the mine. The bright Moon added to the light of their torches, from which the frightened animals fled, wondering what this new human whim might signify.

Alas, no trace was discovered.

All this happened a long way from Felifax's "fort." No echo of the hubbub could reach as far as the humble hut of bamboo and palm-leaves where the object of the search was breathing feebly. By the light of a lamp that was more than rudimentary, the two fugitives from the temple of Kali were watching over their patient.

Tears were flowing silently from Djina's eyes. The shadow in which she was sitting prevented Felifax from seeing these tears–but would he have noticed them even if Djina had been in the full glare of the light? It was as if his eyes were hypnotized by the young white woman stretched out on the bed of leaves–and his pupils expressed such ecstasy, such adoration, that the little Hindu girl's heart had been broken. They had never held such an expression for her. She understood, alas, that the love of which the beautiful books from the temple spoke in such exalted tomes had suddenly taken root in him. And that love was not for her! It was directed towards the foreigner: a girl with nacreous skin, a daughter of the conquerors, against whom she had heard so many curses directed.

For his part, the young man was beginning to understand the strange disturbance that he had felt for a long time in his impassioned reading of *Kalidasa*–a disturbance he had felt even more strongly as he clasped the lightly-clad body of the young Englishwoman to his own naked torso. Love, whose impact he had long awaited, had finally struck him–and in a soul such as his, that sentiment could not be other than violent, profound and potentially eternal.

He did not want to think about the future, to remind himself that he was a virtual outlaw, a man hunted by the English. He refused to think about the fact that this young woman stretched out in his hut was undoubtedly the daughter of one of the enemies who would strike him down. He was living in the present moment. She was here!

In an hour, a day, or perhaps a week she would come back to life under the care that he was lavishing upon her; then he would see the beauty of her eyes and the dazzle of her smile as he reveled in the sweetness of her voice. For a happiness like that, he was ready to give his life.

At dawn, he was still awake. His body and his iron soul were capable of defying time when necessary. Exhausted by fatigue, and perhaps by weeping too, Djina had gone to sleep.

Meanwhile, at Silver-Hole, a father, demented by frustration, continued his search.

IX

The blow that Grace had received was a terrible one; she remained unconscious for a week–a week during which the devotion of Felifax and Djina never relented for a single minute. The Hindu girl had contrived, in the end, to make her companion see reason, and persuaded him to get a little sleep. Now they took turns to watch over her, although the youth still took it upon himself to keep much longer vigils. He continued to respond ecstatically to that face, so pale and captivating, whose cheeks the fire of fever animated–despite his remedies– to a redness that was so violent as to seem almost artificial.

Head wounds usually heal quite quickly when cauterizing herbs work their customary wonders, but her feverish state persisted. Without that salutary care, continued with regularity, cerebral fever would certainly have set in, carrying away that delicate lily in the full flower of her youth and beauty.

Felifax began to grow desperate, and in his desperation he talked of going to look for a doctor in Benares, whom he would bring by force, if not of his own free will. Such a step would lead to his ruin; he could see that–but it was of scant importance to him. His first and foremost desire was to snatch from the jaws of death the young woman he had rescued, and who had filled his soul.

More confident than he was, Djina had not the same reasons to become insane with worry. She was familiar with the effects of fever. She had often seen young women cared for in the temple. Knowing the dangers to which Felifax would be exposed if he followed up his charitable impulse, she had begged him to wait for a week, promising him that she would raise no objection if there had been no improvement at the end of that time.

The week in question would end that very evening. Djina awaited in terror the arrival of the fatal moment when, in the absence of further equivocation, her beloved companion would hasten towards his ruin, believing that it was his duty. Who could tell what might happen? Could the charitable act of receiving into his hut and caring for the young English girl be reckoned a crime? Anything could be turned against the man they wished to bring down, to do him harm.

Felifax was determined, though. He would go to Benares that evening. He explained his plan to Djina.

Entering the city by night, he would discover the residence of the conquerors' most celebrated practitioner, even if he had to knock on every door. He hoped, however, to be able to find a better way of locating the doctor. Sourina had taught him that, according to English custom, all the information useful to their citizens were displayed, night and day, at the Town Hall. By that means, he would obtain the information easily. He would introduce himself into the sleeping doctor's house by stealth, tie him up in a bundle, and carry him through the jungle to the cabin. Then he would order him to cure the sick woman, or else he would be abandoned to the beasts of the forest. He would keep him for as long as necessary, and take him back to Benares by the same method. By that means, he would not be capable of any indiscretion regarding the location of their retreat.

Djina knew how headstrong Felifax was. He would carry out this mad plan step by step. She feared that it would have deplorable consequences.

The young man had gone out to renew their supplies of beneficial herbs, in order to permit Djina to continue the treatment during his absence. Left on her own, the Hindu girl suddenly shivered; a feeble and halting voice had just murmured, in English: "Where am I? What's happened to me?" And almost immediately afterwards, in a plaintive tone: "How my poor head hurts!"

These words had been pronounced by the injured woman. After seven days of total unconsciousness, she had just opened her eyes, amazed to find herself in that mean, more-or-less rudimentary cabin, with no other ornament than a *sarangi* and a few books.

Djina spoke English fluently, having learned it alongside Felifax. She went to the injured woman and explained to her in a few sentences about her frightened horse, her fall, the intervention of a young Hindu, her removal to the cabin and the care that had been lavished upon her.

"How long have I been here, then?" the invalid asked, fearfully.

"The Sun has set seven times since your mind lost the power of thought, and..."

The Hindu girl had to interrupt herself. Felifax had just appeared, like a young Greek Hercules, at the door of the hut. He was clad only in his fur *langouti*.[31]

The young Englishwoman's dilated eyes fixed themselves upon this apparition with a sentiment that she could not have defined herself. Was it an effect of the fever? Was it some mirage produced by her aching head? He seemed to her to be a supernatural presence, and it imprinted itself unforgettably on Grace's memory.

Felifax spoke in very pure English, his voice seeming to sing: "Brahma has answered the prayer of his faithful children! Our joy is great, miss, in seeing you emerge at last from the fever that worried us so intensely."

Subdued by that captivating and musical voice, without even being aware of it, Miss Palmer drank the horribly bitter beverage that Djina had just put to her lips in half a coconut shell. Her eyes could not tear themselves away from the young man. Divining the importance of her emotion from her expression, Djina felt a violent sorrow lacerating her heart. Would the foreigner respond to the ardent love nascent within Felifax?

"Can you tell me," Grace asked, in a breathless voice, "whether it's true that I've been here for seven days, as this girl has told me? That would be frightful!"

"My sister Djina is not mistaken. A week has, indeed, gone by since the moment when I picked you up in the jungle."

"And you haven't informed anyone that I'm here?"

"How could I have done? I have absolutely no idea who you are. There were no papers in your pockets to inform us as to your identity."

"You should have gone to Benares to inform the police. That's what one does in such cases." Grace had scarcely pronounced these words when she felt a sharp pang of regret, for a painful contraction had overtaken the features of her two saviors.

In a voice that was more serious and bitter, Felifax explained: "I was planning to go in search of an English doctor this evening and bring him here. Since I have not taken the step that is, it seems, indispensable in such cases, important reasons must have constrained me. If I were able to acquaint you with those reasons, miss, you would not reprove me for that omission."

She had caused him distress. Understanding that, Grace attempted to make her voice as gentle as possible, in order to appease that pain. "Pardon me, I beg you, for my stupid reaction. The reason for it is that I have a dearly beloved father who doubtless thinks me dead and must be in despair. I must go to find him right away!"

The last tisane proffered by Djina was already taking effect; the patient's head was less painful, and a soft warmth was circulating in her veins, seemingly giving her back her strength. With the aid of the two young people, she raised herself up slightly, but her eyes immediately became clouded. She felt herself fainting into her hosts' arms.

"It will be impossible for you to take a step for two or three days," Felifax said. "What is more, it will be necessary to take everything that we give you meekly. Then, perhaps, you might try to go out–on condition, however, that you do not too far. Where is your father? Is he in the jungle?"

"My father is..."

The young woman stopped, reflexively. She had just realized that the man kneeling beside the bed was undoubtedly the singular being for whom her father was searching. He and his companion were remarkably similar to the description the doctor had given. She could not reveal the true identity of her father to her rescuer and inform him that her father was the man charged with his arrest. To cover up her hesitation she pretended to have suffered a slight fit of weakness, passing her hand over her bandaged forehead. She continued: "My father is at the silver mine excavated in the jungle at the place called Silver-Hole."

Felifax had often been in the vicinity of the mine, avoiding it carefully; he knew exactly where it was. He had often cursed the Europeans who had come to disembowel his domain. He nodded his head to signify that the place of extraction was known to him. Then there was a pause, until he started, seeing a flood of tears run from the injured woman's eyes. Trembling with emotion, he inquired gently as to the cause of her distress.

"I'm thinking of my father, alas–of his despair, which will have to be further prolonged. If only I could let him know that I'm alive..."

It would be impossible to send this information; she guessed as much in seeing the forest-dwellers' expressions darken. She fell silent then, although the flow of her tears redoubled.

The young man gazed at her with ardent eyes, in which a great compassion was legible. A violent struggle began within him. He could calm her distress with a single word–but it would sacrifice the liberty that was so dear to him.

"Miss," he said, in a grave tone, "your father will be informed this very day. He shall know that his daughter is alive, and will soon return to him."

A fugitive flicker of joy passed over the young woman's face, and was then extinguished. This time, reflection had made her think of the danger run by the handsome and generous young man. "Friend," she said, "permit me to address you thus, since I understood, just now, that you had powerful reasons for not going to Benares to inform the authorities of my accident. The same reasons, I suppose, still apply in opposition to the step that I suggested."

"It does not matter, miss. It is a matter of setting your mind at rest and bringing your father an immediate release from his great sorrow."

Grace was in a quandary. Knowing her father's inflexible conscience, she doubted that any consideration would prevent him from doing what he believed to be his duty. He would not hesitate to arrest his daughter's savior, without giving any thought to the fact that the reckless imprudence the young man had committed arose from the simple desire to bring him consolation. He would take his prisoner to Benares, even if, as he had said a few days ago, he had then to open the doors of his prison. No, he must not be allowed, at any price, to expose the courageous young man–to whom she felt drawn by an incomprehensible sympathy–to danger.

"No, I tell you," she said, forcefully. "It's too generous. I refuse to let you take such a step. My father's sorrow will be prolonged for three days more, and his joy will be all the greater for the delay."

Felifax's decision, however, appeared to be irrevocable. Handing the young woman a little notebook fallen from the pocket of her riding-jacket, along with a pen that was also her property, he simply said: "Here's the means of writing a sentence to reassure your father as to your fate. To calm your fears regarding mine, I promise to arrange matters so that the message is received without my being seen by anyone. After completing my mission, if I am able to return, I will tell you who I am and the reasons for my initial hesitation."

In view of the tone in which these words were pronounced, Grace nodded her head. It was better to consent, to prevent him from committing an imprudence.

Supported by Djina, she sat up on the bed of dry leaves. Tearing a blank page from the notebook, she wrote a few words of explanation, requesting trust.

It was, by now, about 6 p.m. Felifax got ready to leave, having received detailed instructions as to the exact location of the doctor's room within the encampment and the means by which it could be reached without too much risk of being seen.

After his departure, Grace took another cup of the beverage and went peacefully to sleep, holding one of the Hindu girl's hands in her own.

It was nearly midnight when the guard-dogs at Silver-Hole gave tongue, making such a din that they brought the entire camp to its feet. Bizarrely, instead of hurling themselves upon the intruder–or intruders–they went to ground in every available corner. At the same time, an extreme agitation was manifest among the horses and other animals, which made the old hands say: "Lord Tiger is paying us a little visit; let's see if there's any chance of bagging a nice rug."

They all took up their weapons and set up ambushes in the vicinity of the kennels and the stables–the places most likely to attract the kings of the jungle.

In the room reserved for his use, Sir Eric Palmer was just getting ready to lie down, although he could not sleep. Desolate and inconsolable, the poor man blamed himself for his daughter's death. Why had he accepted this mission? Why had he given her permission to accompany him to India–and then into the jungle? He had just returned from Benares, where he had hoped, momentarily, to find some trace of her.

In response to the racket made in the camp, he too picked up his gun and went out. Having learned the reason for the alarm, he joined his friend the engineer in the ambush set in the most exposed position.

A quarter of an hour passed in feverish impatience, all eyes staring fervently into the darkness. Alas, no sign of the redoubtable predator was manifest other than the tremulous anxiety of the animals.

Eventually, everything became calm. The horses stopped shivering; the dogs stopped growling. The lord of the jungle had doubtless made a detour around the rifles that were waiting for him. Not caring to spend all night lying in wait, the men returned to their beds. Sir Eric did likewise. What a surprise! By the light of his desk-lamp, he saw a piece of paper on the folding table, which had not been there before.

The doctor snatched up the missive, and immediately felt dizzy as a violent emotion gripped him by the throat. He had recognized his daughter's handwriting. It was a trifle shaky, to be sure, but he could not doubt its authenticity. He had to sit down. His legs gave way, weakened by emotion, for the few lines said:

Dear Father, because of an accident your darling Grace has found it impossible to contact you for eight days. She is being admirably well looked after by exquisite individuals. In three or four days, she will be in your arms. It is impossible for me to tell you more. Set aside now the sorrow that my kisses will soon be able to wipe out.

Your darling Grace

At the bottom, below the signature, was a little sign arranged between them to thwart any attempt at deception, should there be any such possibility.

He read the note again. No one but Grace could have written it, that was certain. He recognized the paper from her notebook and the ink from her pen, which was the same as his own. Eight days, it said–exactly the number of days since her disappearance. The ink was fresh, so the note had been written within the last few hours.

He got up, mad with joy, laughing and crying–an extraordinary thing, in a man of his strength and coolness. He ran into his friend's room to tell him the good news and to say that he would go to Benares the following morning, to tell Baber to suspend his investigations.

X

Baber, having been set on that quest, had indeed been looking for Grace, visiting every *purdah* and monastic *zenana* maintained by the high priest and his associates.[32] This search was not without its reasons. The part-time animal-keeper had formed a real affection for Doctor Palmer, and when he had heard of his daughter's disappearance his imagination had got to work. He had put together certain troubling facts that strongly indicated Sourina's involvement.

What had happened was this. The morbid jealousy of Commissioner Napper with regard to the colleague summoned from Europe had led him to do something terrible. Happening to find himself in the company of the autocratic priest of Kali, the police chief had indulged in a little thoughtless gossip, mentioning the imminent capture of Felifax–a capture that was inevitable, promised by a famous detective capable of working miracles, albeit with the aid of persistent good luck.

The chief Brahman was an accomplished psychologist. He understood immediately what sentiments lay behind the highly-placed functionary's chatter, and used his skill to elicit a much more serious breach of confidence–the information that the famous policeman had been installed in the jungle for more than a month.

That was more than sufficient for the shrewd Brahman. Emissaries had immediately been sent forth to get to the bottom of this disquieting news, and had not taken long to ascertain that the man in question was named Sir Eric Palmer, and was installed with his daughter at the Silver-Hole mine.

Sourina's memory was prodigious. He had always read the English newspapers in order to keep abreast of events. He had seen the name of the famous doctor detective there on several occasions, with reference to the mysterious affairs he had cleared up. There could be no doubt–His Majesty's government had decided to send him to Benares to elucidate the secret of the scientifically-inexplicable human phenomenon that had caused such a disturbance among the natives.

Sir Eric Palmer was a man who might capture Felifax and solve the mystery of his birth. More than that, being hardly inclined to encourage Hindu fanaticism, he might dispose of the young man coldly, to prevent him from causing more serious trouble. Sourina's apprehension led him to seek advice. He spoke to his sole confidant within the temple, the Brahman in charge of the tigers. Unknown to him, though, Baber was listening inside one of the little gilded chapels in the cloister.

Although the curious animal-keeper could not hear all of the conversation, the fragments he caught gave him pause. They consisted of these detached words and phrases: *Detective Palmer... jungle... man without pity... danger... Felifax... a daughter... hostage... convent.*

Coincidentally, Baber was informed two days afterwards of Grace's disappearance, by the doctor himself.

The combination of these facts was strongly suggestive. He had called them to his interlocutor's attention, and a faint glimmer of hope had alleviated the amateur detective's anguish. Alas, it was impossible get to the bottom of the matter for the moment. On the one hand, the chief Brahman could not be interrogated directly. On the other, the emissary of Scotland Yard was on a secret mission; that was his primary duty, and nothing–not even the fate of his beloved daughter–must allow that to be compromised.

The next day, Baber learned that Sourina had gone to make a tour of all the Brahmanic monasteries and *mattas* [33] maintained in the name of Kali the Black. He would be accompanied by two or three Brahmans and a few servants bearing gifts. It was child's play for the cunning Baber to get himself selected to accompany his master. He went with Sourina.

The real reason for this unannounced tour of inspection was to find a place of internment for Grace, taken as a hostage in exchange for Felifax–but this was nothing but a threat, although Baber thought it an accomplished fact. For three days, they went from convent to convent; they were very numerous around the holy city. The animal-keeper looked hard, asked questions and eavesdropped on conversations, but he could not obtain any clue as to the fate of Miss Palmer. He did, however, experience a considerable emotion.

In one strictly enclosed retreat, he learned, in an unexpected fashion, of the presence of Sita, the former priestess of the tigers in the temple of Kali–the Sita who had been intimately involved in the religious drama following which his brother Rao had suffered a violent death. He could not see her, alas. He only heard Sourina talking to her, instructing her to continue to keep the secret with the utmost rigor.

On his return to Benares, he went to the Reverend Douglas' house in order to meet the doctor. Sir Eric had just returned to the city; it was the day after the happy moment when he had received news from Grace, announcing her imminent return.

Although he was not a credulous man, Baber's Hinduism led him to advise against taking any further steps before the date indicated in the note.

Meanwhile, in the hut in the jungle, Grace was taking her first meal, after having learned Felifax's fantastic history.

In a heated voice, he had told her about his birth, whose circumstances were still unknown to him, about the princely fashion in which Sourina had brought him up, the supernatural power that he had been given over wild beasts, the extraordinary erudition that he had obtained, and about his misery in being imprisoned while his nature filled him with the desire to live free in the paradise of the tropical forest.

The young woman perceived the nobility of that heart, the beauty of that soul, which hatred had been unable to corrode. All his misdeeds had been committed with but a single goal: to liberate his little companion, who had been unjustly imprisoned.

The three days required to give Grace the strength necessary for her departure passed very quickly. The young woman felt herself attracted, with all her being, towards this young man, who was so handsome, so upright, so loyal. When he finally told her that she could now go to find her father, her great joy was mixed with a profound pain.

She left the next day, at dawn, in company with Felifax, after having bid Djina an affectionate farewell and given her the locket she wore around her neck as a souvenir.

Felifax took the horse by the bridle. Having been looked after every day by the young man, the animal had eventually grown accustomed to the singular scent that had initially terrified it. It no longer showed the slightest inclination to revolt.

They walked for four hours, chatting; a violent emotion constrained their hearts and occasionally made their voices quiver.

When they came near to the workings at Silver-Hole, Felifax stopped and murmured, with difficulty: "Goodbye, Miss Grace. We are destined to part here. You are English, I am Hindu; we are worlds apart. If you deign, sometimes, to remember Felifax, assure yourself that your image is forever graven within him, never to be forgotten."

There was a sob in these final words, which stirred the Englishwoman's increasingly troubled heart profoundly. Without quite knowing what she was saying, as if pressed by an irresistible impulse, she pronounced these words, which were tantamount to an engagement on her part: "Your image is similarly graven on my heart, my dear friend! Grace Palmer cares very little about racial differences, when souls are in harmony. It will certainly be a long time before we see one another again, my father's intention being to send me to Calcutta to pursue my medical studies while awaiting our return to England. Oh well, whatever Indian city I find myself in, I shall come in response your first call. You only need to go to Reverend Douglas, the pastor in Benares, and say to him: 'On behalf of Felifax.' You can be assured of its immediate and secret transmission. Now tell me how I can reach you, in case

I can, in my turn, have an important communication to make to you."

"Along the route, I have pointed out landmarks that will enable my hiding-place to be found. If I am forced to leave it for any reason, information concerning my new location will be under the rock that I showed you yesterday evening. Good-bye, miss; my best wishes go with you."

With an impulsive movement, she leaned towards him, kissed him on the forehead and departed at the gallop, leaving him breathless with emotion. The cries of joy announcing the young woman's arrival at Silver-Hole were soon audible. Then, slowly and with his head bowed, feeling internally torn apart and experiencing an atrocious misery, Felifax went back to his hut, where Djina's tenderness made every effort to re-lieve his great suffering.

For the first time, a secret came between Sir Eric and his daughter.

After the first moments of hectic effusion, Anglo-Saxon phlegm, coupled with the doctor's own stoicism, gained the upper hand. He became the detective again. The mystery had tormented him atrociously for an entire week; his task was to solve it.

He ran up against Grace's desire to maintain silence. She told him that she could not remember where she had fallen, that she had been taken in by poor Hindus in a jungle village, and that they had looked after her devotedly. For eight days, she had been delirious; after that, her first thought had been to notify her father.

"I'm astonished," she added, a trifle awkwardly, "that my letter was not put directly into your hands. The messenger would then have been able to give your further information. Personally, I wouldn't know how to find the place where I fell. I was drowsy all the while the horse was bringing me back."

That could not fool a father who was also a famous de-tective. Sir Eric understood that his daughter was deliberately concealing the location of the people who had cared for her.

As for the wound, which he examined carefully in company with the mine's physician, he was astonished by the admirable fashion in which it had been treated. What unknown colleague had accomplished that quasi-miraculous cure?

The mine's doctor, who had been in India for more than 20 years, talked about old *yogis* who knew all the properties of the jungle plants. Sir Eric could not help thinking of Sourina. Perhaps he had taken Grace away when she was injured, had cared for her by means of his Brahmanic science, and–fearful of the consequences of too bold a move–had released her again. Naturally, he would have sworn her to silence on the matter of what had happened, under threat of taking venge-ance upon her father. And Grace, by no means ignorant of the fabulous powers and irresistible mastery of advanced initiates, would have obeyed the injunctions of the terrible disciple of Kali. So he talked to his daughter about the chief Brahman, and was astonished to see her authentic amazement, followed by sincere hilarity. That was proof enough–Sourina had noth-ing to do with it!

Felifax's name came to mind, but he dared not pro-nounce it. Later, perhaps, Grace would take him into her con-fidence.

The young woman was badly in need of rest. Grace was required to spend whole days on a chaise longue on the veran-dah, looking out in the direction from which she had come after leaving Felifax. Her heart told her that the young man would definitely try to see her again, and because she feared some reckless imprudence on his part, she wanted to show herself to him. Her feminine intuition, or that of a woman in love, was not mistaken. Felifax made the long journey every day, coming to study from afar the woman who had taken pos-session of his heart, his soul and his thoughts.

He was away from the hut all day, never getting back until late at night, prey to a depressing sorrow that moved Djina to despair. The Hindu girl's heart was replete with the treasures of affection. In spite of the immensity of her despair, she was able to repress it into the utmost depths of her being, and always presented a smiling face to her companion. She was able to find words capable of dressing the bloody wounds of that ardent heart.

One evening, Felifax came back even sadder than usual. Grace had left for Benares. He had seen her, with her father, in the little automobile that ferried supplies to the mine. The luggage she had taken with her left the matter in no doubt; even so, the young woman had darted a glance full of sadness at the place where they had parted. What strength of character it had required to prevent him from emerging from the bushes where he was hiding, and to which he had come every day to spend long hours watching her!

Cursing Kama,[34] Djina saw tears in her cherished companion's eyes. Felifax blessed her, in spite of his terrible despair.

XI

Days passed. Once, returning unexpectedly to the hut, Felifax found Djina collapsed in a corner of the hut, weeping with prodigious sobs. His tender and affectionate heart was upset; he leaned over the fragile and delightful girl, shaken convulsively by her sobs, and took her in his arms. Sitting on the ground, he rocked her like a little child.

The previous day, a rather painful scene had been enacted between them.

While they were on the bank of one of the little tributaries of the Ganges that went through the jungle, Djina suddenly heard cymbals and trumpets sounding piercing and deafening notes. A wedding! The bride and groom, not taking the trouble to go as far as Benares to the Manikarni *ghat*–the stairway ordinarily used for such a consecration–were getting married on the river bank.

Curious about everything unfamiliar, Djina took Felifax by the hand and drew him to the riverbank, while keeping completely out of sight.

The primitive orchestra was set some 20 meters from the water. The relatives of the bride and groom were sitting beside the musicians, grouped around the umbrellas of five Brahmans, who were accompanying them. The bridegroom was dressed in red; jeweled pendants and jasmine flowers hung from his pink silk turban, hiding his face, which could be seen nevertheless to be very young.

As for the bride, her face was hidden, in the Muslim fashion. A veil of green silk, sewn with yellow flowers, covered her head and hung down over her breasts. Her bare feet projected from beneath her blue dress, starred with white dots, the soles painted red–an emblem of her virginity. Her toes were ornamented by silver rings, while copper and gold bands gleamed about her arms and legs. She moistened her feet in river water, representing the sacred Ganges.

93

The groom shed his sandals in his turn and–retaining his pink socks–paddled in the mud that is always abundant by the river's shore.

Moved by this ceremony, which she would have liked to be hers, Djina had kept the hand of her beloved in her own. Following the mirages of a dream, she pressed herself against him fondly, seeking a possible embrace. Felifax had knelt down, in order to be better able to hide his tall figure in the bushes. Suddenly, he felt the Hindu girl's bare arms wind around his neck, while two ardent lips were stuck to his in a protracted kiss.

Surprised by this caress, which sent a river of fire coursing through his veins, Felifax did not pull away immediately, and even returned the embrace. What would happen? Djina made the mistake of speaking, breaking the spell. He recognized his little childhood companion, who had disappeared momentarily behind a veil, and pushed her away rather brutally. Then, having risen to his feet, he went back to the hut, without saying a single word along the way.

That evening, he did not want to go to bed under the same roof as his pseudo-sister, doubtless to avoid any further attempt, and at sunrise on the following morning he went away.

That was why Djina was weeping.

Little by little, by means of tender caresses and gentle words, Felifax succeeded in drawing out the secret of that poor little wounded heart. He had, to be sure, perceived the young girl's sentiments in respect of him–sentiments that had little accord with his own. Her kisses had, in fact, an ardor beyond those of a sister for her brother. Entirely preoccupied by his own love, however, he had not examined the matter in depth.

Keeping the delicate creature on his knees, making his embrace more affectionate, he spoke to her softly in a warm tone: "So, pretty little Djina, that's the big secret of your constant sadness and the hurt tone that drives me to despair. Your heart is full of an unfortunate passion, which combats the affection that should unite us. I have told you already, during the first days of our life in the jungle, that you are a dear little sister to me, whom I love, in all the beauty of the word, and whom I shall always keep by my side. *Madama*–the intoxication of lust, who represents the most sensuous aspect of Kama–is impossible between us, you see, little sister."

"Yes," she replied, "because you have given your heart to that accursed Englishwoman. Better that her fall had killed her."

"Don't blaspheme, Djina. That malevolent wish is unworthy of your exquisite soul. You can see that I am not roused to anger by your words; they merely make me sad. I hold, however to that which you know to be true, and I can swear to you upon Brahma that, even if I had never met Miss Grace, you would never have been anything to me but a beloved sister. Reflect on that, my Djina; we know one another too well, we are too long accustomed to treating one another as two children of the same mother. Love comes at a stroke; an affection too long prolonged cannot change into true love. Believe in Felifax, little sister, and look into your own soul."

He observed that the young Hindu girl was unsettled by these wise words. She knew her friend to be incapable of lying, and fully understood that she must abandon all hope.

He hugged Djina to him more tenderly. "Setting aside any carnal sentiment, little sister, a great affection is more beautiful than a violent love, for it endures eternally. Let us go through life hand in hand, living for one another, sharing our joys and our troubles. I do not know what will happen with Miss Grace! Perhaps much suffering for me–but I shall always have the sweet affection of my sister Djina to dress my wounded heart. You may, in your turn, meet a man capable of moving your heart–then you will find your big brother nearby if ever you are in need of aid or protection. For my part, Djina, nothing can ever separate me from you save for death."

"Nor me from you, brother. Your little sister will live only for the happiness of Felifax, and intends to sacrifice her entire life to it."

The delightful creature had understood. Her insensate dream vanished at that moment. She remained in his affectionate arms, and it was her who spoke to him about the pretty Englishwoman. She discovered then what fantastic projects the young man had imagined since the revelation of his great love for Miss Palmer.

Had Grace not said to him that, for her, no barrier existed between and Englishwoman and a Hindu, when their souls were beautiful? That was tantamount to an engagement. He wanted to be worthy of her. What should he do? He still did not know, but he had faith. One day, Brahma would inspire him. Foreigners came demanding that the jungle yield the treasures it contained–well, why should he not do as they did? Had not Sourina revealed to him that the soil of India, especially that of Bengal, hid unimaginable treasures? The colossal fortunes of the maharajahs came from these exploitations, such as the Silver-Hole mine where Miss Grace and her father had stayed. Such mines not only produced silver but gold in its native state, diamonds, sapphires, rubies, emeralds, topazes, beryls, turquoises and many other precious stones.

Sourina knew the secret location of several deposits. He had spoken of it often on occasions when he was seized by the mad ambition that he had long nurtured, but had not revealed to his pupil. Well, Sourina would reveal these secrets to him! He would strip them bare, if necessary. He wanted to be the richest man in the world, more magnificent than any nabob, in order to lay that fortune at the feet of the lovely Englishwoman.

Yes, Felifax was certainly an overgrown child; his extravagant imagination was proof enough of that! But there was such force in his eyes that Djina ended up sharing his intoxication.

"You won't forget your little sister?" she asked.

"Djina shall have everything she desires. She shall dip into her big brother's treasures with both hands. Tell me what would give you the greatest pleasure."

"I am a woman, Felifax, and a Hindu woman besides. I would like jewels."

"Djina, the first money I obtain will be to buy you necklaces, bracelets, rings."

"How beautifully all those stones sparkle! I have often heard the *devadasis* extolling the splendors of certain women, courtesans or favorites. The most beautiful jewels, I have been told, belong to the wives of the Maharajah of Benares."

"Do you envy the lot of those wives, then? They are covered in jewels, it's true, and their hands are idle, but they are at the mercy of the master's desires, and he only gives them the consideration due to highly-priced objects."

"Without envying them, I would love to have their jewels. How I long to wear, for just one day, his favorite wife's jewels."

"Just one day, Djina?"

"Yes, one day. Their perpetual possession might result in my tiring of them, and I would always be fearful of losing them. Come on, brother, let's talk more seriously. This is folly, like all dreams. It would be better if you'd help me prepare our evening meal."

Felifax made no reply. By the gleam in his eyes it was easy to divine that a fantastic idea was germinating in his mind.

After the meal, he announced to Djina: "I'm going to Benares to visit the temple. I need new books for my studies."

Accustomed never to dispute her companion's plans, Djina only advised him to be careful. On this occasion, she did not believe that he was going to the temple–he must have a fervent desire to see Miss Grace again.

Less than three hours afterwards, Felifax was sitting on the bare bank of the Ganges, looking across at Benares on the other shore. Most of all, he was studying the Maharajah's palace, majestically raised up nearby. Between the green-filigreed columns he perceived, on the terrace of the *zenana*, the indolent forms of the monarch's *bayaderes*. The music of *sarangis* was audible, carried by a sensuous rhythm redolent with the scents of vanished glories and lost paradises.

Felifax remained motionless, lost in his dream. It was too soon to act.

Women go to bed late in *zenanas*. Every evening, wives and *bayaderes* wait until the lord and master has decided whether he will summon them for his pleasure, or to soothe his ennui. When the chief eunuch finally comes to say that His Highness has gone to bed, the wives always find it difficult to get up. For part of the night, they remain behind the columns, contemplating the gold-studded sky, the flowing silver of the Ganges and the amethyst of the violet-hued countryside.

It was midnight that evening. The eunuch had already passed through, announcing the master's retirement to his apartments without invoking a smile from any of the wives, when the perforated wall of the terrace overlooking the river was suddenly crowned by a magnificent apparition.

A few cries of fright were quickly stifled. The man—was he a man, or rather a god?—laughed, displaying his marvelous teeth. He radiated such power, such magnetism, that a breath of sensuality passed over every one of those indolent women. Their eyes lit up with desire and they extended their beautiful, jewel-laden arms imploringly.

If Felifax had wanted to fall immediately upon any precious trinket whatsoever, he would have been welcomed like Jupiter by Danaë.[35] That was not his intention. Without appearing to perceive the sentiment to which he had given birth, his eyes seemed to be searching for someone.

Eventually, the embers of his pupils flared up in satisfaction. An *apsara* had just appeared, as dazzlingly beautiful as an idol. Without ever having seen her, he guessed that she was the favorite.

He came forward lightly and silently, and the face of the young beauty lit up, while she withdrew into the brocade-hung room where her bed was. Her beautiful arms were extended towards the man; her red lips invited him to be bold.

Leaning toward her, he kissed her on the forehead, saying ardently: "O thou, the most beautiful of the beautiful, the offer of your love is the most precious wealth of all. Today, however, I ask for something else. I want your jewels–all of your jewels!"

She shivered. This captivating man was nothing but a thief. Her left hand clutched at the ornaments in her hair, while her right attempted to reach the hammer of the gong to call for help.

He divined her intention, and his laughter gushed out. "I do not want to plunder those jewels, worthy attributes of your unmatchable splendor. A little sister that I have has expressed the desire to wear a favorite's jewelry for one day–just one day–and I have come in search of them. Tomorrow evening, at the same hour, they will once again ornament the one whom Brahma has created to increase their sparkle."

"What if I refuse to let you save them?"

"I shall pray that you will be unable to resist my demand."

He would have used force, had it been necessary. He had taken it into his head to satisfy Djina's desire, and he would satisfy it no matter what it cost. The extraordinary result was that the smiling favorite took off every one of her jewels and gave them to the man. She had read the frankness of his expression and surrendered to the charm of his voice, obedient to a troubling, unsuspected scent.[36]

Felifax took the jewels, stowed them securely within a fold of his loincloth, and turned away to retrace the route he had already used once, scaling the palace wall on the Ganges side.

On the threshold, he looked back.

"Tomorrow, queen of beauty, daughter of gods, at the same time, the jewels will be at your feet."

"And what if I ask for something in return when you come back tomorrow?"

"I shall give it to you. What do you desire?"

"You shall know tomorrow."

Without another word, he went across the terrace through the assembly of admiring women, leapt gracefully up on to the stone parapet and vanished into the night.

Djina's dream came true. In her meager hut, for an entire day, she wore the favorite's jewels–but she shivered powerfully at the thought of the risk her brother had run. Never again would she express any desire; he was capable of any audacity.

As on the previous night, the fantastic apparition appeared at the same time on the balcony of the *zenana*. Felifax kept his promise. He passed among the ecstatic women, heading for the favorite's room. Arriving at the threshold, he stopped and recoiled slightly, struck by amazement. The woman was stretched out on precious fabrics, completely nude, holding out her arms to him.

He went forward without further hesitation. Had he not to keep his promise?

Straight away, he took the precious gems out of his loincloth and laid them at the favorite's feet. As he got up again, however, the young woman's cry of fright alerted him to the danger with which he was faced. A company of eunuchs surrounded him, ready to put him to death.

He released his usual burst of laughter, accepting the challenge.

Unfortunately for him, the leader of the eunuchs was reckless enough to lash out at him with the *kurbash* [37] that he was holding in his hand. What a change that wrought! The nascent laughter ended up as a seeming roar, and the fearful women thought that a nightmare was unfolding before them.

The man's captivating eyes changed abruptly. The irises brightened, releasing a dazzling greenish glare; the pupils narrowed and elongated. Within an instant, the eyes were like those of the king of the jungle. At the same time, the characteristic stripes appeared upon his back. These features radiated such ferocity that the eunuchs recoiled, no longer having confidence in their numerical advantage.

Felifax was ready to make the clumsy servant pay dearly for the insult received when the favorite's soft and supplicant voice was raised, saying: "Instead of the discretion that I have asked of you, and which you owe me, grant me this man's life. Flee, in the name of Heaven, and bear away my desire."

He shook his head; the sacrifice was too great. Seeing tears in the beautiful eyes, though, he nodded, suppressing his wrath.

He gained the balcony in a single bound, releasing his laughter once again, and his emotional voice threw back this promise: "I shall come again, beautiful Arzumaud. The sovereign himself, and all his guards, cannot prevent me from laying at your feet the homage of my admiration."

This blasphemy caused a forward rush, but Felifax was already far away.

The following day, the Maharajah summoned the chief of police to his palace and told him the story. He had been warned by one of his wives, who was jealous of the favorite. He accepted responsibility for punishing the women of his harem, but handed over to the English police the problem of chastising the wretch who had been so bold as to violate his *zenana*.

The functionary had no difficulty in identifying the author of the misdeed. That same evening, posters in Bengali were put up everywhere, advertising a reward of 2,000 rupees to anyone who captured Felifax.

A few hours later, an unknown hand had added a further sentence to all these posters, which nullified the effect of the promised reward:

Respect the son of Kali!

XII

The mine at Silver-Hole was plunged into a profound sadness. Doctor Eric Palmer was on his death-bed. For three days, he had fought in vain against the approach of death, overwhelmed by a bilious hematuric fever.[38] It had come on just at the moment when he was certain of putting his hand on Felifax's collar and wanted to make haste to capture him.

Unleashed by the 2,000 rupees promised by the maharajah, a number of police volunteers had set about beating the jungle–and chance, or blind providence, might well favor the incapable. Naturally, the doctor had been informed by Baber of the most recent indiscretion of Felifax the Terrible. Others might think what they wished, but it only made him more sympathetic to the fellow. After the Brahman Sourina, the high priest of Durga the Implacable, he had braved the Maharajah, the principal secular authority, all with a good humor that was bound to amuse an Anglo-Saxon. As a man who put duty before all else, however, the doctor had to complete the mission given to him by his government. Compared with that, sympathy counted for nothing.

His minute investigation of the jungle had inevitably extended to the natural fortress behind which the rebel's hut was sheltered. Still posing as a botanist, he had observed the passage of the stream under the branches and his inquisitive eyes had perceived a tiny scrap of muslin on the tip of an acacia thorn.

As he extended his investigation further, new clues presented themselves to him–among others, the skin of a musk shrew,[39] an animal highly valued by the natives for the taste of its flesh. This pelt, presumably thrown in the water to be carried away by the current, had been caught on a liana. It had undoubtedly come from the interior of the natural fortress, indubitable proof of a human habitation sheltered by thornbushes that grew five or six meters tall.

The doctor detective was alone with John, who was not afraid of anything; he was trustworthy. Rendered circumspect by his previous failure, Sir Eric did not want to put off the capture until the next day, so he gave instructions to John and the two of them went into the stream–only to return at speed.

After five or six steps, in fact, they had been forced to flee. Gavials–crocodiles native to the Ganges and its tributaries–had raced towards them, their enormous mouths gaping wide. The stream could not be the only way in; it was necessary to find the other–but the doctor had been feeling ill all day; he had been shivering from head to foot, and red mists were passing momentarily before his eyes.

"We'll come back tomorrow," he said to John. "I feel a fever taking hold of me. We'll have to set fire to the jungle to flush out the man who's gone to ground in there."

The return to the mine was painful. John had to support his master on several occasions. When they arrived at Silver-Hole, the engineer, who was in the yard at the time, could scarcely hold back an exclamation. Sir Eric's face had begun to take on a jaundiced hue. A quarter of an hour later, the mine's doctor was at his bedside, and his thermometer indicated a 40-degree fever.

At about 3 a.m., Palmer called to John, who was keeping vigil by his bed. In a halting tone he said: "My poor John, I can't go with you tomorrow to complete the capture into which I've put my heart and soul. You must go as soon as possible, in order to get there very early. Lie in wait to see what happens, and try to get a glimpse of the inhabitants of that palace of brambles and lianas. If it proves to be the refuge of the individual in question, go to Benares to inform Baber, at Reverend Douglas' house. It's best that the honor of the capture should go to him."

Fatigued by this long speech, the doctor lost consciousness. John had already left.

Increasingly anxious, the engineer sent word to Grace at the pastor's house by means of the supply vehicle, which brought her back that same evening.

Sir Eric only had brief moments of lucidity; the rest of the time he was delirious. The concession's doctor never left him, even calling out one of his colleagues from the city for consultation. There are cases in which medicine has to declare itself incompetent, injections and potions having no effect. The detective, so famous in England, would fall on the battlefield of his voluntary profession, to die a victim of duty.

Grace read the verdict, despairingly, in the eyes of the physicians. Courageously, she summoned up all her strength, intending to resist the collapse she anticipated. And yet, to the profound amazement of the engineer and the doctor, on the morning of the third day she had her horse saddled, and rode straight into the jungle with all possible speed. The two friends blamed this departure on despair. Neither of them could leave the mine to follow her. In any case, Grace was already too far away.

After two days, John had not returned to the camp. Sir Eric was in no state to worry, while the other inhabitants of Silver-Hole knew nothing about the mission with which he had been charged. The poor devil was a prisoner. Tied up, but without having been subjected to further ill-treatment, he was lodged in Felifax's storehouse. Twice a day, he was released for a meal, but his questions went unanswered.

Faithfully following the doctor's orders, the servant had come to lie in wait to watch over the comings and going from the fortress of lianas, but his task had not lasted long. Lacking his master's skill, he had not been able to avoid the gaze of a man who was always on the alert. Although he believed himself well hidden, he had felt the weight of a human body suddenly descend upon his shoulders. In less than 20 seconds he was rendered helpless, and had the pleasure of discovering the secret passage for which his master had searched so hard. The route was indeed along the stream-bed, through a corridor in which interlaced lianas prevented the approach of the voracious gavials.

To Felifax, the man watching his hiding-place had to be an enemy. However, as the stranger was incapable of striking a blow, he contented himself with putting him out of harm's way and keeping him close by. It would certainly have been easy for him to change his retreat, but he did not wish to because he had an inner presentiment that he would receive a visit from Grace. In that expectation, he was ready to run the most dangerous risks.

One morning, at about 11 a.m., while Felifax was out hunting, Djina remained on her own, standing guard over John. The Hindu girl suddenly heard the name of Felifax called by a familiar female voice. Grace, part way along the route along the stream-bed and terrorized by the gavials behind the woven lianas, was calling for help.

Djina did not regard the Englishwoman with the jealousy of a rival. On the contrary, having made her brother happy, this woman now commanded all her affection. She ran to offer the comfort of her presence, and Grace was soon outside the hut, breathlessly asking where Felifax was.

Alas, Djina's companion was gone for the greater part of the day, and Grace could not wait. She told Djina that her father was dying, and gave her a piece of paper she had prepared in case Felifax was absent. The paper bore these words:

Please help, my friend; come save my father as you once saved me.

Djina questioned her for some time regarding the symptoms of the malady. Then, as the young Englishwoman was in a hurry to return to the dying man's bedside, she assured her that Felifax would respond to her call.

Grace left, with a tiny glimmer of hope in her black despair.

Fortunately, John was deeply asleep in the little storehouse, and the Scotsman slept so heavily that he did not hear his mistress's voice. What would have happened if it had been otherwise? Nothing good, undoubtedly, for Djina would not have had the authority to release her big brother's prisoner, and Grace would have refused to abandon him to his fate.

During the young woman's absence, Sir Eric's condition had remained the same. Could he wait several hours for Felifax's intervention?

Grace interrogated the physician. She declared herself capable of hearing anything. For her, the waiting was unbearable. How much longer could his agony last?

"It's difficult for me to say, my dear child. Twenty-four hours, perhaps–30 at the most, given that your father's constitution is so strong."

At 10 p.m., the physician having administered a further injection, she asked him to leave her alone, saying that she would call him if the need arose. As he had not left his colleague since the onset of the malady, he must need sleep. His presence could not prevent death from completing its work, so the physician obeyed the young woman. He went to lie down, fully dressed, on his bed.

Grace was counting the minutes now. Would Felifax respond to her appeal?

At midnight, there was a sudden alert in the camp: barking dogs, restive horses, a general dispersal. It was assumed that the tiger was visiting again.

On returning from his previous mission, Felifax had told Grace about the manner in which it had been accomplished–by means of the general confusion caused by the assumed presence of a tiger. He had sought an explanation for this particularity himself, and had innocently attributed its cause to Sourina's science.

The young woman's heart stopped beating. She shut her eyes, listening to the camp personnel running to their ambushes, chattering about the king of jungle. There was no doubt; it was what she had been waiting for. When her eyelids opened again, she saw him standing before her. He held a little copper flask in his hand. In a grave voice, he said: "You called me, Miss Grace. Here I am."

With a desperate gesture, she pointed to the bed where her father lay. His hands–the only part of him that seemed to

106

be alive–were gripping the covers in a sinister fashion. According to popular wisdom, that was the precursor of death.

The new arrival came closer. With the aid of the little
lamp that illuminated the room, he examined the moribund
man carefully. Then, having lifted up his head, he forced the
clenched teeth open with the aid of a spoon. Then he introduced a mouthful of the beverage he had brought with him in
the copper flask.

"Do the same thing in an hour," he said to Grace, "and
repeat the dose eight times over, every hour."

"But how shall I be able to make him swallow? I don't
have your strength or skill."

"In an hour, he'll be able to swallow."

"There's hope, then?"

"If Brahma wishes it! The herbs are usually infallible."

"I'm afraid, my friend."

"Have faith, Miss Grace. I'll come again tomorrow night.
But will it be possible for you to leave the camp? A similar
alert every night..."

"Could be dangerous, couldn't it?"

"Not for me. Besides, for you, I'm ready to run any risk.
It's for your father's benefit. To complete the today's medica-
tion, tomorrow I will bring you a saturation. For now, adieu–I
shall take advantage of the commotion in the camp to resume
the aerial route."

"Take care of yourself, my friend, in the name of
Heaven. The Maharajah has offered a reward for your capture–what foolish thing have you done to him?"

"A mere childish prank–a fantasy of Djina's. I shall explain later. I have no fear of the sovereign or his reward. It's
understood, miss? Eight hourly doses–and after that, nothing
at all. Not even the doctor's injections, if possible. I recom-
mend that you empty whatever remains in the bottle on the
ground."

"Farewell, my friend–until tomorrow."

"At the place where we parted–where your lips touched
the forehead of the poor Hindu."

"Greater in my eyes than all the princes of India, or the most illustrious of my compatriots!"

In a gesture of infinite gratitude, she got up and planted a new kiss on the young man's forehead. Three seconds later, he had disappeared, without any gunshot signaling his passage. Felifax had not been seen.

At 6 a.m., the silver-miners' physician, surprised at not having been called, came to see the dying man. The latter had ceased to breathe hoarsely, his hands had relaxed and he seemed to be asleep.

The practitioner took pains to hide his surprise. He observed an improvement, which he could only credit to his own care. To further the cure, he took his syringe and opened a new ampoule. Grace put her hands together and said: "I beg you to wait a little, doctor. I have an intuition that this deep sleep is not harmful." The man of science, disconcerted, agreed to delay his intervention.

Pleading slight fatigue, Grace retired to her room at about 6 p.m. At 1 a.m., she was able to replace the physician again at her father's side. The practitioner had gone through all the phases of self-congratulation. Not only had the death-agony been temporarily suspended, but the slight improvement had persisted.

At the time arranged on the previous evening, Grace went to meet her friend. In his hand, Felifax was holding a second copper flask, whose contents must be taken in four doses.

"After that," he said to the young woman with profound conviction, "your father will be saved; he will regain his health quite rapidly. I ask you, on your honor and on his too, never to tell anyone to what intervention he owes his life."

The young woman swore the oath that guaranteed her eternal silence, and offered Felifax her undying gratitude. As they separated, she could not help mentioning to the *vana-prastha* [40] that her father's servant, John, had disappeared. Given that clue, the forest-dweller recognized his prisoner. He explained the circumstances in which he had found a spy lying in wait close to his retreat, a rifle in his hand.

"He has nothing to fear from me, miss. I shall keep him another three or four days, until the moment comes when I decide to change my retreat. I shall remain here until then. You might have need of me. However, if you demand that I release my prisoner, it shall be done tomorrow morning."

Grace knew the brave John to be very talkative, as stubborn as a mule and obedient to no orders but his master's. Once cured, Sir Eric would continue with his hunt to the end, and she had promised not to tell him that he owed his life to the unfortunate that he was tracking. Moreover, John was fond of money. The lure of the proffered reward might lead him to do something stupid.

"Hold on to our brave Scotsman, and send him back when you judge the time to be right. How shall I find you afterwards?"

"When I release your servant, my new refuge will be chosen. When he returns, look in the barrel of his rifle; you'll find a piece of paper there. The paper will bear two numbers, indicating the day and the hour when I shall come to the Reverend Douglas' house."

"I shall be there. It would be better to send it by word of mouth–writing is dangerous."

This time, she offered her forehead spontaneously. The young man had the strength to brush it with his lips.

At Silver-Hole, they were obliged to believe in miracles. The moribund had cheated Death by his resistance to its sly attacks. As for the doctor, he was exultant, attributing all the credit for the miraculous cure to himself. With what gratitude Sir Eric shook the hand of his colleague at the mine! Fortunately, no one saw Grace's furtive smile.

Sir Eric asked for John. On learning of his disappearance, he felt an enormous distress. Had the brave fellow fallen victim to a wild beast or been struck down by the rebel? What did it matter? The mysterious man would pay for the faithful servant's disappearance; Palmer would begin his pursuit again as soon as he was able to stand upright.

One morning, though, a joyful voice made the invalid shiver. John came back, howling with joy. Under his arm he carried a young spotted deer. Happy to see his master almost back on his feet, he told the story of his capture by Felifax and his rather mild captivity.

"I lacked for nothing, boss; I was cared for by a dainty little Hindu girl with eyes as large as this and a voice like a music-box."

"And the accursed Felifax?" the detective asked.

"A stout fellow, boss, with amazing strength. My God, how well the lianas served him as ropes, and how tightly he tied them! He didn't talk much and never replied to questions. He set me free this morning, at dawn, and told me he never wanted to see me again. He doesn't know me, God damn it! I owe him one—I have to pay him back for keeping me prisoner!"

"Have no fear, my lad—we'll winkle him out. He won't escape us this time."

"We'll have to begin the search all over again, boss—the lad's taken flight. That's why he let me go."

The doctor frowned. Then, quickly recovering his hearty self-confidence, he changed the subject. He was still convinced that he was the man to capture Felifax.

Throughout the conversation, John had kept his rifle in his hands, much to Grace's annoyance—had she not to look in the barrel for the information Felifax had promised? Finally, unable to contain herself any longer, she went to take the gun from the servant.

"Thank you, Miss Grace," he said, cheerfully. "I have to clean it right away, like any good huntsman. I saw a deer passing right under my nose a couple of miles from the camp and I couldn't help saluting its passage with a rifle-shot."

Grace had to sit down, struck hard by emotion. She would not know when Felifax would go to Reverend Douglas' house. If he did not find her there, he might wait, imprudently risking capture by men determined to capture him. She felt tears coming into her eyes. It was impossible, now, to warn him about the annoying difficulty.

XIII

By freeing Sita, the former priestess of the tigers in the temple of Durga, Baber hoped to obtain information about the drama that had preceded his brother's death.

Seventeen years had already passed since his brother's incineration on the banks of the Ganges! For 17 years, Baber had been waiting for vengeance. Methodically and meticulously, not wanting to act until he could strike a sure blow, Baber was well worthy to work with Sir Eric Palmer. The latter was still confined to bed, and his convalescence probably lasted longer than he wished.

The impudent Ralph Napper continued to slander the Scotland Yard ace. In all his reports to the metropolis, and even abusive telegrams, he insisted that the famous detective had failed. These continual digs enraged the doctor, and did not make him any more sympathetic towards Felifax. The offensive against the latter would continue ceaselessly until victory was obtained. On the previous evening, the convalescent had affirmed that yet again to Baber. Before leaving Benares, the agent, disguised as an animal-keeper, had come to report to him. The expert detective, whose eye was normally so penetrative, had not noticed the bizarre smile with which the Hindu responded to the announcement of that imminent victory.

In truth, Baber knew more about it than his patron. For three days running, in the middle of the night, Baber had seen Felifax going into the Reverend Douglas' house. On the last occasion, he had been escorted back to the door by Miss Grace Palmer, who had hastened from Silver-Hole in response to the pastor's summons.

The young woman appeared to be on the best possible terms with the hunted rebel. To do his duty as an affiliate of the police, the part-time animal-keeper should have informed the Police Station, and Sir Eric Palmer in particular. Indeed, the detective would have been able to obtain all the information necessary to complete the operation that was so dear to his heart by interrogating his daughter.

Instead, the sly employee had kept his mouth shut. The outlaw was the child whose mysterious birth had been connected with his brother's death; before making a move against him, he wanted to know more. Now, he was striding along the road to Bhavanour, the village where the convent of Shiva Ardhanari [41] was located. Leaving nothing to chance, Baber had planned his journey so as to arrive at Bhanavour at nightfall; he did not want to be seen prowling around the convent.

During his visit with Sourina, after hearing the name of Sita and making certain that she was a prisoner in this place, he had take careful note of everything. A gesture made by the *guru* [42] in charge of the *matta* to the fervent servant of Kali had been enough to indicate the cell in which the unfortunate victim of the infamous machination must be weeping. Knowing that he could not gain entry by the main door, nor by the stoutly-barred windows, he had resolved to get in by scaling the wall.

The house of Shiva Ardhanari was thus named because of the ruins of a temple near to which it had been constructed. According to the Hindu custom, these ruins had not been cleared away. Their truncated columns stood up like a circle of soldiers guarding a citadel. When Baber arrived at the ruins, it was dark. Without hesitation, he moved between the stones enshrouded with lianas and brambles, and slipped into the necropolis of columns, steles and capitals. He moved towards the only shrine that remained almost intact, adjacent to the wall of the claustral residence–a wall as high as only the inhabitants of India can build. Two similarly intact staircases led to the roof of this shrine, surmounted by a monumental state of the god who was both destroyer and creator, represented by a body that was half-man and half-woman.

Baber climbed up, sliding between the stones, almost invisible in the early darkness. As soon as he arrived, he had taken off his white *langouti* and the piece of white cloth suspended from his shoulder. He had nothing around his loins now but a slender dark-colored thong and a long cord that was exceedingly fine and exceedingly strong.

Having arrived at the foot of the god, beneath which he seemed a mere pygmy, Baber climbed up to the shoulder. Huddled beneath one of the enormous ears, with which he seemed to fuse, he slowly and imperceptibly unwound the cord from around his waist and slid it over the neighboring wall. A smile passed over his lips then; the profound silence of the night had just been interrupted by voices chanting *mantras*. He was not mistaken. In the convent, nightfall was celebrated by offering macerations in the name of Shiva Arshanari. Baber could expect to work in relative peace now; everyone should be in the sanctuary to obtain the blessings of the god.

The wall that the animal-keeper descended along his cord had been constructed with stones from the ruins. They were very dark in color, and their shadow obscured the lithe body, the color of tincture of iodine, which slid down without the slightest instability.

Eventually, he reached the courtyard. Making no more noise than a serpent, he ran towards the three massive constructions constituting the retreat proper. Baber confidently believed that Sita's prison was located in the one sheltering the sanctuary, where the lodgings of most of the cenobites were to be found.

Still silent and invisible, he passed in front of the place where the ceremonial invocations were taking place. Chance was definitely in his favor; he had come on the night of a major invocation–but it was necessary to flatten himself abruptly against a wall and crouch down in a sort of recess.

To the rhythmic beating of gongs, a procession was coming towards the sanctuary, where a few male and female Brahmans were already officiating. This cortège consisted of *yogi* initiates and white-clad *gopis*. Baber could not help shivering. Might Sita not be forced to attend these ceremonies?

With his hand over his eyes, he watched the women pass; they carried baskets in which jasmine, marigold and lotus flowers were heaped. Sita was not among them.

Baber slid through the lamplit corridors like a shadow. Soon he stopped and shivered. A *guru*–a veritable colossus– was standing guard outside Sita's door. Sourina's orders were being faithfully executed. The servant of Kali undoubtedly dreaded some new exploit on the part of Felifax, alerted by some possible indiscretion of the ties connecting him to Sita.

Within range of the Shivaite was a gong whose hammer he held in his hand. At the first suspicion of alarm, a single blow on the gong would bring 20 Brahmans, ready for violent action.

Baber did not hesitate for long; he was utterly resolute. For weapons, he had a *khanjar* [43] stuck in the cord of his tight loincloth and a braid of silk terminating in a slipknot. The latter, as used by the Thugs, Kali's stranglers, is a terrible weapon in the hands of a merciless man.

An oppressive silence reigned in the corridor of massive stones, save for the distant muffled echo of the mantras intoned in the sanctuary. Suddenly, there was a scarcely perceptible choking sound, then the dull thud of a body collapsing on the ground. The passage was free! Baber took the key with which he could open the locked door from the sentry's langouti.

Two minutes later, Sita, so long imprisoned, woke up with a start to see a Hindu beside her, who transfixed her with eyes of fire and said: "I have come to save you. Tell me, are you really Sita, the former priestess of the tigers in the temple of Kali."

Trembling with emotion, the young woman replied: "Yes, I am Sita."

"And you have been imprisoned on Sourina's orders?"

At the name of the redoubtable man whom she hated, tears came to the unfortunate's eyes. Terrified, she asked: "Why speak to me of that cruel man? Are you one of his friends?"

"I am the brother of Rao, the Brahman killed on his orders. He was 18 years old."

Sita started violently at that name and covered her face with her hands. Baber saw tears leaking between her slender fingers. Time was pressing, though; another monk might come to relieve the one who had collapsed lifeless in the corridor. The Hindu leaned over the woman, saying in a tone of inexpressible hatred: "I have come to serve my vengeance, and to invite you to share it. In a few minutes, we can be out of this jail. Will you follow me?"

The recluse continued weeping. She seemed, however, to lend an avid ear to this miraculous proposition.

"Do you know the temple of Kali?" she asked, eventually. "Can you tell me whether there is still a child within that temple? He must be fully grown now. I don't know how long ago I was imprisoned here, but I believe that it has been an entire lifetime."

Baber was seized by an intense emotion. In spite of himself, there was not a muscle in his face that did not quiver. He had reached his goal, and would know the secret of his brother's death. Instead of answering, he asked: "What was this child's name?"

"I called him Rama; [44] it is the name he still bears in the depths of my heart, but the master did not want him described thus. He gave him a bizarre name: *Felifax*."

Baber's eyes gleamed. "The child lives," he relied, softly, "and you would be proud of him. I think that I shall soon be able to introduce you to his presence. Come on!"

He took Sita with him. He found the cord hanging from the wall. Alas, the route would be extremely perilous for Sita. The night air was affecting her; she was not used to its excess, only having been allowed out by day into a confined space.

Baber did not hesitate. Having tested the strength of one of her veils, he used it to bind the woman tight to his own body, and without showing the slightest weakness he commenced his dangerous ascent. The man's muscles were made of steel. He attained the top of the wall despite his burden, pulled up the cord after having detached Sita. They both went on, occasionally brushed by the silent flight of huge bats.

Baber undoubtedly had friends in Bhavanour, for a *verga* harnessed to two humped oxen and covered by an awning seemed to be waiting for them in the ruins. Sita was hoisted up, and the chariot immediately got underway. Less than two hours afterwards, they were in Benares at the moment when the death of the guard and the disappearance of the recluse were discovered at the convent of Shiva Ardhanari.

The monastery was seized then by a veritable terror; vows of silence were forgotten as everyone thought of the terrible anger of Sourina when he learned of the disappearance. The rest of the night was spent searching for the fugitive. No clue remained as to the manner in which the escape had been engineered; there was no breach in the walls or evidence of their disturbance. Baber had done things properly, without leaving a scratch during his ascent.

Baber's hut was situated in a district of Benares neighboring Victoria Avenue, the central thoroughfare of the English quarter. This district, called Bavana, is similarly somewhat removed from the holy city's palaces and temples; it forms a sort of neutral zone between fanaticism and civilization. The fanatics—the Brahmans—do not come so far; the English go through it but never stop there, doubtless fearful of weapons hidden in the midst of that unimaginable desolation.

Sita had been lodged there. She was very well hidden there. No one would ever think to look for her there. Exhausted by all her emotions, overwhelmed by the air and freedom, the young woman consented to lie down on Baber's bed, and went to sleep almost immediately.

Sitting cross-legged on the ground, aided by the flickering light of a lamp, the animal-keeper studied the woman who would finally enable his avenging hand to strike the guilty party. He now expected to hear some drama of love, tragically interrupted by Sourina. The attitude struck by the former

117

priestess at the mention of Rao's name appeared to indicate something of the sort.

Sita was now about 35. She had lost none of her former charms. In contrast to many Hindu women, reduced by frequent childbirth and domestic toil, seclusion had conserved—or even brightened—the beauty of her complexion.

The young woman remained unconscious for more than ten hours. On awakening, she could not restrain a slight exclamation of surprise and joy. The sunlight was flooding into the meager hovel, which seemed to her the most marvelous of palaces. She had just recalled the events of the previous evening. She was free! And there, immobile in front of her, was her liberator.

He was staring at her. The words he had spoken during the night returned to her thoughts, bringing a sudden redness to her cheeks. He had told her that he was Rao's brother—and that name evoked so many painful and abominable memories! On the other hand, to be sure, he had promised to take her to her child.

"You promised that you would take me to my little Rama—the one he calls Felifax?"

"Yes. I promised; I shall keep my promise. You shall see him. In the meantime, you need to know this: the child, now a handsome young man, has fled the temple of Kali to live in the jungle. Since his flight, Sourina has been a target for his wrath."

"He will never be able to repay that wretch sufficiently for the shame and torture that I have suffered."

"You owe your internment to him, don't you?"

"Why do you ask?"

"He had my brother killed at the same time. What crime had he committed then?"

As she had done in her cell, Sita hid her face with her hands. Abruptly, she said to the animal-keeper: "I have sworn to keep that frightful adventure to myself, and to reveal it to no one but my son, who will avenge me—but you are the brother of Rao, whom I ought to loathe... although he too must be a victim. Listen, and I shall tell you the cruel history of my damnation. For your part, you must swear by Brahma to leave the matter of my vengeance to my son. If he cannot accomplish it, then you may strike."

With a gesture, Baber made the requested oath. Then, in an extremely low voice, as if shame had laid a thick veil over her past torment, Sita began her story.

When she had finished speaking, Baber's face bore a distraught expression. Gravely, weighing each word according to its importance, he said: "Sourina will pay for your suffering, your shame and my brother's death. I shall help Felifax to accomplish his vengeance. Listen—there is another who must pay: his accomplice. I shall cross the sea to seek him out in his own country, and the scarf of Kali's stranglers will be his punishment for his frightful crime."

"Will you take me to my son now?"

"That will doubtless not be long delayed. Baber is a man of his word, but your son is in the jungle. He is wanted for a few trivial misdeeds, and a large reward has been offered for his capture. The jungle alone is keeping his secret."

"So I shall suffer further?"

"No, I hope not. I shall try to find out where he is, or to get a message to him."

"The city is dangerous for him, you say? Doubtless Sourina wants to recapture him."

"It's not only Sourina! To avoid any danger, I will bring him to you, if I discover the secret of his retreat."

Baber had suddenly thought of Miss Grace, the means by which she spoke to the rebel, and the end of an overheard sentence: "I will warn you"—which led him to suppose that the doctor's daughter was in a position to help him.

Having instructed Sita not to move from the hut, he went out to keep his promise. He went directly to the Reverend Douglas' house to ask whether Miss Palmer would be returning to Benares soon. If necessary, he would go to Silver-Hole himself.

Grace had just arrived in the city with the supply vehicle, to make a few necessary purchases. She intended to return that evening, for her father was still in need of her care.

On seeing Baber, she offered him her hand. When he asked her about Felifax, she started violently. Why would he say that? Was it permissible for Baber, in the exercise of his police duties, to spy on her actions? Did he want to facilitate the doctor detective's capture, or was he desirous of getting his hands on the 2,000 rupees? Concealing her disquiet behind an affronted response, she replied in a very haughty fashion. The other must not be allowed to intimidate her.

Without seeming to perceive the young woman's tone, Baber contented himself with saying: "Would you care to come with me, miss? I am giving shelter to a mother snatched by me from the captivity in which she was held. For more than 16 years, this unfortunate woman has been separated from her son. If you cannot tell her where he can be found, perhaps you can tell her how he is."

Grace declared herself willing to go with him.

"Put on your nurse's costume, miss, and follow me at a distance. I will lead you to the hut where the poor woman is waiting, in tears."

A few minutes later, Grace came out of the pastor's bungalow and followed the animal-keeper at a distance.

At the end of a quarter of an hour, Grace went into Baber's hut. Her Red Cross costume made such a visit appear normal.

Although the former priestess told her nothing of her dolorous secret, she knew how to adopt a tone necessary to elicit confidences, for Grace explained something rather complicated to her. She was alone with Sita, Baber having gone to the temple of Kali. After such an important event, it was necessary to know what Sourina was doing.

The chief Brahman had just received the frightful news of Sita's disappearance. Prostrate at the feet of the goddess, he implored her protection. For him, no doubt was possible: Felifax had liberated his mother, and she would have no hesitation in revealing to him the secret of his birth. If that were the case, Sourina might well tremble; his life was in danger.

When Baber left the temple again that evening, the high priest was still prostrate. He had offered a great sacrifice, and the tigers were roaring over the joints of fresh meat abandoned to their ferocity.

Baber hastened home. His debtor doubtless knew her son's hiding-place. Vengeance was at hand.

On arrival at the hut, however, the impassive face of the Hindu displayed troubled amazement.

The house was empty. Sita had disappeared.

XIV

Scotland Yard was in turmoil. An unusually long radio-gram had arrived from Calcutta. The report came from the Governor of Bengal himself, and this exceedingly highly-placed individual concluded with the following sentence:

There is no point summoning a detective as renowned as Doctor Palmer, only to see him spend months doing nothing!

This complaint, surely inspired by the policeman Ralph Napper, also said:

The activity of the Indian Government's detectives has been completely nullified by this rather damaging interven-tion. These policemen would have put an end to the exploits of this mysterious man some time ago. To the contrary, the latter, encouraged by this negligence, has dared to attack the Maha-rajah, forcing that prince to complain bitterly about the state of affairs...

The result, in short, was to put the faithful vassal of the crown in an awkward situation. Trouble was in store. Switch-board operators, secretaries and stenographers had spread the news rapidly. Nothing more was necessary to unleash pas-sions.

Sir Eric Palmer was generally admired at Scotland Yard, but his successes had also generated a certain acrimony on the part of the envious. For their part, his partisans loudly pro-claimed that the undesirable person in Benares would not es-cape the ace detective's science. He must, however, be given the time to familiarize himself with an unfamiliar country.

Such was also the advice of Sir Harold Nimbly, the head of Scotland Yard. He had defended his protégé against the Lord Chief Justice, the Attorney General, and all those who dealt with the police from behind desks, unaware of the diffi-culties of their thankless task.

Naturally, not a word was breathed in the radiogram about the illness that had struck the rugged fighter down; there was talk of apathy and incapacity, which was more reasonable. Besides, opinion in high places was more or less unanimous. The mockery sustained by such negligence could not be tolerated any longer. A volunteer operative so pitifully incapable must be recalled immediately and given the sack.

Remaining very calm beneath this storm of protest, Sir Harold Nimbly had replied to the Lord Chancellor: "Your Lordship should not worry about potential mockery. Firstly, public opinion in England does not know the first thing about this business. Secondly, Doctor Palmer is not, in official terms, a policeman. He receives no salary, working in an amateur capacity. I fear that such an injurious decision might well, if word got out, arouse strong feelings. Everyone admires this modest and learned man; he has accomplished veritable tours de force... on occasions when there was talk of your negligence."

"He will, then, suspend his inquiries and let the Benares police do their job in *milieux* they know better than he does."

"Milord, the Indian government itself appealed for the enlightenment of this so-called incompetent! I know Palmer: such an order would make him spring into action. He would abandon his friendly collaboration... and what then? No one can stop him searching for the man, as an ordinary citizen. There might then be a more serious loss of face for our people in Benares."

"At any rate, you will certainly send the Governor of Bengal a radiogram that I shall draw up–without, I hope, adding a single word of commentary."

The police chief was a dutiful man, so he obeyed the order. That was why the airwaves transmitted a veritable reprimand concerning a desperately sick man languishing in his sickbed. The radiogram, received in Calcutta, was relayed to the Police Station in Benares in its entirety. There it was greeted with veritable joy–and, with an alacrity he had never previously displayed, Napper sent it on to the interested party, accompanied with a few hypocritical condolences.

Formidable oaths resounded in the room at Silver-Hole on receipt of this message. Fury was succeeded by profound sorrow, coupled with a violent desire to abandon the whole project, but wise and careful consideration took over. To do that would be tantamount to desertion, and Sir Eric was incapable of that. Repressing all his anger and humiliation, the detective summoned John. He ordered the servant to help him dress and give him two injections of quinine and extract of cola, and then ordered the faithful Scotsman to saddle the horses, saying: "Let's go, comrade. I swear that I shan't pause or rest until I've brought this accursed Felifax to the office of the Governor of Bengal, dead or alive!"

"I'll go with you, Father!" Grace cried, excitedly. "I too have to defend your name and your reputation."

Sir Eric had not the strength to refuse, and Grace departed with the two determined men. In reality, believing in her father's infallibility, the blonde girl wanted to prevent anything unfortunate occurring in the case of a meeting between the detective and the rebel. This time, Felifax would have a difficult task on his hands. He would have to deploy all his resources to escape the clutches of a man determined to capture him.

If the detective could have seen the phenomenal being at that moment–the son of Kali who commanded the wild beasts, the provoker of the Maharajah–he would not have been able to believe his eyes. In a shelter made of bamboo and palm-leaves, a son was weeping for his mother like a little child, while an affectionate sister knelt beside him, mingling her tears with theirs.

Having obtained information from Miss Grace designed to allow her to find Felifax's retreat–which is to say, the reference-points that would guide her to a suitable place in the jungle–Sita had set off bravely, without bothering to wait for the animal-keeper to return.

The directions Grace had given were precise, and that precision was due to Felifax. He did not want the young Englishwoman to walk too far at hazard. Careless of the danger, he did not hesitate to come close to the city. He had said to Grace:

"Every day, I shall hide in the trees. No one will look for me so high up. Besides, I am certain of my aerial escape-route. When I have recognized you, I shall descend from my hiding-place and guide you to my new shelter. There, we shall have the leisure to talk at length."

Grace had been obliged to accept this arrangement. She did not want any further dangerous recklessness.

Since then, the young woman had been unable to get out, because of her father's painful convalescence. She knew, however, that Felifax was standing guard faithfully. She had furnished all these details to the unhappy mother, while giving her, by way of a postscript, a sign of recognition.

Sita had departed, innocently, without any anxiety. Utterly exhausted by walking, however, she had not been able to get very far into the jungle when night began to fall swiftly. What would become of her, alone in the darkness? Fortunately, a few huts were located not far away–temporary shelters for bamboo-cutters and their families. They gave her accommodation for the night. The following morning, the mother–capable of any miracle to find her son–plunged into the forest again, without paying any heed to the advice of her hosts.

Sita walked for nearly three hours, resting for a few minutes every now and again. She had engraved the reference-points in her memory, like a meticulously-traced map. Attentive to the sight of the least clue and watching the ground for snakes, the priestess did not see a glittering silver-filigreed shield suspended six feet above the ground–nor the other sparkling shields shining radiantly in the middle of the road. At the center of each disc something lay in wait: a dark hairy tuft in which two tiny ferocious eyes were discernible.

These beautiful discs were the webs of aryas–the famous venomous spiders whose bite is unforgiving if it is not treated within a minute.[45] Insects and butterflies were held prisoner in these webs.

Suddenly, deploying its long hairy feet, one of the jailers descended an equilibrating thread, and Sita felt a sharp pain in her neck, raising her hand in response. The terrible *arya* had already returned to its fief, and the Hindu woman saw it resume its look-out post. Raised in the temple of Kali and then imprisoned in the Shivaite *matta*, the priestess knew nothing about the treacheries of the jungle. The bite did not seem to her to be very painful, and in her haste to arrive she continued on her way.

Less than half an hour after the arya's attack, Sita felt the first signs of distress. A bloody mist appeared before her eyes, her legs grew weak and she was assailed by a horrid malaise that made her stagger. Despite all that, she forced herself to go forward.

It was then that Felifax, ensconced in his tree, noticed the woman, dressed in dark veils like the *pariahs*, who was walking alone through the jungle, seemingly on the brink of collapse. His compassionate heart was aroused. When he saw her fall, he descended hastily from his tree to go to her aid. As he leaned over her, he felt a slight shiver. Beneath the dark veils in which the woman was swathed, he had just seen the bright splash of a silk handkerchief, in the corner of which the letters G and P were interlaced. How could he fail to recognize that handkerchief? It belonged to Grace; she had had it with her when he had rescued her and cared for her in his hut. Who was this woman, then? A messenger, undoubtedly!

Alas, the unfortunate woman seemed to be in a very bad way. Her eyes were closed, her respiration was halting, and her lips were flecked with foam.

It is necessary to know the symptoms of the malady to render effective treatment, because the arya's bite leaves no trace. Leaning over her, Felifax was searching for the slightest clue when she opened her eyes momentarily, An ecstatic smile immediately illuminated her beautiful face. The voice of blood had spoken; Sita had recognized the one for whom she had come in search. "Rama!" she murmured. "Rama!" And when he made no response, she went on: "You are really Felifax?"

Powerfully moved, the young man nodded. The dying woman raised her hands with difficulty; general paralysis was already setting in. She was able, however, to put her arms around her son's neck, murmuring in a breath: "I am your mother... my little Rama... your mother, imprisoned by Sourina... happiness escapes me... I'm dying."

Stunned by a violent shock, he gasped: "Go on talking. What's wrong with you? I'll heal you. I know the wisdom of the Brahmans, their medicine. Speak–you say that you are my mother?"

She had closed her eyes again. She reopened them. "I'm dying... the bite of a hairy spider..."

"A long time ago?"

"Nearly an hour."

He let out a howl of despair. No help was possible; all of her blood was infected.

Sita felt the paralysis taking hold; she drew him to her again with all her remaining strength, so that he might hear her scarcely-perceptible voice.

"Let me speak... my little Rama... yes, I'm your mother. An odious crime presided over your birth... an English surgeon, with Sourina's help..."

The unfortunate woman perceived that her tongue was becoming heavy, incapable of saying much more. She suffered a choking constriction, and articulated with difficulty: "Sourina... will tell the name... the crime... vengeance... Ba..."

The animal-keeper's name could not be completed. She had ceased to live, without being able to hug the child for whom she had shed so many tears.

It was he who kissed her face, to which the final sleep was already importing its ultimate beauty. Then, maddened by the despair of meeting this mother, who had immediately disappeared, he took the cadaver in his muscular arms and plunged into the jungle. He ran to the hut that had served them as a shelter for several days.

Djina, on learning his terrible unhappiness, found the words of consolation that he needed. She washed and dressed the body for the last time, adorning the dead woman with her poor bracelets and bestowing her most beautiful *dupetta* upon her, in order to permit her to enter *nirvana* in all her beauty.[46]

The long and painful funeral vigil began then, while Sir Eric Palmer and John searched tirelessly for a trail to follow, accompanied by poor Grace, who was tortured by anxiety.

Felifax made the decision that his mother, so briefly seen, would be incinerated with all due ritual, on the bank of the sacred Ganges–but not, however, on the Burning *ghat* specially reserved for such funeral ceremonies in Benares. All day long, he ran through the jungle assembling precious essences: enough sandalwood, cinnamon, camphor and magnolia to build an enormous pyre. He also set about finding men to carry Sita's body. The Brahmanic religion forbids relatives to undertake that final transportation; the only thing they are authorized to do is disperse the ashes in the river.

That evening, therefore, at sunset, the funeral cortège emerged on to a narrow pathway leading down to the Ganges. At the base of this path, the pyre had already been set up, as tall as a hut. Four men from a nearby village carried Sita's cadaver, set feet forward on a bamboo stretcher, down a slope so steep that it was almost vertical. Felifax walked behind them, unsteady with sorrow. Djina held him tightly, in order to communicate all the warmth of her sisterly affection.

The beautiful dead woman went down, the innocent victim surrendered to her indifferent porters. In India, only the soul counts for something; when that has departed, one separates oneself from the remains. When she reached the bank, she was laid down in the mud and half-submerged in the river for her last bath.

Felifax looked at her for a long time then, in order to make a deep impression on his memory of her two closed and dark-ringed eyes, bordered by the black fringe of her eyelashes, her delicately-shaped nose, her full cheeks and her exquisite lips, slightly parted to display her white teeth. Then, the body was laid on the pyre, which was set alight: a nabob's pyre of precious perfumes, which gave off sparks and flames in torment. Sita was in the middle, nothing else of her as visible but one lugubrious foot–just one–silhouetted in black shadow against the firelight.

Kneeling beside the river with fists clenched, Felifax watched avidly as the fire burned down. All the filial devotion from which he had been severed for such a long time seemed to flow through his heart, generating a nameless despair. He thought he saw his mother raise herself up from the pyre to depart as a ritual sacrifice; he closed his eyes, wanting to drive the horrible vision away.

When he opened them again, a long time afterwards, the incineration was over; nothing remained but a heap of white ashes, in the midst of which was a small pile of darker hue. The son threw them into the Ganges while reciting *mantras*. Exhausted, Felifax remained crouching by the waterside, his eyes closed again, better to preserve the image he scarcely knew within his vision.

How long did he remain thus? He could not have said. An iron hand placed upon his shoulder made him start. At the same time, a curt voice instructed: "Don't try to move, Felifax! I arrest you in the name of His Majesty the King of England, Emperor of India!"

Sir Eric Palmer was there, revolver in hand, grave-faced, somewhat regretful of completing the arrest at such a moment–but he did not want to go away empty-handed this time.

He had picked up the trail that morning. The unfortunate youth, overwhelmed by grief, had neglected his customary precautions and the policeman's implacable eye had found it easy to locate him. Villagers, skillfully interrogated, had pointed him in the direction of a young man they had never seen before, going to the river-bank carrying loads of wood.

Initially astonished, the doctor had eventually been convinced that he had the rebel. He and John had separated immediately, each taking a different route to increase their chances of taking him. He had even ordered the Scotsman to shoot if necessary–and Grace, less confident of the servant's coolness, had decided to accompany him. Her father, she was quite certain, would not fire except in the most extreme circumstances, but John, being more impulsive, might do something irreparable.

The doctor had arrived on the bank of the Ganges alone, just as Felifax, kneeling by the pyre, was watching a cadaver burn. Who was the woman? A victim, perhaps? Impossible–his grief and Djina's would have been less emphatic. What relationship, then, had Felifax to the dead woman?

Despite the circumstances, Sir Eric, respectful of Hindu ritual, had refrained from interrupting the funeral ceremony. He had waited to arrest the man who had given him so much trouble until he fell prostrate on the bank of the Ganges, after the dispersal of the ashes.

Felifax did not understand immediately what the man wanted, but when he felt handcuffs–which he had never seen before–around his wrists, he stood up. With a violent gesture, he sent the revolver spinning away, and with all his muscles tensed in Herculean effort, he snapped the police device.

With a rapid reflexive movement, Grace's father retrieved the weapon and covered his captive again. He could not fire, though; he remained nailed to the spot by the spectacle unfolding before him.

The young man, so handsome in his grief a few moments ago, was almost unrecognizable. One of his terrible furies had taken hold of him.

A stranger, profiting from his immense chagrin, wanted to take him away! That was a horrible profanation! He would make him pay dearly for it! Abruptly, he became again what he had been on the maharajah's terrace: a true tiger-man!

The doctor saw his eyes suddenly change into olives of gleaming gold, the appearance of the characteristic stripes on the nude torso and the ferocious rictus of his mouth.

By means of one of his fantastic leaps, Felifax would have been able to hurl himself upon the man and destroy him–but he remained immobile instead. Why? Because he had recognized the father of the Englishwoman whom he loved with all his heart.

Was this father in league with the police, then?

In order to resist the temptation to strangle the other, Felifax wanted to run away. At the same time, the doctor recovered from his stupor, saw him and fired.

Although the bullet left the barrel, it was lost in the trees, because the weapon had been abruptly knocked upwards by Grace. Seeing the danger to which her friend was exposed by the infallible sharpshooter's bullet, she had hurled herself forward.

With a violent motion, Palmer shoved his daughter aside and took aim at Felifax again. The latter, turned to stone by Grace's appearance, had no further thought of flight. This time, he would undoubtedly have been shot down if the agonized voice of the young Englishwoman had not cried: "Father! He's the one who saved me in the jungle. He's the one who prevented death from claiming you when all hope was lost at Silver-Hole! Two nights running, he braved the dangers to bring you the potions that saved you. He made me swear never to tell you, but the danger he's in frees me from my oath. Fire now, if you dare to do it!"

The doctor lowered his hand. He closed his eyes helplessly, prey to a violent struggle between duty and gratitude. It only lasted for a moment before duty secured its dominion–but Felifax was no longer there. Obedient to Grace's injunction, he had vanished, taking Djina with him.

XV

What was Felifax, then? What odious crime had presided over his birth, and why had his mother been so cruelly separated from him?

The high priest of Kali was the only one who knew the solution to the mystery. This is it:

Sourina was a Brahman born and bred. His father was a Brahmaput–a son of Brahma–as was he, and he had become a Mahabrahman, the highest rank of all. Both had been inducted into the cult of Durga in her most terrible form. Sourina had refused to marry. He entertained ambitions that were too great for him to think of founding a hearth, and he had received at his request the necessary dispensation from the Brahmanic college. Although his family would become extinct with him, he believed himself capable of rendering his name immortal.

Of superior intelligence, having attended the majority of Hindu colleges of every language and religion, Sourina had a profound admiration and a boundless adoration for the grandeur of his country. In this situation, he was better placed than anyone else to understand the horror of its conquest and the misdeeds of its English conquerors.

As Hindu fanaticism appeared to be profoundly dormant, Sourina had imagined reanimating it, reaching into its innermost core. To that end, the Brahman maintained the best possible relations with the conquerors. His profound erudition, his surprising skill in assimilation and his impeccable mastery of the English language opened all doors to him. By that means, he was able to make a thorough search for the weak points and vulnerabilities of that strong people. One of his acquaintances was Sir Edmund Sexton, a regimental doctor with the Bengal Lancers, who were garrisoned in Benares. Was their friendship honest and loyal? Be serious! It was an interested camaraderie; the surgeon was destined to serve him some day.

Sir Edmund Sexton, a fervent researcher, had fallen prey to an obsession with human grafting, and he had found an enthusiastic audience in Sourina. Profiting from the liberty that his functions allowed him, the Hindu minister hastened to the hospital run by the surgeon and spent hours on end shut up with him in his laboratory; he was his most fervent disciple.

An idea had, in fact, taken root in the fecund brain of the visionary doctor, capable of conferring an unparalleled glory on the person who realized it. Immediately, he had made a partner of his illustrious friend, whose collaboration seemed indispensable to its success. This time, though, he had not found Sourina as enthusiastic as usual; on the contrary, the Brahman had revolted indignantly. The man who had initiated him into the new science must have lost his mind.

The surgeon wanted to attempt the coupling of a woman and a tiger–a monstrous project that could only have been generated by the brain of a madman. Moreover, the Englishman, not daring to make such an attempt with a woman of his own race, was indubitably soliciting the use of a Hindu woman. That would involve Sourina in collaboration with a new crime committed by the conquerors.

That night, the Brahman had left the hospital full of indignation, asking himself whether it might not be prudent to make it impossible for the surgeon to realize his folly. He knew the Englishman too well; he knew that he was capable of persisting in this insane pursuit. As he made his way back to the temple of Kali, however, reflecting at length, he eventually set his indignation aside. The surgeon's ideas seemed less horrific to him. Thus prepared, he remained in the cloister surrounding the temple for long hours, in front of the tiger cage, thinking hard.

Early the following morning, after having passed a sleepless night, during which he had ruminated the most contradictory thoughts, he went back to the major's house.

"By what means, sir, do you intend to obtain the union that you mentioned?"

"I would use the method of artificial insemination."

"And what would you do with the phenomenon thus obtained?"

"A living proof of my genius, an enigmatic creature, combining the beauty and the intelligence of the human race with the strength and facility of the most redoubtable of felines..." Sir Edmund Sexton, carried away by his subject, launched into descriptions dithyrambic and scientific. Sourina, with no time for sophistry, was no longer listening. His goal in undertaking the experiment was entirely different.

If it succeeded, he would not leave the resultant child in the care of the English surgeon, even if he had to extract him by force. With such a creature, he could shake his contemporaries out of their apathy; he could produce him before subdued crowds as the son of the goddess Kali, sent by her to take back their ancestral lands, and India entire. Stirred up by the call of this demigod, who would presumably bear some physical resemblance to a tiger, they would drive the accursed race into the sea.

The surgeon asked Sourina to procure him a robust and healthy woman, who would offer the best possible chance of success. The Brahman had immediately thought of Sita, an 18-year-old girl of absolute perfection, princely blood and the most complete intellectual faculty. Directly descended from the great Tamerlane,[47] Sita knew that her ancestors had been pillaged by their rivals, and that her parents, ruined by the English domination, had disappeared soon afterwards. As a poor orphan, the sole survivor of that princely line, she had been taken in by Sourina's father, then the master of the temple of Kali. He had seen the high-caste girl as a possible spouse for his son, who was studying at the Brahmanic Institute in Calcutta.

On the death of his father, called to succeed him in the temple, Sourina—in spite of the great difference in their ages—had not wanted to abandon all his father's projects. Preoccupied with the great dream of the liberation of India, however, he had never talked to Sita about the possibility of a union between them. The young princess, now a sacred dancer, could wait. Now, carried away by his titanic project, wait. Now, carried away by his titanic project, he was ready to sacrifice her to Sir Edmund Sexton. The realization of his hatred was nigh.

Very superstitious in spite of his erudition, Sourina wanted to have Sita appointed as priestess of the sacred tigers in advance of the experiment. She would thus be placed under the protective sign of Shiva's spouse. The choice was made by the College of Brahmans, assembled for the occasion of the festival of the goddess. In order not to upset the man who was indispensable to him, the surgeon had consented to wait until then.

Before this severe assembly, the most highly-reputed dancers in Bengal sought feverishly to have the honor of being selected for the privileged position. Sourina could have imposed the choice of Sita, but he did not want that. Such abuse of power was repugnant to him, in contrast to the loyalty of his projects. He had contented himself with indicating to the dancer his desire to see her triumph—and on the day the choice was made she deployed such charm, grace and beauty that she was selected.

Sourina had won. The experiment could take place; the subject would be worthy of giving birth to a rival to God's creatures.

For that occasion, a layman and foreigner was granted access to the temple of Kali. Informed by Sourina that everything was propitious and that the woman selected for the experiment was the most beautiful, they had plotted together the means by which the scientific crime would be accomplished. Sourina had suggested to Sir Edmund that they employ curarine, a vaporous extract of curare, whose properties he had extolled. Not only did its influence render people quite helpless, but it left them completely susceptible to instruction between the first moments when the anaesthetic took effect until the point at which they lost all possibility of movement, without their losing consciousness.

In order to conceal the criminal transfusion from all prying eyes, Sourina had ordered three hours of adoration on

135

the banks of the Ganges that morning, on the pretext of a fit of anger on the goddess's part. That was why, at the time appointed for customary ablutions, the temple was completely emptied of all its residents: *palomen*, *yogis*, *devadasis* and slaves. The only ones remaining were Sourina, Sita and two animal-keepers, retained in case they were needed–but they posed no threat; the cult of the goddess Kali authorized any crime.

When the Brahmans, *yogis*, dancers and slaves returned to the temple after three hours of expiation at Mother Ganges, it was all over.

Five months later, poor Sita, in the midst of atrocious suffering, gave birth to a misshapen monster, which combined human and feline characteristics. Confronted with this deplorable result, Sourina experienced a great disappointment.

The major returned to his hospital in a bad mood. After cursing and mulling over the most extraordinary ideas for four or five days, he called on Sourina, desirous of submitting a means of attempting a new experiment to his approval. He proposed that the imprint left by the artificial fertilization must be powerfully marked in Sita's flesh. Biological studies had demonstrated that the observed characteristics could be reproduced by a second birth.

On learning of this phenomenon, Sourina underwent a complete change, occasioned by renewed hope. He must marry off Sita very quickly–quickly enough to contrive the birth of the Hindu messiah. At first, he thought of reserving that creation for himself. Had not Sita been set aside for him by his father? The child, the issue of their marriage, he would consecrate to Kali, kneading him as he pleased. There were two obstacles. Firstly, he was 40 years old; secondly, he was too well-known. The wife of the high priest could not bring a child into the world without the whole temple getting excited. How could he present the child subsequently as the son of Kali?

He had to find among his disciples a well-formed man with a perfect constitution, utterly devoted to the goddess. He had such a man ready at hand: a young Brahman named Rao, a superb fellow, 25 years of age and with glorious blood in his veins, since he was descended from Baber the Conqueror. Unfortunately for him, reason demanded that the marriage could have no future.

Sourina summoned Rao and the two of them had a long conversation, after which the young Brahman agreed to do everything that his venerated leader wished. He still needed Sita's agreement, because it was important that the marriage should be secret.

The poor girl, still suffering the ill-effects of her earlier torture, could not put up much of a fight against the cunning and diplomacy of Sourina. The clandestine marriage appeared to her a further defilement of a daughter of her caste. Using persuasion and threats by turns, the pitiless man persuaded her of the necessity of the union; it would efface the defilement that had already taken place. The union would only bring about a transient change, for it must be secret–because of her position as priestess of the tigers–and without continuity; Kali could not accommodate any worship but her own.

Sita, devoid of strength, had ended up yielding reluc-tantly to Sourina's will. He had officiated at the marriage, in the strictest secrecy. The young husband, Rao, left the fol-lowing morning, on the priest's orders, to undertake a mission journeying through India.

The clandestine marriage bore fruit. The child would be a consolation for Sita in her life as a spouseless mother; per-haps he would even avenge all her suffering.

The much-anticipated day finally arrived, and Sita brought into the world an admirably-conformed male child, larger than normal. Amazingly, confirming the theories of Sir Edmund Sexton, he bore characteristic black stripes on his back and sides. His lovely eyes changed completely when he became angry, suddenly becoming those of a tiger, and his body gave off a very pronounced feline scent. Two tigresses in the neighboring cages having given birth at almost the same time, their milk was added to the nurture of Sita's child.

Unexpectedly, Rao returned to the temple at that moment. The unfortunate man made the mistake of expressing an intention to see his wife again and to embrace his child. That same evening, having been carried away by a mysterious illness, he had been immediately incinerated on the bank of the Ganges by the other Brahmans. His mother and his brother Baber were unable to obtain any explanation of his sudden death.

For two years, Sita knew a sort of happiness in seeing her dear little Rama–called Felifax from the moment of his birth by his "inventors"–growing older. Alas, it was necessary for her to tolerate the mingling of her milk with that of the tigresses.

Felifax grew with amazing rapidity, appearing to be three times as old as he was. His mind was as prodigious as his strength. One day, on the orders of the chief Brahman–who was haunted by fear of maternal influence on the child destined for a sacred task–he was abruptly separated from the priestess. The latter, despite her tears, prayers and resistance, was secretly imprisoned in the monastery of Shiva Ardhanari– and Sourina began the education of Felifax, whose nature gave rise to every hopeful expectation.

Another person kept watch over the child, just as jealously–but from a distance, because entry to the temple was difficult for him. This was Major Sir Edmund Sexton. He had prepared a long paper on his experiment, but to have it appear with the appropriate impact, it would be necessary to produce the living proof. It was impossible; that good fortune was forbidden him. He sensed the increasing hostility of the Brahmans guarding the temple. Sourina could unleash them, and that made him pause for thought. On the other hand, he was also prohibited from using force. His former accomplice would immediately interpret it as an attack against Hindu religious sentiment, and the Indian government would certainly put the surgeon in the wrong.

Years went by. The surgeon was reassigned to the Army Corps in Bombay, and subsequently recalled to England. This recall was due to new follies perpetrated on the natives.

Confirming all the expectations of his adoptive father, Felifax appeared to be the superman the Indian revolution needed. His power over wild beasts was beyond comprehension; he managed them like domestic animals. This power was exploited for the amazement of crowds. Indeed, he passed his time among the tigers, playing, wrestling and sleeping with them. He made the two most beautiful into his faithful dogs.

These two, having come into the world at the same time as him, were his foster-brothers, so to speak. After their deaths, he had adopted their offspring, adorning them with two terrible names of his choice. The male was Rudra, the god of devouring fire and devastating storms; the tigress was Durgane, a name very similar to that of the destructive sprit. Never had beasts been better named, to the extent that they seemed to be the personal emanations of those deities. Felifax obtained from them an incredible docility to his orders. After his flight into the jungle, it was these two formidable servants for whom he had come in search on the evening of the festival of Kali, scattering the crowds watching the celebrations on the banks of the Ganges.

Such was the mystery of Felifax's birth. Baber had not exaggerated in speaking of a horrible drama.

XVI

We are now in the Governor's Mansion in Calcutta.

"Milord, I have failed in the mission entrusted to me by Scotland Yard. I have had a moment of weakness, in not striking down the rebel I was instructed to arrest. Since yesterday, I have thought hard. My attitude would be the same if I were to be confronted by Felifax again. Not being a paid functionary of the law, and moved solely by my conscience, I have come to explain my conduct to Your Lordship, the representative of my government."

"Worthy conduct!" said the Governor, Lord Chapfain. "As a man, I cannot help approving of you, Sir Eric. You have brought a very complex problem to my attention, and are to be thanked for that. In sum, this Felifax certainly merits the importance that others have attempted to attribute to him."

"He's a youth enamoured of liberty and independence. He has a very good heart, and cannot see suffering without soothing it. He has never made any attempt to undermine the authority of the Indian Empire. If he has avenged himself on Sourina, for reasons we do not know, it has always taken the form of liberating those oppressed by the chief Brahman's authority. As for his history with the Maharajah, it's a childish matter that ought to be laughed off."

"So you're his most fervent defender now, my dear Palmer? In brief, you think that we can only enhance his reputation by persevering in our attempts to capture him."

"That's it, exactly! Your Honor would act wisely in giving orders on that matter. I know nothing about the drama surrounding the birth of this child, whom Sourina calls the *son of Kali*. I'm only certain of one thing: Sir Edmund Sexton is mixed up in the business."

"A learned man–a genius, even! Many men of his sort are unappreciated in their homeland!"

"What role has he played in this affair? God alone knows. You know what he's capable of, and you must suspect a troublesome secret. At any rate, my presence in India will not have been entirely useless if I have been able to convince you of the dangerous futility of arresting Felifax."

"No one will be able to protest," the Governor insisted. "The decisions of the Law are sovereign even for the Hindus."

"Give the order to arrest Sourina, then."

"You don't do things by halves, my dear Palmer. Don't you know that he's the most powerful Brahman in Benares, and in the whole of Bengal? He also has connections in every convent in India. His arrest might provoke a general uprising."

"The arrest of Felifax, son of Kali the Black, might perhaps be worse! Think of what effect the words *son of Kali* might have on fanatical natives. They represent grandeur, veneration, not to mention sacrifice. As I've already told you, I have not the slightest trust in this Sourina, despite the evidence of loyalty he has given. He would not hesitate to exploit the error of an arrest..."

"Stop, my dear Palmer! In such an eventuality, we would have Sourina at our side–I have his assurance on that."

"His, perhaps–not the priests submissive to his orders. Believe me, Governor, the trade of detective makes one mistrustful. I hope with all my heart that my country will not have to put Sourina's loyalty to the test–I would be too fearful of seeing it submerged by the tide of revolt without making the least effort to escape."

"My God, you're hardly reassuring! Will you accept the task of making the necessary inquiries?"

"After the failure of my mission, as Your Excellency will understand, it's difficult for me to accept a similar task. A man like me must succeed; his failure is unforgivable. I'm on the point of deciding to give in to the pleas of my dear Grace and retire to Cornwall. My son, a lieutenant stationed here in Calcutta, has a leave of some months due shortly. I'd like to put him up in our little house by the sea." At this evocation, Doctor Palmer smiled. He had arrived in Calcutta scarcely an hour ago, with the aim of seeing the Governor of Bengal and explaining his negligence with respect to Felifax.

In his radiogram to Scotland Yard, Marquis Chapfain had judged him rather harshly, acting under the pernicious influence of the chief of the Benares police. Since the doctor's first words, he had revised his impression and had treated him entirely amicably.

"Can that be possible?" he exclaimed. "Even if I asked you to clear up a new mystery?"

"Even then–and Your Excellency may judge my regret."

"Unfortunate, very unfortunate! A little while ago, when I was apprised of your visit, I could not suppress a gesture of satisfaction. I thought: Here's the ideal man to clear up this business in Hong Kong, which absolutely defies understanding!"

With a movement more pronounced than he intended, Sir Eric Palmer drew his chair forward. The Governor, having noticed this movement, forced himself not to show it–except that an imperceptible smile flickered across his features, while he pretended to change the subject.

Sir Eric Palmer replied in an evasive manner–but he had taken the bait. Eventually, he could no longer control himself. He asked: "Isn't Sullivan the chief of police in Hong Kong?"

"Yes, I believe so. At least, the memorandum I received this morning bears his signature."

"What's happening out there? Is it anything like this Felifax business?"

"It's less complicated. It's doubtless a simple matter of some bloodthirsty brute. Every five days for a month, at almost the same hour, one of our compatriots has been found lying dead in one of the streets in the European quarter of Hong Kong, struck down in an identical manner: a single blow of a powerful fist at the base of the skull. The blow causes a fatal hemorrhage."

"Who are the victims? Policemen?"

"Not always–sometimes English officers."

"Do the crimes always occur in the same place?"

"No, alas. In different corners of Hong Kong. One fantastic particularity–the poor devil is unfailingly marked with a number in sequence: one, two, and so on."

"Where are we up to?"

"The seventh was yesterday. How far does the villain want the sequence to go?"

"It's settled, Milord Governor. I'm on my way. When's the next boat?"

"My goodness! My dear Palmer, what about your promise to your daughter, your little house in Cornwall, your son's leave...?"

"After this business is over, Your Excellency. Sullivan is an old friend, a loyal comrade; with him, I'm certain to work well. I'm ready to take that boat."

"Softly softly, you old devil! The day after tomorrow, at the earliest. A destroyer's leaving to rejoin the China fleet; if you take passage on her, you'll gain two or three days. You can't imagine the satisfaction it gives me to see you take responsibility for the affair."

"And Your Excellency's decision regarding Felifax?"

"I don't know yet. Despite that telegraph from Benares, I'll suspend the search. Let's hope that this living enigma doesn't get up to any more tricks during the truce."

"I believe I can guarantee that he won't. The boy's mourning his mother."

"That's as may be. I'll also see the Maharajah. I'm beginning to come around to your opinion, that it's better to let things rest. My report to Scotland Yard will be made in that light."

With these words, Lord Chapfain cordially held out his hand to the detective. The latter left immediately to send a telegram to Grace in Benares, asking her to rejoin him without delay. He wanted to see her before his departure for Hong Kong, and to entrust her to the care of his son, James. The lieutenant in the Bengal Lancers would be returning to England in two or three months, and he could take his sister back to her Aunt Molly in Plymouth.

Sir Eric Palmer had not taken the Governor entirely into his confidence, but his assurance of Felifax's tranquility during the proffered truce had been given in the full recognition of its cause. Indeed, a sensational event had take place on the same evening as his encounter with the rebel beside the smoking cinders of Sita's funeral pyre.

Despairing of his weakness and also disarmed by his daughter's confidences, the doctor had judged it pointless to search the jungle any further. He had returned to Benares, instructing John to bring their luggage from Silver-Hole.

Not a word was exchanged between father and daughter along the route. Grace was respectful of paternal meditation, and Sir Eric was reproachful of his beloved child for having kept such a secret from him. Despite his great psychological understanding of the concerns of everyday life, he was somewhat in the dark regarding those of the heart. In the young girl's intervention, he had been unable to see anything but a manifestation of gratitude, quite understandable at bottom. Besides, he would never have been able suppose that a more tender sentiment existed between a young English gentlewoman of uncommonly good education and a Hindu, no matter how pleasing or well-educated he might be.

Needless to say, the Reverend Douglas refrained from telling his old friend about the rebel's visits to his bungalow, and of his meeting, one evening, with Grace. He restricted himself to demonstrating to the doctor the beauty of the gesture by which she had prevented the murder of a human being, especially in the wake of such manifestations of charity and generosity. To his great astonishment, he had prevailed easily; the doctor's logic forced him to acknowledge the justice of the argument.

The effort made by Sir Eric, abruptly wrenched from his sickbed when his painful convalescence had hardly begun, in resuming his arduous pursuit, had not done too much damage. Sustained by nervous tension, he had not even noticed it; the strain did not begin to show until after his return to the bungalow. Afflicted by a slight fever and general weakness, he was obliged to go to bed very early, without taking any more nourishment than a little milk.

Before retiring in her turn, Grace had come to make sure that he did not need anything. After having given himself a double injection of quinine chlorohydrate and cola extract, the doctor went to sleep. Because of the heat, the window remained ajar.

At midnight, the doctor was awakened with a start by a breath of fresh air. The window had been opened wide; a shadow had just leapt into the room and was heading towards the bed from which the recumbent man was watching beneath his mosquito-net...

Soon, the barrel of a Browning was pointing at the invader.

Sir Eric had scarcely been able to suppress a cry of surprise then. The man who stopped still in front of him was Felifax. A profound sadness was imprinted on his handsome face.

There was a silence that lasted scarcely a minute, which seemed like a century. It was broken by the rebel's warm voice. "Sir, I beg your pardon for the manner of my introduction into your room. I did not want to disturb anyone, needing to talk to you man-to-man. I want to tell you that I am at your disposal. I shall surrender myself to you—but before that, it is necessary for me to carry out the last wish of a dead woman. A few hours ago, when you arrested me, I was mourning my mother—a mother whose life has been the most lamentable of martyrdoms. Snatched from her arms by an inexorable will, I have been deprived of the caresses and the gentle affection due to all children. Life might have given us reparation; alas, Brahma did not wish it. The first kiss she gave her son also proved to be her last; she died in my arms of the implacable bite of a hairy arya."

The young man's voice had weakened suddenly; there was another silence. After a few seconds, the voice recovered its strength and continued. "Although mother did not have time to confide the secret of my birth, she indicated the man from whom I could obtain the information. Tomorrow night, I will call upon him to tell me the truth. What will that truth be? I do not know, and I dread it, but I need to know. After that, you will be able to find me in the ruined temple in the jungle. When you discovered me there the first time, you accidentally left one of your waistcoat buttons behind; that visiting card put me on the alert. There you can arrest me. I shall not offer any resistance. I ought not to appear to surrender myself; it will be better for you to come for me."

Astounded by this turn of events, Sir Eric had not made any movement; the youth's demeanor moved him, in spite of himself, and he did not regret the failure of his arrest as much now. Finally, impelled by his loyal nature, he exclaimed: "Don't go back to the ruined temple, my son!"

"But..."

"It won't be me who'll arrest you. There's no point in giving that glory to others, who are incapable of appreciating your gesture. My decision is made; you have nothing to fear from Eric Palmer. Don't let me regret seeing such qualities stifled by rebellion, though."

The young man started in protest. "I have never scorned the laws of your country, sir! I have attacked a man who, in defiance of all rights, detained and maltreated an unfortunate child because she was my constant companion and refused to betray my secrets. I escaped from a gilded prison in order to fulfill my dream of being free to enjoy the beauties of nature! I did not attack the Maharajah's men; I did nothing but defend myself against them. A man struck me with his whip when I had not done any harm, nor committed any sin. My happiness will be in living in the jungle, so beautiful and so captivating, without having to struggle against the spitefulness of men, which is far more frightful to me than my friends the wild beasts."

"I wish with all my heart that you might realize your aspirations, my friend. Once more, believe me, you have nothing to fear from me. Be happy with your little companion, so gentle and pretty, and thank you for having saved my daughter as well as my own ancient carcass. There are debts that are difficult to pay."

Eric Palmer lay back again, as if to prove to Felifax that he was no longer concerned with him.

The next day, he took the train to Calcutta. He wanted to inform the Governor of his decision, and also to plead the rebel's cause.

The following night, Sourina was in bed in the austere cell he occupied in the temple, when he was roused from his sleep by a strange feeling that something was wrong. By the light of the *khojana* [48] that lit his cell all night, he saw before him a tall silhouette, which he recognized.

To either side of that silhouette, connected to it to form a single whole, two other terrifying individuals were discernible: Rudra and Durgane, the royal tigers stolen by Felifax on the night of the festival of Kali.

It was only to find his loyal friends that Felifax had delayed his return to question Sourina. Despite their love of the jungle and liberty, the beasts had followed their friend. All of them–including Djina–had re-entered the temple of Kali by the secret passage known only to the young man.

"Sourina," the youth's voice pronounced, gravely, "you no longer have before your eyes the child you raised and fashioned, but an instrument of justice. My mother, Sita, is dead; her soul has climbed up to nirvana and her ashes have been thrown into the sacred Ganges. Her last words laid an accusation against you and an English physician. Will you tell me the truth?"

"When you know it, will you have the courage to strike the Brahman who has been the most affectionate of fathers to you?"

"Yes, if he is guilty! Except that, since the law of Brahma forbids raising a hand against or shedding the blood of one of his priests, and as my hand might tremble at certain memories, I have brought these two to exact punishment. Ru-

147

dra and Durgane will not tremble; they do not know the law of Brahma."

Sourina was brave. Like the majority of Brahmans, he was scornful of death. Despite that, however, Felifax's declarations disturbed him. He knew that the other was capable of carrying through his vengeance without the least pity. Very quickly, his decision was taken.

In a tone of profound sincerity, he gave the young man an almost full account of the mystery of his birth, which had combined his human nature with a feline one. Naturally, he minimized his own responsibility. According to him, Sir Edmund Sexton had constrained him, by force, to accomplish that horrible profanation. He had been forced to witness the infamy powerlessly, resolved to kill himself in expiation of such a crime–but Kali, the divine source of inspiration, had ordered him to live, in order to look after the son conceived in horror. He had taken the child under his protection, dedicated him to the goddess, to make him the savior of India! Moreover, the Destroyer, spouse of Shiva, had provided proof of her will; she had incarnated herself within the son of her priestess Sita, and had given him the power to prove his divine affiliation to human beings by such undeniable signs as his power to tame wild beasts.

Carried away by his grandiose dream, forgetting that he was on trial, under threat of death, Sourina suddenly cried, with all his enthusiasm: "Ah! To chase from our land these accursed conquerors, profanators of the holiest things, who have made the servants of Brahma into slaves! They have committed crimes without names, killing our brothers pitilessly; every day death strikes anew, not by the blade but by privation and superhuman labor, their diabolical inventions. Our religion has been humiliated and disgraced, our women–our mothers, our sisters, our daughters–appropriated for their amusement. Nothing can resist their force.

"What laid this curse upon your mother Sita, the most beautiful, the most noble, the most pure of the daughters of India, descendant of the great Tamerlane, called perhaps to a higher destiny? Constrained to comply with that scientific madness, I offered him slaves, low-caste *gopis*, *bayaderes* who might have consented in return for rupees. Nothing could divert his will; he wanted Sita, and his medicine has martyrized her odiously.

"This insult to Brahma, the creator god, in the person of his creature, calls for death. That is why I have brought you up so lovingly, shaping your intelligence and developing your physique. I have given you the education of the most learned chief Brahmans, I have instilled in you all the sciences possessed by the most ancient fakirs, I have taught you the supernatural power of dominating crowds, and I have waited until you were 18 to reveal to you the mystery of your birth.

"Yes, I imprisoned Sita; that is a crime, I admit, and I am ready to pay for it–but that internment was necessary to my plan. Her good and gentle soul, innocent of vengeance, would have softened yours and taught you forbearance and forgiveness when it was necessary to instill hatred. Let us leave things to settle down, to be forgotten, then suddenly reappear: the son of Kali issuing a call to arms for the liberation of the people of India..."

Sourina would have gone on had Felifax's grave voice not interrupted him.

"Before making the invading nation pay for the crimes of its conquest, to punish it by annihilation, I have a personal duty to punish the man who made my mother suffer."

"His horror will be even greater, his punishment more exemplary, when he sees the collapse of the glorious Indian empire contrived by the child of his demonic genius."

"I do not want a collective punishment. First, I have to avenge my mother. After Sir Edmund Sexton, we shall see. Sourina, I shall believe what you say, and deprive Rudra and Durgane of the satisfaction of a punishment that would be very agreeable to them. In exchange, I demand that you take me to the surgeon. He shall see then what his science has produced. In order to make him pay for Sita's tears, the child conceived as a result of his infamous machinations will forget his mother's gentleness, remembering only the ferocity of the savant. Where is this man? You must put me in his presence or pay for him."

"Why not let yourself be guided by me, my child? The punishment would be more satisfying."

"Enough! You must have perceived that my decisions are irrevocable and that nothing can stop me. I want to be put into the presence of Sir Edmund Sexton. I give you two minutes to speak—otherwise, deeming you a willing accomplice, I shall open my hands; Rudra and Durgane will then follow their instinct."

"So be it! I will obey you. We shall go in search of this man, in his own country. In the meantime, let me reflect on the best means of accomplishing your vengeance."

"I want everything settled now. Rudra and Durgane will be reinstated in their cage, and I shall return with Djina to the temple—she, it's understood, will never leave me. Will she be free to come and go, even to leave the temple?"

"Yes, my son. You will be safe here. Neither the sovereign Maharajah nor the accursed conquerors would dare to profane the dwelling of Kali in order to arrest you. I shall go to pray at her feet; she will inspire me and then I shall tell you my plan for vengeance."

Felifax's power was such that the two royal tigers allowed themselves to be locked in their cage despite their desire to resist. The temple was soon awake. The news of Felifax's return delighted everyone. Among the animal-keepers, however, one man stood apart, his eyes were devouring the youth.

Baber now knew the causes of Rao's death. Having no further need to work for the police, he intended to stick very close to Sourina in future. Loyal to the oath he had made to Sita, he would leave Felifax to take care of his vengeance, but would be ready to support him. Then again, mistrustful of the Brahman's cunning, he might perhaps be useful to his brother's son, whose beautiful and noble soul had no suspicion of potential treason.

When the time came for the customary ablutions, Djina left the temple with the other women, but instead of heading towards the Ganges, she went to the Reverend Douglas' house. She was carrying a message to Miss Grace from her adoptive brother. The houseboy offered to take her to Doctor Palmer's daughter.

Already up and about, Grace was packing. The evening before, a telegram from her father had notified the young Englishwoman of his imminent departure for Hong Kong and his desire to see her. Despite her desire to stay in Benares, it was impossible for her to disobey the doctor–but a profound anxiety was wringing her heart, because she did not know what had become of Felifax.

The detective had not said anything to her about the nocturnal visit, nor about the steps he would attempt to take in Calcutta regarding the Governor of Bengal. Her father, to be sure, had renounced any intention of arresting Felifax, but Grace knew no more than that–and, far from soothing her anxieties, the decision had exasperated them. The poor youth would be pursued by other policemen avid for revenge.

To depart for Calcutta without seeing the man who had begun to occupy such an important place in her heart was painful for her–infinitely painful. Perhaps her father would want to take her to Hong Kong, in which case she would never again see that unique representative of a fabulous and nameless race, whose rare nobility had captivated her heart.

Djina refused the houseboy's offer. She was content to send the letter. She knew what the missive to Miss Palmer contained, and what distress it would cause her. Was it not Felifax's farewell?

In his firm handwriting, in his perfect English, the desperate young man had inscribed these words:

Miss Grace,

Nothing more can exist between us. As I told you once, you are English and I am Hindu. I now know the circumstances of my birth. My mother was the unfortunate victim of a man of your race. Her memory compels me to act.

151

We will never see one another again, but I shall always treasure the image of the graceful blonde silhouette with the bloodstained forehead, of which I caught sight one day in the jungle, and retain the sound of her sweet voice in my soul...

If, in the near future, you should hear talk of a new and terrible exploit, do not attribute it to the wickedness of my soul, but tell yourself that it is the men of your race, having intended it thus, who are uniquely responsible for and ought to be reproached for the ferocity of

Felifax.

When Djina returned to the temple, her big brother and Sourina were conversing in the Brahman's cell. Soon, she saw them go out, and heard Felifax say with a ferocious joy:

"We depart without delay, then. There, as here, I shall have the most redoubtable of superb wild beasts at my disposal. The entire world will be talking about Felifax, the son of Kali, the king of the man-eaters. Woe betide you, Sir Edmund Sexton–vengeance is on the march!"

The pariah was, in fact, going to turn Europe upside down.

6 frs
DE LUXEPS

Londres
en folie

SUITE À
L'HOMME TIGRE
DE
"FÉLIFAX"

PAUL
FÉVAL fils

Part Two: London Goes Mad

I: A Lord Has Been Carved Up

Freddy, Lord Bencenave's old manservant, could not suppress a cry of surprise that morning when he went into his master's room at 9 a.m. The bed had not been slept in. The glass of sugared water prepared the night before had not been touched, nor had the soporific capsule that his lordship took every night.

Although his master had gone out after dinner the previous evening, the idea that he might have gone off somewhere never entered the loyal servant's head; Lord Bencenave was 60 years old, and might have been reckoned the most orderly man in the world. In addition, he was particularly careful of his health, which had been somewhat damaged by long sojourns in India and South Africa, in the capacity of Deputy Governor. His absence was, therefore, surprising.

Having opened the curtains and the shutters, Freddy uttered a further exclamation of surprise. The clothes his lordship had worn when he went out–his dinner-jacket and silk waistcoat–were there, folded on a chair.

The master had gone to see the monstrous spectacle of Rama's Circus Menagerie, which had been installed at Kensington Palace for several days, and had brought the whole of London running.[49] His lordship rarely went out in the evenings, but this entirely indigenous attraction had been perfectly designed to attract a former functionary of the Indian government.

What did it all mean–the empty room, the undisturbed bed and other troubling evidence? Freddy was convinced that he had heard his master re-enter the house at about 1 a.m. His lordship had opened the door with his key and, as always, had carelessly slammed it shut–of that, the domestic was certain.

However, what confused the worthy man was the care his lordship had taken to fold his clothes; normally, in Freddy's absence, he left them extended untidily on the divan.

Thinking that his master might be in his pajamas in another room, the servant went to look for him. It was all in vain; Lord Bencenave was nowhere to be found.

Having returned to the bedroom, becoming increasingly anxious, Freddy suddenly noticed a luminous line under the dressing room door–there was a small gap between the bottom of the door and the floor. Crouching down, he perceived his master's slippered feet. He must, therefore, be attending to the usual necessities. Reassured, Freddy knocked on the door and turned the handle without waiting for the usual authorization.

To his further amazement, his lordship was not there. There were only the slippers, resting on the linoleum–and, astonishingly, two socks, which seemed to be standing upright within the abandoned slippers.

Having come closer to observe this phenomenon, Freddy suddenly threw himself backwards. Then, emitting inarticulate cries, he sank to his knees. His trembling legs refused to sustain him.

The spectacle was enough to cause great distress in the most intrepid of men. His lordship's feet, still encased in their silk socks, were in his slippers–but nothing more, for the legs had been cut off at the base of the calves. Large pieces of amadou [50] had been placed on the neatly-excised sections, to stem the bleeding.

For more than a quarter of a hour, the unfortunate Freddy was incapable of the slightest movement. He felt faint, and invoked the names of all the saints. Finally, having recovered a measure of courage, he found the strength to drag himself to the telephone in order to inform Scotland Yard of this disturbing enigma.

Less than an hour afterwards, two police officers arrived, accompanied by a constable and an attorney. They were soon joined by a detective, whose deductive powers might be useful to them.

"Hello, Mr. Sullivan," said the attorney to the new arrival. "Here's an affair that seems fantastic and very disturbing. We've interrogated this chap, and nothing he's told us has given us a lead."

The man addressed as Sullivan contrived a smile. Without replying directly to his interlocutor, he had himself taken immediately to his lordship's apartment. The police officers had not yet visited it, preferring to wait for their valued collaborator.[51]

Fortunately, Freddy, conscious of his responsibility, had not disturbed anything. Since telephoning Scotland Yard, he had not returned to the two adjoining rooms.

The officers examined everything with meticulous care. There was, however, not the slightest clue to be found on the carpet, the draperies or the walls. Nothing was visible but the imprints of the servant's shoes, where he had gone to the window to open the curtains, then into the dressing-room and stopped abruptly in front of the frightful pair of feet. It was extraordinary! Indeed, it was difficult to believe that Freddy was involved in this atrocity in any way–an old servant, aged himself, could not have any motive for committing such a crime.

Sullivan, who was lying prone on the carpet searching for the tiniest clue, suddenly called the constable. Then, having pointed out a few near-invisible scratches on the floor, he stated confidently: "The perpetrator is certainly a professional criminal; he has carefully effaced his footprints with the aid of a small stiff-bristled brush. Here is the signature of that household instrument, along with a fragment of one of its bristles."

Traces of the brushwork were found in three or four other places, but no further clue was discovered.

Sullivan and the officers examined the interior of the little townhouse all the way to the door. It was No. 8 Green Street, situated in the charming district of Stoke Newington.[52] Lord Bencenave lived there alone, save for Freddy. As with everywhere else, nothing was visible on the door–not the slightest fingerprint. The exterior of the door seemed to have been wiped with a cloth, even though Freddy had not done the housework that morning. He affirmed, besides, that he had heard the door open at 1 a.m.

Lord Bencenave always carried his house-keys with him. The previous evening, before going out, he had told the old manservant not to wait up for him, because he would not need his help to undress. The old man had gone to bed, and had been woken up by the noise of the door slamming. He swore that he had heard nothing thereafter, even though he had remained awake for more than an hour before going back to sleep.

In pursuing his examination, Sullivan glanced outside. By a happy chance, he suddenly saw two boys playing with a small stiff-bristled brush–a utensil commonly used in England and America for brushing clothes. He called to the boys and asked them where they had found the object. Without any reluctance, they pointed to the corner of the wrought-iron railings in front of the house. They had been using the brush in a game of hopscotch for some time. This circumstance was frustrating for the detective; soiled as it was with soil and mud, the brush could not yield any clue.

Muttering complaints about the fatality that had prevented any light being cast upon the affair, and the humor of apprentice surgeons who used their anatomical specimens to play stupid jokes far too frequently, Sullivan went back to the dressing-room, secretly convinced that the feet could not be his lordship's. He picked up the missing man's footwear, with their macabre contents, and coolly proceeded to take off the socks. Having carefully rendered the white feet bare, he asked the manservant whether he could identify his master's extremities.

Like many well-trained English manservants, Freddy served his master as masseur, hairdresser, manicurist and pedicurist. He immediately declared that the sinister debris was indeed the feet of Lord Bencenave. In order to support his identification he pointed to the regularly-treated corns on each little toe and a long scar on one heel, a souvenir of India. The

Deputy Governor had been bitten by a king cobra during a hunt in the Bengal jungle, and owed his life to the intervention of a native non-commissioned officer who had made a deep incision in order to introduce a herbal antivenom. The scar was still very obvious.

Sullivan went back into the bedroom, certain now that this was no medical students' joke and that Lord Bencenave was dead–or had at least had his feet amputated. He sat down in a large armchair and continued to interrogate Freddy. The latter, who had been in the missing man's service for more than 30 years, had followed him everywhere, including India and South Africa. His blind devotion had prevented him from seeing that his master had any enemies, although his lordship had always given evidence of extreme rigor in the various posts he had occupied, especially in his final job as Lord Chancellor.

After giving up that last post, he had retired from all political and commercial affairs, living a very orderly life and seeing no one but a select group of old friends, all of them highly-placed in society. He went out every afternoon to his club, to read the newspapers and play bridge. He sometimes brought back a fellow member to dine with him, but his lordship was usually in bed by 10 p.m.

At his club and among his acquaintances, he had heard talk of Rama's Circus Menagerie, installed at Kensington Palace. It had been advertised to him as a unique attraction, as much for of its impeccable reconstruction of India as for the quality of its spectacle and the splendor of its animals, presented in all their beauty and ferocity. The former Deputy Governor had been tempted to a modest restimulation of his marvelous memories of the country he had loved. That was why he had gone to see the spectacle the previous evening, having dined early. Knowing that his old manservant had loved India just as much, he had invited him to go, but Freddy, who had been off color for three or four days, had declined the offer. He regretted that bitterly now.

After his master's departure, when his evening's work was done, the faithful valet had gone to bed at 10 p.m. Tired out–he had not slept the previous night because of his indisposition–he had gone to sleep without delay. Reawakened by the noise of the closing door, he had looked at his clock; it was 1 a.m. He had heard footsteps in the corridor immediately afterwards, heading for his lordship's bedroom. Having been instructed not to disturb himself, he had not dared budge. Silence had fallen then, and he had not heard the slightest noise thereafter.

Sullivan, like the other investigators, was in no doubt of the old man's innocence; his despair was not feigned and everything about him testified to his good faith.

"It was doubtless you who dressed your master before his departure for the circus. Can you tell us whether any of his clothing is missing?"

In response to the detective's question, Freddy went to the folded garments. Nothing was missing–not the flannel vest or the least accessory. There was nothing missing from the pockets either. The well-garnished wallet was there. the gold watch with its massive chain, two or three trinkets and some loose change. There were also the house-keys, attached to their little key-ring.

"Milord never took off his two rings," Freddy said. "One had a gold cachet with a baronet's coat-of-arms; the other was platinum, mounted with a magnificent blue diamond, the gift of a Burman tribal chief."[53]

These two rings had not been found. Despite their absence, theft had certainly not been the motive for this singular crime. The jewels would probably be found with the rest of the body–a circumstance that would only add to the mystery's obscurity.

The investigators sealed off his lordship's apartment. In appointing Freddy its guardian, they instructed him to remain at the disposal of the law. They left one of the policemen outside, who was to be replaced every eight hours. This policeman was ostensibly put there to protect the old manservant in case the murderers were to return; in reality, he was ordered to keep watch on the fellow's movements.

As the investigators were leaving the Green Street house, the attorney could not restrain himself from saying to the detective: "Well, Mr. Sullivan, I must say that this is a bizarre case for your début at Scotland Yard.[54] Your excellent friend Doctor Palmer would have been delighted to be called in on it."

"Without a doubt, sir–but Doctor Palmer is definitely finished with the police and mysterious affairs. As soon as he returned from Hong Kong, he handed in his resignation and retired to Plymouth with his little Grace.[55] He's a wise man. I wish I had the means to do likewise. Until I have that privilege, I shall try to be worthy of the man who recommended me to Scotland Yard and put all my effort into the elucidation of this distressing abomination."

The three men shook hands. Sullivan, remaining behind on his own, undertook yet another tour of the house.

The detective was a man of Herculean build–like most of the inspectors at Scotland Yard–about 50 years of age, with a frank and loyal physiognomy. He was eager to mark his return to the Metropolitan Police with a masterly coup. He had just returned from Hong Kong, where he had spent several years as chief of police. Often laid low by malaria, he had finally decided to follow the advice of his friend, Doctor Palmer, and request a transfer back to England.

The celebrated doctor detective had been in China in response to the plea of Lord Chapfain, the Governor of Bengal, who had responded to an urgent demand for reinforcements sent by Sullivan himself. For some time, every five days or thereabouts, at almost the same time of day, an Englishman had been found dead in one of Hong Kong's streets. The victim had always been struck down by a formidable blow of a fist at the base of the skull–an unforgiving blow causing a fatal hemorrhage. All the dead men had been policemen or English officers. Eric Palmer, who had been sent on a mission to Benares by Sir Harold Nimbly, the head of Scotland Yard, to search for a mysterious man named Felifax, had refused to continue his pursuit of that individual because the man had saved his life and that of his daughter.

By way of compensating for that stern refusal, he had immediately agreed to leave for Hong Kong. In less than two weeks, he had succeeded in discovering the killer, a blood-thirsty brute escaped from a prison camp in Australia, having been sentenced to 30 years hard labor for similar crimes. By a remarkable coincidence, it was Doctor Palmer who had arrested him previously, in some dive in Whitechapel. At the first glance, the doctor had recognized the trademark, and had arrested the bandit one evening, despite his threats, just as he was about to perpetrate a further crime. The wretch had sworn an oath to kill a man for every year that he had been condemned to prison.

After this exploit, Sir Eric Palmer, finally giving way to the supplications of his daughter, the delightful Grace, had retired to his estate in Cornwall. Before leaving, though, he had suggested that Scotland Yard replace him with his friend Sullivan, who worked according to the same methods and for whose sterling qualities he had vouched. The suggestion having been accepted, the brave Sullivan had the kind of first case for which he had wished. He was confronted by a crime as frightful as it was incomprehensible, in whose solution he must employ all his science.

II: During the Performance

Eric Palmer's successor belonged to a good school, very dear to the doctor detective, whose fundamental point of departure was: Who? Why? How? As a true son of Wales, though, he was handicapped by a determined obstinacy. Like his famous compatriot, Lloyd George, he could never bring himself to admit an error, and was always ready to think himself infallible.

A confirmed bachelor, Sullivan lived in a comfortable house in Jane Street, a few steps from Waterloo Road. He sublet three rooms there from the widow of a former colleague who had been killed while making a dangerous arrest in dockland. He had been given the address by Sir Harold Nimbly himself, who was glad to help the wife of one of his best agents, fallen on the battlefield. The policeman was in clover there; the widow, who was still attractive, took pleasure in pampering an old ally of her husband's, and possibly nurtured hopes for the future.

Unlike most famous detectives, Sullivan did not smoke a pipe, but he always had a cigar in his mouth–a cigar that he only lit in moments of deep preoccupation. The rest of the time, he gripped it, chewed on it or passed it from one side of his mouth to the other, rolling it between his incisors from one canine to the other.

The brave detective's life was, however, poisoned by two bugbears. The first was journalists, to whom he referred as "chatterboxes," accusing them of hindering the work of the police by their prolixity. The second, and much the more terrible, was his feet, which were afflicted with painful bunions. These epidermal tumors obliged him to wear special, unusually large shoes, which bulged like the knotty trunks of elm trees. With every change of temperature, these parasites put him in a vile temper.

163

For the moment, the weather seemed set fair. At any rate, Sullivan left the crime scene with a spring in his step, saying to himself: "To unravel such an affair thoroughly, it's important to trace it back to its point of departure."

He reconstructed the pattern of events. As he went out, Lord Bencenave had named his intended destination. He had gone to Rama's Circus Menagerie. The first thing was to determine was whether the former minister had actually gone to the place he had indicated to his manservant. It is a long way from Stoke Newington to Kensington Palace, and his lordship could not have used public transport, especially in a dinner-jacket. About 200 yards from his domicile, there was a taxi stand. Simple logic suggested that he would have gone straight there.

As at all the cabstands in the district, most of the drivers were probably regulars, living in the neighborhood and gradually accumulating a steady clientele. Sullivan was not mistaken; having found the person in charge of the stand, he was told that the majority of the drivers were local.

"Do you, by any chance, know Lord Bencenave?" he hastened to ask.

"Very well. He comes here every day to get a cab."

"Has he a preferred driver?"

"Yes. Smell always drives Quickfoot."

"Who's Quickfoot?"

"Lord Bencenave, of course. That's his nickname. His best argument, it seems, has always been to drive his foot into the fleshy parts of his inferiors.[56] For that reason, he acquired the name Quickfoot, by which he's generally known."

"Did Smell drive his lordship yesterday?"

"Yes, at the usual hour. Milord went to his club in Piccadilly. Smell waited for him there, although that was unusual, and—which is even more unusual—he waited for him again that evening after dinner. He had to take him out again."

"Is Smell here now?"

"No, he's on a job—but he certainly won't be long. A real taxi-driver wouldn't miss the tradeswoman who brings his breakfast round for anything in the world. He'll make sure he's here–and look, here he is!"

Sullivan turned round and saw a taxi slow down and come to a halt in the line. It was driven by a stout man with an open face. Called by the stand-manager, he hurried forward to answer the detective's question.

"It's true–yesterday evening I drove Lord Bencenave to Rama's Circus Menagerie. I even offered to stay and wait for him. Quickfoot refused–he obviously hoped to get back to Stoke Newington on the cushions of another vehicle."

The first point was established; the victim had gone to the circus.

That afternoon, the detective presented himself at the Empire Club in Grafton Street, off Piccadilly, a rendezvous for former colonials assiduously frequented by Lord Bencenave. The enigma of the amputated feet was already the sole topic of conversation there, causing consternation among the idlers, the readers and the card-players alike.

Although his lordship's acquaintances condescended to answer the detective's questions, he only obtained a single item of relevant information. Lord Bencenave had been seen ensconced in a box during the circus performance. He had chatted merrily with two or three women, whose names he had not taken the trouble to learn.

Instead of methodically pursuing the inquisitorial principle of Who? Why? How? Sullivan went back home to put on a dinner-jacket. There, he was seized by a sudden fit of anger. Several journalists were installed in the room whose use he and his landlady shared, listening avidly to the good Mrs. Smithson wax exceedingly lyrical on the subject of the admirable detective whom she had the honor of accommodating. He reminded her in so many ways of her dear prematurely-departed husband.

The Press's sources of information are truly precious. It was already known that Detective Sullivan was working on the case, and the love of copy had unleashed the pack upon its quarry. Special editions were relating the fantastic details of the crime; it was a matter that might keep the public panting for several days.

Sullivan's fury put the reporters to flight. For her part, dear Mrs. Smithson was amazed to hear her lodger address her in a rather disagreeable manner. He told her that in future there would no longer be any shared room, that he would confine himself rigorously to the three rooms strictly reserved for his use and to their particular entrance. Devastated by this decision, the brave woman fled to her bedroom in tears.

After having put on his dinner-jacket, continuing to seethe all the while, Sullivan went to Police Headquarters to ask for a young inspector who knew his way around society. He was no longer familiar with the important people on the London scene, thanks to his long sojourn in China.

At 8 p.m., accompanied by an inspector named Stillborn, he bought two seats in box 11 from the booking-office at Rama's Circus.

The vast Hindu establishment certainly merited the craze manifest in London; it was furnished with a luxury unprecedented in that kind of exhibition. Immediately on entering, one sensed that money had been lavished on the installation in great profusion.

The exterior of the Asiatic tent erected in the immense hall of Kensington Palace represented a Hindu temple, judiciously chosen and designed to enchant those very numerous Englishmen who had visited India. It was the Golden Temple of Amritsar, on the shore of the Lake of Immortality.[57]

In addition to his obvious wealth, the proprietor of the circus must have been a veritable magician, and an unparalleled set-dresser, for he had mastered the miracle of reproducing objects with a rigorous exactitude that took seductive effect even before one went in. Hindu workmen of the highest repute, many of them imported for the purpose, had been employed for many weeks in sculpting and decorating the different rooms of the masterpiece.

At the entrance to the hall, an artificial lake had been dug, the exact image of the Lake of Immortality. It was equally delightful, with its rectangular quays in black and white marble. Lotuses floated on the water, where the rich ornamentation of the temple was reflected.

To reach the edifice, one passed along a long causeway, a sort of bridge projecting from the bank. Its mosaic path was bordered with a carved balcony decorated with 20 lanterns with variously-colored shades.

All the divinities of the Vedic trinity of the Aryans and the Khakis [58] were sculpted in the massive columns supporting the entrance to the temple. Those who were familiar with the marvelous country explained to the uninitiated what careful research it must have required to reconstitute that pantheon so faithfully. Between these massive columns stood motionless Hindus, dressed like the natives of Ahmedabad,[59] with long tunics, loose trousers and large turbans in unexpected colors: soft violet, turquoise green, saffron orange.

The incomparable "recreator" of this marvel had placed powerful projectors in the various corners of the immense hall, just under the ceiling. These were directed at the lake, the door of the temple and on the Hindus, painting them with floods of light. They imparted a flare to everything, and reflected from mirrors to produce the illusion of a tropical sun.

Captivated by that magnificent spectacle, which took the breath away, one went through the arch slightly fearful of disillusionment–mistakenly, for the enchantment was redoubled. To arrive at the main auditorium one went through a village reconstituted with truly surprising color. This village housed numerous artisans who were making and selling a thousand trinkets of their own invention, on which the English doted.

Finally, one went into the hall–or rather the jungle. The entire flora of India was represented there, and this flora served to shelter the wild fauna of the land of the Rajahs.

The spectators were placed in a semicircle around this jungle, in which gilded cages were artfully concealed, containing the most magnificent specimens. There were, without exaggeration, at least 60 royal tigers: Bengal tigers in all their savage strength, for they were unacquainted with the methods usually employed by animal-tamers. There were 100 leopards, ranging from black panthers from Java to tree-leopards from the Deccan. In sum, there were all the varieties of the carnivorous fauna of the land of *sati*.[60]

Four enormous elephants were walking majestically around the cages; they had the incomparable prestige of having their entire defenses encircled by gold and precious stones.

While awaiting the commencement of the performance, the crowd chatted, passing on the most extravagant gossip. This menagerie, it was said, had been put together by a consortium of Indian Maharajahs as an offering to the King. After the exhibition, these inestimable inmates would become the property of London Zoo.

Estimates were also made of the fantastic sums dispensed for this installation, whose transportation–600 animals, 400 Hindus, more than 2,000 trees and an incalculable number of large boxes–had necessitated the chartering of an entire cargo-ship.

Sullivan, the professional researcher, had a connoisseur's appreciation of this prefect reconstruction of a country he knew. He had estimated expenses necessitated by such a gigantic labor at several thousand pounds. He could see the red soil of India at the feet of the trees; even the humus necessary to the life of the plants–bamboos, areca palms, flame-trees, araucarias, giant ferns and so on–had, therefore, been imported. All this was, moreover, maintained at a hothouse temperature, and skillfully ventilated.

Our man had not come as an admirer, however. He had to inquire into the probable death of Lord Bencenave, and he strongly suspected that he might discover a thread worth following at the circus. His observant eye examined the people disseminated around him, and his colleague Stillborn named the various important people occupying the boxes and the orchestra stalls for him.

Although it could accommodate nearly 10,000 people, the circus filled up very quickly. The policeman planned to make a tour of the popular enclosures–already filled to bursting–during the interval. There was soon hardly a folding seat free. Apart from box No. 13, neighboring the one occupied by the two inspectors, all of them were full.

During the two minutes before the opening of the spectacle, an enormous curtain, disposed in such a way as to match the arc of the semicircle formed by the seats, was closed. Behind the cloth rampart there appeared to be intense activity. The curtain itself was a marvel to behold. Made of a sumptuous fabric akin to brocade, it was delicately embroidered in the purest style of Ghazipur.[61] It represented scenes from Brahmanic mythology: the various incarnations of Vishnu, the combats of the great Rama and the downfall of the demon.

When the curtain was drawn aside, there was a well-deserved murmur of admiration. The spectators had before their eyes a scene in Jaipur,[62] the roseate city, with the Maharajah's palace in the background. The scene seemed to be endowed with its own sun, thanks to the floodlights, and with its own ambience, thanks to its skillful population with lithe men with thick turbans on their heads, dressed in long coats and loose trousers, and exquisite women scantily clad in the fashion of Roman facia or the *ceste* of Venus,[63] which leaves the torso and the legs free and naked–as seductive a costume as there is. They each wore draperies in two shades of the same color: jonquil on saffron, cramoisy on nacarat,[64] coarse green on sinople.[65] No canephore [66] was as graceful as they were as they carried pitchers destined to be filled with water, with one arm raised to support an earthenware pot with gilded handles or a neatly-rounded copper flagon. The children perched on the hips of some of them did not disturb their sculptural gait.

Then, in the manner of German and American circuses, the spectacle began with a grandiose parade, which seemed to emerge from the Maharajah's palace, comprising the artistes of the company. They were all Hindus, and scrupulously so: fakirs, prestidigitators, illusionists, acrobats, dancers, contortionists, mahoulistes [67] and snake-charmers.

The circus acts constituted the first part of the performance; the second was entirely devoted to the famous Rama, the king of the jungle, in the midst of his untamed beasts. Had Doctor Eric Palmer and his daughter Grace been present, they would certainly have recognized the master of ceremonies as the loyal Baber, devoted affiliate of the Benares Police, by virtue of his hatred for the high priest Sourina–except that, instead of having a bare torso, as he had in Benares, Baber was dressed in a gold-bedecked uniform, having taken on the heavy responsibility of directing the spectacle.

The unforgettable vision encountered by all those who had visited India was magical: fakirs insensible to all manner of tortures and all sorts of cruel tricks; muscular acrobats performing exercises unknown to Occidentals; contortionists producing the illusion of snakes; snake-charmers whose cobras reared up, extending and retracting their hoods. All this was presented within the admirable frame of that Jaipur setting, with the ambience of the native orchestra and the well-trained figurants coming together and posing to give their various tableaux an ardent intensity.

Suddenly, the clarion voice of the master of ceremonies announced: "A festival in the Maharajah's home!"

The magical curtain closed again; the hustle and bustle was renewed, and another scene worthy of the Arabian Nights appeared: marvelous décor representing the great hall of Dewan-i-Khas [68] in the palace at Delhi–another prodigious and scrupulously exact reproduction. What prestigious decorators these Hindus must be, to reproduce the marble, alabaster and different metals in this manner!

Sustained by huge square columns, joined in pairs by exquisite scalloped ogives of shining marble and alabaster, the hall was an enchantment. A thousand incrustations of birds, flowers and butterflies of every color ran lightly along the pillars, climbed the capitals, wound amorously around the coving and vanished into the floral vaulted ceilings, covered in topazes, turquoises and amethysts. In places, the marble, admirably faked, seemed to round off its gleams, harmonizing its pastel shades with the colors of mounted gemstones and displaying its subtle indentations beneath the floodlights.

All this appeared ethereal and charming in the half-light sustained beneath the decorated ceilings. A veritable work of art, advertising the greatest artistes! Even the words engraved in letters of gold–the words pronounced by the great Shah Jehan on first entering this palace of dreams–had not been forgotten, although they were inscribed in English:

If there is a paradise on Earth, it is here. [69]

The actor representing the Maharajah appeared on the magnificent Bukhara carpet then, accompanied by his followers. He took his place on an exact replica of the famous Peacock Throne, and called for the dancing-girls.

There were at least 80, all pretty and graceful, living idols whose amber-colored flesh seemed jeweled. They were capering like elves to the rhythm of cymbals, tambourines and *bansulis*.[70] In the meantime, a few laughing girls carrying baskets came to put necklaces of yellow and white flowers around the necks of the women in the first row, according to Indian custom.

Soon, the principal *bayadere* appeared. Previously unknown to Londoners, her reputed beauty was the talk of clubland. She advanced into the middle of the others, who now struck rhythmic poses. She seemed to everyone to be an apparition covered in diamonds. No one was looking any longer at anything but her, especially her helmeted head. That head sparkled to the point of hypnotizing the spectators. All her companions seemed to have disappeared, giving way to this dazzling sylph.

Her body was as supple as a serpent's, as well as firm and well-formed. Her arms, made for seduction and embraces, were twisting in a serpentine manner, circled by rays of light that were periodically eclipsed, like certain lighthouses.

Her dance was that of a dragonfly. The only audible sounds were the clink of her precious anklets on the carpet and the continuing cadence created by her bare feet, whose unbound toes–almost as agile as fingers–were charged with rings. The dance was more akin to a series of expressive poses, a sort of monologue in mime, with continually alter-

171

nated approaches and withdrawals. She wore no loincloth, but that did not seem at all remarkable. Indeed, depilated in the oriental manner with *rusma*,[71] and masked by a gold thread like the one that hid her breasts, she was no more indecent than a statue–a living statue, with the beauty of vigorous flesh, a color of rose amber.

She mimed a scene of seduction and reproaches addressed to the Maharajah. Behind her, in the background, musicians sang the scene, accompanying the melody with tambourine and flutes, to the chords of viols, cymbals and *vinas*,[72] permitting the bayaderes to activate their poses. Throughout this dance, she attained the acme of the choreographic art–and when she departed, calling to her beloved with her back arched and her lips slightly apart beneath the diamonds attached to her nostrils, exposing her white teeth, she seemed to want to be followed, unable to tear herself away from him. Her arms, her breasts and her enraptured eyes called out to him; she drew him with her entire being, as if she were magnetic.

The curtain closed again, in the midst of the enthusiasm. An ovation followed the marvelous scene, whose magnificence had never been seen before. It was the interval–a further visit to the native village, where the orchestras excited new passions, new interests and new purchases. One could also say new conversations. Sullivan, with his ears pricked, passed close to various groups, but there was very little mention of Lord Bencenave, despite the numerous column-inches in the evening papers. Most of the talk was about the spectacle already seen and the even more beautiful spectacle they were about to see.

Sullivan's curiosity was drawing him towards the popular sections when Stillborn, the young inspector who was with him, suddenly started violently, and exclaimed: "Oh my God–that's too much!" Nudging the detective's elbow, he nodded in the direction of a man of about 30, quite handsome in a rascally sort of way, and of veritably Herculean build, who was about 20 yards away. This fairground pugilist had his arm around the waist of a young woman with the gaudy elegance of a prostitute.

"I'll bet 200 pounds that's Blood-drinker," Stillborn said.

The two policemen threw themselves forward, but a movement of the crowd, undoubtedly deliberate, abruptly hid the man and his companion. When they arrived at the place where they had seen the couple a few seconds before, the two seemed to have vanished into thin air. There was no longer anyone there but individuals of a more or less shifty appearance, whose mocking smiles testified to their satisfaction in having outmaneuvered the police.

"God damn it–he recognized us too quickly," the young inspector groaned.

"You, certainly, but not me–he couldn't have seen me before. Now I'm marked in my turn. Who is this Blood-drinker?"

"An escaped convict, condemned to life imprisonment for murder."

Sullivan asked no further questions. There was nothing they could do about it–the escapee was in hiding. They went back to the boxes, a bell having announced the imminent end of the interval.

When the detective took his seat again, the next box, No. 13–which had been empty until now–was occupied by an elegant young woman of about 25, of remarkable beauty and refined manners. Stillborn told him that she was Lady Deborah Moorhen, a rich divorcée.

At the pronunciation of that name, the young inspector saw Sullivan get up, go through the corridor into the neighboring box and lean over the young woman, who was a trifle surprised. The policeman's motive was professional. In fact, he remembered having heard one of the missing man's fellow club-members declaring that the former minister had spent a few moments in Lady Deborah Moorhen's box.

In Box No. 13, leaning over the boldly-exposed legs, Sullivan ventured to say: "Pardon me, Madam, for introducing myself, contrary to custom; I am the detective charged with the inquiry concerning the tragic disappearance of Lord Bencenave. If you saw him yesterday, could you give me any clue, no matter how slight?"

The young woman's face became mournful. "I am at your disposal, sir," she said, in a harmonious voice. "His lordship was an old friend of my father's, who honored me with his affection. We spoke during the interval yesterday for about ten minutes. He kissed my hand again at the exit from the circus, but the crowd carried us in different directions. Just as I was driving off in my car with my friends, I noticed him again, doubtless searching for a cab."

"He had left the circus at that point?"

"Yes, he was standing on the opposite pavement. My friends saw him too. I can give you their names if you have any interest in them."

"Thank you, Madame. I shall permit myself to remember that promise if the need arises." Bowing politely, the detective went out of the box.

As he resumed his place, the embroidered curtain disappeared again. An enormous grille had been raised between the spectators and the jungle, which now appeared in all its splendor. This grille closed off the hall to a height above that of the tall trees. Cries and laughter were heard, and a multitude of gamboling monkeys appeared, turning the most beautiful somersaults and executing the most ludicrous contortions.

Suddenly, there was a general flight of the simian tribe. An impressive silence followed, and a ripple of frantic applause ran around the hall. A tall, young Hindu with the bronzed face of an Apollo, his athletic and well-proportioned body almost nude—for he wore nothing but a *langouti* about his loins—had just appeared in the jungle. As he emerged from the bushes, the formidable vision that brought forth such an enthusiastic response became visible. He was holding two monstrous royal tigers by the scruff of the neck: two Bengal tigers with ferocious faces, subjugated by that grip and that powerful will.

He appeared thus, like the vanquisher of the Nemean lion,[73] almost supernaturally handsome with his fiery eyes, so redolent with harmony and superiority that the applause had not yet died down.

At that moment, Sullivan turned mechanically toward the box occupied by Lady Deborah Moorhen. The young woman was standing up, her long, slender, ring-embellished hands clenched on the edge of the box. Her eyes, like her attitude, evidenced such passion for the man in the jungle that the policeman suppressed a smile, and could not help murmuring: "Rama is the fire and that woman the kindling; passion blows and catches alight. Who knows? The animal-tamer might not find it so easy to subdue this two-footed wild beast."

Then, in response to the Hindu's call, all the tiger-cages opened, as if by magic, and their inhabitants rushed out, avid for the hunt: 60 tigers leaping and roaring, without the least inclination to submission. The man was no longer moving, and his formidable grip now had difficulty keeping hold of his two intimates, who wanted to leap away with the other tigers.

In strange emulation, the young animal-tamer seemed to be seized by the same mad desire for liberty; the audience saw him release his favorites and leap into the midst of the wild beasts, his bounds as powerful and magnificent as theirs. He had no fear of their attacking him, seizing him and over-whelming him as he muzzled their enormous yawns, or left them open without the man-eaters dreaming of closing them.

Like two faithful greyhounds, the two giant tigers, Rudra and Durgane, followed him every step of the way, ready to intervene if they had to. The precaution was unnecessary; the man seemed to be taking an ebullient revenge on the sowers of death, the drinkers of blood.

The breathless crowd followed the spectacle anxiously. What powerful divinity could be protecting this creature, sparing him from the blows of those slashing claws, visibly furled at the ends of enormous paws, and from those cruel teeth, ready to close upon his flesh? What supernatural force animated his muscles, which could be seen bulging beneath his brown skin, allowing him to brave their mortal embraces and lie down next to his roaring adversaries?

There was nothing in the world to compare to this exhibition. Emotion tightened the throat, paralyzed the limbs. An almost painful silence stunned the immense hall where the greatest and the least were gathered. There were only the roars of the hunt–the raucous exhalations of the wild beasts–bursting forth in a funereal fanfare.

In response to a cry–a commandment, an imperative order–everything became still. Rama had stood up very straight and the tigers crouched down, creeping towards him.

"Here, Rudra! Here, Durgane!" he was heard to call.

The two giant tigers came to place themselves to either side of him.

The emotion was redoubled again when a pretty and slender young Hindu girl, about 14 or 15 years old, was seen coming forward. dressed in the manner of John the Baptist, her delicate bosom was hidden beneath a panther-skin. Without manifesting the slightest emotion, she passed among the carnivores and came to place herself within the left arm of the beast-master.

She seemed to be indifferent to the great gaping mouths directed towards her, and scornful of the huge covetous eyes staring at her tender flesh.

The enthusiasm was unleashed then; it was the finale of the spectacle. In the midst of the applause, people began to get up and vacate the vast hall–except for one delightful young blonde woman, about 20 years of age, who remained in her seat in the orchestra stalls, repeating as if in ecstasy: "Felifax and Djina: I wasn't mistaken!"

Grace Palmer had recognized her friends from the Benares jungle.

III: The Hostess

Living in Plymouth with her father, the daughter of the famous doctor, Eric Palmer, had been able to read numerous details in the newspapers concerning Rama's Circus Menagerie, and dithyrambic eulogies about the extraordinary animal-tamer who was the uncontested master of the most savage wild beasts. In this portrait, she had recognized Felifax and had experienced a sudden desire to resume her medical studies in London.

She ought, however, to be happy now. Was it not the case that her father was no longer exposed to the blows of the wretches he had been pursuing for such a long time? Undoubtedly! But there was a more powerful memory in her virginal heart: that of the man, as admirable as he was extraordinary, whom she had met in the Benares jungle, whose soul was as beautiful as his body. That virginal heart had spoken.

As a loving daughter, she had obeyed the instructions her father had given her when he departed for Hong Kong. She had come back to England to live with Aunt Molly–but her thoughts had remained elsewhere. And here was Felifax, in London. Perhaps he had put together this menagerie in order to see her again?

She still had his farewell letter, piously conserved, and took pleasure in rereading the words that it contained.[74] He had not come to see her again after sending it, perhaps to execute the terrible exploit of which he had spoken, in order to avenge his mother. That vengeance had presumably been exacted upon an Englishman. She would have liked to know more, to try to prevent the calamity. The execution of such a project might have been disastrous for Felifax. In England, things did not work as easily as in Bengal. Here, criminals did not escape punishment.

When she had told her father about her desire to go to London, he had smiled, and had not opposed her departure.

Happy with his decision to retreat, with delightful times spent fishing in the sea with his faithful John, or in his garden, the famous detective had not the slightest intention of following her. He did not even read the newspapers, no longer having any desire to worry about Scotland Yard. All that he knew came from the articles that Grace sometimes read out to him. Once she was gone, he decided not to read anything, to remain ignorant of everything. He did not want to have any temptation to involve himself in things that did not concern him.

Having arrived in London by a morning train, Grace had gone directly to their old apartment, retained as a *pied-à-terre* in the capital. That same evening, she was at the circus. Baber had been the first Bengali she recognized, in the person of the master of ceremonies; after that, she had impatiently awaited the appearance of the one for whom her entire heart was crying out.

Finally, the moment had come. Then, alas, she had seen her beloved's gaze directed towards a box, with an affectionate smile–and in that box was Lady Deborah, fascinated, seized by a passion that was an avowal. Her heart cruelly stricken by the thought that there was some connection between this woman and Felifax, she had hidden her face in order not to be seen. Now, she followed the flow of the crowd. She strove to keep the image of her friends from the forest hut before her eyes, happy not to have been mistaken and conserving hope for the future.

It was indeed Felifax and Djina who had appeared, living as they had in their jungle kingdom. They were received rapturously by India's conquerors. Felifax had taken the name of Rama given to him by his mother, the gentle Sita. His gaze not only dominated wild animals; it was turning the heads of all the women in England.

Every night, invisible in a corner hidden behind the scenery, an ascetic at the height of his powers, dressed in the European manner, had a bizarre smile on his lips. His eyes, whose fire was barely contained, stared at the spectators with naked hatred. This was Sourina, the chief Brahman of the temple of Kali; he still entertained his dreams of hegemony. It was to this prestigious magician that Rama's Circus owed its creation; this exhibition was to be part of his vengeance. He had put the best craftsmen to work for months to create these marvels. He wanted to attract all the highly-placed people in London to the circus, and for that he needed a spectacle without precedent.

Plunging both hands into the almost inexhaustible treasures of the temple of Kali, Sourina had made all the plans and had organized every aspect of the spectacle. Meanwhile, he had sworn never to show himself. He wanted to remain in the wings, unknown to anyone–especially the English. He had even succeeded in entering England without being included in the list of the troupe that had been submitted to the authorities, as the law required. A policeman had come to make sure that the remitted list was correct. The number recorded was rigorously exact, and the investigator had never suspected that the supreme commander of the important caravan had been smuggled in. By the same token, he never suspected that the monumental statue of the goddess Kali placed in a temple of prosperity had hidden the man whose religious authority was respected by all the inhabitants of the subcontinent.

In addition, Sourina had taken precautions in Benares. So far as anyone knew, he had departed on a religious tour of the country; in any case, how could the authorities be anxious about the Brahman minister who was such a loyal friend of England?

Behind this mask, he had put the circus in the name of his adoptive son, now called Rama, and entrusted its artistic direction to Baber. The simple animal-keeper had been promoted over the heads of many others–but while, on the one hand, no one disputed Sourina's orders, on the other hand, the high priest was ignorant of the mortal hatred that Baber nursed with regard to him.

The troupe, having been gathered and hired by the faithful servant of Kali, was entirely devoted to him. It included numerous Brahmans, a company of *devadasis* and *bayaderes*

179

from the temple, supplemented by the best dancers in the sub-continent, and even the priestess of the sacred tigers. By means of prodigious eloquence and cunning, he had obtained the authorization of the college of Brahmans, who were gener-ally opposed to public exhibitions by the sacred dancers. In the meantime, Felifax took responsibility for the animals; he went into the jungle to search among the most redoubtable and most untamable. Naturally, the young man's two favorite tigers, Rudra and Durgane, made the voyage; he was attached to the couple by a great affection. Had he not drunk the same milk as their parents, who had died in the temple some years before?

In the end, this enormous troupe had embarked for Europe, taking up an entire ship.

Since its arrival in London, Rama's Circus Menagerie had revolutionized England. Although Sourina had abandoned its general direction, he had jealously conserved its moral di-rection. His Brahmans and his dancers were rigorously subject to the rites of the religion of Kali. As in Benares, the high priest wanted to continue offering sacrifices–blood being in-dispensable to the celebration of the cult of the infernal god-dess–but Felifax had pointed out to him, quite rightly, that such a custom might attract opposition from the local authori-ties. Slaughterhouses were strictly regulated in England, and the infringement of that regulation might be dangerous. Then again, fresh blood tended to excite the wild beasts. Although he had nothing to fear from them, it was possible that the ani-mal-keepers might suffer accidents; such accidents were trivial matters in the temple in Benares, but they were now in Europe, where they might take on more serious proportions.

Sourina had eventually fallen into line with this advice. Sacrifices had been suspended, and replaced by longer *man-tras*. The carnivores were fed on horsemeat brought every day from abattoirs by an accredited supplier, and Djina had been given responsibility for the upkeep of the temple.

On that particular day, however, the Hindu girl had been upset. The high priest had definitely gone beyond Felifax's instructions. While performing her duties that morning, she had noticed fresh blood at the foot of the statue of the goddess. She could have sworn that the blood was not there the previous evening. What was more, she had also found further traces of blood on the bars of a cage–undeniable proof that the tigers had eaten during the night, for their cages were carefully cleaned after their 5 p.m. meal, in advance of the evening performance. Sourina must, therefore, have offered a sacrifice. She had to inform Felifax of that. All day she had tried in vain to tell him about it. It had been impossible to obtain a moment alone with him.

In the evenings, after the spectacle, she often remained with her beloved brother, reminiscing about their happy times in the jungle. She took advantage of that to tell him what she had seen. The young man knew from experience that it was futile to tackle the high priest head on, and decided not to talk to him until the following day. In any case, Sourina had gone out, as he did nearly every night.

By virtue of some strange telepathic phenomenon, Felifax and Djina started talking about Miss Grace Palmer. They had no suspicion that she had been so close to them that evening, or that she was just arriving home at that very moment, her heart painfully swollen by her love.

Meanwhile, Chief Inspector Sullivan was pursuing his inquiries and sorting out his findings. At that moment, he was in a taxi, following the route from Kensington Palace to Lord Bencenave's house. He would then do it on foot, to ascertain how much time the victim had lost between his exit from the circus and the time indicated by his manservant as that of his re-entry to his room.

The brave detective was furious, and with good reason. Never before had his unlit cigar been passed back and forth so often within his mouth. He cursed journalists, those terrible chatterboxes, and gossiping women–his landlady in particular. One of the evening papers, appearing at 8 p.m., had given an elaborate description of the detective Sullivan, including his biography, his portrait and his past exploits. There was even a description of his domicile, the number of rooms he occupied and details of his personal property. He was hailed as a great man, and the article spoke openly of the tremendous sympathy he inspired in his landlady, Mrs. Smithson. The policeman's fury was overflowing.

Despite this painful embarrassment, he was not in the least neglectful of his investigations. He arrived back home at 4 a.m., sweating and muttering complaints. His feet were killing him. The weather had changed, and the walk from Kensington Palace to Stoke Newington had been the last straw.

His first priority was to take off his shoes and record the evening's observations in his notebook. All of a sudden, though, as he sat down at his writing-desk, he had a violent shock. There was a hand on the note-pad, cut off at the wrist.

The hand bore two rings. One was solid gold, inscribed with a baronet's coat-of-arms; the other was platinum, set with a magnificent diamond. They were Lord Bencenave's rings!

This macabre message was accompanied by an article cut out of the *Evening Blackbird*. It stated that the missing man's rings might be the vital lead in tracking the murderer down. What was going on? The criminal, obviously a professional and a very clever man, evidently had not wanted to give the police that opportunity, and had made haste to return the compromising jewels. But how had the hand arrived on the detective's desk?

Careless of the late hour, Sullivan knocked on Mrs. Smithson's door. She did not take long to appear, clad in a modern floral nightgown that was, naturally, too short. Her doll-like face was still swollen by sleep. She had seen nothing and heard nothing. No one could have got into the detective's room by way of the main entrance. Besides, Sullivan had locked the communicating door himself.

The side door, by which he had just come in, bore no trace of a break-in. That left the window, which was slightly ajar–but Sullivan's rooms were on the second floor, overlooking the street; it seemed impossible that the wall had been scaled, and a ladder could not have been set up in a street that carried so much traffic even at night.

There was no longer any question of sleep for the detective; his rage further amplified, he set about searching for new clues. He was avid to shine some slight ray of light into the profound darkness of the mystery.

There was an important lunch that morning at the Seals Club.[75] Lady Deborah Moorhen, the president, was entertaining a non-member–a person about whom she had said nothing, even to her best friends.

The Seals Club had been founded ten years before by the rich divorcée. At first, it had only included her innumerable admirers, but it had broadened little by little; a few young wives and pretty unmarried women had been admitted. Nowadays, admission to the club was the most fervent desire of all fashionable young people of either sex. Indeed, for these thoroughly modern individuals, avid to be talked about–whether for some scandalous action, some glorious eccentricity or some passionate infatuation–Lady Deborah was the hostess of choice.[76]

Married at 20 by exceedingly rich parents into one of the great families of England, she had found that union a cause of the blackest disillusionment from the very first minute. Her spouse was in the grip of a demanding mistress, a married woman of considerable influence at court. By virtue of that fact, the latter held the career of her young admirer in her hands. Although the lady had consented to the union, it was with the expression condition that it should never be consummated.

A slave to the flesh and the word he had given, the husband had forced that insulting continence upon his wife for two successive years, a spouse in name only. Finally, at the end of her tether, the delightful creature had issued an ultimatum demanding that her honorary conjoint should fulfill his marital duties, but had been refused again. She had then decided to provoke a scandal that would rebound primarily upon the authors of her deception.

She rarely went to Rotherhill, the estate in Sussex where—under the pretext of hunting–her noble spouse often met his mistress, sometimes spending several days together. One night, however, accompanied by numerous friends from the aristocracy and the gentry, Deborah had surprised the couple in flagrant conversation and scornfully thrown the woman out of the house. Then, quite brazenly, she had taken a young officer from the Prince of Wales' entourage as a lover. No one blamed her for it.

The relationship was short-lived; two sensational duels had taken place in quick succession. The first, between the young favorite and the guilty husband, resulted in the grievous wounding of the prince's officer. The second was between the victor and the husband of the great lady who had been so abruptly expelled from Rotherhill; this time, the weapons favored the offended party, and left Deborah's spouse in a piteous state. As soon as he had recovered, he had the unpleasant experience of hearing his divorce granted and was then expeditiously dispatched by His Very Gracious Majesty's Government to a remote outpost in Nigeria. He had died there two years later of malaria.

Having resumed the name of Moorhen, which was that of her own family, Lady Deborah had nursed the young officer wounded on her behalf with great devotion; then, as soon as his convalescence was concluded, she had not hesitated to tell him that their affair was over.

Such a scandal, and consequent divorce, inevitably conferred upon the young woman an undeniable reputation for originality and snobbery. Her admirers became much more numerous. Some malicious tongues alleged that Lady Deborah had had a great many affairs, but that was mere gossip. In fact, the divorcée maintained the decorum indispensable to her name, and others gave her the reputation of being as glacial as an ice-field.

This time, however, it was impossible to deny that the president of the Seals Club seemed to be under the sway of a serious infatuation. As they awaited her arrival, in the company of the guest about whom nothing was known, the members of the club discussed this remarkable development amongst themselves.

Although the name of the chosen individual had not been spoken aloud, no one was in any doubt that it was the animal-tamer Rama. The Hindu was the only man who combined the attributes of Adonis and Hercules. He had turned every female head in the three kingdoms–those constituted by the common people, the gentry and the nobility. They all knew that Lady Deborah Moorhen, along with her friends in London's high society, had been in the audience at the first performance of the circus. Every evening since, box No. 13 had been reserved for her. Meanwhile, the animal-tamer had been showered with flowers and sumptuous gifts by the rich divorcée.

To begin with, Felifax had been amused by this pursuit; he had distributed the flowers among the women and passed the gifts on to Djina. The image of the lovely Grace Palmer was too profoundly rooted in his heart for him to break his vow of eternal love. To be sure, logic commanded him to forget the young Englishwoman, from whom he had separated for so many reasons. The forgetfulness that he was trying to cultivate had been the principal factor in the attention he paid to Lady Deborah's pursuit.

For his part, Sourina had encouraged him strongly to respond to those advances. The shrewd Brahman saw his adoptive son approaching the age of 20; his strength and power had been increasing for a long time and he was bound to feel the ardors of puberty. In order for him to play the future role for which he was intended, it was necessary to distract him from a sincere love that was capable of obstructing the mighty project. On the other hand, the healthy soul of Felifax would not allow him to fall in love with this flighty woman, or yield to the seductive wiles of any other infatuated imperialist female; it revolted against any such depravity. This provided Sourina with a potential opportunity; he might profit from this repulsion by using it to obtain a firmer anchorage within Felifax's mind for the fundamental element of his mighty ambition: to kick the English out of India.

Despite the appeal of his senses, there was one thing that held Felifax back. He owed his feline ascendancy to the scent of the tiger species. Grace Palmer had revealed that particularity to him, although her love for him remained undiminished. She had even promised him to devote all her medical expertise to the discovery of an antidote designed to obliterate that *bizarrerie*.

The young animal-tamer feared the possible consequences of this emanation. It might become an obstacle; his delicate feelings would find it difficult to bear a sudden withdrawal of affection caused by that bestial resemblance. For that reason, he stubbornly refused Lady Deborah's repeated invitations. The divorcée must, however, have been able to perceive the perfume mentioned in jest by Catullus;[77] she had often been close to him at the moment when he appeared in public, naked save for his *langouti*. After all, the snobbery of the woman was easily adequate to enable her to find a perverse intoxication in that animal odor.

Sourina's science had eventually formulated a plant compound, based on sandalwood and magnolia, with which clothes could be impregnated, ameliorating the force of nature. Then, Felifax had finally accepted an invitation to lunch at the Seals Club in Greenwich offered by his young admirer.

She had come to pick him up at Kensington Palace in her luxurious Rolls Royce–and to prolong their *tête-à-tête* had instructed her well-trained chauffeur to take a very considerable detour.

Greenwich is situated six miles downstream of London Bridge on the bank of the Thames; the place is frequented by water sportsmen keen on yachting, rowing, swimming, diving and water-polo. When the Seals Club had established itself there, Lady Deborah Moorhen had bought a property on the waterfront, and as the club's resources were so very great, had further embellished it over time, making it into an enchanter's palace.

The arrival of the president, flanked by the hero whom everyone had anticipated, was an occasion for applause. The Hindu seemed perfectly at ease in European costume and a silk turban artistically wound about his head, making the regularity of his features and the velvet splendor of his profound eyes even more prominent. He expressed himself in impeccable English. His warm and charming voice disturbed and captivated, even contriving to soften some of the raucously emphatic concluding syllables of the language of Shakespeare.

His education was faultless. During the meal, he proved to be a perfect man of the world, replying tactfully to questions, and supplying interesting anecdotes that were colorful and lively. He radiated sympathy, forcing the most reluctant rebels to capitulate. In sum, no one knew what Rama might be. The pomp and ostentation of his exhibition created the presumption of a considerable fortune. Many rumors concerning him were doing the rounds. In any case, he had no reason to envy the Hindu sovereigns on the grounds of education and distinction. He owed that to Sourina–during the three months preceding their departure for England, the Brahman had confided him to one of his many friends in the European society of Calcutta. Without meeting any resistance, the young man's assimilative mind had adopted the best of that worldly education, just as it had set aside with perfect tact that which seemed to him to be shocking.

For these snobs, Rama was a veritable prince. He gave them proof of it! After the fashion of the sovereigns of India, the young man insisted on giving each of his fellow guests a small souvenir of his first contact with elegant society and worldly cant. Lady Deborah was delegated to give each of the invitees a precious stone of his choice: a ruby, sapphire, topaz or opal. They came from Sourina's store-house, and had been donated by the chief Brahman himself. He had not abandoned his dreams; like Egypt, he wanted liberty.

These stones were contained in a golden casket, intricately contrived and precious. When Lady Deborah had finished the distribution, the young man activated a small catch that operated a false bottom. This revealed a flawless diamond of awesome clarity, intended for the hostess.

Sourina's plan was not lacking in ingenuity. His adoptive son Rama assumed by this gesture the status of a supernatural being in the eyes of people who were highly likely to mention these opulent souvenirs in the most select drawing-rooms.

Deborah whispered a few words to a quartet of her inner circle of clubwomen and, profiting from the diversion contrived by these obliging souls, drew her future conquest into a little private room.

IV: A Woman Cut into Pieces

One cannot hurry destiny. Was the hour called forth by the divorcée about to sound? No! At that exact moment, someone knocked repeatedly on the door of the little room. The voice of one of the clubmen called through closed door: "Chief Inspector Sullivan of Scotland Yard wants to speak to Lady Deborah Moorhen urgently!"

Obliged to interrupt the duet that had barely begun, the reluctant president had to see the detective.

Sullivan had been pursuing his inquiry with the cold tenacity of duty. The forensic examiner, having carefully examined the macabre debris, had curtly declared: "The human feet submitted to me–which, given the identifying marks, can only be those of Lord Bencenave–have been separated at the calves, half-way up the tibias, using a butcher's saw for the bones and a specially-sharpened knife from the same source for the flesh. These two sections, properly executed by a man of that trade, were made after the death of the victim."

This information, emanating from the mouth of an authority, constituted useful information. Sullivan immediately had the idea of consulting the list of convicted men upon whom the extreme severity of the former Lord Chancellor had come down most heavily. Naturally, they were numerous. It was necessary to see if there were any butchers or chefs among them, or any other tradesmen used to handling saws and knives. The forensic examiner had repeated several times over his insistence that the neatness of the section was the undeniable signature of a professional.

The performance at Rama's Circus Menagerie had finished at midnight. Freddy, his lordship's manservant, was sure that his master–or, rather, the assassin carrying the clothing and the funereal debris–had arrived back at 1 a.m. It had been necessary to establish the means by which the victim had intended to go home. It was also important to recover the body,

but everything in due course! With patience worthy of a detective, Sullivan had made the journey by car, by bus and on
foot.

Now, at that hour of the night, when the streets were
clear of traffic, it took less than an hour to get from Kensington Palace to Stoke Newington by car, but there was not
enough time to make the journey on foot. Lord Bencenave, it
must not be forgotten, was over 60–besides which, according
to his acquaintances, he never walked anywhere. There remained the bus. If he had used this last mode of locomotion,
Lord Bencenave would have been forced to use two services,
the first from West Kensington to Liverpool Street Station,
getting off at Charing Cross, where he would catch the bus
from Victoria Station to Stoke Newington, which would set
him down ten minutes from his home.

Sullivan, like the other investigators, believed that the
crime could not have been committed at Green Street. He was
satisfied that his lordship had been killed somewhere else,
with the intention of putting investigators off the scent by
transporting his clothes back to his home. The murder and the
butchery must therefore have been carried out with great rapidity, in order that everything else could be done within the
hour.

The most likely hypothesis was that the former minister
had found a car put at his disposal, driven–without his knowing it–by one of his former judicial clients. The latter had
taken him to some remote spot, where he had killed him,
doubtless with the aid of accomplices. While two assassins
were occupied in disposing of the rest of the corpse, a third–
the most skillful–had taken his lordship's clothes and papers to
Green Street, without removing anything. The revenge was
amply characterized by the delivery of the two feet of the person whose penchant for kicking people had earned him the
nickname Quickfoot.

The initial hope that a key clue might be provided by the
rings had quickly been annihilated by the subsequent deposi-
tion of the hand on Sullivan's own desk. The latter had

worked unremittingly for hours attempting to find some evidential trace, but in vain. He was faced with powerful opposition; the funereal messenger had acted in exactly the same manner as at Green Street; everything had been carefully effaced. The detective had convinced himself that the window must have been used for the nocturnal visit, but that was mere supposition; no proof emerged to corroborate it.

It is easy to imagine the consternation generated at Scotland Yard, and the feverish gymnastics performed by Sullivan's cigar. Extraordinarily, he had even been seen to smoke several of them in succession–certain proof of his preoccupation.

Why had he come to Greenwich? Quite simply, to see Lady Deborah, whom his lordship had visited in her box at the circus on the night of his disappearance. Perhaps she or her friends might have noticed some shifty individuals prowling around the old man or waiting for him near Kensington Palace.

The detective had initially gone to St. James's Park, to the divorcée's town house. There, orders being scrupulously obeyed, the servants had pretended not to know where their mistress was to be found. It had required threats made by Sullivan and the fear imposed by the police on the lower orders to convince them to reveal that she was at the Seals Club.

This first step taken by Sir Eric Palmer's replacement was not entirely unproductive. One of Lady Deborah's acquaintances believed that he had seen several cockneys, with their caps or hats lowered over their faces, including two women of equivocal demeanor. They seemed to be waiting on the pavement near his lordship. That was all–no precise description. There had been too many people in the neighborhood of the circus.

After apologizing for his impromptu visit to the Seals Club, Sullivan withdrew, refusing the glass of port that he was offered. He had not been surprised to find the animal-tamer Rama in a *tête-à-tête* with Lady Deborah. He had almost expected it; the great lady's attitude in the course of the perform-

191

ance at the menagerie had given notice of that *dénouement*. Privately, he could not help thinking of the Hindu as the mirror of the fair.[78]

After the detective's departure, it proved impossible for the amorous lady to recover the situation she had so carefully contrived. Her friends had invaded the room and the murder of Lord Bencenave had taken over the conversation.

Felifax did not read newspapers and had no interest in London gossip, so this was the first he had heard of the crime. At 4 p.m., he asked if he might leave, because he was accustomed to visit his animals at that time and help feed them, to prevent bloody skirmishes.

Retained by an important meeting of the club, Lady Deborah put her car at the disposal of the fascinating animal-tamer. She could not contain her joy; he had accepted an invitation to dine with her. She was quivering with excitement; she sensed that her victory was at hand.

At midnight, Lady Deborah's luxurious car was outside one of the rear entrances of Kensington Palace, exclusively reserved for the use of the Hindu artistes. On the lookout behind the lowered blinds, the rich divorcée was impatiently awaiting the arrival of the man for whom all of her exacerbated senses were ardently desirous.

Finally, she shivered like a cat presented with a saucerful of sugared milk. The tall silhouette of a man appeared from an unexpected direction. He was clad in an ample black overcoat in the latest style. His head was enveloped by a black turban in which a sparkling cabochon gleamed.

In order to avoid the crow of curiosity-seekers and numerous admirers who jostled one another every evening to touch or call out to the idolized animal-tamer, Felifax had made his exit by another service door. Now he was hastening towards the siren's car. He both feared and hoped, simultaneously, that her enchantment might free him from the spell cast by the tenacious memory of the young blonde Englishwoman that filled his heart.

In fact, only a few paces away from him, the lovely Grace was incorporated in the crowd of excited fanatics that was moving restlessly and crushing one another. Instead of watching the exit from Kensington Palace, her eyes were staring feverishly at the car with the closed blinds. Her amorous heart had divined the presence of an enemy therein. Having been in London four days, she had come to the circus every night, and every night she had been able to observe the increasing desire of the great lady and the attraction experienced by the man who, for her, would always be the noble, handsome and unique Felifax.

The lovely Grace Palmer was suffering horribly. An internal voice cried out to her, telling her to show herself and cut this excessive flirtation short. On perceiving the divine youthfulness that had awakened his heart, the son of Sita would forget the beauty and flashiness of the other woman, for whom he could not possibly entertain the same sentiments. It would be a battle between the heart and the senses, and she had no fear of combat. In the elevated soul of Felifax–especially now that it was deprived of the pagan atmosphere of India–the flesh could not possibly triumph; the result was not in doubt. Every evening she came to the circus with the intention of crying out to the young man, to tell him the depth of her sentiment, that she loved him to the point of torment. Alas, at the last moment, she only hid herself more completely behind the spectators seated in front of her in the orchestra stalls.

Now, she realized, it was all over: the great lady would complete her victory. A reflex precipitated her forwards. It was necessary to prevent that. She ran, calling out to Felifax. Alas, it was already too late. The young Hindu had reached the car, and two beautiful bare arms, with slender white hands whose fingers were ornamented with rings, had seized their prey.

As it moved off, the car's wing brushed the unfortunate Grace, who was nailed to the spot, incapable of the slightest movement.

That same night, Inspector Sullivan was relentlessly rooting through the slums of St. Giles's and Whitechapel. He was following up what he believed to be a promising clue.

During the day, a bloodstained handkerchief had been brought to him. The handkerchief was embroidered with the initials B G under a baronet's crown. With the handkerchief was a short metal rod–a steel of the sort used by butchers and chefs for sharpening their implements. The steel was spotted with blood.

The handkerchief had been shown to old Freddy, Lord Bencenave's manservant, who had formally identified it as the property of his poor master. The field of investigation seemed to be narrowing down. These two pieces of evidence, remitted to the inspector, had been found at the mouth of drain in a notorious street in Whitechapel. That proximity seemed to indicate that someone had tried to dispose of it. The arrival of a witness had doubtless precipitated a movement that had left the mission incomplete.

Among the convicts who had cause to complain about the severity of the former Lord Chancellor was a murderous butcher nicknamed Blood-drinker. Thanks to a fortuitous combination of circumstances, despite the sentence passed and the steps taken by Lord Bencenave, he had been able to avoid the rope, and the threats he had made against his accuser were a matter of common knowledge. He had made no secret of his intention to have his skin, sooner or later. On the eve of his transportation to penal servitude in Australia, the wretch had succeeded in escaping from prison and had not been recaptured.[79] Ten months had passed since then; the police had come to the conclusion that he must have left London, or even England.

These coincidences were, however, so troubling that Sullivan succeeded in persuading himself that the man, having gone to ground in Whitechapel, must have organized Lord Bencenave's murder with the collaboration of other thieves on whom the terrible Quickfoot had passed sentence. All of a sudden, he had recalled the encounter at Rama's circus, in

company with Stillborn, when Blood-drinker had been escorted by comrades and a loudly-dressed woman. Murderers
often return to the scenes of the crimes. Moreover, whether it
was autosuggestion or a mirage, a policeman on duty at the
circus on the night when the former minister had been there
was sure that he had recognized Blood-drinker among the
spectators' he had added: "The man rushed off on seeing me."

There was also the testimony of one of Lady Deborah
Moorhen's friends. He had seen shifty-looking individuals
accompanied by dubious women near his lordship on the
pavement opposite the circus. Was that not enough to put a
detective on the scent?

It was the trail of the sinister butcher that Sullivan had
been following all night, in the company of two of his well-
disguised subordinates.

He returned to his lodgings at 9 a.m. to have a well-
earned meal. He had just opened the door when the ringing of
the telephone precipitated him towards the receiver. Sir Harold
Nimbly required him urgently at Scotland Yard; another disturbing event had occurred.

Without losing a second, the harassed Sullivan went back
down the stairs he had just climbed, and ran to do his duty as
fast as his feet–execrably painful after a night of walking–
could carry him.

One Kate Vernon–the housekeeper responsible for over-
seeing the domestic staff in the household of Lady Vertemer,
the owner of a large private house in the Strand, near the corner of Trafalgar Square–stated that she had arrived at 7:30
a.m. to find the staff sound asleep. Surprised by this anomaly
in the house of a woman whose strict habits included early
rising, the housekeeper had hastened through the house in order to wake the staff. The two chambermaids, the valet, the
cook and the kitchen-girl were still in bed, all of them in their
respective rooms. Lady Vertemer's paid companion was also
asleep in a large armchair in the small bedroom contiguous
with her ladyship's own bedroom; she remained unconscious.

195

Panic-stricken, the brave Kate tried to bring the servants to their senses. Being unable to do so, she ran to fetch a neighbor who was a physician, Doctor Hobgoblin. The latter came without delay. After much difficulty, he succeeded in restoring a measure of consciousness to the paid companion. In response to her immediate plea, the physician demanded to be let into her ladyship's bedroom. Contrary to habit, the door was locked, and the key–as they perceived at that moment– was clenched in the fingers of the recently-awoken woman.

Without saying anything more, the doctor took the key and opened the door. Lady Vertemer was lying in her bed, covered up to the chin, She made no movement as the newcomers entered. Her two white arms, still very neatly-shaped and decked with bracelets, were outside the bedclothes. Her delicate hands, with rings on the extended fingers, lay quite still on the lace coverlet.

The position of one of these arms attracted the doctor's attention. On his instruction, the housekeeper opened the shutters while he went to the bed. As he made out Lady Vertemer's features more clearly, he started. He reached out towards the nearer of the white limbs... horror!

It was cold, with the rigor of death. Scarcely had his fingers touched the arm when it rolled aside, impelled by the contact. It had been neatly severed at the shoulder. The other arm, over which he leaned, had been similarly separated from the torso.

Violently distressed, Doctor Hobgoblin lifted up the bedclothes. The head ensconced in the pillow had been cut beneath the lower jaw and a couturier's mannequin had been laid out in the bed to simulate the body.

What an excess of frightful discoveries! The physician's heart was hammering.

The housekeeper recognized the mannequin as having been taken from the sewing-room. Doctor Hobgoblin turned to interrogate the paid companion, but had no opportunity. She suddenly collapsed on her feet, falling back into the kind of

196

lethargic sleep that still claimed the other residents of the house.

Kate Vernon, half dead with fear, offered a confused explanation of her surprise at discovering, on arrival, that there was no one in the servants' quarters. Allowing her to ramble on, Doctor Hobgoblin set about communicating with Scotland Yard. Having been put through, he gave a few details and demanded that the police come immediately. Once that was done, he thought it best to tell the housekeeper to leave the house until otherwise instructed.

The senior staff of the Metropolitan Police could hardly help establishing a connection between the means employed in this crime and the death of Lord Bencenave; that was why they immediately summoned Inspector Sullivan.

This time, the police commissioner, Sir Harold Nimbly himself, wanted to take statements with the detective. It was necessary to wait until 2 a.m. for the servants to awake–and it was futile, for none of them was able to say anything about what had occurred. They had gone to their rooms at 11 p.m. The paid companion had left the victim at about the same time; her employer had gone to sleep while she was reading to her. She had then gone into the neighboring room to wait for 1 a.m., the time at which she gave her mistress–an inveterate morphine-addict–a final calming injection. Before the prearranged hour, however, she had been overtaken by an imperious somnolence, just as the other servants had, without being able to offer any explanation. She had never experienced such a heaviness before, although she got up early every day.

The physicians and chemists brought together under the direction of Doctor Hobgoblin for the purposes of the inquiry strove to identify the powerful anaesthetic that must have been used. They had to confess their failure; there was no trace of the etheric odor of chloroform, or the bitter almond odor of ethyl chloride.

In the same fashion as the Stoke Newington crime, the room where the human remains were found was in perfect order; there was no trace of footprints on the thick woolen carpet. It required all of Sullivan's science to discover, as he had at Green Street, tiny scratches made by a clothes-brush and a few particles of soot. The faker of Glozel could not have done better.[80]

In the fireplace, there were infinitesimal striations on the blackened interior wall; the murderer, or murderers, had gained access by that means. A particularly telling point was that there were no bloodstains on the funereal debris. The excision of the arms, like that of the neck, had been quite clean and, as in the case of his lordship, large pieces of amadou had been positioned to stem the effusion of blood.

Where had the body gone? Where had the macabre operation taken place? These questions remained unanswered. As for the motive for the crime, it was not theft, no jewelry having been removed. Lady Vertemer had been in the habit of sleeping with rings on her fingers, superb bracelets on her wrists and a magnificent pearl necklace—an antique—around her neck. There was also a platinum chain bearing a very valuable pendant. The latter jewel, a unique piece, was a turquoise the size of a hen's egg, engraved with the face of a roaring tiger with its mouth agape, with teeth of diamond and eyes of emerald; a ruby tongue completed the marvelous work. There were legends attached by rumor to this fantastic jewel. Some said that it had been given to her by a Maharajah to warn the lady had been very dear, others that she had stolen it from a Maharani who had died of cholera.

The former version seemed more plausible; Lady Vertemer had been a great beauty who had gone to India with her husband, a highly-placed official. Widowed at 30, she had not wanted to leave a country where it was easier for her to live, her fortune not being very considerable. Free, beautiful and something of a coquette, she had attracted a good deal of scandalous criticism, without worrying about it in the least, being welcomed in spite of everything into the highest society.

Having returned from India after several years in possession of a greatly increased fortune, she had acquired the house in the Strand and was reputed to possess marvelous jewels.

She had acquired her companion during the final years of her sojourn in Rajputana,[81] when she had been the favorite of a powerful Maharajah, motivated as much by cupidity as by ostentation. It was there that she had developed the habit of not taking off her jewelry while she slept.

Given that the murderers had not touched the jewels, the murder must, in consequence, be a drama of vengeance or a sadistic crime. But what had become of the body? The disappearance, one after the other, of two bodies of which nothing was found but certain parts, exhibited with infernal cruelty, was beginning to subject the unfortunate Sullivan to a torture of his own.

An agile young inspector explored the chimney flue. Its clean state led him to think that someone might have passed through it, but that was all. Although it was permissible to suppose that the man who had arrived by that route had opened one of the windows overlooking the Strand for his accomplices, there was no proof of it. However, there could not have been numerous comings and goings without attracting the attention of the policemen on duty at the corner of Trafalgar Square.

The house, it was observed, also had windows overlooking a side street off the Strand named Pretty Lane which was usually deserted. The crime could have taken place there. It was searched without result. Doctor Hobgoblin and his colleagues were unanimous in declaring that the cuts, very neatly made with purpose-designed instruments, denoted professional skill on the part of the operator.

Then, the sight of an eye-popping clue, found beneath one of the windows overlooking the side street, brought an exclamation of joy from everyone. Two admirably clear footprints had evidently escaped the murderers' precautions, the clothes-brush having obviously neglected them. With the avidity of hunting-dogs, the sleuths pounced upon this ray of light in their darkness. There was a general stir. Everyone's eyes went to the feet of the chief inspector, who felt himself growing pale.

The unsuspecting murderer had walked through the soot; the imprint of his feet was very obvious, and showed a strange peculiarity. He wore special shoes, identical to Sullivan's, squared at the end with a slight upturn to protect the painful bunions.

By an instinctive reflex, the inspector lifted his feet to assure himself that their soles were not stained with soot. Sir Harold Nimbly could not help saying to him, with singular irony: "Eh! Might you, by any chance, be one of this sinister carver's accomplices, Sullivan?"

The addressee of this remark forced a humorless smile. It was easy to see the unease that had taken hold of him. That discomfort was redoubled when the head of Scotland Yard made a further discovery: a fragment of masticated tobacco-leaf originating from a much-chewed cigar. This time, Nimbly knitted his eyebrows.

No, it was impossible that Sullivan, an upright policeman with nearly 30 years of loyal service, could be the companion of a murderer, The coincidences were alarming, though, and might give rise to a good deal of suspicion.

The poor detective had a intuition of what was passing through Sir Harold Nimbly's mind. He could not withstand the battery of stares directed at him. Losing control of himself, he cried in a tone vibrant with truth: "Tell me what you're thinking, sir, I beg you. You know I'm incapable of such an abomination, don't you? If the opposite is the case, I'd rather blow my brains out in front of you!"

"That would not be a solution," said the commissioner, "and would not prove your innocence! On the contrary, it would speak against it. The murderer, or one of his accomplices, might very well suffer from your disagreeable infirmity, and might also, by an unfortunate coincidence, share your obsession with chewing cigars. Then again, someone could have stolen a pair of your shoes–have you got several pairs at home?"

"Certainly, Sir. I always have three or four pairs at a time."

"Have you thrown any away recently?"

"No, not since my return to England. When I left Hong Kong, I got rid of all useless baggage. If you would consent, sir, to accompany me to my lodgings, I will see at a glance whether a pair of shoes has been stolen, with the aim of injuring me and distracting the inquiry."

"Your word is sufficient, my dear Sullivan. All the same, to show you that I have no ulterior motive, I shall accompany you as soon as the statements have all been taken."

Half an hour later, police cars deposited the investigators outside the detective's lodgings in Jane Street. Poor Sullivan had lost his habitual composure; he was in a start of profound depression, and did not even notice the cars containing the accursed chatterbox journalists following the police cars, avid for news and indiscretions.

The detective let the visitors in by his own door and led Nimbly into his dressing-room, where the wardrobe containing his shoes was situated. On entering the dressing room, he let out a new exclamation of horror: the washbasin was brimful of water that was tinted blood red! Without a doubt, someone had washed bloodstained hands therein. And that was not all! The mirror was smeared with red, as was the linoleum. The hand-towel, rolled up on the marble, was similarly stained.

Like a madman, Sullivan ran to open the wardrobe. Although his four pairs of shoes were there, one of the pairs bore recent stains of grey dust. On the soles, moreover, very obvious traces of soot could be distinctly made out.

The poor man's emotion made him collapse into a chair. He was choking. He felt an iron claw clutching at his throat. The watchers thought he had been stricken by apoplexy and hurried forward to unfasten his collar and offer him the necessary care. He remained inert for nearly ten minutes, incapable of pronouncing a word, having no breath with which to speak. The commissioner's secretary had the bright idea of calling Mrs. Smithson. The frightened widow arrived in a hurry.

Nimbly was increasingly anxious. He called the landlady over and said to her, with all the authority of which he was capable: "My dear Mrs. Smithson, through your late husband, you are still somewhat affiliated to our administration. In memory of that brave man, fallen on the battlefield, I appeal to you to rack your memory and reply to me with total loyalty."

Surprised by such a preamble, the widow—the evocation of whose dear departed had brought tears to her eyes—began to tremble. She promised.

Then, showing her the basin full of bloody water and the stained hand-towel, the head of Scotland Yard demanded: "Have you seen anyone suspicious prowling around Inspector Sullivan's apartment?"

"Alas, sir, it's difficult for me to reply. In a fit of bad temper, my lodger decided to bolt the communicating doors between his lodgings and mine. On the other hand, he has opened those that I sealed up a long time ago. I've heard nothing in his rooms. I was at the cinema yesterday evening with a neighbor, Mrs. Buster. When I came back in, at midnight, there was no noise at all—complete silence. Mr. Sullivan wasn't in."

"What time did he come back?"

"I don't know. About 9 a.m., I saw him leaving the house, running as fast as his poor feet could carry him."

"You don't do his housework?"

"I beg your pardon, sir, but this morning Mr. Sullivan must have been in a great hurry. He didn't give me his keys, as usual."

Nimbly shook his head. Decidedly, the coincidences were becoming more and more worrying. He turned back to Sullivan, who had recovered his composure, although there was cold sweat on his face and his depression was intense.

Sullivan made the effort to get up and go towards his superior. "I beg you, sir," he said, "to accept my resignation. With the suspicions that might weigh upon me, I cannot continue to remain under your orders."

"Then, Sullivan, I am obliged to place you under arrest."

The detective started violently. It was a thunderbolt, the collapse of his life. Seeing his consternation, the commissioner took pity. Putting his hand on Sullivan's shoulder, he continued: "I had not completed my statement, Sullivan. By submitting your resignation, you would appear to be implying that you were admitting your guilt, and I would be obliged to treat you as I would this wretched murderer. The devil with that! Don't throw in the towel–stand up straight, return the enemy's blows by giving as good as you get. For myself, I believe in your innocence because too much evidence is stacked up against you. A detective of your experience, used to unraveling the most complicated mysteries, would not have acted like a child in bringing here those whose job it is to seek out criminals. You would, at least, have got rid of this abundance of accusatory evidence. You must persevere, and not rest until you have discovered the guilty party. For your honor, for that of the police, and for the public's peace of mind, that is your duty!"

Moved by his superior's forbearance, Sullivan–momentarily incapable of the least effort–allowed himself to be guided by the other. Nimbly did not wish to leave him alone, dreading some rash move on his part. A suicide attempt would leave Scotland Yard in the most inextricable mess. He stationed two inspectors in the lodgings and one on the landing. Having given them very strict orders, he got back into his car to return to his office.

For her part, Mrs. Smithson went back to her own part of the house, alarmed by the turn of events and the suspicions that were weighing on her lodger. Alas, the distress of the brave woman with the excessively tender heart was contagious. Two reporters in the employ of a sensational newspaper paid her a visit, and obtained from her a burlesque tale worthy of their hire. Sullivan was about to experience some very bad times.

V: In the Manner of Hercules

Felifax loved poor people and children more than any-thing else. Could there be a better proof of the beauty of his soul?

He had insisted that Sourina distribute a significant part of the circus receipts to the indigents of London on a daily basis. In addition, he had a good number of seats allocated to the unfortunates–who needed the diversion–every Sunday, the day of rest. He carried these invitations himself into the poor quarters of the city, in company with Djina and Baber. It was not long before the name of the famous animal-tamer became extremely popular.

He did the same for the children. Thursday matinées were exclusively reserved for the capital's schools. For Feli-fax, the enthusiastic cries of the excited kids was worth a thousand times more than the applause of the elegant crowd. At his own expense, he sent sweets to the vast swarm of boys and girls. Djina and the other Hindu girls handed them out.

Sourina never made any objection to these acts of char-ity; on the contrary, the philanthropy of his adopted son was integrated into his plans. Besides which, the priest of Kali never showed himself in any circumstances. He spent entire days in his private niche in the statue of the goddess, presiding over the religious observances of his Brahmans and the other Hindus.

Nearly every day, however, Sourina went to spend some time in the Oriental gallery of Kensington Palace. There, be-fore the proof of the conquerors' rapacity, he indulged his hatred at leisure.

All these jewels, all these statues, all these weapons and all this finery had been plundered from the sacred land. The Maharajah Runjeet Singh's golden throne was stolen. The presence of those images of the gods and living saints was profanation and vandalism, as was the Koh-i-Noor, the eye of light torn from the face of Shiva, That standard of Ayub Khan, taken at the battle of Kandahar, was the souvenir of a massa-cre.[82]

The old Brahman never failed to conclude his visit by pausing before a plaything that had belonged to Tippoo Sahib,[83] representing an English officer being devoured by a tiger. This image brought out all his hopes and dreams so well. Immersed in its contemplation, the carnivore took on in his eyes the appearance of Felifax at the head of an India in revolt, and the English officer was multiplied to represent the conquerors, massacred or fleeing before justice on the march.

On the afternoon of the day when the funereal remains had been discovered in Lady Vertemer's house–just as the unfortunate Sullivan, scarcely recovered from his shock, was swearing not to rest until the murderer was discovered–the immense hall of Rama's Circus was resounding with joyous clamor.

The hall was buzzing with unaccustomed animation: there were invalids on crutches or in wheelchairs, convalescents and poor devils sustained by nurses, even stretchers transporting unfortunates raised from their deathbeds by one last effort in order to come to applaud the spectacle that had excited the whole of London. Rama was putting on a benefit performance for the hospitals of London, for which he had obtained the cooperation of the Guildhall. The Lord Mayor had in fact, decreed that numerous special buses would collect and transport the patients from the various hospitals.

The best seats, even in the boxes, were reserved for the worst cases, but some of the boxes were occupied by the Lord Mayor and the consultants, physicians and administrators of the hospitals. Lady Deborah Moorhen ornamented her own box. Her presence was perfectly understandable; in order to participate in the animal-tamer's generous gesture, she had made a donation of a thousand pounds. Thanks to her gift, every invalid would be able to take a way a souvenir of the day: tobacco, pipes and lighters for the men, trinkets and baubles for the women. Djina and the young dancers made that distribution too. The unfortunates' joy was indescribable, as was the pleasure reaped by the amiable daughters of a blessed land.

On this occasion, Lady Deborah Moorhen had assisted in the performance from the beginning. Several guests were present in her box: three men and three women. The oldest of them, a wizened man of 60 with a dark complexion, was taking a great deal of pleasure in the spectacle.

Hidden in the scenery, Sourina looked out into the hall, as he did every day. This time, as he looked into the beautiful divorcée's box, he shivered violently, and could have been heard to murmur: "It's Sir Edmund! The accursed Sexton! I've not given him much thought since my arrival in England, saving him up for last. What a pity the hall is so full of unfortunates–what a delight it would have been to inform Felifax of the presence of his mother's torturer! It would have been a great pleasure to suggest that he release his tigers into the crowd. Let's be patient. I shall not point out the man yet; the longer the little one aspires to his vengeance, the more complete it will be. Then nothing will stop his avenging arm; he will rack his brains for a punishment appropriate to the gentle Sita's executioner. Doubtless he'll feed him to Rudra and Durgane; the man who wanted to create a tiger-child will perish beneath his claws."

The great Brahman seemed to have forgotten that he was at least equally guilty; had he not aided the surgeon-major in his science and his opportunity to execute the most odious of crimes?

Suddenly, as if Brahma–or perhaps the bloody goddess Kali–had heard the horrible vow of their minister, there were cries of fright, and the dancers fled in mid-ballet. An enormous tiger, bounding and roaring, appeared in the middle of the stage, intoxicated with its freedom.

The audience, believing it to be part of the performance– a scene skillfully contrived in accordance with the enchantment to which they had been subject since the outset–was unworried. The applause and acclamation was immediately redoubled. The beast seemed nonplussed by such a thunderous reception, and stopped in its tracks–but that hesitation was brief. It crouched down, and made a new bound towards the spectators, who finally understood. Terrified cries came from every corner of the immense hall. An indescribable panic took possession of the audience.

The walking wounded and the convalescents knocked over their infirm and weaker comrades; cripples raised their crutches, trying to open out a passage; the impotent howled in distress.

Bravely, the Hindu ushers threw themselves in front of the unfortunates forming a rampart with their bodies. Under the influence of Felifax, these native souls had acquired the beauty of self-sacrifice, and dared to confront their age-old enemy, the terrible man-eater that claims thousand of victims in India every year.

The tiger was now in the midst of them, among the front row seats, which were smashed to pieces by its movements. Its huge paws lashed out at the reckless individuals who were attempting to bar its passage. Several had already bitten the dust, bleeding profusely from deep wounds inflicted by the implacable claws.

The disorder was at its height when a powerful voice suddenly took over. It said, commandingly: "Ladies and gentlemen! For Heaven's sake, don't move! Don't scream!"

Under the influence of that authoritative voice, stamped with confidence and majesty, there was a moment of calm. The escaped tiger shivered, pricking up its ears. Then a supernatural being appeared, nude save for a *langouti* around his loins, bounding in the same manner as the wild beast. In three of four fantastic leaps, he placed himself in front of the feline just as it crouched down again.

Felifax, preparing for his public performance, had heard the terrified clamor and had come running. Djina, opening the door, had cried: "Quick, Felifax–Sindhypo has escaped. People are being killed in the hall." With hands free, without a weapon, he had precipitated himself forwards. Now he was face to face with the redoubtable adversary.

The tiger, its appetite excited by the blood of the wounded Hindus, whose scent was in its nostrils, did not seem inclined to obey its master. It was licking its scarlet chops and beating its flanks with its tail. Without roaring, it pounced. But Felifax had anticipated the cunning leap; his muscular arm shot out and his steely fingers closed on the scruff of the carnivore's neck, grabbing it in mid-air.

The fight was on: man against wild beast. What a great spectacle! What capital excitement! Not the struggle enacted every evening in the caged jungle, where the animal-tamer's power subdued the innate ferocity somewhat–no, the raging battle of a mad beast against a fully conscious man who had strength, courage and intelligence to draw upon.

To prevent the worst, Felifax knew that he must be the victor. He had no doubt of it; he would prevail.

The panic was suspended momentarily; a mortal silence descended now as everyone was concentrating on the action. Women hid their faces so as not to see and put their handkerchiefs in their mouths so as not to scream. Alone of her feeble sex, Lady Deborah followed the contest. The man she loved would probably perish. A wonderful attraction, indeed! [84] What a morbid delight for a seductress of her species; what a truly exciting spectacle for her atrophied senses!

Another person was similarly following the scene with tenfold interest. It was the oldest of the friends invited into the divorcée's box. He was breathless, as if prey to a kind of ecstasy. Just at that moment, he saw the characteristic stripes appear on the animal-tamer's body, while the handsome face became ferocious and his pupils, which were elongated in the shape of an olive, were streaming with phosphorescent light. Wrath, the instinct of defense acting upon Felifax's nature, had brought out the stigmata of the ascendancy wished upon him by men.

Skillfully, evading the furious thrusts of the claws that were trying to tear him apart, the animal-tamer was still maintaining his grip on the nape of his rebellious adversary. Muscles as taut as metal cables stood out beneath his bronzed epidermis. He held at arm's length the frightful gaping mouth that reached jerkily towards the prey it intended to devoir,

In that merciless *tête-à-tête*, however, the son of Sita had calculated that victory would go to the most resilient. The beast was employing all its strength and all its weapons at once. One well-directed blow would have been the death of him–and in the meantime, he could only use the five digits of one hand. Within a limited period of time, his strength would suddenly give out, with a convulsive and painful contraction of the muscles of his arm. The general anxiety was at its height. No bullfight or combat of large wild animals had ever congealed the blood of spectators so forcefully. For honor, with everyone's life at stake, it was necessary to bring it to an end.

Intelligence came to the aid of Djina's foster-brother. Taking advantage of a moment when Sindhypo, with a supreme effort, was trying to reach him, convulsively distending its foam-flecked gaping mouth, Felifax seized a pair of opera-glasses from the hand-rail of a nearby box with his free hand and immediately hurled them into the monster's gullet.

Now, taking advantage of his adversary's suffocation–the creature lacked the means to get rid of the opera-glasses blocking its throat–the animal-tamer seized Sindhypo beneath the shoulders and drew himself up to his full height, holding the creature tightly and locking its hind legs between his muscular thighs. That done, having forced apart the carnivore's front legs and placed them on his own shoulders after the fashion of Breton wrestlers, he abruptly planted his head upon the node of the tiger's throat, beneath the reclosed jaw. He was sheltered now from fangs and claws alike. Then, clasping his hands behind his prisoner's neck, he began to squeeze, steadily and powerfully.

Soon, just as Theseus had defeated the Minotaur and Hercules had accomplished one of his most difficult labors in stifling the Nemean lion, Sindhypo was seen to collapse lifeless. The supernatural vigor of Felifax had repeated the famous exploit; the bloody monster was dead. Its back had been broken by the irresistible vice.

After a brief moment of amazement, there was a long sigh of relief; then acclamations and cries of gratitude broke out everywhere. Anticipating a flood of thankful people surrounding him, the animal-tamer–who was covered with his own blood, having sustained numerous superficial scratches–disappeared, while his comrades carried the wounded Hindus away.

Fortunately, no serious harm had come to the spectators. The coolness of the nurses and medical orderlies had prevented a catastrophe; the damage was limited to bruises and a great deal of emotion. The clarion voice of Baber put an end to the uncertainty by announcing that the program would continue after the intermission.

Lady Deborah, still shaking all over after having joined in mentally with the fury of the combatants, left her box along with her friends. Her intimacy with Rama granted her entry backstage. She wanted to congratulate him, and to dress his wounds with the fire of her passion.

Fearing that they were too many, the Hindu posted at the door blocked their way. He tried to prevent the divorcée and her courtiers from going in, but Lady Deborah insisted, and one of the others hastened to declare: "I am Sir Edmund Sexton, a hospital surgeon; the wounded might have need of my services."

This was true. Sexton had been seated in Lady Deborah's box in his capacity as chief surgeon at several London hospitals, including Charing Cross Hospital, the London Hospital and St. George's Hospital. This madman was more possessed than ever by his mania for creating miraculous transformations of human nature. No longer being able to exercise it in the colonies, he had found a marvelous experimental field among the poor devils delivered to his pitiless scalpel. Very busy at his various hospitals, he had not yet visited Rama's Circus Menagerie, and had profited from the need to observe a few grave illnesses affected to satisfy his curiosity.

On his arrival in the auditorium, having been noticed by Lady Deborah Moorhen–with whose father he had been ac-

210

quainted–he had found himself unable to refuse to share a box with someone he had once dandled on his knee. For her part, the lovely woman was happy to rediscover an old friend lost to view for many years.

In the wings, Felifax, disdainful of his own wounds, was occupied with the men who had fallen victim to their courage.

Sourina, his broad-brimmed hat lowered over his eyes, was watching the Brahman physicians attending to their needs. Suddenly, he had a shock. Lady Deborah had just arrived with her entourage. Sexton was there! He feared that the situation might be irreparable. The lady would head straight for Felifax and introduce her companions to him. What would the young man do on hearing the name of his mother's torturer pronounced? Hurriedly, he whispered a few words to one of his yogis and went to the young man. How could he prevent the animal-tamer from speaking to the woman who had held him in her trap for several days? Nothing the high priest could say would turn him away from that siren.

He suddenly thought of something capable of making Felifax forget everything else, and muttered in his ear, in Bengali: "My son, while you were so unsparing of your courage, I saw in the auditorium, vainglorious and in good health, the man who submitted your mother to the most odious of outrages. That man was the cause of all her suffering–he tortured her to make you into a monster!"

The effect was brutal. Lady Deborah Moorhen was already drawing near, but she stopped dead, absolutely petrified. For the second time, the captivating face had just transformed itself, taking on a strange resemblance to the terrible muzzles of Durgane and Rudra. He let out a raucous cry–which might have been described as a roar–and hurled himself toward the hall. Then, lowering his hat over his eyes again, Sourina slipped away, not wishing to be seen and recognized by his former accomplice, the one-time surgeon-major in the Indian army.

The precaution was unnecessary; Sexton could no longer see anything. A force independent of his volition had fixed his eyes upon the animal-tamer, and his brain was making a mental calculation. This marvelous Hindu, this elegantly-proportioned Alcides with the face of a demigod,[85] must be the same age as the child conceived by his own genius—as Felifax, for whose birth he had risked everything. He remembered him presenting the same symptoms as a baby, until the age of three, whenever he had thrown a tantrum, already striking fear into everyone.

Could there really be any doubt? He was in the presence of his superhuman creation, of his glory—inaccessible to others because he was the rival of God! He would request a meeting of the Academies of Science and Medicine in order to present them with the living outcome of his genius: a man who added to beauty, natural elegance and intelligence the power of indomitable musculature and magnetic fascination: he could command wild beasts!

He was about to run towards the young animal-tamer when the yogi to whom Sourina had whispered a few words came up to him and spoke a few words in Maharashtri, a Hindu dialect employed by Sikh soldiers. The surgeon spoke the language fluently; he had invariably employed it in former times in his conversations with Indian natives.

"Take care, *Sahib*. Your name must not be mentioned in front of Felifax. Your life is at stake!"

The surgeon's excitement was cut short. He trembled. The great Brahman, his accomplice, must have denounced him to the young man, accusing him of every crime. That ferocity whose frightful stigmata had just been revealed to him, that irresistible force that he had seen at work, might perhaps be turned against him, without his being able to stop it. Could one prevent a tiger from biting and tearing apart its prey?

He felt a sudden shock, of the kind popularly known as "someone walking over his grave," and he turned to Lady Deborah.

"What did that Hindu say to you?" she asked. "You must know him—he spoke to you in his own language, didn't he?"

With a violent effort, Sexton contrived to suppress the anxiety that had gripped him, and replied, with a piteous smile: "You're not mistaken, my dear; I knew him in Calcutta. He served in the Bengal lancers; I had occasion to treat him several times. These Bengalis have a truly astonishing memory for faces." Then, desirous of fleeing the wings, where he no longer felt that his life was safe, he drew the divorcée and her friends away, trying to make a joke but lacking the ability. His humor rang false.

The group passed in front of the place where Sourina was hidden, as was his habit, at one of his lookout posts. The Brahman called to one of the ushers.

"Zara, go station yourself outside the box occupied by those people and keep your ears open. You speak English well, do you not? You were an interpreter at the Woodland Hotel in Delhi, yes? Well, take careful note of everything they say about Rama–perhaps they will call him Felifax–and repeat it to me at the end of the performance."

After making an affirmative sign, the man set out to follow the cheerful group.

There had never been anything comparable to the success that Rama's performance obtained before that breathless audience. That was only just; his presence of mind and inimitable courage had recently saved many of them from an abominable death.

When he left the jungle with Djina, in the midst of frenetic applause, Djina drew him to their favorite corner and told him with the utmost seriousness: "Brother dear, Sindhypo, whose bones you broke just now, had drunk fresh blood last night. This morning, once again, I found traces of blood at the foot of that statue of Kali. Sourina has made a sacrifice."

"Are you sure, Djina?"

"Absolutely certain. The bars of the beasts' cage bore evidence that Bava, the head animal-keeper, hastened to erase when I arrived."

Felifax's state of mind disposed him to anger. Without hesitation he went to Sourina's niche.

The high priest was in conference with Zara, the Hindu instructed to spy on Lady Deborah's box. Zara had just repeated one of Sexton's remarks: "Dear friend, I don't want to cast any doubt on the qualities of this superman. I, more than anyone else, ought to qualify them as superior. On that subject, you shall have amazing revelations one day. Before then, milady, would you care to arrange for me to be in his presence, in your home, so that I might study him at leisure? There is, however, one express condition: you must not mention my name to him."

"What was the woman's reply?"

"Swearing the required oath, while laughing, she promised to invite Rama to her country house in Rotherhill."

Felifax arrived at that moment. After Zara was dismissed with a gesture, the young animal-tamer began by reproaching the great Brahman for breaking his word in the matter of sacrifices. He had been able to establish for himself the state of excitement in to which fresh meat put his beasts; a horrible catastrophe might have resulted.

The priest of Kali let him speak, venting his spleen. Eventually, he said: "Yes, my son, I realize that. Although I was wrong, that sacrifice to the goddess was necessary to obtain the means of finding the trail of the accursed man. I believe I did well by immolating two goats. Kali answered my prayer the same day by setting your mother's torturer before my eyes."

"Ah yes! Let's talk about that–the wretch has vanished again."

"I know where to find him. Patience, my son–a few more days will only serve to make your vengeance more refined. It will take place in front of witnesses. The civilized world shall understand the infamy of the conquerors."

"Ah, I'm looking forward to that day. My mother's ashes are crying out for it, and I am in haste to fulfill my oath."

"His hour is nigh; I swear it to you in Brahma's name. Now, another matter–you have told me several times of your desire to go with Lady Moorhen to visit Rotherhill, her country house in Sussex. Until now, I have opposed that fancy in the interests of our spectacle, which would not be the same without its principal attraction. The greater number of employees are, however, complaining of exhaustion. Since our arrival in England, they have not had a single day's rest. I have therefore decided to close the circus the day after tomorrow, for 48 hours. On that day, the festival of Kali will begin in Benares; we shall respect it here. It will be an ideal occasion for our coreligionists to honor the cult of the goddess, while everyone gets some rest."

That same evening, Felifax passed on this news to Lady Deborah. Glad to have her lover all to herself for 48 hours, she decided to leave the following day in order to prepare a delightful holiday for her guest. He would join her as soon as the circus closed, along with Baber, in the capacity of his steward. They would leave London after the performance.

As she did every evening, the divorcée waited outside Kensington Palace in her sumptuous motor car; her intimate friends were prattling in cars that were no less luxurious. They were going slumming in Whitechapel–a sort of tourney of grand dukes that was very fashionable among the London gentry, perpetually avid for strong emotion.

Meanwhile, a poor soul was suffering the martyrdom of that departure for Cythera. As if propelled by an invincible force, Grace Palmer's footsteps drew her towards the continual renewal of her torture. She set out with the intention of showing herself and defending her poor love, but she never dared to complete her plan.

The previous evening, when her tearful eyes had been fixed on the point where the magnificent cars had disappeared, a soft voice had murmured nearby, in a slightly exotic accent: "Oh, Miss Grace, do you love him still?"[86]

She had turned round, shivering. Djina was there, and came to take her affectionately in her arms, standing on tiptoe to kiss her on the cheek. The young Englishwoman immediately responded with a sincere hug. She would have someone to talk to about her pain: a friend who knew about the love born under the Indian sun between two people of different races, but with an equal beauty of soul.

Persuaded that the unhappy young woman was happy to confide in her, Djina led her into the backstage area of the circus, where a room had been reserved for her on her brother's orders, tastefully furnished and hung with elegant Srinigar cashmere in delicately harmonized shades.

They agreed between themselves to meet at the stage entrance again, and that Grace would come to see Djina on the day after Felifax's departure. They decided, in addition, not to tell the young man about their meeting. It seemed best neither to get in the way of his plans nor to enter into a struggle with his entire character.

Sir Eric Palmer's daughter left Kensington Palace a little less sad; the man who was making her suffer, she had been assured, retained a large place for her within his heart. Now, she understood his thinking. She realized the excessively loyal motives that had made him write his farewell letter. At the end of the day, those motives could not be irrevocable. Her desperation was now mingled with hope.

VI: The Sweethearts' Bar

The special editions of the newspapers, appearing a few hours after the butcher's new exploit, had not treated the police gently. Sullivan, for his part, would remember that.

The greater number related the troubling coincidences encountered in the detective's lodgings. Several had the good will to attribute them to the fiendish Machiavellianism of the murderer, but one of them addressed questions directly to Scotland Yard, overtly laying an accusation against the unfortunate policeman. This was the *Daily Herald*, the organ of the Labor Party. Its reporter had doubtless taken to heart Sullivan's harsh words referring to chatterboxes, and other characterizations that were even more severe, and remembered the threats issued when he had been chased away from his lodgings. Now he was joyfully taking his revenge, at the risk of making a false charge.

For an entire column, the reporter waxed lyrical about the imprint of footwear that was unique throughout the Empire, about the traces of soot found in the victim's home and on the soles of shoes found in the detective's apartment. He merrily described, in captivating detail, the bathroom where the murderer had "arranged"–the irony was obvious–the bloody washbasin, the bloodstained hand-towel, the spattered mirror and linoleum. He terminated his indictment by demanding justice, even if the honor of the police must suffer. He reproached Sir Harold Nimbly for wanting to protect a criminal with his immunity and demanded an immediate arrest, the sole means of preventing further crimes.

It is easy to imagine the lamentable state of the chief inspector as he read this comminatory essay. It required all his superior's authority to calm his fever and prevent him from going to execute the miserable pen-pusher. Instead, having excoriated himself with a terrible fit of temper, he went out with no intention of doing anything reckless.

A few hours later, it must be admitted, he had accomplished a great deal, making considerable progress in his inquiries, to the point of asking for reinforcements to his team and giving detailed instructions for the provision of efficacious assistance in making an arrest that he expected to be difficult.

That night, under the protection of Stillborn, an inspector on special duties appointed by Scotland Yard in response to a request from the House of Lords, Lady Deborah and her entourage ventured into the ill-famed districts of London. The illustrious animal-tamer Rama and his court of flatterers visited music halls, public houses and other drinking-dens,[87] and various dives in Whitechapel, St. Giles and Docklands.

Although the more-or-less depraved minds of the pleasure-seekers appeared to experience an unhealthy satisfaction, fascinated by the display of vice and misery, the young Hindu's was overtaken by an immense pain and a violent scorn. So this was what these people were like, who–posing as conquerors–wished to offer themselves as a model to the people of India, whose morals were so pure. Beneath their cloak of civilization, they sported infamous vices, of which they seemed proud. At that moment, the Son of Sita admitted the bloody theories and barbarous dreams of Sourina; it all seemed preferable to letting his country sink to this degree of corruption.

In response to their repeated demands, Stillborn–whose secret function was to steer clear of places that were too dangerous–had eventually consented to take them to an ignoble dive called Sweethearts' Bar.[88] It was certainly the most infamous tavern that it is possible to imagine, frequented by odious shrews and young "free spirits" ready for anything, and also by scoundrels escaped from hard labor and other prison-fodder, all incessantly in search of evil to do.

The arrival of the band of well-dressed gentlefolk, including half-naked women in their silk dresses, covered with jewels, provoked a stir among these dregs of humankind. The eyes of the men were covetous, while those of the girls and the

218

termagants glittered with hatred as they stared at the white throats hung with pearls and the gem-encircled wrists. Hands moved nervously towards pockets, groping for knives or revolvers. Some of the bandits even took a few steps towards the group.

The inspector was getting ready to whistle in order to summon the policemen who were patrolling the quarter when Felifax, confident in his prodigious strength, placed himself resolutely in front of the women. Fortunately for the thieves, who were already disposed to fight against a dangerous explosive, one of them recognized him. He whispered: "Lower your hands–it's that Rama."[89]

More or less everyone had heard talk of the hero of the day and his charity. His combat against Sindhypo in the course of the benefit matinée was already legendary. There was an immediate recoil, both admiring and prudent. However, one drunkard with a ruddy and bestial face three-quarters covered by a thick beard came forward to curse the curious idlers, and immediately captured the inspector's attention.

To make an arrest in this place and on this occasion could have awkward consequences. Stillborn understood that, so he tried to calm the reckless fellow. Then he stepped back in amazement, recognizing conventional police code-words. He was advised to take his snobs away, because there was going to be an incident, perhaps even a veritable battle, in the course of which his cockney aristocrats might catch a bullet or serve to sheath a knife.

The drunkard was none other than Sullivan. Having learned that the butcher Blood-drinker came to Sweethearts' Bar every night, he was on the lookout for him. As if satisfied to have got the better of the cop, he went to sit down again with three other drunks of similar quality, who seemed to be unconscious, slumped forwards on a gin-soaked table.

Sullivan was absolutely convinced that he was on the track of the murderer of Lord Bencenave and Lady Vertemer; the analysis of the facts and his secret deductions had confirmed his hypothesis. With regard to the first crime, that belief had a professional basis: the butcher's hatred for the former minister; the death-threats uttered in the presence of numerous witnesses; the exceedingly neat fashion with which the excision of the feet had been carried out. This extended as far as the pieces of amadou commonly employed in abattoirs to treat accidental cuts, and similarly abundant in various workshops.

With the second crime, these presumptions had attained reality. Lady Vertemer, a lady of very high status, had been compelled to keep intact a certain reputation–a superficial renown, for she had still not been disarmed, from a frivolous point of view.[90] In order not to lay herself open to criticism from her peers, she sought the desired compensations in a shadier milieu. Perhaps she even experienced a perverse sensation in feeling death so close at hand. To this effect, she utilized the services of a former servant turned tout.

Her ladyship's companion and confidante had ended up revealing this particular in the hope of facilitating the discovery of the guilty party. She was almost certain that she knew who the criminal was. It must be one of the intermittent visitors of the former favorite of a Maharajah. She had orders to let them into the house by an unused service door. That door gave out into Pretty Lane, the side-street leading to the Strand.

In one of the descriptions given of three or four of these nocturnal moths, Sullivan believed that he had recognized that of the drinker. There was nothing impossible in that; the butcher was a superb male specimen–with bestial and cruel features, to be sure, but with an athletic body very adaptable to the pleasure of an intoxicated woman.

In a truly scientific manner, the detective, once set on that track, had rooted through the criminal files for two or three hours in order to acquaint himself with the places frequented by the brute before he was sentenced to death–a sentence commuted to life imprisonment with hard labor.

Sullivan had seen the villain at Rama's Circus the day after the murder of Lord Bencenave. At the moment when his colleague Stillborn had pointed out Blood-drinker to him, he had not had the slightest suspicion of the importance that the wretch would shortly acquire. However, his glance, as sensitive as photographic film, had registered him, and that indication had been reinforced by anthropometric data kept in the police files. He had even pinned down certain details of the villain's secret life before his sensational arrest by Doctor Palmer.

A woman of easy virtue, about 40 years old, known by the name of Gypsy, was thought to be the butcher's mistress. She had a pawnbroker's shop, primarily for fencing stolen goods, and had done everything for the wretch during his sojourn in prison. That particular world has its code of honor. After being compromised and deprived of the convict's living, Gypsy had the right to expect some gratitude on his part. A miscalculation! Since his escape, the churl had taken care to avoid her.

Our old flame [91] had attributed this negligence to a perfectly possible fear that the place in which she made her living was under strict surveillance. Not wanting to believe that she had been betrayed, the forsaken woman went in search of her forgetful swain. When she succeeded in finding him in his new retreat, she found that she had been replaced and was sent away so unceremoniously that the bruises still showed more than two weeks later. In spite of this, she continued to love the bloody ingrate and to send him subsidies.

Sullivan thought that he ought to be able to profit from this tenacious blindness. Presenting himself at the pawnbroker's establishment while she was overwhelmed by despair, he spoke in the following terms: "I'm an old cell-mate of Blood-drinker's from Newgate.[92] I'd like to cut him in on an important job with no danger attached."

With the aid of this skillful subterfuge, his cunning disguise and a few pipes borrowed from the judiciary domain—which gave his words a certain gloss of truth–the detective had obtained some half-confidences. The butcher went to the Black Eagle and the Red Eye, two establishments with a sinister reputation. These items of information might have led

221

him astray if he had not learned, by some miracle, thanks to a jealous discussion between two women, that the individual for whom he was searching went to the Sweethearts' Bar every night. That was why he was waiting for him there, with three of his best men, ready to attack.

The quantity of sinister faces encountered in the bar with the poetic name had warned him that a capture would be difficult, if not impossible. These cut-throats would not hesitate for a second before combining forces against their sworn enemies, the policemen, and exterminating them pitilessly. In spite of that, he had not thought of retreating for a single instant. That was why, having seen Stillborn come in with the company of revelers under his protection, he had played the drunk in order to warn him to leave the place, and to ask him to send serious reinforcements with all possible urgency.

Without too many recriminations–for they were already sated with bleak amusement–Lady Deborah and her friends were about to obey when the door of the dive was pushed open, giving passage to Blood-drinker. Almost a giant, he was a fine representative of bestial vigor. Above his bullish snout, bloodthirsty sparks seemed to glisten in his inexpressive eyes. He was carrying a rather voluminous package in his hand, wrapped in a bloodstained cloth. Thrown on the table, this package made a metallic sound. Sullivan and his men shivered.

The butcher's suspicious gaze inspected the room, and immediately noticed the gentlefolk who were about to leave. A covetous gleam came into his ferocious eyes at the sight of the half-naked women and the display of jewelry. He went towards the group, swaying at the hips and saying: "Hello, beautiful ladies. Has Blood-drinker's arrival put you to flight, then? You're mistaken, my little dears–he's a true connoisseur of fresh flesh, and you wouldn't spoil his collection of lovers."

He addressed himself primarily to Lady Deborah, the most beautiful and the most heavily begemmed. The latter smiled, her senses already aroused by the burning gaze of the "Terror." The man's enormous hand, still red with blood, reached out towards the aristocratic lady's pale-skinned throat; at the same time he leaned over her to give her a kiss with his gin-soaked lips.

The other thieves laughed heartily. Blood-drinker certainly had a way with him when it came to talking to women, even the richest ones. But the brute never completed his movement; despite his height and weight, he was lifted from the ground by an arm as irresistible as a gorilla's, and thrown clear across the room. A catapult could not have done better.

Felifax had been unable to watch his hostess soiled in that fashion, and had intervened.

In spite of his fall, Blood-drinker was on his feet quickly, a revolver in his hand. Some of his associates moved as if to go to his side; others went to block the exit. The wretches scented prey.

At Sullivan's table, one of his subordinates, pretending to be very drunk, got up and staggered towards the door. He reached it. The drinker, who was scanning the room with his large bovine eyes, took a sideways step and commanded him to stop in an authoritative manner. The rogue was not one of the regulars, and the convict's entrenched mistrust recommended that he take every precaution. The drunkard did not appear to have heard him, though. He opened the door. A gunshot rang out and a bullet went through the disobedient man's arm. The drinker had unanswerable arguments at his disposal.

At the same time, a voice cried: "Hands up!"

Three men were standing upright, revolvers in hand: Sullivan and the wounded man's two companions.

The small number of the policemen gave courage to the criminal gathering. Thirty men were soon ranged alongside Blood-drinker, the majority armed with revolvers, the others only having knives–although the latter would be terrible weapons in their expert hands.

Profiting from the disorder, Stillborn, who was responsible for Lady Deborah and her friends, made haste to get them outside and entrusted them to the inspector who was already wounded. "Go on, old boy," he said. "Take my clients to the nearest station and sound the alert! You're wounded, and thus at a disadvantage. I'll go help our comrades."

The young policeman, whose arm hung inert, knew that he would be most useful to Sullivan by going to raise the alarm. He obeyed, following the socialites, who were literally panicking. Their number was, however, one short; Felifax had not wanted to leave the room.

After exchanging a few words, the thieves decided to give no quarter; all the Scotland Yard operatives must die. As he gave the order, Blood-drinker noticed that the socialites had gone. Releasing an oath, he ordered some of his associates to pursue them–but they found the guide ready to kill them rather than let them pass.

And the battle commenced.

Gunshots were fired back and forth. Some cut-throats bit the dust, but also two of the detective's companions. The little finger of Stillborn's right hand was amputated by a bullet. Sullivan alone remained unscathed, continuing to fire. Soon, his revolver was empty. He was done for.

"Save your bullets, fellows," Blood-drinker ordered. "This bankrupt cur isn't worth the trouble. We'll drench him in gin and light him up like a bowl of punch!"

This sally was greeted with a loud cry of joy and a gale of laughter. The rascally horde advanced on the lone man. The latter folded his arms, awaiting death. The face of the drunkard who had turned back into Sullivan–for he had forsaken his disguise–even acquired a smile. He was glad to die on the battlefield: that death would wash away the stain of the odious accusations leveled against him.

His end, it appeared, was not yet inscribed in the book of destiny. A vengeful fury fell into the middle of the group of executioners; a kind of roar astounded them. Within three seconds, six men were floored, struck down as if by a sledgehammer.

Felifax had joined the dance.

The valiant and loyal soul of the son of Sita could not stand by and watch that dastardly assassination. The detective's attitude in the face of death, having compelled his admiration, had caused him to execute his prodigious bound. Now that he was unleashed, it was a ferocious beast that the assassins had before them.

Sullivan, soon seeing this unexpected aid arrive, recovered his will to live. He leaned over, searching for one of his stricken colleagues' revolvers, but he did not get up again. Blood-drinker stunned him with a blow from the butt of his gun. He was unable to continue his work, though, because the Hindu's vice-like grip crushed his shoulder, forcing him to drop his weapon.

Just at that moment, a band of policemen erupted into the room. The gunshots had alerted them, and they had raced to the rescue. All resistance was now futile. A cry of rage escaped the butcher's throat; the battle was lost, thanks to the action of the accursed animal-tamer. He would pay dearly for that intervention. Wriggling free, he opened his knife with a rapid flick and threw himself forward.

The fool! The hand with the weapon was seized in midair by fingers of steel, and his broken wrist fell alongside his body, putting him completely out of action.

Holding his head in his hands, Sullivan got to his feet. Still half-stunned, he saw his would-be-slaughterer vanquished and heard Felifax's voice say, softly: "Take delivery of your prisoner, sir. Your courage has certainly merited his capture."

In a trice, the fuming butcher was led away by the policemen. Sullivan breathed easily. When he turned round to thank his savior, Felifax was already going through the door. Inspector Stillborn, although wounded, had had time to say to the policemen guarding the exit: "Respect the Hindu, or he'll make you pay. Besides, he's one of ours."

A telephone call summoned three armored vans. Less than half an hour afterwards, the fish netted by the operation were leaving for a long holiday. As for Blood-drinker, he had the honor of his own wagon.

What had become of the package thrown on the table? Someone opened it just in time, because an accomplice was about to make it disappear. It contained a butcher's tools: knives of varying length, saws and a chopper, stained with blood. There was also a sharpening steel, similar to the one recovered from the gutter in Whitechapel along with Lord Bencenave's bloody handkerchief.

There was no doubt that the drinker was the murderer. He was taken to the offices dedicated to measurement and anthropometry. Sir Harold Nimbly wanted to interrogate him personally first thing in the morning. During the intervening hours. he was softened up and grilled in every possible fashion. They used persuasion, intimidation and the various more-or-less violent means employed to force criminals to confess. They obtained no result whatsoever.

The drinker told them that he did not know what they wanted him to say. The tools he carried? Well, yes, he used them for illicit practices, but not for murder. Working for a gang of horse-thieves, he was responsible for slaughtering them and cutting them up for horsemeat dealers–a philanthropic service for the gentry. But he refused to denounce his accomplices–leaving the task of discovering them, he said, ironically, to Mr. Sullivan, the great policeman who was so skillful at forging crimes... and criminals.

Despite these denials, no one thought there was a shadow of doubt as to his guilt. If they let him stew for a while, he would stop playing dumb one day, and begin to make restitution for his crimes. In the meantime, the semi-accused Sullivan received the congratulations of his superior, and was fêted at Scotland Yard.

VII: More Human Remains

As they had done for the exploit of the "leader of wild beasts" at Kensington Palace, the local and national newspapers tried to outdo one another in celebrating the victory of the police. They lavished dithyrambic articles upon the man whose name they had dragged through the mud the previous evening. Sullivan became the eminent detective, a worthy successor to Doctor Palmer, and the troubled capital breathed more easily.

Since the Green Street affair, people had asked themselves anxiously whether they might be in the presence of a new Jack the Ripper. The surgical decapitation in the private house in the Strand confirmed that dread. Then again, the arrest of the sinister butcher, still carrying his bloody tools, suggested that there might have been a third victim. This supposition took on substance when policemen working in the docks reported having encountered three individuals carrying a large package on their shoulders, wrapped in imitation leather, which appeared to be stained with blood. The parcel had been suggestive of a human body. They had gone forward to apprehend the carriers, but the latter had had time to leap into a motor boat, which seemed to be waiting for them, and flee.

London conserved a certain anxiety within its tranquility. The monstrous pork-butcher's accomplices, who were still at large, must be capable of imitating him. However, the optimists had the upper hand. All would be well; the exploits of the brilliant detective Sullivan would continue along the same track; the entire gang would soon be captured.

Doctor Eric Palmer, retired in the manner of a sage in his little house in Plymouth, was enjoying his rest. He continued in his refusal to read the newspapers or to hear about their contents. He did, however, hear about the sensational arrest and the triumph of his successor. His sister Molly talked about

227

nothing else. An aging spinster, her delight in reading was redoubled by a passion for gathering all the facts.

When the confirmed spinster had first mentioned it, the doctor had not protested. On the contrary, he declared that he was delighted with the success of his old comrade. But when he was apprised of all the details, he shook his head and his sister heard him murmur:

"Once again, Sullivan is badly mistaken. Blood-drinker is not guilty of these crimes. Firstly, that dullard would not have taken so many precautions. Secondly, he would not have left the jewels, and especially the money, behind. His mistress, Gypsy, the pawnbroker, has international connections who would have taken the jewels and found the means to sell them on at a good price. Yes, it's a grave error. Sullivan really should have asked himself the definitive questions: Who profits from the crime? Who has an interest in the crime? Who benefits therefrom?"

Molly started at these words and asked her brother in an anxious voice: "So, Eric, will you go to London yourself, or write to Sullivan?"

"Oh no! It's no longer my concern. When I was put on a case, I wouldn't tolerate any intrusion into my affairs. I would have refused any advice from a superior or a colleague, ready to defend my mission with my fists. I don't want to expose myself to Sullivan's fists. He's a good man; I'm certain that he'll realize his mistake on his own. Besides, guilty or not, Blood-drinker has merited hanging for a long time. Already condemned to hard labor for life, he'd be in Australia if he hadn't escaped a few months later while I was in Benares.

"Now, my dear Molly, in the name of Heaven, don't tell me any more of these stories. I don't want to worry myself sick over other people's mistakes. I promise you faithfully that at your first attempt to tell me about affairs in London concerning crimes, murderers and detectives, I'll set off in my boat in search of a desert island, or for a voyage that will last six years, like that Frenchman Alain Gerbault."[93]

Grace's aunt knew her brother's implacable will, and she swore to respect his orders. The meal was completed in total tranquility.

Sir Eric Palmer's foresight was, alas, only too well-founded. Less than 30 hours after Blood-drinker's arrest, a further incident shook the population of London all over again.

Miss Dorothy Mason, a singer and dancer at the Store Street Music Hall, had just opened her eyes and was stretching her limbs when she stopped abruptly and recoiled, let loose frightful cries. This was the reason: facing her, on her nightstand, was a grimacing severed head, together with a right hand cut off at the wrist.

The head, she knew, was that of General Ferund, the former colonel of a regiment of Sikhs in India and former commander of the militia at Pretoria in South Africa, presently the commander in charge of British Military Prisons.

In his various posts, the superior officer had been notorious for a severity tending towards cruelty, In India, he had had a large number of native soldiers shot, accusing them of attempted mutiny. It was said that in South Africa, during his first campaign in the war for the Transvaal, he had mercilessly executed a number of prisoners. Later, as commander of the militia, he had been equally disdainful of human life. Finally, since his appointment as the commander of British Military Prisons, a veritable reign of terror had been launched at his instigation–which went, it was rumored, as far as hanging prisoners without trial. While he rarely spoke, his written orders were laconic sentences and his signature was a virtual sentence of death.

A price had been put on his head by the condemned.

Although he was married and the father of grown-up children, the pretty dancer Dorothy Martin had been his official protégée for two years. He often came to the charming apartment at the corner of Bedford Square in which he had installed her, scarcely 50 yards from the music hall whose star she was. The officer had his own room in the artiste's residence: a room separated from Dorothy's by the dining-room and a bathroom.

The evening before, General Ferund had come, as usual, to see the dancer's performance. After returning home, they had had a light supper and had gone to bed at 1 a.m., each to their respective rooms. And then, in the morning, Dorothy found this most odious exhibition on her night-stand. The young woman's cries roused the neighbors, who came running.

Contrary to habit, the door of the apartment was not locked, so they had no difficulty in reaching the dancer's bedroom, to find her half-dead with terror. Two of the neighbors fainted on seeing the frightful remains. Three of the others–all men–went into the General's room, expecting to find a decapitated corpse. Amazingly, the room was in perfect order. The victim's clothes were there, neatly folded in the manner of an old military man. Nothing seem to have been disturbed. There was no trace of a struggle on the turned-back bed. The dent produced by a horizontal body was visible, but there was no body...

Seized by misguided zeal, the neighbors set about searching for the sinister remains, swarming everywhere and turning everything upside down. Soon, one of them realized that they were committing a grave error. They had not notified the police at the outset and had taken on a task that was incumbent on them. This realization hit the well-intentioned but disorderly mob like a cold shower. They had to communicate with Scotland Yard without further delay.

Sir Harold Nimbly was already undertaking a further interrogation of the butcher Blood-drinker. The inquisitors seemed to be about to use the most extreme methods of extracting confessions from criminals. This was not, of course, the torture so dear to the Inquisition–the rack, the vice, thumbscrews, the collar, the boot, and so on–but in order to maintain a less cruel appearance, modern tortures are more refined, being primarily moral.

A telephone call suspended the session. In consequence of the information furnished by the person at the other end of the line, it appeared that a new crime had been committed, identical to those of which the accused had been charged.

Sullivan turned green. This was too much. He and others went by car to Bedford Square. There, the policeman became very angry on seeing the mess that the neighbors had made. No mistake was possible. These mutilations were the murderer's signature; this had been perpetrated by the same hand as the preceding crimes. The sections had been made with an identical cleaver and large pieces of amadou were still placed on the cuts to stem the blood-flow.

Not a meaningful clue had survived the deluge of imprints made by the volunteer policemen. However, in one of the seams of the carpet Sullivan found an entire strand of couch-grass and a clothes-brush similar to the one found in the hands of the boys in Stoke Newington the morning after the murder of Lord Bencenave. Similar traces had also been found in Lady Vertemer's house.

What did it signify? Had Blood-drinker been telling the truth when he swore by his great gods that he had nothing to do with these crimes? In that case, had one to give credence to his other affirmations: that he had been slaughtering and butchering horses stolen by his accomplices?

On analysis, some of the blood taken from the drinker's cleaver had indeed proved to be animal blood, but there were also particles of human blood. "That's nothing!" the butcher had explained. "A mate cut himself trying to help me!"

There was great consternation in London when special editions of the *Times* and the *Daily Mail* announced that another mysterious crime had been committed. Fear took hold again. It was not the man arrested... so who was it?

Naturally, the *Daily Herald* took the opportunity to chastise Sullivan. How had the great detective let himself by fooled on this point? It was a great pity that he had been awarded so many undeserved eulogies, and hailed as the suc-

231

cessor of Sherlock Holmes and Doctor Palmer, only to end up with a fiasco on this scale.

The public is made thus; those it elevates to a pinnacle it demolishes with equal rapidity, endlessly repeating the story of the idol with feet of clay. The man who, the evening before, had been on the point of being carried aloft, was no longer good for anything but being thrown to the dogs.

Although poor Sullivan had not merited the eulogies, he did not deserve so much scorn. His first deductions on the subject of the butcher had been well-founded and plausible. He explained that again to Nimbly when he returned to Scotland Yard with the macabre remains of General Ferund–remains that were added to the others in the Metropolitan Police's black ice-house.

Another important piece of evidence had just come to light. On the evening of the Green Street affair, Blood-drinker had been seen prowling around Lord Bencenave's house. He had even asked a taxi-driver whether the lord ever went out at night. On the other hand, Sullivan was sure that Lady Vertemer had received the butcher in her home at night on three or four occasions. What was more, he had found a letter in the victim's papers in which the wretch asked for money, in a manner that was hardly friendly and shot through with threats. To all this evidence had been added the sticky tools that he had been carrying at the time of his arrest.

"The error was inevitable," declared the fallen idol. "Doctor Palmer himself would have been misled."

Confronted by his subordinate's despair, Nimbly tried to comfort him. He knew how the song went; the papers would crow joyfully over the judicial error. Nothing could be done against that music but to stiffen one's spine and wait for the storm to blow over. In the meantime, one had to do something useful. As some had warned, the murderer could have had accomplices skillful enough to substitute for their leader. Might they be seeking to devalue all the evidence gathered in the course of previous investigations by committing similar crimes? There was no need to throw in the towel. Blood-drinker must be interviewed again, to persuade him that his version was believed. His confidence boosted by his certainty of having "put one over on the cops," he might be tempted into some imprudence. Then, what a triumph Sullivan would have, what a revenge for the institution: a demonstration of the loyalty and skill of the upholders of the law, and the vanity of the critical stings of impudent journalists.

His spirits somewhat lifted by the calm admonition of Sir Harold, immediately after his return Sullivan went to the butcher's cell. While letting him believe that the accusations against him would undoubtedly be dismissed, he asked point-blank: "What were you doing in Green Street in Stoke New-ington on the eve of the murder, and why did you ask questions about Lord Bencenave going out at night?"

With the utmost cynicism, born of the relief caused by his inquisitors' *volte-face*, the drinker replied in a malevolent tone: "I was planning to settle Quickfoot's hash. Someone else beat me to it, and I regret it. Even so, there's an ace in the game–I couldn't have done it better. That pedicurist's self-respect must have taken a whack from some part of the old jumping-jack's boot. I applaud his jape with all my heart. I wish I'd done it myself."

"You haven't told me anything about your nocturnal in-terviews with Lady Vertemer. Why did you send her a threat-ening letter?"

"That's easily understood, Mr. Sullivan. The girl wasn't in the first flush any more, and the kindness of a man like me–for I only have to crook my little finger to have the most beautiful girls in Whitechapel rolling at my feet–merits, you must admit, considerable compensation. The old *rupee* [94] was very tight-fisted; I had to remind her of the proprieties."

"So you would have murdered her pitilessly?"

"No, I certainly wouldn't have gone that far. I'd have slapped her about a bit, to put the wind up her enough to make her crack–which is to say, to fork out a respectable number of guineas. I'm a patriot–I like the King a lot, especially in gilded effigies. That's OK–the dismemberer seems to know the game. While admiring his science totally, I can't help wishing he hadn't. He's cut the grass of revenge from under my feet and killed my hen that laid golden eggs."

"And General Ferund–do you know him?"

"And how! There's a very nasty bird. He might meet the same fate as his friend Quickfoot some day. Between ourselves, there's many a brave lad in England who'd put an end to his mania for writing terrible decrees without appeal if they were to run into him. Or has he already encountered the minor inconvenience of being sliced up? If that's the case, three cheers for the slicing machine!"

Sullivan made no response to the wretch's sarcasm. Although his wish had been granted, there was no point in telling him. He left the cell and went back to work. It was a matter of not losing any of his notoriety.

In Plymouth, Molly Palmer nearly fell off her chair when she read the details of the Bedford Square incident in the *Exeter Mirror*. So her brother had been right when he said that Sullivan had made a mistake! She wanted to tell him so when he came back for lunch, but as soon as she pronounced the first word, he told her to be quiet. When she insisted, he got up from the table and went out in his boat until nightfall.

Doctor Palmer, who was known everywhere as "the king of detectives" had got it into his head that he did not want to hear any more talk of police; he knew only too well what he was like. To his mind, the only way of dismissing his regrets regarding the vocation that had filled him with such passion was to live in the most complete ignorance of thefts and other felonies. To that end, he would not even try to open the shutters of his windows.

For her part, Grace Palmer, who was still in London, never mentioned mysterious affairs in her letters. She was too afraid of seeing her father set off on a campaign and lose in a few days the salutary effects of his months of good rest. That was why she did not reply to her Aunt Molly's questions imploring her for various facts. She rejoiced in hearing the old lady tell her that the doctor did not want to hear talk of what was happening in London, and that he spent his days at sea, returning therefrom with a formidable appetite.

VIII: The Stranglers' Cord

Lady Deborah Moorhen had left in the morning to go to her country house. Despite her insistent pleas, the animal-tamer had declined to accompany her. He would not leave London until after the evening performance. There was, therefore, an entire day to pass without seeing the disturbing conqueror of feminine hearts.

The Hindu had good reasons for acting thus. Firstly, he did not wish to abuse Sourina's permission and lose the circus the benefit of an auditorium that was always full to overflowing. Then again, and more importantly, he did not want to risk causing offense to the beautiful divorcée's friends–for he had to take into account the feline odor emitted by his skin. He countered it quite well with the aid of a perfume fabricated by Sourina, but he was anxious about the strength of the effluvia. Lady Deborah had not found it unpleasant as yet–better than that, she seemed to find it a perverse condiment–but would her invited guests take the same view?

The emanation was stronger at certain times: on awakening in the morning, in spite of washing; after staying too long in a closed room; when he was angry or irritated. People who were not forewarned could become uncomfortable and make unkind comments that he found hurtful. It was better to avoid the possibility.

The country house at Rotherhill was only 60 miles from London. The fast car put at his disposal by the young woman could cover that distance in less than an hour and a half. There was no need to hurry. That is why he had not had the car sent round to the stage door; he preferred to pick it up at the house in St. James's Park.

Put in a slightly bad mood by the thought of making the journey alone, Lady Deborah was relaxing in one of the admirably-upholstered corners of her comfortable Rolls Royce, staring into the distance. It was not long, however, before her mind turned to the countryside around Upper Norwood, whose fertile valley was the summer retreat of London's inhabitants. Without thinking about it, she began counting off the places they passed through: Purley, Redhill, Reigate and so on. She passed through the Forests of Worth and Tilgate. Finally, at Burgess Hill, she met up with the friends who were waiting for her. They wanted to take her to Brighton; there was a big party at the casino in honor of the Prince of Wales. The young woman was resistant to the attractions of the great seaside resort. As the mistress of her household, she did not want to leave anything to chance, and the tempters ended up following her to Rotherhill.

About 20 people had accepted Lady Deborah's invitation. By various means of locomotion–cars, carriages, on horseback and even by aeroplane–they came together at the appointed hour at Rotherhill, situated near the unhistoric little village of Crow, virtually all of whose inhabitants were in milady's service in some capacity. Among their number was Sir Edmund Sexton. One of the first to arrive, the surgeon had dropped everything, so impatient was he to spend a few hours in the company of the man he believed to be entirely the creation of his genius.

The rich divorcée's country house seemed modern but had a history, once having been part of Lord Buckingham's estate. It was even said that the musketeer d'Artagnan and Cyrano de Bergerac had stayed there when they came to England to save the son of Anne of Austria.[95]

Rotherhill, surrounded by a marvelous estate and a dense forest, was primarily noted for its proximity to Brighton, whose beach was very fashionable. In her invitation, the hostess had advertised a wild boar hunt, and every respectable Englishman is keen on such diversions. The danger one runs therein is great sport.[96]

On the first evening, a succulent dinner prepared by the Seals Club's chef–specially imported for the occasion–put everyone in a good mood. The Moorhen cellar was famous, and the heiress had not wanted to abandon the family tradition.

The steward in charge of his mistress's considerable fortune was responsible for maintaining it, and acquitted himself marvelously.

Despite the general liveliness, Lady Deborah gave the signal to beat the retreat at midnight. It was necessary not to forget the following day's hunt, which might be tiring and replete with ups and downs. The chief huntsman had, in fact, located several boars, including one sow with six young and one old solitary male. The latter had been hunted many a time already but its ferocity and cunning had always defeated the dogs, of which it had disemboweled at least half a dozen.

There was another motive behind the signal to retire. The amorous woman wanted to wait up for Felifax; an entire day of separation seemed to her to be a century and she wanted to see him as soon as he arrived.

The car she had put at the animal-tamer's disposal was a French car–a very fast Hispano-Suiza bought three months earlier. With little traffic encumbering the route at night, it ought to be able to make the journey in little more than an hour. At 3 a.m., however, Felifax had still not arrived.

Exhausted by fatigue, Lady Deborah ended up sinking into a leaden slumber. It was the steward, who stayed up on her instructions, who received the Hindus on their arrival at 4:35 a.m. He led them to their respective rooms, which were situated next to one another.

In fact, driven at breakneck speed by a chauffeur who was something of a daredevil, the car had devoured the 60 miles in less than 50 minutes. By forcing the pace in this way, the eccentric mechanic had hoped to throw a scare into the people who, without a care for his sleep, had kept him waiting from midnight until 3:50 a.m. at the gates of Lady Moorhen's house in St. James's Park. The rendezvous had, of course, been arranged for midnight. What could Felifax have been doing in the meantime?

Lady Deborah was so happy to see her hero again that she did not even interrogate him when she came to tell him, on the following morning, that the departure for the hunt was imminent. The servants had already woken everyone else and brought them breakfast.

Although he had had scarcely three hours sleep, Felifax exhibited no trace of fatigue. As for Baber, insomnia had no effect on him; he was made of iron, and as soon as he got up he came to rejoin the young man in his room.

Meanwhile, Lady Deborah's steward was attending to the preparations with Kilkenny, the chief huntsman, renowned as the best in all England. Having entered the service of Lord Moorhen, Deborah's father, at an early age, he had soon become famous among the rich householder's numerous guests. No one knew better than he how to organize a beat or an all-out chase, and no one knew better than he how to sound the *whoop* announcing the animal's death.[97]

Very advantageous propositions had been made to Kilkenny by various proprietors of hunting establishments–offers he always refused with the same stubbornness. The huntsman intended to remain faithful to the house in which he had first gone into service, and in which he enjoyed the greatest liberty. He loved his job, and milady's immense estate was marvelously endowed for all kinds of hunting, from foxes to wild boars, the latter being quite abundant in the locality. Having unlimited credit at his disposal–the lady's aristocratic pride demanded that everything be irreproachable–the chief huntsman had assembled, at great expense, a remarkable pack of running dogs, from the kennels of the Essex Union and the Duke of Buccleuch.[98] They were admirably conformed, howled well and went head-to-head with the largest beast with great courage. The stable was no less remarkable; it contained some 20 cobs, specially trained for the drag.[99]

In their eagerness for this rare and exciting diversion, the guests of Rotherhill had got up early, each one desirous of choosing his horse in advance. Sexton and two or three gentlemen of a similar age were not hunting, but they had left their rooms because the departure of a hunting-party and its dog-pack is an occasion in itself, even if it is not a royal one. Above all, the surgeon wanted to see Felifax. As the latter must have arrived during the night, he was itching to be able to contemplate proudly that to which he continued to refer in his own mind as *the product of his genius*.

While awaiting a few latecomers, the majority of the hunters surrounded Kilkenny, telling stories of various trails they had followed. In his opinion, it was necessary to let the sows with litters alone. They should also forsake the old solitary male, several of the best dogs still being debilitated by recent wounds occasioned by his terrible tusks. According to Lady Deborah's instructions, they ought to get on the trail of a little company composed of three third-year boars and thee others somewhat older, of which one in particular was a superb specimen, whose head would make a magnificent trophy.

Baber had appropriated an excellent mount and had reserved a speedy chestnut for Felifax. The latter had not yet come out of the house; he was chatting with Lady Deborah.

Soon, cries of joy greeted the appearance of the young woman on the steps. Deborah replied to them with a smile. Putting her foot into the stirrup, she gave the signal to depart. The acclamations were abruptly interrupted in an inexplicable fashion. All the horses gathered at the foot of the steps were showing signs of sheer terror; their ears were laid back, their limbs were tremulous and they were trying to escape from the hands of the grooms. They were kicking and whinnying, grouping together in a quivering mass.

The two groups of hounds that made up the pack began howling in terror. These dogs, which had been ready for action a few moments ago, yapping impatiently and wagging their tails joyfully, now presented a lamentable spectacle. Trembling in every limb, they pulled in their tails and crouched down as low as they possibly could.

No one knew, with any certainty, of any cause capable of provoking this surge of fear. No one was inclined to attribute it to the presence of the animal-tamer Rama. Was it a coincidence? He had just appeared at the top of the steps, his tall and symmetrical figure molded into an elegant sporting jacket and shod in high boots of supple yellow leather.

Only Baber and Sir Edmund Sexton might have been able to explain–but the surgeon's eyes had met those of the Hindu, and his tongue was utterly paralyzed.

Felifax knew immediately what was happening: this emotion on the part of animals unused to the proximity of large wild beasts was due to him. Alas, when he had accepted the invitation to participate in a boar-hunt, he had not given any thought to the hazards of his inconvenience. It had been scented by the dogs' sensitive noses and the instinct of the horses. Now it was too late to retreat, at least from the revelation of a secret that he wanted to guard jealously.

Felifax's intelligence gave rise to rapid reflexes. The best means of calming the effect was to suppress the cause. He must act to terminate it without delay–and without prompting minds to reflect, and perhaps to suspect. He had to act without hesitation. Standing close to the balustrade of the steps, he saw the stallion that Baber had reserved for him about four yards away, snorting and rearing up. "Release the bridle!" he called to the groom, who could no longer hold on.

With a fantastic leap, describing a semicircle above the barrier, he landed in the saddle astride the horse, whose name was Briskly. The animal sagged beneath the jarring weight; then its hocks tensed, and it departed at a mad gallop. Immediately, there was an inexplicable general relaxation.

"You must excuse Rama, milady," Baber hastened to say. "It's a method of mounting a horse that he learned in India. He was unable to resist it when he saw the animal giving signs of nervousness and indiscipline. It should not delay you; follow his lead and he will rejoin the hunt." In a low voice, to be heard by Lady Deborah alone, he added: "Rama is undoubtedly the cause of the dogs' and horses' terror; living constantly with wild animals, he has developed an ambience of his own to counter their subtle odor. He would be devastated if your guests perceived that particularity, as they would have, had he not immediately set out to subdue Briskly."

The divorcée gave him a slight smile of complicity. She had known about that animal odor from the very first; his ambience might have been the principal cause of her passion. If her guests were to reflect on the subject, they might well guess Felifax's secret; it was necessary to occupy their minds. That was why she cracked her whip, while looking at Kilkenny.

The huntsman had attributed the disturbance to stormy weather. The animals having recovered their composure, he obeyed his mistress and gave the signal to depart.

Sir Edmund Sexton had followed the scene with glittering eyes and a rapidly-beating heart. They incident gave even more weight to his experiment; he would include it in his report to the Academies, and his glory was certain. As soon as the hunt had departed, he went back up to his room. He was eager to get to work without further delay.

The cavalcade reached the forest in good order. The dogs, their tranquility restored, trotted gaily along, guided by the hunters on horseback. In the lead, Kilkenny headed straight for the trails he had found the evening before, which led to the lairs of the condemned animals. When he judged that the time was ripe, he had the dogs released, and they immediately gave voice. It was the signal to stream away. They threw themselves forward like a flock of pigeons, while Kilkenny cried at the top of his voice: "Follow them! Follow!"

Huntsmen and huntswomen charged after them, Lady Deborah at the head—accompanied by Baber, who did not want to leave her side. They were leading the chase, but their eyes were searching for Felifax rather than anything else. Why had he not come back?

The Hindu, as Baber had supposed, had not made any attempt to halt Briskly's vertiginous course, although it would have been easy enough. The powerful grip of his hands could have mastered that madness, while his formidable thighs would have been able to bring the runaway animal to ground without the aid of spurs, but he was not trying to rejoin the hunt; on the contrary, he wanted to avoid it.

Nature stirred up a reverie: *Grace, the jungle!*

His mount came to an abrupt halt, projecting him on to its withers. He had been paying so little attention that his feet slipped out of the stirrups and he was thrown to the ground. His quick reflexes allowed him to fall adroitly, and he found the cause of this new alarm in front of his eyes.

An enormous wild boar was there, defensively poised, extending its verrucose snout towards him, with its long sharp tusks yellowed by age. It observed him with its ferocious little eyes, its stiff hair raised in anger forming a kind of ruff around its hideous head

Felifax shook his head; such an animal was not capable of frightening him. In the Bengal jungle, he had faced more fearsome adversaries, including buffalo and wild oxen. He ignored it, and got ready to run after his horse. Liberated from its rider and taking wing in fright, Briskly was indeed making off with all possible speed.

The young man had turned his back on the animal; he was about to race off when he was suddenly thrown back on the ground by a violent shock. The boar–the old solitary male, advertised by Kilkenny as being so savage, had hurled itself upon the person who had been so imprudent as to provoke it in the vicinity of its lair.

Momentarily stunned, Felifax was not immediately aware of what had happened to him. He felt a violent pain in his leg, where one of the tusks had struck him. Fortunately, the blow had been deadened by his boot, whose leg had a long tear in it, as had his riding breeches. Blood was visible on the leg scored by the trenchant tusk.

Hot and stinking breath on his face warned him of further danger. The solitary male had made a half-turn and come towards its fallen enemy again. It was sniffing him before trampling him and stabbing him with its terrible weapons.

Felifax scarcely had time to turn the thrust aside. He was already covered by a heavy and hairy mass whose strength was unexpected. He wanted to get rid of it, but could get no purchase on the thick hide. The enraged beast was lashing out incessantly with its tusks, ripping the huntsman's garments to shreds and even causing some damage to his epidermis.

Then, Felifax had to set about vanquishing this animal with which he was completely unfamiliar–warthogs, the close cousins of wild boars, are not found in India. It was impossible to attempt to strangle the beast, its enormous neck being defended by rigid bristles, or to repeat the embrace he had used to crush Sindhypo, because the body was too fat. The animal-tamer had instead to defend himself against the excited animal's furious assaults.

This was surely an exact replication of Stone Age combats when man and beast had been in competition. Still, our ancestors had spears of seasoned wood and stone axes to aid them. Felifax had nothing but his hands and his enormous strength. He did not even have the help of his feline odor, which struck terror into other animals. The wild boar did not know that odor, for its species possessed two senses that were rather subtle: hearing and smell.

In spite of all this, the combat could not last long, and had to end with the victory of the son of Sita. He played a new trick, which would have made a crowd cry out in admiration. With a skillful movement, he was able to seize the creature by the two hind legs. Tensing his muscles in a supreme effort, the king of the jungle succeeded in lifting the solitary boar off the ground and whirling it around above head height. The enormous and ignoble head slammed into a stout tree, which shook under the impact.

The fight was over. The man had won. The beast did not even contrive a final shudder.

A smile extended across Felifax's face. He was pleased with himself. Leaning over the solitary boar, he studied it with an amused eye. Then he readjusted his clothing as best he could. His waistcoat had suffered most of all, the sharp tusks having inflicted large rips upon the cloth. He cast it aside casually and continued on his way. He would have to go back to the house on foot, since his horse had fled.

A journey of a few miles did not worry him; he had grown used to much longer and more difficult journeys in the jungle. Scarcely had he taken 20 paces, though, when he turned to retrace his steps. With a childish laugh, he leaned over the boar and, without undue effort, hoisted it to his shoulders. "I must not forget," he said, merrily, "that Deborah invited me to a hunt. I ought, therefore, to bring back a little game."

He departed with a supple stride, seeming hardly aware of the burden he carried on his shoulders.

Kilkenny had conducted the hunt as a consummate huntsman should; the dogs had led the pursuit of the doomed male brilliantly, immobilizing it until one of Deborah's best friends, fulfilling the function of master of the hounds, had dispatched it with his hunting-knife. A foot was awarded as a trophy to one of the divorcée's circle, and the hunt went back to the house, leaving Kilkenny to take care of bringing back the head and throwing the entrails to the dogs.

The young woman was slightly anxious; for the entire duration of the pursuit through the forest she had not perceived the slightest trace of Rama's passage. Her anxiety increased further on her arrival at Rotherhill. The young Hindu's mount had returned, covered in sweat, but without its rider. What had happened to him?

Although he did not show it, Baber shared her apprehension. He knew that the animal-tamer was capable of overtaking the best horse at a run. If he had let his mount come back in this fashion, perhaps it had been impossible for him to recapture it. He must be wounded! In order not to dampen the spirits of the satisfied hunters, he made every effort to reassure Lady Deborah. If the animal-tamer had not returned in an hour, he would go out to look form him personally, with the hunt's beaters and people from Crow.

When the hour had passed, the man they were waiting for had still not arrived. Baber was getting ready to leave with his volunteers and two dogs when he heard a loud cry of amazement. A man was coming into the courtyard, and his appearance was such as to generate a powerful emotional response.

Very tall, with his clothes torn, his muscular torso covered by a bloodstained shirt that was virtually in tatters, the man was carrying an enormous wild boar on his shoulders, whose weight did not appear to inconvenience him at all. At a leisurely pace, he came up to the hostess and deposited the boar at her feet.

"Pardon me, milady," he said, cheerfully, "for having hunted alone–truly, I did not have time to go look for you."

There was a moment of stunned silence. Lady Deborah, trembling with emotion, could not help asking, in a tone that betrayed her infatuation: "Oh, my God! Are you hurt, my dear Rama?"

He laughed heartily. "A few scratches. Mr. Black Pig would not let things lie–he took out his annoyance on my clothing, and has suffered somewhat in return."

Everyone now surrounded the young man and peppered him with questions. With good grace and the greatest simplicity, he told the story of his combat with the wild beast. The men were flabbergasted, while emotional tears washed away the ladies' makeup. Kilkenny, incapable of containing himself, cried: "It's the loner! Ah, sir, you've accomplished the greatest feat of venery one could ever hope to see. They'll be talking about this for a long time in Sussex."

It was indeed a feat to stupefy the brave man and all the connoisseurs of his kind: to put an end to a boar of such strength without a weapon, and without the assistance of dogs, seemed a supernatural achievement. Each of the hero's new exploits surpassed the preceding one.

The latter did not seem to be paying attention. He was chatting with Lady Deborah, who was still trembling at the thought of the danger he had run. When the testaments of admiration became too demonstrative, he insisted on removing himself, in order to wash and put on new clothes. Baber, who had already come out, went ahead of him. Sir Edmund ran to his room in order to record the fabulous combat in his report.

The conversation in the drawing-room was interrupted by a telephone call from London. The butler at the house in St.

James's Park felt it his duty to warn his mistress about the new exploit of "the carver" and give her the details of the murder of General Ferund at the home of the dancer Dorothy Mason.

The hunters were stricken by distress, feeling shivers down their spines. What a series of atrocities! Was London going to be obliged to endure this Reign of Terror, despite the efforts of the impotent police? An evil omen! The day that had begun so well would, alas, terminate in tragedy.

Felifax, still by reason of his feline odor, excused himself from attendance at dinner. He told Lady Deborah that he had a slight fever, brought on by the bruises he had received in his fight with the solitary boar, A quiet day and a good night's sleep would put him right again, permitting him to take part in a motoring rally organized by the socialites for the following day.

Despite her annoyance, the hostess had to respect the reason. She knew that it would be useless to argue. She said that she would send Doctor James to see him. It was, in fact, Sir Edmund who had given her this insidious advice–what a marvelous opportunity it would be to examine his subject thoroughly, while pretending to care for him! He had to think again; the animal-tamer refused the consultation. His wounds were purely superficial, and Baber could treat him more effectively than the most illustrious surgeon in the world, with the aid of fast-acting unguents from the land of his ancestors, which he always carried in his luggage.

All afternoon, the wild boar's adversary stayed in his room. Baber took advantage of the opportunity to leave the house and go to meet a car with its blinds drawn. Sourina and two Brahmans were in the car. After giving the high priest an account of what had happened the previous day, Baber made a mental note of very explicit new orders.

On the eve of the rally, Baber, seated next to Sexton, encouraged him to drink; it was not difficult. Like many an Englishman who had spent a long time in the colonies, the surgeon was a hardened drinker. Finding his glass constantly full, he emptied it speedily. There was a general tendency in the same direction, Lady Deborah having instructed her butler to pay particular attention to the wines and liqueurs. Strong cocktails had been absorbed before dinner, and the entire table was in a state of foolish merriment, save for the circus director, who was as sober as all his race.

After the toasts, Baber retired on the pretext of going to keep Rama company. Actually, instead of going up to the animal-tamer's room, he went out of the house and headed for a little gate in the grounds that was never used by the staff. Behind that gate, Sourina and another Brahman were waiting, both dressed in black in the European style. Baber had turned up the collar of his dinner-jacket to hide his white shirt. The three men returned to the modernized house, hiding behind various trees and bushes.

Once they were within the walls of Rotherhill, Baber guided them to an immense gallery serving as a library, which extended along the length of one wall of the house. One gained access to it by numerous doors, hidden by thick curtains. When the circus director had installed Sourina behind one of these curtains, from which he could see and hear what passed on the other side, he went up to Felifax's room.

It was empty.

The young animal-tamer had gone out with the idea of taking a stroll through the grounds–but as he passed the drawing-room, it seemed to him that he had heard his name spoken, to the accompaniment of bursts of laughter. Surprised, and desirous of setting his mind at rest, he had slipped into the gallery. There, hidden behind a curtain, he had pricked up his ears. Three yards further along, Sourina, Baber and the Brahman, similarly hidden, were also listening. Although Felifax was ignorant of his adoptive father's presence, the latter was aware of his, having seen him come in.

The conversationalists were talking about the fright experienced by the horses at the moment of departure for the hunt; each one was suggesting a hypothesis more grotesque than the last, amid a chorus of quips. Suddenly, Sexton raised his voice, taking his listeners by surprise. The alcohol had gone to his head, causing him to set prudence aside.

"Would you like to know why the horses showed signs of demented disquiet?" he said, rapturously. "It's perfectly simple–they scented a tiger."

There was an explosion of good humor. Lady Deborah went pale, recalling the words pronounced by Baber: *Rama is the cause of this terror...*

The drunkard continued: "You're saying to yourselves: *that's crazy; there are no tigers in Sussex*. Dear friends, there is a tiger-man! A tiger-man made by me, by my genius–a tiger-man about whom the entire world will be talking. My creation–my glory!"

A smile of savage joy illuminated the face of the eavesdropping Sourina, who murmured: "No more need to tell Felifax the name of his mother's torturer: the wretch is bragging about it as an achievement. He has just pronounced his death-sentence–the child will execute it."

In the drawing-room, everyone was having a good time. The doctor's ramblings were generating much merriment. Fearful that the animal-tamer might suddenly come in, the hostess tried to make the drunkard shut up, but it would have been easier to hold back the tide.

"Yes," he cried, "Surgeon-Major Edmund Sexton has worked the most stupendous of miracles! It was 20 years ago, in Benares, that I, God's own rival, obtained a child from the most beautiful of Hindu women and the most beautiful tiger in Bengal. Sita, as she was called..."

Baber took a step forward. Sourina held him back; he had just heard something like a stifled roar from behind the neighboring curtain. He anticipated an explosion.

Felifax was about to go into action!

The unfortunate young man had indeed heard the infamous confession trumpeted like a feat of prowess. At that moment, he had suddenly become the great beast of which the torturer might perhaps have dreamed. With what joy would he avenge that dear martyr! The man had wanted a tiger; his wish would be granted–he would tear him apart with his fingernails and his teeth, sating himself with blood like his feline father, Rina. He was about to throw himself forward, but he stopped, breathing hard. A gentle vision had just passed before his eyes like a flicker of light; it was a delightful blonde silhouette which seemed to be begging him to suspend his justice.

Miss Grace Palmer was an English woman. Could he strike down an English man? Why not?–she would certainly forgive the action when she learned its motive.

Placed in front of one of the doors of the library gallery, Sexton was continuing his rambling discourse, facing his audience with his back to the curtain. He had the appearance of a fairground barker advertising a phenomenon. Suddenly, the gawkers amused by his speech thought they saw something strange. The surgeon was dying; his features contracted in a horrid fashion; his eyes turned up and his tongue stuck out, as if he were being choked. His face became purple. Both hands went convulsively to his neck, as if to remove something. Some even thought they saw a slender black cord around his neck, forming an irresistible garrote.

"The necklace of the Thugs–Kali's stranglers!" murmured one trembling voice.

It was not possible. Even so, Sexton collapsed without a sound, like a rag doll. Before anyone could go to his aid, there was a horrified recoil. Through a gap in the curtain two brown hands were advancing, extending slowly. They seized the body and drew it back behind the curtain.

These hands were those of the animal-tamer Rama. The witnesses identified them, without any opposition, by means of the ring worn on the little finger of the left hand. That ring had been admired by everyone, for its strangeness; it was a diamond cut in the Hindu form–which is to say, triangular–bearing the sign of Kali.

Amazement paralyzed the witnesses of the tragedy. Then there was a rush toward the curtain. When its heavy folds were lifted, they expected to find Sexton's body behind it–but, to their further violent astonishment, the library was empty.

The servants came running in response to vehement appeals. The house was searched from top to bottom, without revealing its secret. The animal-tamer Rama and his artistic director Baber had both disappeared.

All the lamps and lanterns were requisitioned to illuminate the recesses of the grounds. The search was eventually abandoned when the former surgeon-major's head was discovered in front of a little garden-gate that was never used, as well as his freshly-severed hands. Around the neck, the cord of the tragic sectarians was still visible; the rest of the body was missing.

There was an atrocious groan. Lady Deborah Moorhen had just fainted.

IX: A Dangerous Arrest

On the morning after this hideous drama, at about 10 a.m., Chief Inspector Sullivan, accompanied by numerous policemen, presented themselves at Rama's Circus Menagerie. In his pocket was a warrant, properly made out and signed, for the arrest of the animal-tamer and his director. They had been charged with murder, committed upon the person of Doctor Sexton, the chief surgeon of the London hospitals.

As soon as the horrid discovery had been made, one of the guests at Rotherhill, a person of influence at the English court, had contacted Scotland Yard by telephone. Put in communication with the officer on duty, he had narrated the essential details. Sir Harold Nimbly had immediately made a discouraging connection between this affair and the two preceding ones. He also ordered that Sullivan should be sent to Crow with all possible speed.

The detective had just got back to his lodgings. He was dejected, having no further information regarding the bloody triple mystery. As it did to his superior, the tragedy of Rotherhill appeared to him to bring a glimmer of light.

In the meantime, a council was held at Lady Deborah's country house. No error was possible; the strangulation was the work of Rama the animal-tamer. Unexpectedly, the hostess was the most enthusiastic of all to accuse the man she had adored passionately two hours earlier. This was because she was thinking of the deplorable scandal that would be set off by the abominable crime committed in her residence by a man who was said to be her lover. A great English lady is willing to do anything to avoid malicious gossip.

Her voice having become authoritative, she had called upon her guests not to give any credence to Sexton's drunken ramblings, and not on any account to mention his fabulous tale of creating a tiger-man to the police. The surgeon's manias were proverbial. Now, if these manias might be supposed to have inflicted cruelties on a Hindu woman, the crime would then pass for an act of revenge. The honor of the victim would be sullied, and perhaps also the honor of the Empire. Anglo-phobes would not hesitate to use such calumnies to attack the Mother of Dominions.

Belonging as they all did to the aristocracy and the gentry, the others thought along the same lines as their hostess. In order to whiten the victim, one must blacken the criminal. Thus, the import of the witness-statements was agreed before the arrival of the judicial inquisitors.

When the police arrived, the divorcée, the first to be interrogated, carefully avoided any mention of the intimacy that had existed between herself and Rama. She explained her invitation to him as a whim of snobbery, a desire to play to the gallery. She even slipped a singular lie into her testimony; according to her, the Hindu had repeatedly solicited the invitation as soon as he had heard that Sir Edmund Sexton would be present–certain proof of premeditation.

With a disconcerting perversity, she insisted on another fact: Rama must have been very late in taking the car that was supposed to bring him to Rotherhill at midnight, because he had not arrived until 3:30 a.m.

She gave evidence of a surprising precision in relating the death of Sexton and the terrible identification of Rama's ring. The guests' depositions agreed with hers. They also agreed in emphasizing the complicity of Baber, who had disappeared after dinner, doubtless to make preparations for the crime.

When these depositions had been carefully written down and signed, the police passed on to the examination of the human remains. Sullivan's eyes brightened. The work and the precautions were identical to those applicable to the remains of Lord Bencenave, Lady Vertemer and General Ferund, with the exception of the pieces of amadou–but the latter detail could be the result of a lack of time.

There was no revelatory trace in the gallery. The footprints in the soil of the grounds had been effaced with the aid of a tree-branch. On following these traces outside, the property, marks made by car wheels had been found. The strike had been organized in advance!

Sullivan now made haste to return to London and arrest the wretched author of this sequence of frightful crimes. What relief the pubic would feel at the announcement of this sensational cast of the net, and what a spectacular revenge on the sarcasm of the press! His superior would approve of his promising Lady Deborah Moorhen the utmost discretion with regard to any relationship between her and the murderer. An official press release sheltered her from commentary and permitted the police to take the leading role. Already on the track, an engine-failure had prevented them from arriving in time to save the unfortunate surgeon.

Lady Deborah breathed easy, much relieved. Everyone in the house having retired, she went to bed, eager for a good night's rest, and fell into a peaceful sleep. She had pride and sensuality, but no heart.

In the car, on the way back to London, Sullivan explained to Nimbly that his first impressions had led him to the circus after the murder of Lord Bencenave. Although he had allowed himself to be sidetracked by the decapitation of Lady Vertemer, he thought he saw everything clearly now. The former favorite of the Maharajah could have fallen for the animal-keeper, whose masculine qualities had reignited her former passions. Rama had executed her, like Sexton, for sadistic motives, his indubitable fortune rendering his victims' jewels and money irrelevant.

As for General Ferund, there was near-certainty. The Hindu's lateness in taking the car was conclusive. During those three hours he had accomplished his near-daily butchery. The animal-tamer was half-savage, a vampire, who might well take pleasure in drinking the blood of his victims and doubtless in tearing apart their bodies. A similar fate would have been reserved for Lady Deborah Moorhen; one fine morning, her macabre remains would have been found. The unfortunate woman would have paid dearly for her sentimental whim.

Now it was over; the handsome Rama would pay his debt to justice. Scotland Yard's detectives would be the envy of the entire world.

Sullivan, of course, owed his life to the animal-tamer whom he was avid to arrest and whom he would willingly have struck down with his own hand. The Hindu had prevented him from being killed by Blood-drinker and his gang, and had arrested the escaped convict himself. These actions, far from working to his advantage, had, on the contrary, activated the detective's hatred; in accomplishing them, the Hindu must have been seeking impunity.

Sir Harold Nimbly threw a little cold water on the ebullience of his subordinate. Would they be able to find the animal-tamer again? Would not the latter flee, having been unable to accomplish his crime with the customary mystery? Would not his money, his menagerie and his personnel permit him to do whatever he wished?

An intense fever then took hold of Sullivan. The chauffeur was already driving at a reckless speed, but he called him a tortoise and told him to put his foot down. On arrival at Scotland Yard, he immediately sent agents to watch the doors of Kensington Palace, discreetly but with specific orders to prevent any of the Hindus from going out. In the meantime, he had to fume and fret, gnawing his cigar, waiting for the Lord Chancellor to sign the arrest warrant. Once he had the precious piece of paper in his hand, he rushed out and made his entrance at the circus at 10 a.m.

As on every other day, the whole troupe was at work. The acrobats were practicing new turns, the dancers were studying new steps and Djina was organizing a parade of the sacred elephants, whose star would be the immense Manaor.

Sullivan only had 15 officers with him, but 30 well-armed policemen were waiting outside, ready to intervene. In addition, a direct telephone link had been established between the administrators of Kensington Palace and Scotland Yard. One word would suffice to send police cars flying to the aid of the detective and his men. They had to expect resistance from the Hindus, who might well oppose the arrest of their directors.

Baber had just arrived. He came to meet the intruders and asked them politely what they wanted, entry to the circus being prohibited between performances. He was immediately surrounded by the officers, and Sullivan put a hand on his shoulders, pronouncing the formula of arrest *in the name of the King.*

Baber shivered slightly and asked: "Would you like to tell me, sir, the reason for this arrest?"

The Hindu's *frisson* had not escaped the detective. He smiled; the clown had nerve!

"If you hadn't so kindly made a jigsaw puzzle of the surgeon Sexton," he muttered, "you'd have been able to ask him, as well as the other victims dispatched by Master Rama and you to a paradise that's not even worth as much as the Soviet one."

Intense emotion brought an ashen tint to the bronzed face of Ralph Napper's former auxiliary; it was his way of going pale. At that moment, the officers surrounded him. He had, however, the time to exchange a glance with Djina, who ducked under one of the elephants and disappeared. The gymnasts, illusionists and snake-charmers had already gathered together, menacingly. Did they intend to liberate the director, beloved for his gentleness? Sullivan saw the danger, and stood up to it. Baber was handcuffed and a man ran in search of reinforcements.

The Hindu had an enigmatic smile on his lips; it was a matter of gaining time. His face cleared completely when he saw the barrier forming the cage that separated the spectators from the animal-tamer and his beasts go up. He alone had noticed this maneuver, for the officers were watching the artistes who were threatening to throw themselves forward. He had time! The railings were in place, and Felifax came forward within the immense cage, holding his two favorite tigers, Rudra and Durgane. Then, the partition having been opened, the royal tigers bounded out and came to group themselves around their master.

Beads of sweat formed on Sullivan's forehead. He was petrified. A strong curse escaped his lips and was echoed by all the officers. Baber raised his voice again, though, to say with a semblance of respect: "Here is the animal-tamer Rama, Master Detective. You can now fulfill your mission!"

Felifax had been lost in thought in the wings when Djina had come to warn him of the danger. The previous night, while he was drawing away from Rotherhill in a car obtained by Baber, he had sat beside his director. The car belonged to Lady Deborah. Baber had borrowed it from the estate garage, but in his overexcited state the young man had not noticed that. Not having spoken a word during the entire journey, as soon as he had arrived at the circus he had gone back to his own quarters, situated behind the menagerie. Then, in order to avoid a possible search, the former animal-keeper had driven the car to the house in St. James's Park and said to the porter: "This was agreed with your mistress."

On discovering the reasons for Baber's arrest, Djina had come to inform her beloved brother, adding: "They have come to apprehend you too!"

The animal-tamer's face reflected his surprise. His first thought was to give himself up. The accusation would not stand up, and he would soon be released. But a rebellious impulse brought him to his feet, crying to Djina: "Order the grille to be raised and let the tigers loose!"

Now, striking an attitude of calmness, although he was prey to a ferocious anger, the leader of wild beasts waited in the midst of his formidable animals, in glacial silence. There was not a roar or a snarl from the carnivores, but their mouths yawned hungrily at the intruders, who were all hiding behind Sullivan.

The latter advanced, livid with excessive emotion, and after muttering through clenched teeth "Let's get down to business!" [100] he cried in a hoarse voice: "In the name of the King, animal-tamer Rama, put an end to this joke and surren-

257

der. You have to answer to British justice for all your monstrosities."

Felifax raised his voice in his turn. "Having no monstrous action to my account, Mr. Sullivan, I shall not surrender. Are innocent men arrested? I respect the name of King George but my companions are independent subjects and they will protect me."

A mere click of his tongue sent the redoubtable animals rushing forward against the bars of the grille that had been raised between them and the strangers. There was a concert of roars. He maintained his powerful grip on Rudra and Durgane, his family-members, who wanted to bound forward with their fellows. He resembled some occult deity ready to descend upon humankind.

The seasoned police officers, though unafraid of death, to which their dangerous trade exposed them every day, felt ill at ease. They would have been willing to hurl themselves against the Hindus, risking a bullet, a dagger or strangulation, but they had no defense against these man-eaters. Sullivan stiffened himself against the ambient panic and terror, and took advantage of a brief lull in the roaring to say: "Be careful, Rama–you're entering into a rebellion against your King, and you'll be treated accordingly. We are the stronger..."

"Ah! So that's your morality! You are the stronger! A fine sort of justice! So be it–I accept the challenge. If I must yield to that, my friends will have time to demonstrate their expertise. Yes, I am a rebel against the King, being a king myself–of the jungle. Here are my subjects! Ah, my lambs! Ah, my dear tigers, my brothers, here's a nice dinner for you! English beefsteak, very fresh, and as much conquerors' blood as you can drink. What a feast–what carnage! O Kali, how worthily your festival will be celebrated!"

Then he turned toward Sullivan. "Mr. Sullivan, I give you ten minutes to release Baber and get out. When those ten minutes are up, the grille will be lowered again. Nothing will separate you then from the jungle and its fauna."

An officer had departed for the administrative offices of Kensington Palace as soon as the first words were spoken, however. He telephoned Scotland Yard and demanded reinforcements with all possible urgency.

A minute before the expiration of the deadline, the klaxons of police cars were heard. A moment later, a hundred uniformed policemen armed with rifles erupted into the auditorium. At the same time, machine-gunners were setting up their weapons.

Then, Sir Harold Nimbly's men saw something admirable: a little Hindu girl passing through the unchained wild beasts and coming to stand by her adopted brother's side in order to die with him.

The young man had tears in his eyes now. He saw weapons aimed at his friends, ready to kill. Had he the right to sacrifice all these animals, which he had brought out of the jungle with the intention of taking them back one day? Had he the right to expose Djina–who, he knew, would refuse to abandon him? And all for the stupid pride of refusing to surrender.

Sir Harold Nimbly, who had come with the reinforcements, came forward. Moved despite everything by the courage of the man, and addressed him in a voice that he strove to keep soft: "You can see our armaments, Mr. Rama. Your redoubtable pupils, before being annihilated, will certainly take the lives of a few brave fellows whose only sin is to be obedient to their duty. All the same, the law will prevail. Behind these squads there are others, and others still. Believe me, enough blood has been spilled; your good will might win you a good deal of indulgence."

With an imperious gesture, the animal-tamer imposed silence on his roaring flock, and his voice rang out with a manifest honesty that struck all his listeners, save for Sullivan, who was determined to prove his own wisdom. "Gentlemen," he said, "I have no need of indulgence, being innocent of the crimes that you wish to attribute to me. I surrender, not to superior force–my people have no fear of death–but because I do not want my friends to be the victims of my stubbornness."

As he did every evening, he sent his beasts to their gilded cages and leaned over the heads of Rudra and Durgane to kiss them. The grille slowly retreated into the ground. Then he took Djina in his arms and said to her in Bengali: "Dear little sister, I swear to you on my mother's ashes that I have not committed any crime. When you are able–which is to say, after my condemnation or my death—-you must go to find Miss Grace Palmer. Tell her my whole story, as Sita confided it to us before dying. Reveal to her the odious crime of the man whom I am accused of killing. Add this: *Miss Grace, despite his ancestry, Felifax never spilled blood. The thought of you and his adoration of you prevented him from taking vengeance. He loved you with all his heart and begs you to pardon him for the treason committed against you.*"

"She has already pardoned you, brother; she knows the only reason for your relationship with that woman. You hoped to forget her while you thought yourself unworthy of her. Be certain that she loves you as much as you can love her."

"Have you seen her, then?"

"Yes–we meet every night."

The unhappy youth let his head fall forwards. Grace had come to London, and, like a fool, he had run after unhealthy amours when he could have had the purity of her exquisite soul. He could not blame bad luck. He hugged Djina and kissed her several times, saying: "A few of these kisses are for her."

Then, having broken the embrace, he went to offer his wrists to the police commissioner so that he might be handcuffed,

Despite his skepticism, Nimbly felt a tightness in his chest as he was confronted by the abnegation of that singular and superior being. "Mr. Rama," he said, "it is for the court to judge your crime; for the moment, you are merely accused. You enjoy great celebrity in London, and I want to avoid taking you through the crowd of your admirers as a prisoner. Give me your word of honor that you will not try to escape, and you may go out by a side door with myself and Inspector Sullivan. My men will go the other way."

"You have my word, sir. I will answer equally for my friend Baber."

At a gesture from the commissioner, the handcuffs were removed from Rao's brother. Felifax addressed a few words to the natives, instructing them to wait silently, without any protest, for the decision of the court. He gave them particular instructions as to the care of his beasts. Then he went out with Baber, flanked by Nimbly and Sullivan. On seeing them go, Djina sank to her knees sobbing.

Hidden behind the scenery, as was his custom, Sourina had been following the scene, His heart had begun to beat feverishly when Felifax had threatened to unleash his beasts. Now, as pale as death, he foresaw a dark future. Were his extravagant plans about to founder?

VIII: The Rape of Newgate

Grace Palmer had resumed her medical studies. Surprisingly, though, she seemed to have abandoned medicine itself in favor of toxicology. To that end, she had made contact with a great friend of her father's, Doctor Hanson, a distinguished chemist and toxicologist. Glad to be of some help to the daughter of his old comrade, the savant had admitted her to his laboratory, installed in the Chemical and Geological Society premises at New Burlington House in Piccadilly.

With the ardor and intelligence she brought to everything, Grace applied herself to research into blood-poisoning and the means of countering it. This laborious assiduity was a powerful side-effect of her chagrin. As soon as the Faculty opened, she was at her desk, and did not leave until late. At midday, she ate in a lunch bar in Dover Street that was mostly frequented by intellectuals.

Every day, she met a young fellow of 25 or 30 there named James Macfull, a reporter for the *Daily Herald*, the official organ of the Labor Party, who had a bright future ahead of him. By an amusing coincidence, this journalist was the one who had attacked Sullivan so violently in return for his lack of cooperation. When he came to lunch one day, he brought the sensational news of the murder of the surgeon Sexton and the arrest of the animal-tamer Rama. The fellow was slightly annoyed to be obliged to make honorable amends to the detective, but as he was essentially honest, he had written a eulogistic article congratulating him on putting his hands on the murderers.

On hearing him recount the frightful details of the strangulation, Grace felt a constriction in her heart. Was it possible that Felifax, whom she had placed above everything, could have committed such an abomination? O dolor! A passage from his farewell letter came to mind:

If, in the near future, you should hear talk of a new and terrible exploit, do not attribute it to the wickedness of my soul, but tell yourself that it is the men of your race, having intended it thus, who are uniquely responsible for and ought to be reproached for the ferocity of... Felifax.

No! Her love rebelled; an action so odious was impossible on his part. He must be the victim of an abominable error. That idea became more firmly fixed in her mind when she heard Macfull enumerate the series of crimes imputed to the bloodthirsty animal-tamer. Then, moved to vehement protest, she cried: "Rama is not guilty, at least in respect of Lady Vertemer–unless his accomplice was a very highly-placed lady."

Then, at the journalist's alarmed reaction, she found the courage to tell him a part of the story of Felifax in India, and her certainty that, on the night of the crime in the Strand, the animal-tamer had been in Greenwich at the Seals Club, in the company of an aristocratic lady. She knew all the details of that supper thanks to Djina, to whom Felifax confided everything,

Extremely interested, and foreseeing a sequence of sensational stories, Macfull agreed to do nothing for the time being and to await more ample information that Miss Palmer would obtain from her acquaintances at the circus. Then abandoning her laboratory work for the first time, the outraged blonde girl took a cab to Kensington Palace. She knew she would find Djina there.

The Hindu girl threw herself into Grace's arms and their tears mingled. driven to desperation by the thought of what had happened to her beloved brother, Djina thought it best to bring forward the mission he had entrusted to her. She told her white-faced friend the story of Sita's torments and Sexton's odious crime. She repeated Felifax's last words: "*You will repeat to Miss Grace that despite my ancestry, I have never spilled blood. The thought of you and his adoration of you prevented him from taking vengeance. He loved you with all*

*his heart and begs you to pardon him for the treason commit-
ted against you."*

Gentle relief flooded the heart of the pretty English-woman. Her presentiments had not been mistaken, then–the object of her desires was innocent.

At that moment, a Brahman came into Djina's apartment and told her in Bengali that the master wanted to see her. No name was pronounced. Was there any need? The little dancer left without delay; she knew that the high priest of Kali did not like to be kept waiting. Grace had not had time to tell her that she believed in him.

The Hindu was innocent; that would be perceived, and he would be released. Suddenly, though, she thought: *English justice is very expeditious! Besides, Scotland Yard is deter-mined to see a guilty man in its prisoner; it will make a strong case. He'll be judged as such, and hanged. There's only one hope! The real murderer must be found in time.* This reflection brought her father's name to her lips. He alone could carry out that overwhelming and urgent task. He alone was capable of demonstrating to the police that they had made a mistake. He alone would have the science necessary to save the man she loved. Alas, Doctor Palmer had sworn an oath not to involve himself any longer in the affairs of London. She knew from Aunt Molly's last letter that he had threatened to leave on a long cruise if anyone mentioned the police to him.

Well, she would go get him herself. Everyone gave in to her, even her father–and she would save the honest youth to whom she had given her heart.

From the nearest Post Office, in the conventional lan-guage that she and her father had formerly employed between themselves, she cabled: *Help, father dear. Felifax arrested for crimes of which he is innocent. Sullivan relentless. Danger of death. Trial will be rapid. Am waiting. Grace.*

And the appeal for help departed through the atmos-phere.

Grace Palmer had good reason to be afraid. Scotland Yard was in a hurry to put an end to the story and satisfy public opinion.

By 3 p.m., the discomfiture of the police was quite considerable. The special editions included all the details furnished by Nimbly and Sullivan, but abstained from the least comment. There was no praise at all, nor even a sigh of relief. The animal-tamer Rama had become such a personality in a matter of weeks, had made himself so popular by his courage and his charity that they refrained from saying anything against him. They even seemed to regret that he was the guilty party, the sanguinary brute, the cynical carver.

The *Daily Herald*, generally so prolix, gave evidence this time of a disconcerting banality. It merely related the facts, and terminated thus: *The man believed to be the murderer has been arrested, along with his presumed accomplice.* Not a word about the sensational arrest or the bravery of the officers ready to risk death to apprehend the guilty man in the midst of his wild beasts. A dramatic account of it had been given to the reporters, but the papers that related the fact said: *At the thought of seeing numerous policemen pay with their lives for the victory of their superiors, the young animal-tamer abandoned all thought of self-defense and heroically gave himself up.*

Men are always susceptible to flattery; the disappointment of seeing their feats of arms passed over in silence provokes anger. The unfortunate Felifax found this out in the course of the interrogation to which he was subjected that afternoon. Sullivan and Nimbly showed themselves in their true light as torturers, not averse to any measure to force confessions.

Very calm at first, determined to prove his innocence, the animal-tamer denied any participation in the crimes with which he was charged. He listened with surprise to the recital of the evidence indicating his guilt and laughed like a child. A blow of Sullivan's fist reminded him that one does not mock the police in such a fashion.

The detective thought his last hour had arrived when, despite his height, he was lifted up by an invincible force and held aloft at the end of an arm, dancing in mid-air. He owed his salvation to the arrival of a number of policemen who came running in response to a bell sounded by Nimbly. Assailed by a dozen robust fellows, the animal-tamer shook them off without much effort, sending them rolling against the walls, knocking half of them over with a few nudges. The careless punch had reawakened his atavistic ferocity.

Violent blows from a rubber truncheon eventually put an end to his defense; he collapsed unconscious. The brutes were then able to shackle him with solid chains and beat him unmercifully. When he recovered consciousness, the torture began again. The policemen, tranquilized by the solidity of the chains holding the prisoner, doled it out with joyful heart. The thrashing was hideous, but it did not evoke the least complaint.

At the end of four hours, the animal-tamer was taken back to his cell, without anything having been obtained from him. Instead of the poised youth, determined to defend himself calmly, who had been taken out, it was a rebel who was put back in. Plans of escape and vengeance were already running through his mind.

The telegraph is a marvelous invention, especially in England, where records are always beaten. An hour after being deposited in a London office, Grace's telegram arrived at Plymouth and was given to Miss Molly.

The latter was never permitted to open a dispatch addressed to her brother. The doctor had put out to sea that morning to fish, as he did every day. Fortunately, she knew where his anchorage was. Impelled by an irresistible force, she ran to the harbor to find the owner of a motor-launch used for sea trips. She climbed into the fast vessel without hesitation and had herself driven to the place where her brother was fishing. He gave a cry of amazement on seeing Molly. He feared that here had been a serious accident; when she gave him the telegram, however, he frowned.

What was the significance of this piece of paper? An appeal from Scotland Yard, no doubt, ordering him to London urgently. Another mystery to elucidate. He had sworn to stay away–and, in order not to be tempted by the interesting attributes of the affair, he crumpled the telegram into a ball without opening it and threw it into the sea.

At the same time, he said to his astounded sister: "I don't know what's keeping me from doing the same to you. Your obstinacy in throwing me back, by telling me things I don't want to know at any price, is revolting!"

He expected to see terror in the old spinster's face, but instead, he was flabbergasted in his turn. Without a word, Molly threw herself into the sea and dived after the telegram.

She was an outstanding swimmer, like the majority of English coastal residents. In spite of her skirt–which scarcely hindered her, thanks to the current fashion–she set off in pursuit of the ball of paper, plunging beneath the surface. A sentiment stronger than her had forced her to this unexpected gesture; since her brother did not want to know what the telegram said, she had every right to know what it contained.

The doctor was not of the same opinion. As soon as his stupor passed, he turned to John, his faithful Scotsman, who was sitting in the bow of the boat and said to him curtly: "Get that paper before Molly, and destroy it!"

John, as was well-known, never disputed one of his master's orders. He dived in head-first and swam vigorously.

It was a brief but passionate struggle. John, a champion at the crawl, caught up with the old spinster and they both grabbed the coveted paper at the same time. Unfortunately, the telegram, softened by the sea-water, tore, and each of the adversaries came away with a part of it. A slave to the orders he had received, the servant destroyed the piece that he had in his hand. Miss Palmer, on the contrary, in fear of a further attack, unfolded hers. What she read made her cry out in fright.

Her emotion was such that she sank like a stone. This time, without orders, John went to her aid and brought her back to the boat, where the doctor was anxious. What could have been in the telegram to cause such a reaction?

The old woman's hand still held the piece of paper snatched from destruction. As soon as he had cast his eyes over it, the detective cursed loudly. He had just read what remained of the truncated telegram:

Help, father dear... Danger of death... Will be rapid. Am waiting.

And it was signed by Grace!

Was it possible? Was his child, his dear beloved, in danger? And he, stupid old idiot, had almost destroyed that call for help, that S.O.S.!

Leaving John to look after his sister, he hauled up the anchor, hoisted the mainsail and the jib, and set himself at the tiller to head for land at full speed.

Palmer's boat was a speedy one; it arrived at the quay very quickly. There the doctor shouted to John: "Take Molly back to the house, I've only just time to catch the express. Join me in London with my suitcase."

A few minutes later, the express left Plymouth Station. Wedged in a corner, with his eternal pipe in his mouth, Doctor Eric Palmer, once again the inspired detective, was already in search of deductions.

The districts of St. Giles's, Whitechapel and Docklands, always animated, seemed that evening to be host to an extreme agitation. A sort of password was gliding between mouths and ears, sidestepping the policemen on duty, and numerous groups of people seemed to be converging on the same point. The password was meticulously observed, the secret rigorously kept and the mysterious spoken words received general approbation. They made eyes glitter with anger.

About 10 p.m., an astounding rumor spread through the various districts of the West End and the City, while telephone calls came from every direction, alerting the police. Ten thousand, 15,000 or 20,000 people, it was said, were laying siege to Newgate Prison and freeing the inmates. It was also said that four gigantic elephants were marching at the head of the mob. The massive doors, proof against all ordinary assaults, had not been able to resist their formidable pressure.

The rumor was perfectly true. The poor people of London–the "Family," as they termed themselves–were going to the aid of the man who had shown them such generosity and whose daily deeds relieved so many miseries. This was what Sourina had wanted to order Djina to do when the little dancer's conversation with Grace Palmer had been interrupted. He had asked her if she could tell the London poor of the danger their benefactor was in, and beg them to prevent the greatest of judiciary errors.

What would the Hindu girl not have done to save the brother she thought was lost? Yes, she knew where to go. She knew the places where Felifax and she had gone nearly every day to hand over their money so that it could be distributed to the deserving. It was not to official agencies, but to the sorts of societies formed by the poor themselves, where the share-out would be conducted with the greatest honesty.

These "paupers' clubs" were numerous in the populous districts. When the Hindu girl presented herself there, she was welcomed enthusiastically. Yes, they would snatch their benefactor–the brother who had bent down to their distress–from the hands of the law. They would do it because his sister said that he was innocent. They would have done it even if he had been guilty, for the victims were people of little concern to them: a former Lord Chancellor of implacable severity; a Commander of Military Prisons, cruel and bloodthirsty; a surgeon at the hospitals, a torturer of poor wretches; a sensual female aristocrat who spent lavishly on her vices but was ignorant of charity. Yes, even if he were guilty, his crimes against over-stuffed aggressors attracted the admiration of the people; they were naught but vengeance, a merited punishment.

Sourina had put a considerable sum of money at Djina's disposal. The *devadasi* had all the trouble in the world persuading those who wanted to march for honor to accept it. The rendezvous was arranged for 10 p.m.; a few men were commissioned to fetch Djina at the agreed moment, in order not to lose precious time looking for her. Since the young woman's departure, messengers had been dispatched in every direction to alert supporters; these were responsible for rallying the comrades.

It went like clockwork. The people can always raise a mob when it is a matter of doing the law a bad turn. The poor people marched for their benefactor, but there were also villains from Whitechapel and the Docks. They came running out of hatred for society, with the hope of demolishing the "Bastille" where their comrades had stuck out their tongues at the end of a rope.

Within a few minutes, an entire plan of attack had been formulated. One party of assailants was to gather at Holborn Viaduct, another near the Church of the Holy Sepulchre, at the square tower where the bell is tolled for executions at Newgate, and a third in the vicinity of the Post House and Christ's Hospital. At 9:45 p.m., each group would start moving, by different routes, towards the Old Bailey–which is to say, towards Newgate Prison.

By way of publicity, Rama's Circus Menagerie sent out its elephants nearly every day to amble majestically through the streets of London, objects of general curiosity. Their appearance that evening was a trifle surprising, Rama's arrest being common knowledge, but no one read anything into it. They were content to watch them pass, without noticing that the giant Manaor did not have his usual *mahout*.

In fact, Djina, dressed as a young Hindu male, had taken the *mahout*'s place and was skillfully wielding the *ankus*–a pointed iron rod which, placed in a carefully-maintained small wound, steered the enormous animal. She had prepared the elephants for a public promenade, but she had dispensed with a *howdah* and was perched on Manaor's head. She was going to Felifax's aid. Her voice did not tremble at all when she gave the command to set off on the march and the journey across London began.

The further they advanced, the greater Djina's anxiety became. Would she succeed?

The men responsible for guiding her had calculated the journey-time well. They had no need to pause on arrival at the Old Bailey; crowds were running from every direction. Although the few policemen on duty in the district had been able to see what was happening, an immense crowd–men, women, children and old people–surged like a sea towards the main door of Newgate, without a murmur, let alone a shout. The instruction to maintain strict silence was followed rigorously.

In the first rank, the four elephants stopped in front of the door, their little black eyes shining, as if they were aware of the good turn that they would perform in freeing their eternal friend. Suddenly, the oppressive silence was broken by a female voice crying out in the language the elephants understood: *"Turuth! Turuth!"*–meaning "Break! Break!"

The two largest elephants, side by side, set their irresistible heads against the massive oak door, solidly reinforced with iron, and pushed with all the force of their imposing mass. There was a loud crack, but the door resisted. The third and fourth elephants came to lean on the other two; the cry of *"Turuth!"* resounded again. This time, the unhinged door fell inwards with a loud noise.

The prison guards came running from their station, but the elephants went into the alleyway on the command *"Dutt! Dutt!"*–which meant "Step Over!" Behind them was an innumerable crowd.

The frightened Governor went up to his office to telephone for help, but in vain. All the telephone lines from the prison had been cut a few minutes earlier. How could this rolling mass be held back? How could the guards open fire without hitting the women and children mixed in with the crowd?

A male voice called out, quite calmly: "We are masters here! In less than five minutes, if we wish, the doors of all the cells will be opened and the prisoners freed. We do not ask for that; we only want the animal-tamer Rama, the benefactor of the poor."

The officer commanding the guard-post could not accede to such a demand. He wanted to intimidate the crowd, and ordered his soldiers to take aim at the elephants. He had to respect human life, until he received new orders. A salvo was fired.

The bullets failed to penetrate the thick hides, except for one–doubtless stray–which hit Moota, one of the younger pachyderms, in the eye. The animal leapt forward and fell heavily. As it did so, its trunk plucked the officer who had given the order to fire from the ground. He would have been broken like a straw, but death claimed Moota before the fatal destruction was complete. The officer fell back unconscious, badly injured.

A vengeful trumpeting began. The other three elephants, irritated by the bullets, raised their trunks, intent on trampling by way of reprisal. In response to Djina's order, the *mahouts* went to great pains to calm the beasts and avoid carnage–but the defenders of Newgate retreated before that invincible advance.

A few men, former inmates of the prison, got into the cell-block. An old warder, driven into a corner and doubtless intent on preserving his life, surrendered his keys and pointed to the animal-tamer's strong-room. Secretly, he would not be displeased to be rid of that terrible inmate, who had broken his restraining shackles and attacked the grille forming the door of his cell.

When Felifax saw the people who had come to set him free, he released a mighty shout of joy and threw himself outside. Then, stopping in his tracks, he said: "Thank you, my friends, I shall not forget what you have done. But wait–I am not here alone; there is my faithful friend Baber, as innocent as I am. There is also another man, whom I helped to capture,

272

who also appears to have nothing to do with the crimes of which he has been accused. He is called Blood-drinker, and ought to be set free. I shall tell him how much I regret the impulse that made me protect the policeman Sullivan. That pig gave me a beating by way of thanks, and he shall be paid in kind."

Five minutes later, the three prisoners were in the courtyard, surrounded by their liberators, going out of the prison. The crowd was densely packed around them. They wanted to prevent the police from recapturing them, if they were inclined to try.

Blood-drinker, utterly flabbergasted by what had happened to him, heard the story from a comrade and moved close to the animal-tamer to whisper to him: "Old fellow, I'll forget the day you broke my arm–you've given me handsome compensation. In return, listen to the advice of one who knows the police very well. If you go back to your circus, you're cooked. They'll have you, even if they have to destroy the place and everything it contains. Come with me to Whitechapel–you'll have this whole army to defend you, and it'll take the police months to root through its thousands of hidey-holes. That'll give you time to make yourself scarce."

With an energetic handshake, Felifax gave him to understand that he accepted the offer, and asked in his turn: "Can I get a van tomorrow evening?"

"Yes, I'll get you that easily."

Then the animal-tamer drew closer to Manaor and said to Djina in Bengali: "Tomorrow evening, at 10 p.m., when you hear a vulture's cry repeated three times, release Rudra and Durgane. Before then, have their cage placed at the entrance giving out on to Exhibition Road and don't do anything else.[101] I'll find a means of getting further instructions to you. Now, get the elephants trotting and go back to the circus."

She cried: "I've seen Miss Grace. She loves you, and believes that you're innocent..."

The general noise drowned out what followed. There was a stir among the crowd surrounding them. The police, warned by the Post House, were coming at a run–but how could they reach the guilty parties in that human ocean, where women and children were in the majority? The agglutinated mass of bodies was as impenetrable and irresistible as the tide, rendering any arrest impossible.

Guided by their *mahouts*, the docile elephants followed the regression of the crowd, over which they towered. Soon, on arrival at a crossroads, they disappeared at a trot in response to the command "*Chai!*"–which means "Turn." Frightened people scurried out of their way.

Scarcely had they returned to the menagerie when the police came to demand the elephant-conductors. No one appeared to understand, posing a difficult problem. Would it be necessary to arrest all 600 of the Hindus in the troupe?

The officer in charge knew the native mind well enough to be anxious about the consequences of a mass arrest. The worshippers of the Trimurti [102] were people who would be cut to pieces before they would betray their brothers. Besides, the policemen felt distinctly ill-at-ease in the menagerie. They could hear the numerous carnivores, snakes and raptors roaring, snarling, whistling, yelping, howling and bellowing behind the bars of their cages. They knew the story of Rama's arrest; none of them wanted to serve as beefsteak for those inmates.

The officer telephoned headquarters. He received the order to blockade the circus tightly, and to arrest anyone who tried to leave or enter. A "spider's-web" was immediately formed–but Felifax was not shut up in Kensington Palace. Lost in a sea of people–swimming, so to speak, underwater–he had succeeded in reaching Whitechapel at the side of the drinker, who had become a respectful friend of this supernatural force. An hour after leaving Newgate, he was hiding in one of the butcher's retreats, where the police would surely never find him.

He gladly accepted the food they were enthusiastic to serve him. He had had nothing to eat since the previous day; Sullivan and Nimbly had decided to weaken him by means of hunger. He ate with a good appetite and then made clear his need for sleep. He could rest without fear; Blood-drinker and his comrades were watching over the benefactor of the Paupers' Clubs.

Despite his satisfaction in being free, there was one thing that worried Felifax greatly–Baber was not with him. Everyone said that they had not seen him again after leaving the prison. Had the poor fellow been recaptured, or had he gone back to the circus with the elephants? Manaor held Felifax's uncle in great esteem; he was capable of carrying him away.

Meanwhile, Djina told Sourina what had happened. Never before had the chief Brahman's implacably cruel eyes reflected such satisfaction. Visions of liberation were already rising up within him: civil war in London, the city set on fire and its streets running with blood. His pupil would march at the head of the people, taking revenge on the conquerors for his mother's torture. Sourina would know when the right moment came to take him away, so that his prowess, cleverly exploited in India, would cause the entire people to rise up for liberty and the extermination of the accursed race.

"Kali, thou art the most high! Kali, thou art the most powerful!" he murmured. And he prostrated himself at the feet of the grimacing goddess, in a prayer that would last all night.

Grace Palmer was in the offices of the *Daily Herald* when the news of the invasion of Newgate arrived there. As the daughter of a policeman, she immediately thought that if Felifax agreed to leave, it would be tantamount to a confession of guilt. She did not even utter a sight of relief because her father would have more time to discover the truth. The reporter Macfull told her over dinner that the affair would be carried forward with drums beating. The unfortunate animal-tamer would not be able to cut the hangman's rope by this means. In Britain, when it is deemed to be necessary, the law operates without the least delay.

As soon as they heard that the London poor had stormed Newgate, the journalist went to do his duty. Grace went with him, taking advantage of his press pass. In addition, should the need arise, her name would be the best password possible, Eric Palmer being considered as an extraordinary person, the most famous policeman in the world.

She saw the mass of people swarming back to it refuges in Docklands, Whitechapel, Houndsditch, Bethnal Green, Spitalfields and Shoreditch. She saw the wild determination in their faces. They retreated one step at a time before the policemen, turning their backs to truncheon-blows, but without yielding a single cry.

Grace inferred that too much blood would be spilled in recapturing the man the people had freed. Her father was direly needed–he alone was capable of averting that slaughter. She was sure of his science; he would clear Felifax, and save the poor from a potential massacre at the same time.

After leaving the *Herald* offices, where she had helped Macfull write a front-page article that would cause a sensation in the morning, Grace arrived home at 2 a.m. Sir Eric Palmer was not there yet, but a telegram announced his imminent arrival.

XI: Sir Eric Palmer Returns

Since the arrival of the Circus Menagerie in London, newspaper circulation had increased steadily. First, there had been the amazement generated by the wild animals, then the handsome animal-tamer's success with the ladies, and finally the bloody exploits of the monstrous carver. There had seemed to be no hope of further increases in circulation–but it reached unprecedented levels on the day after the assault on Newgate Prison. The papers were literally torn from the sellers' hands, and the presses kept rolling until their spools gave out.

The nobility, the bourgeoisie and the shop-keepers feared at first that there had been riots by the unemployed, a mass descent upon the rich quarters, looting and burning. When they found out, however, that the demonstration had been limited to the release of a prisoner who, despite his misdeeds, retained a certain sympathy, they were reassured. As people in England are always getting excited about bets and extraordinary performances, they finished up declaring that the event was *quite extraordinary*.[103]

Lady Deborah Moorhen and her guests at Rotherhill were the only ones trembling in fear. If Rama knew about their relentless accusations, he would certainly not be incapable of carving them up in their turn. Their morbid anxiety left them in no doubt of the Hindu's guilt. Each of them used what influence he had to obtain protection.

Papers of every political shade disseminated the unexpected "goodies." Several, under the influence of Scotland Yard, treated the mass demonstration as a sinister manifestation of anarchy. According to them, Rama's flight proved his guilt. But the majority took the thing more light-heartedly, almost excusing the accused for breaking out. An indiscretion had alerted them to the intentions of the Lord Chief Justice regarding the expeditious closure of the affair; they claimed that such a demand for execution was unworthy of a civilized country.

Among the latter was the *Daily Herald*. It must have quintupled its circulation, with not a single copy unsold. Macfull's reportage was truly remarkable. Slipping into the crowd, he had found out about the grave ill-treatment unexpectedly inflicted in the course of the interrogation of the prisoner, and the chains in which he had been bound–whose marks he still bore, along with the bruises of blows inflicted with revolting brutality. He demanded the application of powerful sanctions against those who had thus dishonored the law. He reminded his readers of the tragedy of the Inquisition, and called Sullivan "the licensed torturer."

Curiosity and passion were excited most of all by an article entitled *Open Letter to an Aristocratic Lady*, which was constituted thus:

To Lady D. M.

A very noble and wealthy lady

Almost all the queens of History had numerous favorites. Times have changed, and today's queens have become simple, useful and affectionate, having but one end on Earth: the happiness of their subjects and the education of their children. It is, therefore, the turn of the bourgeoisie to ape the Majesties of old, to replace authority and grandeur with wealth and snobbery.

Yes, queen of wealth and empress of snobbery, you, O noble lady are one of them. Your cast-offs are countless; one could make a small army of your former favorites. Now, you have desired to add the spice of exoticism to your sensations, for the velvet eyes of a certain animal-tamer, as handsome as Rama himself, have lent a few palpitations to your dried-up heart.

That was your right, beautiful seductress–but right should not be forgetful of duty. Why, given the accusations brought against him, have you not declared that on the night of Lord Bencenave's murder, at the hour when the crime as committed, you met him at the door of Kensington Palace, on the Exhibition Road side? That conversation in your car lasted until 2:30 a.m.

Why have you not said that on the night of Lady Verte-mer's murder, the accused was dining with you at a nautical and social club of which you are the sovereign? That supper did not end until the early hours of the morning. Why have you kept silent regarding these facts, which would have made an incompetent and narrow-minded policeman reflect? Why, on the contrary, have you made sure that this loyal creature was brought down? Because, as you know, his respect for your honor prevented him, in spite of everything, from revealing your shared secrets. Do not play the part of a petty Margue-rite de Bourgogne [104] *–do the right thing. You have among your acquaintances a person influential at court; his complic-ity has allowed you to crush an innocent man. Well then, with his help, repair the damage you have done. Obtain for the accused the right to a proper and open trial.*

We shall not hesitate to make this tribune a pulpit for the defense. Until we are satisfied, we shall continue to publish our open letters and sensational revelations.

The brave fellow had signed it: *James Macfull*.

It is easy to imagine the divorcée's rage when a copy of the *Daily Herald*–which she had never been in the habit of reading–was brought to her by express delivery. The article was ringed in blue pencil. A violent attack of nerves was the result of reading it. Then, innumerable telephone calls from her friends began to arrive.

Her namelessly castigated admirers placed themselves at her disposition for the correction of the impudent journalist who posed as a judge, and to get rid of him if the need arose. They were assuming that the article was grotesque nonsense. Although that was the opinion expressed by gentlefolk, the public thought very differently, and became far more sympa-thetic to Rama.

Sullivan's own blood had curdled in his veins, and he owed his life to the enlightened care of Mrs. Smithson. A tele-phone call had arrived immediately afterwards which shook him again; he was told: "The prisoner Baber, not having escaped from Newgate yesterday, demands to make important revelations."

Despite his agonized feet, Sullivan went down his stairs four at a time. Within half an hour, he was listening to the confidences of the director of Rama's menagerie. This time, he was exultant. The Hindu confessed to all the mysterious crimes, which he had perpetrated out of hatred for the English, at whose hands he had suffered greatly. He had taken pleasure in killing Lord Bencenave, Lady Vertemer and General Ferund, who had mistreated him in the course of their service in India. As for Sir Edmund Sexton, he was also the man who had strangled him and carved him up, to avenge his brother Rao, who had been martyrized in the course of a fantastic experiment, made for the sole purpose of demonstrating Sexton's science.

Trembling with joy, Nimbly, Sullivan and the two attorneys who were present posed numerous questions. To what extent had Rama been his accomplice? How had the murders been accomplished? What had become of the victims' corpses? Baber only answered the first question: "Rama took no part in these affairs, of which he was entirely ignorant. He had already left Rotherhill, in order not to hear Sexton insulting Hindus. I caught up with him a little later. An indefatigable walker, the animal-tamer had not hesitated to make the 60-mile journey from Rotherhill to London on foot. As I was in a car, I overtook him, and did not breathe a word of what had happened. By virtue of that, his astonishment when they came to arrest him is perfectly comprehensible, as is his resistance. He knew from hearsay the kind of justice that the conquerors deliver. In those circumstances, you will understand why he was so eager to follow his liberators."

Having decided to make these revelations to establish the innocence of his marvelous nephew, Baber had not wanted to profit from the deliverance. He would have made his confession immediately if anyone had deigned to interrogate him, but the interrogation had been limited to Rama. He refused to answer the other questions, swearing that he would never say anything more and demanding to be executed as rapidly as possible.

An eager accumulator of evidence of guilt, Sullivan threatened to force the Hindu to talk. Then, having rolled up his sleeve, Baber took a steel paper-knife from the table. He transpierced the bare arm completely in several places, and did it without losing his indefinable smile. "You can subject me to torture," he said, "but nothing will oblige me to weaken. I shall not say a word."

Confronted with this ferocious evidence of his insensibility, the questioning was suspended. Baber was taken back to his cell, where the prison doctor came to attend to him.

Then, with all possible speed, Sullivan went to his office and set about writing a press release. His was a veritable triumph; the guilty party had confessed; he would muzzle the scribblers and give that rascal Macfull a clip round the ear.

He was so absorbed in his article that he did not hear his office door open, nor see that a man had come in. The newcomer came to stand behind him and read over his shoulder. All of a sudden, the inspector started. A mocking voice said: "Good morning, my dear chap. You aren't going to send that tissue of nonsense to the press, are you? You're insistent, then, that the police should continue to be held up to ridicule?"

. Sullivan turned around, as if he had been bitten by a snake. Doctor Eric Palmer was there, smiling. It was he who had made the cutting remarks.

Although Sullivan had ability, he was not lacking in grievous faults: he believed himself to be infallible, was possessed of immeasurable pride, and tended to forget to be thankful. He forgot, therefore, that he owed his position as Chief Inspector to Doctor Palmer, and replied vehemently: "My work doesn't concern you, since you're not on the case. You might like to stop joking."

"Agreed, Sullivan. But I still have the right to amuse myself by discovering the real guilty party and proving, dear Sullivan, that you're a birdbrain, as the *Daily Herald* says."

A furious anger took hold of the detective. "You're jealous!" he howled. "Jealous because someone has surpassed you in clarifying this affair."

"No, old fellow. If I had put my nose in after the first crime, you would simply have been my assistant, and..."

"Do you think so? You don't know, then, that your stock has fallen at Scotland Yard since your failure in Benares?"

"Fortunately compensated by the arrest of the Hong Kong slaughterer–made on your behalf, old boy." Palmer's voice had hardened; nothing was more calculated to bring out his character than an accusation of mediocrity. "You silly fool, in the affair in question, I explained to Lord Chapfain, the Governor of Calcutta, that I had motives that a man like you cannot grasp. His loyal and good soul understood immediately. You have just insulted a friend who has done a great deal for you and is ready to do more. I wanted to tell you, charitably, that you are in error and that I have come to help you."

"Go to the Devil! I have no need of your obsolete science. You're finished, old chap–replaced by a younger man!"

"By a younger man I've recommended–you're right. Be careful you don't drown in your own saliva, *old chap*, and good day to you!"

This was said with considerable sarcasm. Sullivan struck a boxer's pose, ready to affirm his superiority. Palmer, however, made no response, having already departed and closed the door.

The doctor hesitated in the courtyard of Scotland Yard for a quarter of an hour, tempted to let events take their course–but he thought of Grace and of his vocation. He loved her too much, and that held him back. Then again, it pained him to see the police ridiculed and on the point of committing an unpardonable error.

He told himself that he had been so happy in his little house in Plymouth, along with his fishing boat, with John for his crew. How tranquil it had been between the sky and the sea, being gently rocked by the lapping waves, spending nights beneath a gold-powdered sky, with the soft song of the wind in the rigging... a poetic ideal! Why had he plunged back into the inferno of London, to be jostled at every step, to hear trumpets, horns, bells, street-traders crying out, cockneys arguing–to suffer the fever of the immense city?

He reached the main gate. As he stepped through it, he remembered his arrival at the house he had abandoned more than six months ago: Grace's distraught greeting, throwing herself into his arms, sobbing, confiding at the same time the secret of her heart and her desperation. He had been initially startled by the confession of love, about which he was dubious. But how could he, a defender of the equality of men and of races, oppose the accomplishment of his theories? He did not even have the pretext of Felifax's guilt to license an objection, because he knew him to be incapable of black-heartedness.

He did not give the possibility any more credit when Grace told him the story she had had from Djina's lips that morning. His honest soul was revolted by the infamy of Edmund Sexton; could one take refuge in science to commit such atrocities? For a son to take revenge on his mother's torturer was excusable; it was a formidable extenuating circumstance, without taking account of the possible atavism of his feline ancestry. However, in spite of that, Palmer refused to believe in Felifax's crime. A man like that would not attack his enemy treacherously–he would strike him down face-to-face. His profound psychology was certain of not being mistaken. He had come here to demonstrate the inanity of those accusations to Sir Harold Nimbly.

Unlike Sullivan and many others, he had the advantage of knowing Felifax, who had saved his life in the Benares jungle, as he had saved Grace. There was a debt to be paid; he must not fail in his task. He must save him from the gallows and bring the real guilty party before the judge.

Another man might have thought his mission ended. Had he not just read Baber's confession over Sullivan's shoulder, absolving the animal-tamer from all guilt? Well, no. Baber's confession was false. Palmer had got to know the man in Benares, as an affiliate of the police, and believed in his honesty. Events might perhaps prove otherwise, but if that were the case, he would admit that he had been wrong, while having the satisfaction of having done his duty.

Suddenly decided, he retraced his steps and went up to the commissioner's office. From the welcome he received, he deduced that Sullivan had preceded him. Although the other remained affable, he sensed that the commissioner was somewhat restrained. When he explained that he had come to place himself at the disposal of Scotland Yard for the complete clarification of the troublesome mystery, he was amazed to be told: "I'm awfully sorry, my friend. You put in your resignation despite my pleas; you picked out your successor yourself. I was quite happy to make it official; you'll understand that it's impossible for me to go back on it."

"Sullivan isn't infallible, sir; anyone might have been taken in as he has..."

"You alone can see clearly, I suppose?"

Palmer understood the sarcasm; it lashed him like a whip. For the first time, he felt compelled to defend himself and replied harshly: "I believe, sir. that I have sometimes given you proof of my... luck. In any case, when I stuck my nose in an affair, the police were not treated as they are today by virtually all the newspapers. Yes, sir, I alone could have seen clearly, for I would have looked for the solution in its causes. Your Sullivan has not done that."

"We have the guilty man's confession."

"Do you believe it, Sir Harold? In that case, I understand the arrogance of your Chief Inspector. Send his report to the papers, then. Their customary laughter will become a great tumult, aimed at you. Before long, the true culprit will be dragged to the Gemonies–by me!"[105]

"For that, Palmer, it's necessary to be authorized by us. Don't count on it!"

A bitter rancor swelled in the heart of the man who was normally so good and calm, and made him aggressive, almost to the point of spite.

"Do you believe, Sir Harold, that your investiture is so very necessary? The master of us all, the great Sherlock Holmes, often acted without the support of your services. I have striven to follow in his noble tracks. I am minded to imitate him again."

"At ease, Sir Eric. Sherlock Holmes, you know, without being officially invested, could always rely on a sympathetic response when he asked for our services. It will not be the same for you; I shall give orders accordingly."

"So be it! I accept the challenge. Keep your services, Sir Harold, I don't care. I could offer you a tournament; I would have the support of the entire press and public opinion–but no, I have too much respect for the administration with which I have collaborated for more than 25 years to cut it off at the knees. My inquiries will be discreet; I shall break no windows, and before long, forgetting what you have said, I shall bring you the name of the guilty party."

He made a farewell gesture, and went down the stairs muttering to himself. What had he got himself into? What a fool he was to get into a fight with the administration, when he ought to have been doing battle with the fish in the Channel. But the triumph of justice sustained him; he would put everything into the job and emerge victorious. It would certainly be very arduous without the aid of various police services, but bah! He would proceed carefully and overcome the difficulties.

To begin with, he went to the cold room that served as a morgue, where the macabre remains of the carver's victims were kept. Among policemen, Sir Eric Palmer was considered glorious, so when he learned that Sir Eric was taking an interest in the affair, the keeper of the cold store greeted him joyfully and let him in.

For nearly an hour, as a detective and a doctor, Palmer examined the collection of arms, hands, feet and heads. He studied the fingernails, eyelids, tear-ducts and corners of the mouths with the aid of a magnifying-glass, and an enigmatic smile passed over his lips.

"Kerrigan," he said to the attendant, putting an affectionate hand on his shoulder, "you and I are old comrades. Could you devote yourself entirely to me?"

"You can depend on it, Sir Eric. You got me this job, and brought me out of poverty. Thanks to you, I've been able to educate my children..."

"I need the help of a brave man such as you, and it pains me to have to ask you for a small favor. Kerrigan, no one must know that I'm working on the case and that I've been allowed to examine the victims' remains."

"You can count on me, sir. I'll be as silent as the grave. It's the least I can do."

"I still have to ask a more serious favor. Are you still living in the lodgings adjacent to this station?"

"Yes, sir."

"Well then, one night this week, will you let me into the laboratory, along with your frozen specimens? I'll need about two hours with them."

"Whenever you wish, Sir Eric. The laboratory shutters are closed every night. No light will be visible outside. No one will suspect your presence. What does it matter, anyway, if there are consequences? The place is yours, since you gave it to me."

The detective shook the brave man's hand and went out, heading for his own residence. He would allow himself until tomorrow to reflect and to re-read the details relating to the murders provided by the various newspapers.

After the doctor's departure, Sir Harold Nimbly felt ill at ease. The damned fellow had unsettled him considerably. Why was he so sure that the guilty party was still running around? He seemed damnably certain of what he said.

The head of Scotland Yard knew the doctor, who was called "the king of detectives" the world over, very well. He said nothing lightly, and when he got involved in an affair, it was with the certainty of bringing to a successful conclusion. His stubbornness was proverbial; nothing got in his way in the pursuit of the truth. Then again, what further scorn would be poured on the police if the detective, free and working in secret, succeeded in proving a new and painful error? However, as he could not go back on his decision, he resolved not to hinder him in any way. To that end, he telephoned Sullivan to tell him to stay calm and to hold on to his press release until he received further orders. It was better not to say anything about Baber's confession.

The Chief Inspector took this blow so hard that he went home feeling ill, with all the symptoms of jaundice. It was a splendid opportunity for Mrs. Smithson to prove the extent of her affectionate devotion to her cherished lodger.

Grace had not yet come in when the doctor got home. He found John there with his luggage, brought from Plymouth. The Scotsman had resumed his duties and was already busy cooking the evening meal. The stout fellow said: "Miss Molly does not seem to be thinking about her bath any longer. She's waiting for news of her niece."

A telegram was sent immediately to reassure the aged spinster and inform her that all was well.

Grace was at the *Daily Herald*, where James Macfull was amusing himself in a child-like manner. The reporter had just received his sixteenth challenge to a duel since that morning. Lady Deborah Moorhen's courtiers and flatterers had come one by one to demand reparation for the injury his article had done to a lady.

The journalist's mocking reply had been the same in every case: "The status of the person I designated under the name of Lady D. M. is of scant importance to me; in any case, she conducted herself disgracefully. You must have very little respect for her to have recognized her so easily."

"No jokes, sir. Yes or no–will you agree to stand and fight?"

"Are you so determined on a duel? I don't see anything inconvenient about it, I suppose—on the contrary, it would be remarkable publicity for my paper. Indeed, it would no longer be able to hide the designated woman behind simple initials. Moreover, everyone would then see that one of Mr. Sullivan's chatterboxes is capable of dying on the field of honor on behalf of the press. You'll have to wait until I've made a list of all the challenges. I'll number them in sequence; it will certainly be a fine and numerous society, for I've only just begun my campaign."

"We shall stop it in advance!" howled the gallants.

"By suppressing me? Reassure yourselves, gentlemen, that my death will not suppress the effect; there's a whole heap of brave lads at the paper ready to continue it—and behind them, all the journalists in England and the entire world. No one muzzles the press!"

What objection could be raised to that? The greater number of the matadors were disarmed. Lady Deborah promised unlimited favors to the man who could put an end to the campaign and put down its author, but in vain.

Without the least disquiet, Macfull prepared a new article with the items of information gleaned by Grace. The latter returned home in time for dinner and, during the meal, her father told her what had happened at Scotland Yard. The young woman's thankful kisses recompensed him for his decision.

"My dear Grace," he asked her, abruptly, "are you going to work with Hanson tomorrow at his laboratory in New Burlington House?"

"Yes, daddy—we have some experiments to do."

"I shall have need of his intelligence one evening this week and I'll seek him out. Tell him that."

After dinner, they chatted. Suddenly, shaking out his pipe, Palmer asked: "Would you care to take a turn around Kensington Palace, my darling? I'm curious to know how Sullivan has organized the blockade of the circus."

The young woman was ready in an eye-blink, and a car carried them towards the important monument. Without showing himself overtly, Palmer made the tour. There was certainly no lack of policemen, who were having some difficulty moving on numerous curiosity-seekers. There was, however, nothing hostile in the crowd's attitude, merely a simple desire to see.

The blockade was solid; no one could go in or out. The rule was bent, however, for the knacker's lorry bringing the joints of horsemeat necessary to feed the animals.

On the side of the lorry Palmer read:

Fred Maclean

Horsemeat Dealer–Bethnal Green

Moreover, he heard one of the delivery men explaining to a policeman that the meat was late because of the size of the order.

The doctor detective wanted to go all the way around the building. A few escapes might have been contrived during the surveillance, but they would be difficult. He and Grace arrived in Exhibition Road as the monumental clock on the Oratory Church chimed ten. The church was the most beautiful edifice in London built in the Renaissance style, and was situated to the east of South Kensington

At that moment, a strange cry echoed in the darkness.

"It sounds like a vulture," Palmer remarked. "Undoubtedly a signal!"

He had not finished his sentence when cries of fright suddenly broke out and they saw two bounding masses coming out of Kensington Palace, breaking through the police cordon and disappearing into a small van stationed a short distance away. It departed immediately at breakneck speed.

Felifax had done as he had promised; he had come in search of Rudra and Durgane.

XII: The Cold Room

Eric Palmer worked with rectitude; Sullivan would have been well-advised to follow the same method, into which he had been initiated. Palmer never hurried. He never made up his mind until he had given a matter a great deal of thought. Having arrived home after his excursion to Kensington Palace, Sir Eric went to bed and to sleep.

It was different for Grace; what she had seen frightened her. The two tigers fleeing from Kensington and meekly getting into the van could only have been Felifax's favorite tigers, Rudra and Durgane, about whom Djina talked constantly. Although they obeyed the animal-tamer like pet dogs, their ferocity might be terrible if he released them. What did the young man intend to do with such fearful auxiliaries? Might he not declare war on society and set himself outside the law, in spite of Sir Eric Palmer's efforts to prove him innocent.

She passed an almost sleepless night, but departed early nevertheless for her laboratory, after a light breakfast with her father.

Without hurrying, the doctor went out at 9 a.m. and headed straight for Downing Street. He presented himself at the Department of Colonial Administration–specifically, the India Office. He knew that he would find numerous friends there. They gave him the most charming of welcomes and gave him the use of a special office. There, he was given access to the files concerning the sojourns in India of Lord Bencenave, Lady Vertemer, General Ferund and Surgeon-Major Sexton.

Renowned as the queen of colonial powers, England has not usurped that reputation. It is, in fact, impossible to find a more complete organization. Every English citizen departing for a colony or a dominion is immediately entitled to a dossier in which all his actions are recorded, however simple. What is recorded there, above all else, is the nature of his relationship with the natives: the manner in which he treats them, and the manner in which he is regarded by them. It is necessary to provide work for an army of policemen supported at great expense in the different protectorates. That institution achieved its masterpiece in the India Office. The entire life of the subcontinent's colonists is contained in its files.

The esteem in which Doctor Palmer was held warranted the rare favor of being allowed to see all the dossiers, which he went through with extreme care. From time to time, he could have been heard to murmur:

"Quite bizarre!"[106]

The India Office, a powerful and well-equipped organization, is also responsible for relations with Hindus resident in the Metropolis. Special functionaries are allocated to this service, and have a duty to visit the natives for whom they are responsible. After spending more than an hour with the files on the carver's victims, the doctor detective went to the relevant office and asked to see the list of Hindus making up the staff of Rama's Circus Menagerie. A few minutes later, he was not only presented with a complete list, but also their photographs and fingerprints. He examined the names and studied the photographs one by one. Several times more the habitual phrase escaped his lips: "Quite bizarre!"

Palmer was certainly demanding that morning, for he asked to see the functionaries responsible for the circus, and when he was introduced to them, he interrogated them.

"All the Hindus are recorded on this list?"

"Yes, sir. We've checked and rechecked, and are continuing to do so twice a week. The list is rigorously exact."

"You're certain that every man and woman resembles his photograph?"

"Without a doubt, sir. They were not only photographed on their departure from Calcutta but again by the anthropometric service on their arrival in London, with new fingerprints. Here are the ones made here–you may compare them."

With admirable patience, Palmer compared the 600 photographs taken in Calcutta with the 600 taken in London, and then did the same with the fingerprints. There was no difference. His exclamations of "Quite bizarre!" became even more expressive.

The doctor was not yet convinced. He went to the office of the senior civil servant, and sent a radiogram, in the conventional cipher, to Lord Chapfain, the Governor of Bengal, asking for an immediate response.

Content with his morning's work, he ate a large lunch, for he had the appetite of a man used to the open air. Then, at his usual pace, he left for Stoke Newington to visit Lord Bencenave's house in Green Street. His second expedition was to Lady Vertemer's townhouse in the Strand and Pretty Lane. He finished off at Bedford Square, where the apartment of the dancer Dorothy Mason, the friend of Genera Ferund, was carefully examined by his expert eye.

He was surprised not to encounter any objection to his investigations on the part of the police officers keeping watch on the crime scenes; on the contrary, they offered to help. Had Sir Harold, then, not issued any orders concerning him? He was glad of that. It would have been painful for him to set himself against the Administration. In spite of it, though, he decided not to make use of the services of Scotland Yard and its various items of machinery.

It was 6 p.m. when he got home. While waiting for dinner, Sir Eric Palmer set about reading the newspapers. Astonishingly, none of the dailies reported Baber's confession. This was proof that his observations had been taken seriously. The laborious report compiled by Sullivan had been suppressed. A broad smile lit up his face. His prestige was still effective.

All the papers devoted several columns to Rama and his crimes, but there was no incitement in the articles, no demands for the presumed murderer to pay the supreme penalty. What was said about him was recorded disinterestedly, and was mostly fantastic. Some said that he was the son of a powerful Maharajah. Others asserted that, in spite of his youth, he had been educated by fakirs and had become a master of all the occult sciences: suspended animation, levitation, and–above all–hypnotic domination. Yet others claimed to have it from a reliable source that he had been forced by the sect of Thugs, the famous and feared stranglers, to assist in human sacrifices, and that he had sworn an oath to obey their destructive deity.

Sir Eric Palmer skimmed through this gossip. He knew the secret of Rama's origin now, and his psychological knowledge gave him a profound insight into its implications. He read James Macfull's articles in the *Daily Herald* much more attentively, however. The latter, with journalistic shrewdness, refrained from reporting imagined details and there was no malice in his copy. He sought to sow doubt in the minds of his readers with regard to the accusations made against the animal-tamer, following up on the alibis he had mentioned in his open letter to Lady D. M.

As he had promised, Macfull continued his revelations and–without specifying his source–gave a precise account of the wild boar hunt organized at Rotherhill. He recounted the fabulous feat accomplished by the accused in killing a reputedly ferocious solitary boar with his bare hands. He gave specific details of the dinner: the libations had been more than numerous; by the time the toasts were made, everyone was intoxicated, especially the surgeon Sexton.

In a further open letter to Lady D. M., even harsher than the first, he asked her to explain the advice she had given to her guests: firstly, not to make any mention of Sexton's lamentable ramblings preceding his murder; secondly, to be unanimous in giving testimony against the animal-tamer Rama–testimony whose substance had been agreed between themselves.

He ended by addressing the Lord Chancellor:

Can Your Lordship tolerate such persecution? Are the rich allowed to do that for which the poor are severely punished by the law?

How angry the divorcée was when she read this! How had the wretched journalist learned all these details? She was sure of all of the people who had been at Rotherhill that evening–none of them was capable of betraying her thus. Then she remembered that she had dismissed a young waiter on the day after the crime. What had he done? He had spoken enthusiastically about Rama, declaring him incapable of having committed the crime of which he had been accused. Yes, that was the source of the most recent *coup*. She began to dread further and more intimate revelations from the man, who had been in her service for three years. He had been witness to numerous orgies.

She had good cause to tremble. The first thing the waiter had done on arriving in London was to seek out the journalist who was not afraid to attack the aristocratic lady head on. He had taken great pleasure in giving him the results of his covert espionage, without omitting any scabrous secret. James Macfull was a man of honor. He did not wish to make use of the latter weapons, dragging the moral turpitude of a highly-placed woman of such puritan appearance into the light. He only published the details relating to Sexton's death. This new article provoked a second explosion of interest.

Anticipating its success, the *Daily Herald* had tripled its print run; even so, by 10 a.m. it was impossible to find a single copy for sale in the whole of London.

Palmer had a connoisseur's appreciation of the quality of the article. He was not unaware of the friendly relationship established between Grace and Macfull, and had decided to talk to the fellow in the case of excessive ill will or open hostility on the part of Scotland Yard. The two of them would increase the *Daily Herald*'s worldly renown by means of a campaign waged against the Administration and the lamentable errors it had committed.

Grace interrupted him in his reflections; she had been wandering around Whitechapel in the hope of obtaining some news of Felifax. Alas, she came back empty-handed, having not heard the least hint of gossip anywhere. Even the march on Newgate seemed to have been a mirage–but the police presence seemed to have been reinforced. The young woman was worried. Would the animal-tamer get into a fight with the policemen? The latter's orders would be very strict in that regard, especially since the escape of the tigers. The order must have been given to shoot without warning.

Exhausted by her excursion to the populous district, and by her lack of sleep the previous night, Grace ate sparingly and went straight to bed thereafter. Nature reasserted its rights; she fell into a profound sleep almost immediately.

Palmer stayed up smoking in his study. At about 10:30 a.m., he left the house, accompanied by John, and was driven to New Burlington House, where Hanson ought to be expecting him. The savant had, in fact, replied to the young woman's announcement that her father might have need of his services: "I'll be working on my experiments for much of the night; Palmer can find me at the New Burlington laboratory until 1 a.m."

On seeing his old comrade–who he had not seen for six months–come in, Hanson shook his hand effusively. He had regretted the great detective's premature retirement more than anyone else. He admired him, and it pleased him greatly to see him return to the breach.

"My dear friend," Palmer said, "I need the benefit your science to help me to elucidate the troubling mystery of the carver. I swore not to get involved any more in police matters, but it's a matter of my darling Grace's happiness, and–at the same time–of paying a debt of gratitude owed to a loyal fellow with a magnificent soul."

"It's unnecessary to tell me all that, old man. You have need of me; everything I possess is at your disposal. Where are you taking me?"

"To see some dead people!"

"Well, that's not the most amusing call to pay, and they certainly aren't in Piccadilly Circus–so where are your dead people to be found?"

"In the cold room at Scotland Yard."

"Why aren't we going by day, when the mortuary [107] doesn't seem quite as sinister?"

"Ill-will on the part of the service, annoyed by..."

"Really! I'm yours, Sir Eric–what shall I bring?"

295

"Reagents for researching toxins in the human body, especially those permitting their precise identification. John will come with us to carry them."

Professor Hanson had the requested accessories ready in a trice. Once John was loaded up, the three of them quit New Burlington House.

Kerrigan, forewarned of the timing of their visit during the day, accompanied them to the mortuary. The building was situated in Scotland Yard and its entrance was in the street, next to the Black Museum where the famous collection of all manner of objects used in crimes is to be found. The three men had no need to go into police headquarters, but they had left their vehicle at Charing Cross for the sake of prudence.

Kerrigan led them into the little laboratory used for autopsies, and put the refrigerated box containing the sinister remains at their disposal. Hanson examined them carefully. As Palmer had asked, he began by making the same observations.

"My dear Palmer," he said suddenly, "I concur absolutely with the opinion you offered en route: the victims, save for Sexton, were anaesthetized before being cut up, doubtless to avoid too much loss of blood, and for another reason, which the inquest will doubtless establish."

"It is still possible to identify the nature of the toxin?"

"We shall get there! The reddish rings that we observe on the nails, the abnormal whiteness of the region around the tear-ducts, the tumefaction of the eyelids and the violet foam dried up in the corners of the mouth reveal a violent poison, perhaps not in large enough quantity to kill on being introduced into the bloodstream, but powerful enough, at any rate, to immobilize a human being for several hours."

By means of the apparatus brought by John, the professor took minute samples from the remains, analyzed them with mathematical precision, and finally declared, after an hour of labor and scientific research: "It isn't possible for me to specify the exact composition of the anaesthetic, but I can assure you that it contains extracts of curare. I can even affirm that these extracts were vaporized near to the subjects and absorbed by inhalation. Look at Lady Vertemer's nostrils, and General Ferund's."

Palmer's face was a curious sight at that moment; it shone with extraordinary brilliance. "Tomorrow morning, Hanson," he asked, "can you come with me to Lady Vertemer's house in the Strand? Everyone there slept for a long time. Perhaps it was caused by your poison."

"Listen, my friend–if the thing exists, we'll find traces of it. They can't escape my means. We might profit from performing the same operation at Lord Bencenave's house and General Ferund's."

"Now, Hanson, would you like to examine the sections and tell me if you notice anything."

"Yes, I'm astonished by their neatness; one might have thought that they were done with a guillotine. They weren't made by a saw; the bones exhibit none of the splintering invariably left by a surgical saw or any other sort."

"I'm glad to hear you say that, and I think I've guessed the kind of instrument that was employed. I hope to have confirmation within 48 hours. Now, my old comrade, let's not prolong our visit. Everything has gone well thus far; let's not leave the brave Kerrigan to endure his anxiety any longer."

The apparatus was repacked, and half an hour later each of the savants was in his own home.

Meanwhile, something alarming was happening. During his periods of police work, Palmer sang as he got undressed, and the song he sang that night was his own composition:

Stubborn old Sullivan
I'll drown you in your spit! [108]

Ah, if the doctor had been able to see his old comrade at that moment, he would have taken pity on him. Sullivan was receiving a visitor at that inappropriate hour, and his nocturnal visitors were by no means ordinary; they comprised a man and two tigers.

Felifax, reiterating his *coups* in Benares, well able to frighten the most courageous man to death, had decided to pay the detective back for the blows he had received from him.

Making use of the van that one of Blood-drinker's friends had put at his disposal, he had departed with Rudra and Durgane for Jane Street, where the policeman lived. The address given by the newspapers in the course of their dithyrambic eulogies was now known to anyone who feared him.

Shut up inside the van with his two terrible auxiliaries, the leader of wild beasts held them in his steely grip and murmured friendly encouragements to prevent them from roaring. Motor vehicles were not a means of locomotion with which tigers were familiar; Rudra and Durgane did not seem to care for it overmuch. The driver was in his seat and beside him was a silent individual with a vulpine face nicknamed Master Key by virtue of his ability to get through any door without making the slightest sound. The latter had been briefed by Blood-drinker and instructed to gain access to the detective's house, if possible without waking him up.

Sullivan was sleeping deeply, somewhat sedated by a soporific tea administered by Mrs. Smithson. In order to be closer to her lodger while attending to his jaundice, the widow had reopened the communicating door and was ready to come running in response to the faintest call.

Despite the profundity of his sleep, Eric Palmer's successor was woken up by warm breath on his face and a strong odor. After opening his eyes, he shut them immediately, releasing a stifled groan. He believed that he was still in the grip of a frightful nightmare. He had just seen a tiger's muzzle no more than a foot from his face, with a tongue lolling out of its gaping mouth, and large phosphorescent eyes, green with yellow striations, staring at him.

Reopening his eyes for a second time, he saw the same scene–accompanied this time by a vibrant voice that he seemed to recognize.

"Mr. Sullivan," it said, "you forgot the other day, during my interrogation, that I am a Hindu. In my country, an insult is always repaid, even if it requires centuries. Moreover, a severe punishment is reserved in India for those who respond to favors received with hatred. In Whitechapel, I prevented you from being lit up like a torch, your precious person being inundated with gin. You thanked me by striking me in a cowardly fashion, while I was tightly chained on your orders. Why?"

Sullivan was brave, but he had gooseflesh nevertheless. Before his eyes, now fully awake, was the most terrifying of spectacles: the tall figure of the animal-tamer Rama was standing over his bed, restraining his monstrous felines with his powerful hand.

It was thus that Felifax had shown himself in Benares, giving everyone the impression of being the son of Kali; conscious of the terror imposed by that vision, he was desirous of imposing it upon the mind of the policeman before making him pay for his mortal offense. Quite calmly, he continued: "Mr. Sullivan, I asked you why you struck me in a cowardly manner. I repeat my question for the second and last time. The next time, I shall instruct my two friends to interrogate you, and I ought to warn you that they have not eaten well today."

Sullivan sat up with a violent start, and murmured in slightly strangled voice: "How do you expect me to be able to reply, when you interrogate by means of terror?"

"And you, Sullivan, by means of cruelty! I still bear the marks of your blows, and those of the chains that you imposed upon me."

"With a criminal of your type, one does not take chances."

"I shall not discuss that question with you, but with my judges–at least, I shall hope so. I gave you my word that I was innocent. I shall not insist on that, but I intend to punish you for your ingratitude."

"By having me eaten by your tigers? The procedure is more cowardly than those you reproach. Firstly, there is no ingratitude on my part–rather you have made me suffer in trying to direct accusations against me. Nothing could redeem the tortures endured by an honest man like me at the thought of being taken for the most dastardly of murderers. Ah, you're a master! To remove my specially-made shoes from my home and use them to plant incriminating footprints, then to replace them in my wardrobe after having used them at Lady Verte-mer's, accompanied by a bloodstained towel. That's why I hit you–your intervention in Sweetheart's Bar in Whitechapel no longer counted for anything; all that remained was my anger at having you in front of me."

Felifax listened. The policeman pronounced these words in a strained voice; tears appeared at the corners of his eyes at the memory of those frightful moments, at the memory of the shame afflicting a loyal servant suspected of the most heinous of crimes. The young animal-tamer's generous and compas-sionate soul was moved. He recognized the man's sincerity.

But Rudra let out a roar. He had seen Sullivan make a move towards the service revolver set on his night-stand. The roar halted the movement and brought Mrs. Smithson running. In her sleep, she had taken it for an appeal by her sick lodger.

On her entrance into the room, confronted by a vision that she would never forget in her entire life, a stifled moan escaped her throat. She collapsed in a heap, unconscious.

It seemed that Rama had not seen her. He was staring at Sullivan. The softness of his voice astonished the man on the brink of a terrible death. "Sullivan, I came here with the idea of giving my friends a meal worthy of them–cutlets of English policeman–but Brahma has put into my animal-keeper's body the soul of a gentle creature whose life was nothing but one long martyrdom, thanks to one of your compatriots. I cannot see suffering; I cannot spill blood. Think on those last words, master detective, and do not treat your prisoners as badly in future–there may be innocent men among them."

Using his prodigious strength to drag away the two re-calcitrant felines–desolate at the loss of an abundant supper–he left the room and went back to the vehicle. At that moment, a police patrol hurried toward the van, intent on asking for some explanation of why it was parked at the corner of Waterloo Road.

The van departed like a whirlwind before the policemen were able to bid it farewell with a few pistol shots.

Sullivan, still flabbergasted and trembling like a leaf at the peril he had just been in, was at the telephone, demanding to speak to Sir Harold Nimbly. He brought him up to date regarding the provocation to which he had been subjected. He demanded a force large enough to track the man who had dared to threaten him in his own home to his lair in Whitechapel or St. Giles's. The detective definitely had a heart of stone, and would never be able to comprehend the elevation of a soul.

XIII: A Titanic Struggle

"In conformity with my promise, Sir Harold, I am bringing you the name of the carver and have come to ask you for an arrest warrant."

Doctor Eric Palmer had just been introduced into the office of the head of Scotland Yard. This fashion of self-presentation caused the commissioner to start. He looked at the genial detective with wide eyes. Would he merit once again his nickname of "the king of detectives"? Having had no news of Palmer since their last interview, and no other interested party having notified him of the detective's movements, Nimbly had assumed that the other's resentment had died down. But here he was, four days after his intervention, announcing his success with impressive certainty.

After a pause of five or six seconds, necessitated by emotion, Sir Harold asked: "What is his name?"

"That of a man very powerful in India, a religious leader whose influence is limitless. Until now, he has been taken for a faithful friend of England–he is, however, her deadliest enemy."

"You're speaking in riddles, Sir Eric. What is the man's name?"

"Sourina, overbrahman, high priest of the cult of Kali."

"Where is this person?"

"At Rama's Circus Menagerie."

With a hasty movement, the police commissioner opened a file to take out the list of Hindus making up the troupe, with the intention of consulting it.

Palmer stopped him, with a smile on his lips. "Useless, sir. Sourina's name is not on that list. Yes, there have been a few defects in the operations of the India Office, however legendary their efficiency may be. The minister of Kali has been here since the first day, and he is undoubtedly the secret promoter of the exhibition."

Unnerved by his interlocutor's confidence, Sir Harold asked, with a slight residual reticence: "Are you certain of what you're saying?"

"If I were not, sir, I would not be here. You need be in no doubt; I say nothing without proof. I have seen Sourina myself."

"When was that?"

"Yesterday evening, while delivering meat to the wild beasts."

"What are you telling me?"

"The exact truth, sir. Yesterday evening, I was a delivery man for Maclean's Horsemeat Shop in Bethnal Green, official supplier of Rama's Menagerie. I saw the high priest."

"Could you have been mistaken?"

"I watched him for more than an hour one morning in Benares, in the course of his ritual ablutions. I was disguised as a beggar then. The least of his features is engraved on my memory."

"What you're telling me is amazing. I hardly dare believe it. In any case, the denounced individual is so important that I can't make a decision without the assent of the Lord Chancellor."

"So be it, sir. The important thing is not to beat about the bush. I believe I detected a certain anxiety in Sourina–he could escape us."

"Even so, it's necessary for us to pause for reflection, Sir Eric. The director of the circus has made a formal confession."

"You did not dare to tell the press that, and you did well. It is false–utterly false, believe me–and solely dictated by his devotion to Felifax."

"What's that name again? Felifax?"

"Excuse me, sir–I mean the animal-tamer Rama. Before this evening, you shall know what the name signifies and that the animal-tamer is that man. I know Baber, having worked with him in Benares. He was working for the police. I would have given you a guarantee of his honesty and his innocence if you had deigned to listen to me a little during my first visit. I can tell you this: he is Rama's uncle, although the latter still does not know it."

"But why accuse himself in his place–since, according to you, the young animal-keeper has nothing to do with the murders?"

"The animal-tamer has led a life very far from the circus. Confronted by the case made by Sullivan, Baber was able to believe that one he loved like a son was prey to a madness. He was afraid that an over-expedient justice might be meted out to Rama on the gallows at Newgate. With the fanaticism typical of his race, he wanted to displace the rope to his own neck."

"That's hard to believe!"

"You don't know the Hindus! If we had time, we could interrogate Baber. I'm almost certain that I could get him to admit his subterfuge."

"Why don't we do that?"

"Because we don't have the time. Trust me, sir–let's go to see the Lord Chancellor."

"You're persuasive to the point of nullifying my own judgment, Sir Eric. Let's go."

"We might take Sullivan. The poor devil treated me as a veritable enemy, but he's worked so hard. It would only be just to let him share in the honor a little."

"You're a good and loyal man. Unfortunately, Sullivan is busy today with a particular vengeance. He has sworn to capture Rama, who paid him a nocturnal visit along with his two tigers–to which your protégé nearly served him as lunch. He's taken it to heart."

"Why not leave the boy in peace? Sullivan ought to be happy to be still alive."

"I can't blame him. This Rama has intolerable manners. His rebellion, won't last long, I promise you that. In the meantime, let's leave Sullivan to his own devices–he hasn't captured his quarry yet."

A few minutes later, Nimbly and Palmer were received by the Lord Chancellor. The latter was alarmed, and had his colleague at the India Office summoned. The departments were immediately thrown into turmoil, to the great annoyance of the doctor detective. Once again he regretted not having proceeded with the arrest on his own authority, leaving explanations until later.

Numerous telephone calls were exchanged between the Lord Chancellor, the Treasury and the residence of the President of the Privy Council. Finally, after two hours of delays that set his teeth on edge, the doctor, Sir Harold and several police officers arrived at Kensington Palace.

Remembering the violent reaction to Rama's arrest, the police commissioner thought they ought to take every possible precaution. The amateur detective dissuaded him.

"Prudence is unnecessary, sir. The Hindus won't release the animals in the absence of the tamer; they'd be the first victims!"

"Your Sourina might have escaped, though."

"That would have been difficult, sir. I ought to make a confession on that subject. By using your name, yesterday evening, I had the surveillance tripled and the cordon drawn more tightly. A cat could not have got out."

As they went into the circus, they were immediately confronted by a strange sight. The whole company of Hindus–acrobats, riders, animal-keepers, snake-charmers, artisans and dancers alike–was gathered in mourning before the statue of Kali, which had been brought into the hall.

A corpse, already stiffened by death, was laid out on a kind of catafalque at the foot of the statue. Palmer cursed–the cadaver was Sourina's. Believing that a trick might have been perpetrated by the terrible minister of Kali, he threw himself forward. No doubt was possible, alas! Death had done his work for him.

As a doctor, the detective employed the standard means of examination. He consulted the face and fingernails of the corpse for the tell-tale signs that were already visible on the funereal remains. Then, leaning towards the stunned Nimbly, he said: "Will you have Professor Hanson summoned. He'll confirm my observations. The man has killed himself with curare."

While an officer went to telephone New Burlington House, Nimbly made a roll-call of the Hindus, identifying them with the aid of the list and the photographs. Palmer was right, as usual; Sourina was surplus to their number.

As Djina's name was called, the doctor had the little dancer set apart. Grace had vouched for her faithful friendship and the honesty of her character, made in the image of her adoptive brother. He was questioning her in a paternal manner when Grace arrived with Professor Hanson. She had been at the laboratory and it was she who had taken the telephone call ordering the scientist to Kensington Palace on Sir Eric's behalf. Knowing that her father was in the process of fighting his last battle, the anxious young woman had come with the professor. Why were they asking for Hanson, who had no connection with the police? She ran to Djina, took her in her arms, and proved her utility in being accepted as a confidante by the Hindu girl.

Sourina had been visible anxious for two or three days. He had been warned by a Bengali employed in the India Office that the celebrated detective Sir Eric Palmer was inquiring about the composition of the circus troupe. The evening before, one of the employees of the horsemeat shop had been allowed to enter the private enclosures while delivering the meat. Seized by a great anger, and suspicious that he was a policeman, Sourina had had the man brutally expelled by his Brahmans, whom he held responsible for the fellow's curiosity. Palmer could not help smiling. He recognized the delivery man as himself. He had borne the insults and injuries without protest, having just learned what he wanted to know.

Finally, two hours before the arrival of the police, Sourina had been informed that a warrant for his arrest had been requested, and that preparations were being made for an exemplary punishment. Without losing a minute, he had conferred with his senior Brahmans, given them their orders, and had retreated into a private place in the improvised temple of the goddess Kali. Half a hour later, the news of his death threw the entire troupe into consternation. The priests decided of their own accord to render to his body the supreme honors due to a great pontiff and faithful servant of the redoubtable incarnation.

When Djina had been told that Sourina was the author of the crimes for which her childhood friend had been imprisoned, the girl became livid and began trembling from top to toe. By force of persuasion, pleading the necessity of proving Felifax's innocence, Grace drew grave revelations from her. In a choked voice, Djina ended up confessing that she had observed bloody traces at the foot of the statue of Kali, although Rama had formally prohibited the ritual sacrifice of goats. She also mentioned the droplets found on the bars of the cages of certain tigers, more ferocious than the rest, when she was certain that those bars had been cleaned for the evening performance. The tigers must, therefore, have eaten during the night– an inexplicable thing! Indeed, after the wild beasts' daily meal, no meat remained in the menagerie, to avoid exasperating them.

Now that she thought about it, Djina remembered that that these bloody traces coincided with the mysterious murders. Rama, informed by Lady Deborah Moorhen, had mentioned them to her. At this evocation, the auditors of her confidences felt a shiver. It was futile to look for the cadavers now; the victims had been sacrificed to Kali. After having separated the limbs for disposal at the domiciles, the remainder of each corpse had provided a feast for the tigers. Where could one find a more secure hiding-place? There was no fear of indiscretion; the carnivores' stomachs would not yield up their secret.

"And here is the instrument used in the crime," Palmer put in. He had just taken up one of the sacrificial knives kept, according to custom, in the pedestal of the statue. "With this tool, gentlemen, he could cut off the limbs with a single stroke." The doctor thought that he could detect doubt in his companions' eyes. He insisted: "You can take my word for it,

sir. I've seen it done many times in India. The Brahman sacrificers sever the head of a zebu with a knife like this, as sharp
as a razor and as heavy as a guillotine. Should I furnish proof
using one of the legs of this villain's cadaver? That would be
rather appropriate.

Nimbly opposed the suggestion. He had seen a ferocious
gleam in the eyes of the praying Brahmans at the mention of
the sacrilege. The fanatics were the kind of people who would
die to a man to defend the venerated body. It would be necessary to fight, and a fight would be utterly futile now. By this
suicide, the guilty party had made the most formal of confessions. Professor Hanson had confirmed the cause of death as
curare, the most implacable of poisons. Diplomacy required
that he should not annoy the natives gathered around the
corpse; the repercussions in Benares would be too great and
complications were always to be feared on the part of a fanati-
cized population.

Suddenly, Nimbly cried: "My God! We must go tell Sullivan to stop his campaign against Rama. It will be necessary,
my dear Sir Eric, for you to take the fellow in hand. His testimony is invaluable–he must be able to tell us a great deal
about these affairs."

"Quite wrong! He cannot know anything about the
abominations of his adoptive father; he would never have tolerated them. Yes, I'll run to Whitechapel to prevent a massa-
cre. I'll take Grace, whose intervention will be worth more
than all the police in the United Kingdom."

The young student was of the same opinion. She urged
her father to go; the idea that the man she loved was in danger
filled her with anxiety. At that moment, Djina begged her:
"Take me with you, Miss Grace. My presence might be useful
to you, and I no longer feel safe here. I read my condemnation
in the terrible eyes of the Brahmans a little while ago. They
will never forgive my revelations and will make me pay for
them. I don't want to die before seeing my beloved brother
again."

After consulting her father on the matter, Grace brought the Hindu girl along. They leapt into a police car, leaving Nimbly to see to the closure of the circus. The men on surveillance were called in and the natives put under armed guard. The prostrate Brahmans continued to revere the body of their patriarch.

The vindictive Sullivan had sworn to have the hide of the animal-tamer Rama. Cleverly, he had spread rumors in Whitechapel and the other eccentric districts that a reward of 2,000 pounds sterling had been promised for the rebel's capture. The claimant would receive full remission of his sentence if he were in the hands of the law. By force of supplication, the policeman has persuaded Sir Harold Nimbly to ratify this promise.

The head of Scotland Yard had espoused his Chief Inspector's cause for two reasons: the siege of Newgate Prison and the criticisms of the press in general and James Macfull in particular. In addition, he could not tolerate the danger created by the two liberated tigers.

There is within the criminal class a solidarity unknown anywhere else, but there are false brothers too. The latter must carry out their betrayals in secret, for fear of reprisals.

One of Blood-drinker's former lieutenants, nicknamed the Weasel, bore a grudge against the butcher. Sentenced in his absence to a term of seven years hard labor, he told himself that with 2,000 pounds he could expatriate himself without fear of the Australian prison camps, where punishment for his treason would await him at the hands of his former comrades. He went to see Sullivan.

Events having made him circumspect, the policeman started out fearing a trap, but when the informer had offered to remain hostage until after the operation, he quickly gained confidence and hastened to make the necessary dispositions. Did he not have a free hand in the matter?

The Weasel was, above all else, jealous of Blood-drinker. Before the butcher's escape, he had been in command of his gang, and had acquired a taste for the profits of that viceroyalty. But now, relegated to the second rank–reduced, so to speak, to nothing, while the other rubbed his nose in it with his lavish spending and his conquests–he deeply resented his fall. He gave all the necessary information, explaining in detail how it would be necessary to proceed in order to be successful, and asked to be placed in protective custody. The wretch did not intend to risk his own neck, or the execution reserved for informers in the world of cut-throats and killers.

The operation would take place at 3 p.m. At that hour, robbers tend to lie low, and are more easily gathered in the nest, while honest laborers and housewives are hard at work, minimizing the risks in Whitechapel.

Blood-drinker's lair, in which Felifax was living, was situated in the middle of a sordid terrace named Donkey Street. The house sheltering the butcher and his guest had one floor reserved for the animal-tamer and his two beasts, which were locked up in a room next to his own. He had to make incessant efforts to prevent them from roaring; their characteristic odor mingled with the street's usual stink, not adding perceptibly to the air's pollution. They were well-fed; the whole gang, mobilized by the thought of the force that such auxiliaries could give them in their way of life, kept them abundantly supplied. Thefts of meat had doubled.

Blood-drinker believed that he was safe in his fortress. In any case, had it not been for the Weasel's treachery, no one would ever have thought of looking for him there.

Used to mounting large-scale operations during his service in Hong Kong, Sullivan, scornful of the jaundice that made him resemble a lemon, had organized the attack in a masterly fashion. The brutal butcher's sentries would not be able to give any warning until ten minutes before the operation.

Suddenly, police cars with armored bodywork surged into the neighboring streets, literally blockading Donkey Street. Fifty policemen armed with revolvers and rifles invaded the houses, while four machine-gunners were installed in pairs at either end of the street, ready to rake the narrow thoroughfare.

By now the alarm had been given. Blood-drinker's faithful allies came to group themselves around the butcher, who immediately understood the magnitude of the surprise attack and ordered the retreat. The house had several exits. He advised Rama to find a new retreat. The latter seized the napes of Rudra and Durgane's necks in his fists and they got under way. A chorus of oaths from the first to leave warned them of the futility of flight.

Indeed, the informer had done a thorough job in telling Sullivan about all the exits. They were powerfully covered.

The drinker was a true commander; he examined his little band and took note of his lieutenant's absence. The Weasel was missing; that told him everything. "The filthy Weasel's sold us!" he cried. "Comrades, we have to surrender. Many of you have little on your conscience, and won't be long detained at His Majesty's pleasure. Those will have a sacred duty to fulfill as soon as they get out–they must execute the traitor. Swear it!"

Without exception, their hands were raised. The Weasel would not enjoy the wages of Judas in peace.

Sullivan soon saw a dozen bandits coming out of the designated house, their hands in the air, surrendering discreetly. Once securely handcuffed, they were taken to the cars–but neither Blood-drinker nor Rama was among them.

The butcher had remained by the side of the wanted man. He knew that he could expect no consideration from the police; that being so, he intended to defend the man whose strength and supernatural power he admired to the death. "Comrade," he said, "we're in a bad situation. A cur's tongue has sold us. If we can get out of this street, I know a paradise where the cows won't come. Do you want to risk the whole package?"

"Let's do it."

"You'll have to launch your two rockets on the sheep. We'll take advantage of the stampede to make a run for it."

Felifax nodded his head affirmatively, but the drinker could see that his magnificent black eyes were moist. He leaned over the two beasts he held in his fists and murmured to them in Bengali, as if the creatures could understand him: "Rudra, Durgane, my dear brother and sister, the ferocity of men is threatening us, and we might be going to die. Pardon me for having dragged you away from the gentleness of the jungle."

He kissed them on their muzzles, and felt their rugose tongues return his caress. Then, marching with them into the narrow corridor, as far as the door of the house, he launched them forward, crying: "Djaya Rudra! Djaya Durgane!" The Hindu word corresponds more or less to expressions used to excite hunting-dogs to hurl them after their prey.

The two men got ready to leap out in their turn–but a sinister noise slit the air: *tackatackatack, tackatackatack, tackatackatack.*

"Ah–the pigs have got machine-guns!" the butcher howled.

They had not anticipated that. Almost in unison, two dolorous roars drowned out the noise of the deadly evil.

Careless of the danger, Felifax threw himself outside, followed by the drinker. He cried out in despair. Rudra and Durgane, scythed down in mid-leap by the implacable machine, were stretched on the ground side by side, as they had always lived since birth.

Without trying to hold back his tears, the man knelt down by his beasts. He saw their great luminous eyes fixed upon him. Those eyes were full of despair for a distant country they would never see again; then their brightness vitrified. One final slight shudder shook each magnificent body and the souls of Rudra and Durgane went up to the nirvana of the jungle.

Overwhelmed by misery, Felifax got to his feet unsteadily. Bullets were flying past his ears. What did that matter? Blood-drinker, seeing that he was done for, had opened fire; the police were responding–but Sullivan had given orders that

312

Rama must be taken alive. The policeman wanted to have the satisfaction of making him pay for his nocturnal visit, and of seeing him hang. The hail of bullets died down.

It made no difference to the butcher. He had been hit in the chest three times. His clenched hands groped for the wounds, as if to stem the blood, while he croaked: "Avenge me, Comrade–death to the pigs!" He collapsed in the course of a final blasphemy. Blood-drinker would never endure the prison-camps of Australia.

Still mortified by the death of his favorite tigers, Felifax seemed to be stupefied, but Sullivan's voice made him shiver.

"You're finished, Rama!" cried Mrs. Smithson's lodger. "My turn to laugh!"

The young animal-tamer appeared to have suffered an electric shock. He let out a burst of laughter like a roar, and his voice growled: "No mercy this time, Mr. Sullivan–the deaths of Rudra and Durgane demand vengeance." He gathered himself to pounce.

The policeman understood; the threat was not vain. Changing his tactics, he hastened to cry: "Fire on him! Kill him! That's what he wants!"

The rifles were raised, the revolvers aimed, ready to fire as soon as the anticipated leap was launched.

The shots were never fired, though. A stentorian voice commanded: "Halt, in the King's name!"–and Palmer ran through the ranks, followed by Grace and Djina.

It was Sullivan's turn to let out a howl of rage. The accursed doctor had arrived again to snatch his vengeance away from him. Prey to a sort of dementia, he pointed his revolver at his former comrade and fired.

The two young women cried out in unison. A man had fallen, but that man was not Sir Eric Palmer. It was Felifax, gravely wounded in the chest while saving the life of Grace's father for a second time. Just as he was about to hurl himself upon his mortal enemy, the animal-tamer had been stopped by the intervention the doctor detective, who was marching forward with Grace and Djina. At the same time, he had per-

313

ceived Sullivan's action. Too far away from the gunman to turn the weapon aside, he had made a formidable leap worth of his feline ancestry, placing himself in front of Grace's father just in time. He had taken the bullet destined for the king of detectives.

The other police officers lost no time in disarming Sullivan. Doctor Palmer, crouching over Felifax, shook his head sadly; the wound appeared to be fatal. Grace and Djina, their arms around one another, were sobbing brokenly.

Fortunately, a motorized ambulance was standing by to receive wounded policemen. With infinite care, the unconscious animal-tamer was carried to it.

Palmer instructed one of the officers to make the necessary arrangements for the bodies of the drinker and the two tigers, and then to inform Sir Harold Nimbly of what had happened. Satisfied that it would be done, he got into the ambulance with the wounded man, along with Grace and Djina.

Felifax was taken to Charing Cross Hospital, where Palmer had a friend who was an eminent surgeon, who had already been alerted by telephone.

XIV: The Amateur Detective

That evening, there was a meeting in the quarters of the Lord Chancellor. In the magnificent office next to the ministry were the President of the Privy Council, the minister responsible for relations with the Dominions and high court judges. They were waiting for Doctor Eric Palmer, whose praises were being loudly sung by the newspapers.

Sir Eric arrived at 10 p.m., with a satisfied expression on his face.

"Gentlemen," he began by saying, "I have the pleasure to inform you that, if no unexpected complications arise, Rama will survive his wound. Don't be surprised that I take so much interest in this Hindu, who might, with good reason, seem suspect to you. He has acquired the habit–and that's the right word–of saving my life. I shall soon acquaint you with the measure of that steadfastly loyal man and the grandeur of his soul."

The Lord Chancellor accepted this with a smile. "Above all else, we want to know how you came to suspect the high priest of Kali, Sourina. The Brahman's eminent status obliges us to make a very detailed report to the Indian Government. It will be published in the various states of the subcontinent, so we must prove that his arrest, had it been effected, was backed by a powerful case. We must be more careful than ever not to offend the religious sentiments of the natives, all the more so as Sourina was considered a fervent friend of our country."

Palmer smiled enigmatically. He was enthusiastic to give satisfaction to his peers.

"Gentlemen, permit me a slight digression, which appears to me to be indispensable. I shall get to the subject that interests you very quickly, in any case.

"I admit, perhaps to my great shame, that I was determined to ignore everything that might be happening in London in the judiciary field. When my daughter returned to London

315

to continue her medical studies, I found myself even more detached from the world. My unmarried sister Molly, excited by various facts, tried to force me to take an interest in the mystery of the carver. I ended up threatening to disappear if she continued.

"I knew, however, about the arrest of Blood-drinker for the murders–committed without any associated theft, although that would have been natural. Knowing that, I gave my opinion: Sullivan was mistaken. Respectful of my strict orders, my sister had remained silent about the further exploits of the sadist, when I received a telegram from Grace calling me to London with the utmost urgency.

"As soon as I arrived, she told me that Rama–who had been known to us in Benares under the name of Felifax, and had saved both our lives–was accused of the murders.

"The greatest of my abilities, gentlemen, is psychology, and I had been able to gain a full appreciation of the man's healthy rectitude. Sent to Benares in your service to research the mystery created by Felifax, I resigned my mission. I did not want to trouble a man who was incapable of harming English property and had never done any harm to anyone. Far from it–he sought to help the oppressed. The only person injured by the affair was Sourina, the high priest of the temple of Kali and the young man's adoptive father, who had no wish, in any case, to make any complaint against the child he had raised. He intended him, we may suppose, for a task of which I have not been informed.

"My deductive system permitted me to study this Sourina. At the very first glance, I felt an instinctive suspicion of this person awaken within me. My presentiments, gentlemen, are rarely mistaken.

"On my recent arrival in London, my daughter told me about the carver's crimes. My conviction was formed immediately: neither Felifax nor Baber–two Hindus with whom I was thoroughly acquainted–was guilty of these hideously-embellished crimes. Having been to warn Sullivan and Sir Harold Nimbly of the erroneous nature of their accusations, I set about reading the newspapers, without exception. I drew my conclusions logically. All four victims had–and this is extremely important–held important positions in the subcontinent and had left behind more-or-less painful memories of various misdeeds committed against the indigenes. It was necessary to start from that direction.

"I spent the following morning at the India Office, where the files are kept that record the activities in the colony of every citizen of the United Kingdom. I asked to see the reports on Lord Bencenave, Lady Vertemer and General Ferund. I had no need of Sexton's dossier, being already familiar with the excesses committed out there by the former surgeon-major, the perpetrator of a supremely odious action of which I shall soon inform you.

"After careful study, I discovered a very detailed report on the subject of Lord Bencenave's involvement in a rather serious matter dating from some 20 years ago. His lordship, who was then Deputy Governor of Bengal, had been the recipient of a severe reprimand for having, in the course of a religious ceremony, given a young initiate a kick 'in his honor,' as was his habit. The kick–especially its placement–was, especially to a native of high caste and the son of a high priest, an unpardonable offense. Lord Bencenave had continued to offend in this manner, aggravating his offense.

"Now, gentleman, that Brahman initiate was named Sourina, the son of the minister of the temple of Kali–a very important position, which he would hold himself after his father's death three years later.

"As for Lady Vertemer, I made a similar discovery of an item related to a matter of sacrilege. The beautiful lady, the favorite of a Maharajah of Rajputana, had appropriated a magnificent jewel ornamenting the neck of a statue of Durga the Black in a forest temple. Engraved on this unique jewel, a turquoise of astonishing dimensions, was the head of a roaring tiger with its mouth agape, with diamonds for teeth, a tongue modeled in rubies and eyes of emerald. This is definitely the jewel discovered in Lady Vertemer's house, is it not? Now, a

dubash [109] came to reclaim this gem from the indelicate Englishwoman. The latter, confronted with the great lady's refusal, had the temerity to raise his voice, in the name of the
palomen, and was slapped twice. This interpreter was named
Sourina. Three years later, the Maharajah died mysteriously,
but Lady Vertemer had already taken the mailboat to return to
England.

"Finally, in the Ferund dossier, I discovered that the general, when garrisoned in Bengal, had signed a order for the
execution of several yogis and a devadasi, whom he accused
of having organized a Sikh rebellion–an accusation subsequently shown to be false. The yogis were Sourina's disciples;
the dancer was his sister.

"Armed with these valuable items of information, my
conviction was confirmed..."

"What about Sexton?" the Lord Chancellor put in.

"Soon, milord, when I come to Felifax. Armed with this
information, I repeat, I hurried to the office dealing with Indians presently in England. There, the list of the circus personnel told me absolutely nothing. It was then that I cabled Lord
Chapfain, the Governor of Bengal, asking him whether
Sourina was in Benares at present–and if he was not there, to
give me the exact date of his departure.

"That same evening, accompanied by my friend Professor Hanson, the celebrated toxicologist, I went to the refrig-
erator room–where, after a careful examination, the master
confirmed my previous observations. Before being cut up, the
victims had been anaesthetized with the aid of curarine. At the
same time, we noted the singular neatness of the sections,
which bore no trace of saw-marks. Immediately, I thought of a
Hindu sacrificer's specially sharpened knife.

"The poison employed leaves tiny crystals. We found
them on the clothes worn by Lord Bencenave on the evening
of his murder–almost certain proof that the victim had been
surprised in the street, when Sourina or his accomplice had
cleverly contrived to cause him to breathe in the toxin. A dose
sufficient to stun him would permit him to be led away under

the pretext of helping him, in case of curiosity on the part of passers-by.

"We found more of these crystals in Lady Vertemer's central chimney-flue; they must have been the cause of the heavy sleep afflicting all the lady's servants. We also found them in the curtains of the bed where General Ferund and Dorothy Mason slept.

"I was already in possession of a sheaf of troubling evidence, knowing that Sourina had used curarine–an extract of curare obtained by its vaporization–during an operation carried out by the surgeon Sexton. I shall return to that.

"Finally, Lord Chapfain's reply arrived. Sourina had been absent from Benares since a date noticeably similar to that of the menagerie's departure. At the temple of Kali, it was thought that he was on a religious mission in the subcontinent.

"The conviction increased, but I wanted it to be irrefutable, in order to avoid any possibility of error. Maclean of Bethnal Green was the butcher who supplied horsemeat for the wild beasts; I went to see him and he employed me in the capacity of an extra delivery man. I was dispatched on the very first evening. Leaving the other employees to unload the meat, I slipped into the menagerie's private quarters. As luck would have it, I was able to see Sourina.

"My eyes could not have deceived me; it was definitely his strong and implacable face, and especially his authoritative voice, whose impression was retained by my eardrum. He perceived me and had me unceremoniously thrown out–no matter; the observations I had already made were interesting. By that means, I had noticed this: the statue of Kali ornamenting the temple was hollow, and its interior was softly padded. I understood then that Sourina had been able to leave India in the strictest incognito, and how he had entered England without being entered in any list of those present.

"I regret that my curiosity put him on his guard. He was forewarned in due course that a warrant for his arrest had been requested. That is why, seeing that he was lost, he preferred to give himself to death by means of the poison he knew so well..."

The audience was hanging on Palmer's every word. The Chancellor of the Exchequer asked: "In your opinion, have the victims' corpses been destroyed?"

"Your lordship can take that for granted–destroyed by the teeth of wild beasts after having their throats cut at the feet of Kali the Black. All these people had insulted the goddess or her disciples, Lord Bencenave had offended Sourina with his feet, Lady Vertemer with her hands and mouth–had she not insulted Kali in the person of her interpreter? General Ferund had signed the sentence of death with his right hand and had given the firing squad the order to fire himself. Sexton had conceived a notion in his malevolent brain and executed it with a surgeon's skillful hands. *All these members had committed sacrilege*, and were anathema. But why the comedy of returning the members to the homes of the victims?

"The religion demands that the profanatory part of the body may not be admitted to the purification. I can guarantee you this: surprised and anaesthetized, the victims were transported entire to the improvised temple secreted in the menagerie or sanctuary. They were cut up according to the rites of sacrifice and were sent home to be placed in their sinister settings. The menagerie had the use of three cars. The removal was effected by means of a door giving out into Exhibition Road, strictly forbidden to the circus personnel.

"Sourina was a visionary; at the same time as accomplishing his vengeance, he wanted to spread terror throughout the country he execrated. There was nothing wasted; the bodies had been given to the tigers, Kali's favorite incarnation–that is more than adequately demonstrated by the testimony of Djina, the sacred dancer who was Rama's childhood friend. She noticed traces of blood at the foot of the statue and also on the cages of the beasts, and the nights on which she discovered them were the nights of the murders."

"But how could Sourina keep track of everyone's movements?" asked the minister in charge of the India Office.

"Ah! I forgot to tell you, gentlemen, that we have arrested an interpreter at the India Office by the name of Sunsalla. He is a fervent disciple of Sourina and we found some interesting correspondence in his home. He has, in any case, made a complete confession, in a spirit of reckless bravado. This man prepared the way for the crimes; Sourina's infernal genius did the rest, and contrived the ambush at poor Sullivan's lodgings in order to further inflame public opinion. If the murder of Sir Edmund Sexton, carried out by his hands in a fit of reckless fury, had not occurred, the sequence of crimes would have continued. A dozen important people would have been targeted."

"Sourina could not have carried out his vengeance alone. He's no longer young enough to have accomplished such gymnastics."

"You're right, sir–but he commanded a troupe of acrobats unique in all the world. Terrorized, they blindly carried out his orders–even the most incredible."

"Will there be further arrests, then?"

"I see no purpose in that. It would be necessary to arrest the entire troupe, for we shall never know the names of the accomplices who carried out the instructions, nor exactly how the feats were executed. Better, in my opinion, to repatriate the entire troupe–who, having received the warmest of welcomes in England, will be able to propagate their careers elsewhere."

At that moment, a constable arrived to inform Nimbly that Sourina's corpse had been placed in a galvanized and hermetically-sealed triple coffin. Sir Eric was astonished by this ceremony, so the police commissioner gave him a brief explanation. A delegation of Brahmans had asked to see the Chancellor of the Exchequer, with a view to obtaining authorization to take their pontiff's body back to Benares. The high religious status of the dead man required that his body be burned on the bank of the Ganges, the sacred river, at the foot of the Burning Ghat. The chancellor had conceded that right.

Then, fearful of the anger of the mob, which might attack the porters, holding them to be accomplices to the murders, the Hindus had implored and obtained the right to an immediate departure. The India Office had confirmed the order. A large cargo-vessel was due to depart the following day for Calcutta; a large contingent of police would escort the troupe to Southampton overnight and put them aboard, with the body of their high priest. The only ones to remain in England would be Baber, Djina and Felifax, the last-named retained by his injury. Naturally, the troupe would not be taking anything back from the circus or the menagerie.

Once the commissioner had affirmed that it was indeed Sourina's body that had been sealed in the galvanized triple coffin, Palmer made no further objection, even though he thought the departure precipitate. He could not prevent himself from murmuring: "I shall not rest easy until after the *sati*, when the ashes are floating in the Ganges. That diabolical Brahman is easily capable of escaping from his own coffin!"

As his listeners were clamoring for the story of Felifax, the doctor asked for permission to bring in Baber, who had been released from prison that afternoon.

The brother of Rao told these horrified highly-placed persons the story of the crime perpetrated by Sir Edmund Sexton against the gentle Sita–a crime whose consequences had included the death of his brother. He did not know about the series of murders carried out by the high priest, or his hatred would have denounced him. As the avenger of Sita and Rao, he regretted not being able to strike down the chief Brahman himself. He confirmed Palmer's discovery; Sourina had indeed entered England secreted in the hollow statue of Kali.

"Felifax–or Rama–gentlemen," Palmer concluded, "was destined to defy the infernal genius of his mother's torturer. Instead of the bloodthirsty and ferocious nature appropriate to his feline ancestry, he had inherited the loyalty of his real father, the Brahman Rao, who was a son of his caste with a noble and honest mind. He similarly inherited the beauty and gentleness of his mother Sita, a descendant of the great Tamerlane. Then again, he is a scholar of amazing erudition.

"Alas, he retains certain feline traits. First of all, his tigrine scent, from which stems his great authority over wild beasts. He also has prodigious strength and supernatural agility. Then again, when he becomes angry, his eyes change to become feline and characteristic stripes appear on his body.

"Now, gentlemen, I can admit to you that, despite these blemishes, I feel a great affection for the boy, who is entitled to be called the savior of the Palmer family. As soon as he is better, I shall consent with all my heart to his marriage to Grace. The love these children share is rare."

Every hand was extended in congratulation to Eric Palmer. Once again, he had proved the science of the English police, and Britannic pride in him was fierce. The Lord Chancellor told him that the King had asked to see him on the following day.

Palmer could not prolong his visit, however; he was in a hurry to return to Charing Cross Hospital, where Grace and Djina were waiting beside a bed of pain. This time, he took Baber, who was tremulous with emotion at the thought that his brother's son might be in danger.

In the meantime, millions of lines printed by the rotary presses of England's newspapers, telephone and telegraphic cables–including submarine cables–and the Hertzian airwaves were informing the entire world of the new glory of Eric Palmer. The modest man himself, indifferent to fame, was merely a father anxious for the happiness of his daughter, merely a humble human being desirous of repaying to a noble soul the new debt of gratitude that he had contracted.

XV: The Coffin was Empty

Two months have passed. We are in Plymouth.

Felifax, resolved more firmly than ever to keep the name of Rama bestowed on him by his mother, had completed his convalescence. The vitalizing sea air, and—more importantly—his admirable constitution, had worked a miracle. He had once again become, so to speak, the near-supernatural man that he had been before his injury.

As soon as it was safe to move him, Doctor Palmer had taken him to his little house in Cornwall, where he could continue to give him the necessary care. Grace and Djina had shown themselves to be the most devoted of nurses. Rama had allowed himself to be easily convinced that the difference between races was nothing but an empty phrase when souls are beautiful. Encouraged by Palmer, they had both discussed an imminent marriage.

After the departure of Sourina's remains, a *scrivener* had brought a sealed envelope containing his will. He had left part of his considerable fortune to his adoptive son, consisting of cash and precious stones, all deposited in English banks in India. A significant part of that fortune had already been transferred to England, augmenting the receipts of the circus. The greater part of Sourina's wealth remained the property of the temple of Kali, where his mad dreams survived.

Baber had been instructed by the bed-ridden animal-tamer to liquidate the circus menagerie. The magnificent scenery was given to the Hindu museum in Kensington Palace; as for the animals, their fate was easily settled. Rama would have liked to repatriate to the jungle from which he had taken them, but Palmer had succeeded in persuading him to abandon that plan. The government would have opposed it. The wild beasts were enemies of humankind; every year their victims were very numerous. It was impossible to set "man-eaters" at liberty. Baber had been forced to dispose of the magnificent animals. Firstly, London Zoo had been given its pick of them. Others had been donated to the zoological gardens of the various European capitals, and the rest were sold to menageries for the benefit of the Paupers' Clubs of London. Rama had not forgotten his friends.

Then, one day, Palmer and Grace returned to the capital. The young woman resumed her studies with Professor Hanson, searching for a formula that was dear to her heart. The doctor had been summoned to collect a prize for his efforts that crowned his magnificent career. A public subscription opened by the *Daily Herald* would give the "king of detectives" proof of the gratitude of his fellow citizens.

In fact, surpassing all expectations, a veritable fortune had been gathered. James Macfull, the promoter of the idea, knew of the doctor's passion for the sea, and had acquired a nice pleasure-yacht. The remainder of the subscription, deposited in a bank, would pay for the appointment of a ten-man crew. On the day when this testament of sympathy was to be presented, a large crowd of people invaded the bank of the Thames at Woolwich where the yacht was moored. An immense acclamation greeted the detective who had put an end to the nightmare of the carver.

Palmer had never been so moved. He was even more emotional when the Prince of Wales came in person, on the King's behalf, to award him the Military Cross [110] in recognition of his services. His Majesty wished to consider the man who was used to risking his life for the tranquility of his equals as a soldier.

The felicitations were redoubled, but the doctor sidestepped them. He had just perceived Sullivan lurking in a corner, not daring to come forward. Racked by remorse, the Chief Inspector was but a shadow of his former self. Palmer took him in his arms and gave him the accolade,[111] restoring a measure of tranquility to that desperate soul.

A few days later, Rama and Djina, summoned by a long letter, arrived in London with Aunt Molly. The old spinster had been smitten by a veritable adoration for the handsome animal-tamer, and for his gentle little sister. She did not want to leave them, but she came to assist in the preparations for her niece's wedding.

Doctor Palmer had, indeed, decided not to put off the marriage any longer, for Grace's researches had been crowned with success. With the aid of the celebrated toxicologist Hanson, she had discovered a serum which, taken by subcutaneous injection, could suppress a feline odor. Weeping with joy, the young animal-tamer, who despaired of that blemish, wanted to begin the experiment immediately.

Finally, one morning, in the largest room in the Guildhall, the Lord Mayor of London presided in person over the union of Miss Grace Palmer and Rama Tamerlane. The bride's witnesses were Sir Harold Nimbly and Professor Hanson; the husband's were Baber and... Sullivan. The young Hindu wanted to give the unhappy policeman striking proof that he was forgiven.

In a corner of the room, hidden amid the crowd, Lady Deborah Moorhen, seized again by her passion, had come to watch the ceremony. She was already formulating the most fantastic plans for trying to win back the love of a young man who was as handsome as Antinous.[112] The foolish lady was unable to comprehend the honesty of his soul and the inanity of her hope. Rama knew no other love than that of the exquisite Grace. There was no religious ceremony. Rama, in memory of his tutor, did not want to abjure Brahmanism, and Grace had understood his feelings admirably.

That evening, the entire family embarked on the *Grateful* to depart on a long cruise. Djina never left her foster-brother; she would be Grace's little sister. The *Grateful* put out to sea. By the light of a magical sunset, Grace and Rama commenced the most beautiful of amorous duets...

The radio crackled. Eric Palmer took receipt of a cablegram from Benares, It informed him that the body of the high priest Sourina had been ceremonially burned on the bank of the Ganges. The doctor could not help releasing a sigh of relief. That devil of a man was still preying on his mind. His anxieties were, however, well-founded. The authorities in Benares had been deceived. The galvanized and hermetically-sealed triple coffin was empty on arrival in Bengal; it was the body of a Brahman, immolated for the occasion, that had been burned on the Burning Ghat.

What had become of the terrible Sourina?

Felifax
by Hank Mayo
(2006)

Afterword

As with many of the elder Paul Féval's novels, *Félifax* uses a two-part structure; it is very much a game of two halves. Although the first part sets out with the manifest intention of hybridizing the detective story with Tarzanic fantasy, it soon runs into an awkward problem.

In order to develop the character of Felifax–to explain his origins and to show him participating in the romantic idyll of life in the jungle–he must be at liberty. The detective sent to discover his secret cannot be allowed to catch up with him too quickly, because it would prevent important aspects of that work being done–and also because it would also inhibit the development of the subplot in which Felifax and Grace Palmer fall in love (as they must).

For these narrative reasons, poor Sir Eric Palmer–having been explicitly advertised as the king of detectives and the natural heir of Sherlock Holmes–is required to spend most of the first part of the story failing to achieve his supposed ends. This contrivance eventually requires him to be confined to bed with acute malaria for much of the time he spends in India.

One of the advantages of the two-part structure, however is that it allows a pause for thought and for the setting of a new course. Once Felifax's character has been established, he can then be redeployed in what is, in essence, a very different kind of story. Part Two is, therefore, framed as a robust murder mystery, and Palmer's unusual impotence in Part One becomes a key plot element, as he is deliberately removed from the action so that his belated return to solve the mystery and tidy up the plot will give him a chance to shine all the more brightly.

The attempted hybridization was, of course, always bound to fail. Adventure fiction and crime fiction pull in different directions, and the Tarzanic sub-genre is such a refined form of adventure fiction that it pulls harder than most in a direction the detective story cannot follow. In narrative terms, the triumphs achieved by Sir Arthur Conan Doyle and Edgar Rice Burroughs, like those of almost all successful novelists– prestigious as well as popular–are won primarily by managing the viewpoint of the stories, and the two sub-genres require markedly different points of view.

Doyle solved a problem that none of the French writers of crime fiction ever had: how to manage the flow of information during the gradual elucidation of a mystery in such a way as to maximize the reader's avid curiosity. By positioning Doctor Watson as a close observer of everything Holmes does, and making his understanding of the logic of the great man's actions perennially faulty, Doyle maintained and manipulated the suspense generated by the reader's continual attempts to figure out what the detective might be thinking–a very difficult task to perform using an omniscient narrative voice or using the detective as a viewpoint character.

Burroughs, on the other hand, *had* to use an omniscient narrative voice, because it was vitally necessary to his project that the reader must always know far more about the bigger picture in which Tarzan is contained than Tarzan can know himself. dramatic tension is created in Tarzanic fantasies by means of the reader knowing far more than the central character, and thus being able to see the potential for him to make terrible mistakes–or to fail to perform vitally necessary actions–because of the awkward extent and shape of his ignorance. It would be exceedingly difficult, if not impossible, to combine this narrative strategy with Doyle's.

Féval *fils*, not unnaturally, employs the simplest fallback position, using the omniscient narrative voice by default. This inevitably causes the detective story element of the novel to lose much of its energy, when it finally gets going–no reader, even in 1930, could ever have been taken by surprise by Palmer's eventual revelations. Moreover, the author's continual attempts to direct the omniscient narrative voice in such a way as to cultivate the kinds of narrative suspense typical of detective fiction drastically weaken its execution of the narrative task to which it is better adapted: that of developing the character and designing the existential predicament of Felifax.

The narrative voice is thus helplessly caught between an urge to under-inform and an urge to over-inform; it ends up giving too much away wherever it ought to be sparing in its account of detective discoveries, and not saying enough whenever it ought to be building and shaping the margin between what Felifax knows and what the reader knows.

Given this fundamental problem, it is hardly surprising that the younger Féval's attempts to hold a consistent storyline as his plot unfolds are not very successful, or that the improvisations he introduces in order to adjust its course become increasingly desperate. As is usual in such situations, it is the minor characters who suffer. Poor Baber, introduced as an ingenious man hell-bent on revenge, loses both his sense of judgment and his motive force as he is sidelined and virtually forgotten. The even-more-unfortunate Sullivan, initially introduced as a brutal device for removing Palmer from Benares, then becomes a fall guy, compelled to make all the wrong moves that Palmer will have to correct in the nick of time–and few fall guys in the history of popular fiction can ever have fallen quite as far, or quite as messily, as he does. Even Sourina is forced into the background as the plot develops, where he becomes lost in the shadows, and the narrative's final move–which attempts to open the way for a further exercise in hybridization by borrowing the essence of another 20th-century literary archetype, Fu Manchu–falls flat in consequence.

All of this is bound to annoy a sensitive reader. The most awkward narrative problem Féval *fils* has to negotiate–the management of the story of Rama's birth–is handled in a singularly maladroit fashion. Instead of taking the opportunity presented by the narrative to let the reader eavesdrop on what Sita tells Baber, Féval *fils* takes the option of letting the narrative voice tell the reader directly what the circumstances were. One result of this is that the reader never finds out exactly how much Baber knows about his brother's fate and the reasons for it–but however much or little it is, it is hard to explain why he does not share the knowledge with Felifax.

If Baber had told Felifax what Sita had said to him–which Felifax must have been very eager to know, given the tragic inadequacy of the information Féval *fils* allows Sita to give him directly–Felifax would surely not have fallen for Sourina's lies and would not have refrained from taking the vengeance that was his due. The fact that Baber refrains from polishing off Sourina himself is supposedly due to the promise he gave Sita to let Felifax have first crack at him–which makes it all the more puzzling that he withholds the information that would have allowed Felifax to fulfill his mother's ardent desire.

Whether such narrative fudges can be forgiven or not depends, of course, on the charity of the individual reader, but it is worth noting that they underline an awkward moral problem with which writers of popular fiction were always having to wrestle: the problem of whether, and how, heroic characters ought to be allowed to revenge themselves on villains.

The struggles that afflict Felifax's conscience whenever he is tempted to let himself go are really the author's struggles, and it is not surprising–even if some readers will find it difficult to forgive–that the author continually evokes *deus ex machina* devices to prevent Felifax from acting on his own inclinations lest it sully the spotlessness of his noble soul.

Popular fiction has always been caught on the horns of a dilemma in respect of plots that hinge on the desire for revenge; the priorities of melodrama demand that the moral debits incurred by the villains are cranked up to the maximum, but the priorities of conventional moralism demand that heroes should not discharge them by taking a great delight in tearing the aforesaid villains limb from limb; this problem becomes particularly acute when one's hero happens to be a tiger-man, and the younger Féval's evasions are bound to seem a trifle pusillanimous.

For my own part, the only aspect of the plot that I find unforgivable is the unhesitating nature of the stigmatization of

Sir Edmund Sexton as a dangerous psychopath far beyond the pale of any possible sympathy. I agree entirely that he ought to follow the principle of informed consent, and that his daring experiment was therefore badly-conceived, but I cannot agree that the mere idea of creating a tiger-man deserves the extreme kind of *yuck* reaction to which it is subjected by the author and his hero. If I had been Felifax, in fact, I would like to think that I could have looked at the matter of my nature a trifle more coolly, and wondered whether a process that had produced such a fine specimen as myself might not have a lot to be said for it, perhaps warranting further research–provided, of course, that one could obtain interested volunteers rather than pressing unwilling victims into service.

Perhaps, in a better world–or, a least, a better novel–Sexton could have been credited with a little more common sense and imagination, and allowed to mature into a biotechnological genius capable of transforming humankind, or at least animalkind, for the better. On the other hand, I have to remember that the novel's reflexive prejudices were almost universal in its own day, and admit that have not been much ameliorated even in the early years of the 21st century. Such is life–or, at least, melodrama.

Notes

Introduction

[1] Translated and released by Black Coat Press as *John Devil* (ISBN 978-1-932983-15-9).

[2] Two volumes already translated and released by Black Coat Press as *The Blackcoats: 'Salem Street* (ISBN 978-1-932983-46-3) and *The BlackCoats: The Invisible Weapon* (ISBN 978-1-932983-80-7). A third volume, *The Blackcoats: The Parisian Jungle*, will be released in 2007.

[3] Two Rocambole plays translated by Frank J. Morlock have been released by Black Coat Press as *Rocambole* (ISBN 978-1-932983-57-9).

[4] Three volumes pitting Arsène Lupin vs Sherlock Holmes have been released by Black Coat Press as *The Hollow Needle* (ISBN 978-0-9740711-9-0), *The Blonde Phantom* (ISBN 978-1-932983-14-2) and *The Stage Play* (978-1-932983-16-6); *The Daughter of Fantômas* (ISBN 978-1-932983-56-2) is also available from Black Coat Press.

[5] Translated as "The Monkey King" in the Black Coat Press anthology, *News from the Moon* (ISBN 9781-932983-89-0). The story features none other than Captain Nemo.

[6] The elder Féval's own stage play adaptation of *Les Mystères de Londres* was translated by Frank J. Morlock and released by Black Coat press as *Gentlemen of the Night* (978-1-932983-81-4).

Part One

[7] Féval *fils* has *Dourga-ponjah*, although the "n" is presumably a misprinted "u" (the original version of the story was probably a handwritten manuscript recorded in haste). The *Durga-puja* lasts for nine days, around the beginning of October, and involves a considerable amount of extravagant mer-

rymaking. Durga "the Inaccessible," like Kali "the Black" and Chandi "the Fierce," is one of the malignant forms of the Hindu mother goddess whose milder manifestations include Devi and Parvati.

[8] A *bayadere* is a temple dancer, although the term eventually broadened out to encompass any singer/dancer working in a similar style.

[9] Féval *fils* adds his own parenthetical note identifying *arak*– which he renders as "*arrack*"–as *eau-de-vie*. In its narrowest definition, it is distilled from rum and flavored with local fruits, but the term was used much more generally in British India to refer to any kind of hard liquor.

[10] The word *ghat*, derived from one signifying a mountain pass, was adapted to describe the steps descending to the river that served as jetties used for ritual bathing in Benares and other locations on the Ganges.

[11] The name given by Féval *fils* to this character in the original French novel was "Sir Ralph Kidnapper," a distracting and unlikely surname for a chief of police.

[12] The printed text has *dobaski* here and *debaski* when the term is used again, at a point annotated in Note 63. The "k" may be a misprinted "h," occasioned by the same careless handwriting as the error observed in Note 7, and the "e" in the second instance is surely a misprinted "o"–the version borrowed into English is also given in Webster as *dobash*, although I have used dubash because it is the more usual variant. Féval *fils* adds his own definition in the text, which I have translated.

[13] Féval *fils* adds a parenthetical note signifying that this term means Brahmans, but it is not among the Indian words borrowed into English recorded in Webster or the OED and it does not feature in Thomas Craven's *English/Hindustani dictionary*. It crops up again on two occasions, where I have similarly let it stand.

[14] Féval *fils'* parenthetical note defines *gopis* simply as *femmes* (women). Again, Webster records no equivalent English adaptation.

[15] Féval *fils* has *commissary*, which is the most obvious English equivalent of the French *commissaire*, but I have substituted the term most likely to be employed in the relevant context.

[16] The reference must be to the Baber or Babur (1483-1530) who was allegedly a relative of Timur-Leng (see Note 47) and the founder of the Mogul Empire in India. That Baber was a Muslim and could not have qualified his descendants to be Brahmans, but Féval *fils* is generally insensitive to the distinctions between Indian religions.

[17] A *devadasi*, like a *bayadere*, is a dancing girl attached to a Hindu temple.

[18] Féval *fils* has the more colorful *la tarantule de greffes humaine*; I have used the English phrase with the closest metaphorical significance. The notion of accomplishing quasi-miraculous results by means of grafting animal tissues into human subjects had, indeed, been lent a sensational fashionability in the period when Féval *fils* wrote the novel by virtue of publicity given to the experiments of Serge Voronoff. Voronoff proposed that the major component of human aging was the decline of the endocrine system, and that virility could be renewed in male patients by the transplantation into the abdominal cavity of testicles derived from various ape species (christened "monkey glands" by the press). It eventually transpired that any advantage that may have been conferred by the renewal of the patient's testosterone supplies was offset by the fact that the transplanted glands were often infected with syphilis.

[19] Féval *fils* adds his own note here to define *kimki* as domesticated elephants.

[20] The word rhizome, which exists in both French and English, signifies a root-like stem; rhizomes are usually manifest in clusters at ground level.

[21] Féval *fils* adds a parenthetical note identifying *apsaras* as winged female *génies* (nature spirits); they are the water-nymphs of the Hindu paradise.

[22] A *lamba* is a kind of loincloth.

[23] Féval *fils* uses *arroyo* where I have substituted "stream." Although *arroyo* is not a French word and is familiar in Americanized English, it is usually used with reference to watercourses that have run dry; the various ones indicated here are certainly full of water, so the substitution seemed reasonable.

[24] Tanagra was a town in ancient Greece, some 25 miles from Athens, whose necropolis was excavated in 1874, revealing a host of beautiful terra-cotta figurines; it is to one of these that Djina is being compared.

[25] In fact, a *sarangi*–Féval *fils'* *sarangue*–is more like a viola than a mandolin, more often played with a bow than plucked.

[26] The text has *naharatti*, which is obviously a transcription error for *maharatti*–a term rendered correctly in part two; I have substituted the usual English term for the relevant language, *Maharashtri*.

[27] Kalidasa was reputedly the greatest India poet of all time; his dates are uncertain–the estimates current in the younger Féval's time ranged from the first century B.C. to the seventh century A.D. Kalidasa was certainly the author of the classic drama *Shakuntala* (first translated into English, to great acclaim, by the famous botanist and colonial officer Sir William Jones in 1789) but many of the other works attributed to him were probably by other hands. I have translated Féval *fils'* *mélopée* as "refrain" because that is what he means; its immediate English equivalent, melopoeia, is not used in quite the same way on the rare occasions when it is used at all. Strictly speaking, melopoeia is the art of inventing melodies, but the French version can be used to refer to any repetitive melodic composition.

[28] Féval *fils's* *larmier*, for which I have substituted "cornice," exists in English as well as in French, but it seems to me that he might be using it a trifle carelessly. In an architectural context, the word can refer to various kinds of teardrop-like pendant structure, including many that might be suspended

from a cornice–the horizontal part of an arch–but it would be very unusual to find a larmier big enough to hide behind unless it was still attached to its supportive structure.

[29] It is not obvious how the stream contrives to flow in both directions, but it does seem to.

[30] Cinchona, also known as quinquina, is the Peruvian tree from whose bark quinine is manufactured; it was deliberately introduced into India in order to provide supplies of tonic water and anti-malarial medicine. It is unlikely that cinchona trees would have been growing wild in more-or-less untracked jungle, although Felifax obviously contrived to find one. A febrifuge is a medicine intended to combat fever.

[31] Like a *lamba*, a *langouti* (or *langooty*, as Webster renders it) is a kind of loincloth; at the time when the novel was written, it was still the standard dress of many Indians of the lowest rank.

[32] A *purdah* is a screen designed to hide women from public view; *zenana* is normally synonymous with harem, although the modifying adjective is all-important in this instance.

[33] Féval *fils* does not define *matta* at this point in the text, but when the term recurs in Chapter XIII, he adds a parenthetical note defining it as "convent."

[34] Féval *fils* adds a parenthetical note defining Kama as love; he is a Vedic personification very similar to the Greek Eros, often represented as a winged boy armed with a bow and arrow.

[35] Danaë, the mother of Perseus, was visited by Zeus/Jupiter in the form of a shower of gold.

[36] I am not entirely certain why Féval *fils* uses the adjective *insoupçonée* (unsuspected) here, but the implication is that the favorite's perception of the relevant odor is subliminal. (The idea of pheromones had not yet been popularized when the story was written, so Féval *fils* deserves due credit for anticipation if this is, in fact, what he means.) Although there are several other passages in the novel that imply that Felifax's feline odor is clearly distinguishable, there are also several

encounters in which one might expect it to be noticed (as, for instance, by Grace and Sir Eric), but where no mention is made of it in the text. The likelihood is that Féval *fils* simply forgot about it at one or two points where he might have been expected to call attention to it–but he also suggests at one point that it is variable, and it is slightly surprising that he did not take more advantage of that possibility. The fact that Felifax's presence invariably has a distressing effect on animals is, of course, not incompatible with the possibility that humans only perceive it subliminally, unless Felifax is in a state of arousal.

[37] The word kurbash (Féval *fils* renders it *courbache*) comes from Turkish; it refers to a kind of whip used as an instrument of punishment in the Ottoman Empire.

[38] Hematuria is blood in the urine; adding the adjective "bilious" makes no medical sense, but Féval *fils* is presumably attempting to imply that Sir Eric's symptoms are wide-ranging.

[39] Féval *fils* has *rat musqué*, but he must mean the Indian musk shrew rather than the American muskrat.

[40] A *vanaprastha* is a forest-dweller. The term is often used in the context of a philosophical account of the supposed four phases of a man's life, but in that instance, it refers to a post-maturity in which men are tempted to become hermits in order to put the stresses of work and family life behind them. It is obviously being used in this instance as a straightforward description of Felifax's way of life.

[41] Ardhanari means "half female"; this version of Shiva symbolizes the unity of the generative principle.

[42] Féval *fils* adds a parenthetical note here defining *guru* as a priest of Shiva, although the more general reference of the term is to a religious instructor.

[43] Féval *fils*' parenthetical note describes a *khanjar* (he has *kandjar*) as a *poignard solide* (stout dagger), although the weapon's principal distinguishing feature is the curvature of its blade.

[44] Rama is the hero of the *Ramayana*, an epic poem composed describing a war between the Aryan invaders of India and the kingdom of Ceylon. In the poem, Rama's wife, whose name is Sita, is kidnapped by the King of Ceylon and has to be rescued; the name has, therefore, considerable personal significance for the former priestess, especially in her present circumstances.

[45] *Arya* is a Sanskrit term equivalent to the English "noble;" its most common derivative is "Aryan" (see Note 58). I am unable to make a reasonable guess as to exactly which spider species Féval *fils* intends to indicate.

[46] A *dupetta* is a kind of long scarf or shawl. The reference to *nirvana* is a trifle misleading; the term's Hindu usage differs slightly from its more familiar Buddhist reference, indicating the extinction of the flame of life and reunion with Brahma, but remains a destination that is only achieved at the terminus of a long sequence of incarnations.

[47] Tamerlane is a Western corruption of the name of Timur-Leng (Timur the Lame), a Tartar conqueror originating from Samarkand, who ravaged India in 1398. He had previously conquered much of central Asia and Persia in an attempt to reconstitute the empire once assembled by Genghis Khan, from whom he claimed descent. He is just as unlikely as Baber to be claimed as an ancestor by a prestigious Brahman.

[48] Féval *fils* has *cojana*; I have altered the spelling to correspond with the way Indian words are usually rendered in English, although no dictionary I have been able to consult recognizes either formulation. Its intended meaning is obvious from context.

Part Two

[49] Kensington Palace–a former royal residence–was opened to the public before Féval *fils*' novel was written, but it was not a venue of popular entertainment. One might infer at this point that the circus is in a tent pitched in Kensington Gardens close to the palace, but subsequent references leave no doubt that

the circus really is set up inside the palace–a highly unlikely circumstance.

[50] Amadou is a spongy substance made from a fungus. Commonly known as "German tinder," because it was often used in fire-making devices before the invention of safety-matches, it was also employed as a styptic to inhibit blood-flow. Although Féval *fils* introduces the room in which the feet are found as a "dressing room" (giving the phrase in English), he subsequently refers to it as a *cabinet de toilette*–which can mean the same thing, but can also mean an *en suite* bathroom. If the latter is the intended meaning, the implication is that the feet are positioned as if the person to whom they belonged were sitting on the toilet.

[51] Féval *fils* has *magistrates* where I have substituted "police officers." His grasp of British police procedure is a trifle shaky; in France, the primary duty for the investigation of serious crimes falls to a court-appointed *juge d'instruction* (investigating magistrate), who can call upon the services of subordinate agents, and the author is evidently assuming (wrongly) that something similar happens in England. His reference to an "attorney" accompanying the policemen (which I have left in place) derives from the same misunderstanding.

[52] Féval *fils* has *le joli quartier de Newington*. He must mean Stoke Newington, situated between Tottenham and Hackney, although it was not conspicuously *joli* (pretty) at the time the novel was written (or at any other time).

[53] If the victim were a mere baronet, he would not be known as "Lord Bencenave" but as Sir Something-or-other Bencenave, but Féval *fils* is obviously unacquainted with the conventional use of such titles within the English peerage.

[54] Féval *fils* actually has the "attorney" use the word "whimsical," given in English, but adds a parenthetical note translating it into French as *bizarre*. I have retained the latter word, which seems more appropriate.

[55] It becomes obvious here–although there remained some ambiguity about it in Part One–that Féval *fils* believes Plymouth to be in Cornwall. It is, in fact, in the county of Devon. There is also a region of Brittany called *Cornouaille* and the French routinely use that name (sometimes rendered in the plural) to signify either or both of two regions vaguely defined by their former employment of one of the Celtic languages. Although the younger Paul Féval was born and brought up in Paris and the Féval family was not originally from Brittany, Paul Féval senior was exceedingly proud of the distant association his mother's family had with the ancient Breton aristocracy, and liked to think of himself as a true Breton. The elder Féval routinely retained a measure of sympathetic fellow-feeling in the treatment of British Celts in his works, which did not extend to Englishmen of presumed Anglo-Saxon or Anglo-Norman descent; his son's insistence on making Sir Eric Palmer a "Cornishman" and Sullivan a Welshman–despite their names and all other cultural appearances–may reflect this prejudice.

[56] Féval *fils* presumably means to imply that his lordship is fond of delivering kicks up the backside rather than anything more intimate and damaging, but members of the British aristocracy are capable of anything–except, perhaps, consenting to be driven around on a regular basis by a driver named "Smell."

[57] The Golden Temple of Amritsar is one of the most important focal points of the Sikh religion; it has been repeatedly destroyed by Muslims and rebuilt. The name Amritsar (Amrita Saras) was originally that of the lake on whose shore the temple stands; its literal meaning is something like "pool of ambrosial nectar," but it is commonly referred to in English as the Lake of Immortality.

[58] Féval *fils* has *aryas* and *cakias*. Although the usual French derivative of the former term is *aryen*, there is no doubt that he is referring to the original meaning of the term rendered into English as Aryan. Long before its corruption by the Nazis,

Aryan meant a member of the upper castes of India (it was subsequently adapted to refer to members of a racial group that probably occupied the Iranian plateau before conquering and occupying most of India). Although "khaki" only exists in English with reference to the color of army uniforms, the term was originally derived from a Hindu word (meaning "dust-colored") that was routinely used to refer to the presumed descendants of the original population of India before the Aryan conquest–i.e., the dalits, often stigmatized as "untouchables."

[59] The city of Ahmedabad–now more usually spelled Ahmad-abad–had been one of the most important in India in previous eras; it was the capital of an administrative district in British India. located on the west coat north of Bombay. Amritsar is much further north, in the Punjab.

[60] *Sati*, often rendered in English as *suttee*, is a custom by which wives were sometimes immolated on a husband's funeral pyre–a practice that the British rulers of India tried hard to suppress.

[61] Ghazipur was a district within the Benares division of British India, located on the River Ganges.

[62] Féval *fils* has Jepore, a spelling often used in English language references of the time, but the more familiar spelling was also in use then and is invariable today. Jaipur was then a native state in the Rajputana region of British India, celebrated for its architecture.

[63] Féval *fils* includes his own footnote here, not so much to define *ceste* (a Greek term for a bridal girdle, of a type worn by Aphrodite) as to offer a comment on its significance in the context of his description; he quotes three lines from a poem by Théodore de Banville which translate thus: "*While Venus de Milo, the living sculpture / Without pronouncing a word, undid her girdle, / And, in their majesty, unveiled her bare breasts.*" Of the various possible meanings of *facia* (more usually spelled *fascia*) the one intended is the Latin equivalent of *ceste*.

[64] Cramoisy (the direct English equivalent of Féval *fils'* *cramoisie*) is a profound red not unlike crimson; nacarat–identical in French and English–is defined in Webster as "the color of geranium lake," which tends towards orange.

[65] The reference is to the Heraldic sinople–which is a shade of green–rather than the color of the mineral of that name, which is dark red.

[66] A canephore was a Greek basket intended to be carried on the head, or an artistic representation of a basket-carrier on an item of pottery or a mural.

[67] The word *mahouliste* does not appear in any dictionary that I have been able to consult, so I am unable to specify the kind of circus performer to which it is supposed to refer, although its similarity to "mahout" suggests that it may have something to do with instructing elephants.

[68] Féval *fils* has *Diva-i-Kas*; the Dewan-i-Khas was the hall of private audience in the magnificent palace built by Shah Jehan in the mid-17th century when the Mogul Empire reached the peak of its architectural achievements.

[69] This is a slightly better English version than the one Féval *fils* gives, and is also a more accurate rendition of the French version he gives in parentheses thereafter.

[70] I have been able to find references confirming what is obvious from the context–that a *bansuli* (Féval *fils* has *bansoulis*) is a musical instrument–but none that offer more specific information.

[71] *Rusma* is a depilatory compound made from orpiment (arsenic trisulphide) and quicklime; its side-effects must surely be uncomfortable.

[72] A *vina* is an Indian musical instrument that had initially resembled a seven-stringed harp, but had been remodeled long before the 20th century as something more like a guitar, with two resonating gourds at either end of the fingerboard.

[73] Killing the Nemean lion was one of the 12 labors of Hercules.

[74] At this point, the book version of *Londres en folie* reproduces the text of the letter in full, but this is obviously unnecessary in a single volume edition, so I have omitted it.

[75] Féval *fils* gives this name in English (as *Seals-Club*), adding a note translating it into French as *Club des Phoques* (the kind of seal indicated is the marine mammal). Although the younger Féval's readers could hardly have been expected to be aware of it, *Le Club des Phoques* was the title of the *nouvelle* that had been his father's first important publication, in the Avril 1841 issue of the prestigious *Revue de Paris*.

[76] Féval *fils* attempts unsuccessfully to render the last-named alternative into English as *very-fond*.

[77] Féval *fils* adds his own footnote here, which translates as: "Catullus said jokingly of Silva: 'The curt scent that is, in you, a resident goat...' " The Roman poet Catullus was very fond of such earthy references, and I have not been able to ascertain which of his works is the source of this one.

[78] Féval *fils* misquotes the conventional phrase as "of the fair mirror."

[79] British convicts were no longer transported to Australia in the 1920s, but Féval *fils* is merely continuing the tradition of his father's melodramas, which continually harp on about the practice.

[80] Féval *fils* has *le tombeur de Glozel*; Glozel was the site of a notorious and highly controversial architectural "discovery" in 1924 when a number of stone and ceramic artifacts were uncovered that bore undecipherable inscriptions. The majority opinion was and is that it was a hoax, but a small core of believers still insist that the objects were Neolithic in origin and evidence of a hitherto-unsuspected culture.

[81] The printed text has Radjpootama but the "m" must be a mistranscribed "n." Rajputana was the collective name given in British India to a group of 20 native states in the northwest–including Jaipur–which had been taken over by the Mahrattas after the collapse of the Mogul Empire.

[82] Runjeet Singh (1780-1839) was the Maharajah of the Punjab, who organized his petty empire with the aid of the French before making a treaty with the British. The Koh-i-Noor diamond (whose name means "mountain of light") was acquired by Queen Victoria in 1849 as a result of the Treaty of Lahore, which concluded the Sikh Wars; it had previously been in Afghanistan and Persia, and had probably belonged to the Mogul emperors before that. Ayub Khan, a younger son of Shere Ali, became a claimant to the Afghan throne after his father's death and used opposition to the British as a means of gaining popular support before being defeated in 1880 at the battle of Kandahar and overthrown the following year.

[83] Tippoo Sahib, or Tipu Saib (1749-1799) was one of the most successful of the Indian princes in putting up long and stern resistance to the British; his forces won several notable battles before his final defeat by Cornwallis at Arikera in 1791; he ceded half his dominions thereafter, but continued to conspire against the colonial regime and renewed his opposition in the year of his death.

[84] Féval *fils* renders this phrase in English; I have left it untouched, partly because it is a calculated echo of his father's account of the advertisement of a circus in London in *La ville vampire* (available in a Black Coat Press translation as *Vampire City*, ISBN 978-0-9740711-6-9), but mainly because the strange implication it carries–however startling it might seem– is fully intended, as the following sentence demonstrates. I have, however, altered the subsequent phrase rendered in English, *really exciting*, to "truly exciting," because the latter reads better.

[85] Alcides was Hercules' family name.

[86] Féval *fils* gives this speech in English, then adds a parenthetical French translation. I have changed his "always" to "still," that being a more apt translation of his *toujours* in this instance.

[87] Féval *fils*' list is "*dancings, les public-house's, les spirit-shop's, les tap's*," which anticipates the increasing fashion-

ability what would now be called the greengrocer's apostrophe but is otherwise far from *au courant* with contemporary slang. His father had made much in *Jean Diable* (available in a Black Coat Press translation as *John Devil*, ISBN 978-1-932983-15-9) of a sign he claimed to have seen in London in the 1840s advertising "Will Sharper's Spirit-Shop," but it seemed unlikely even then. Féval *fils* adds his own footnote explaining that his last three terms refer to "*tavernes, boutiques à liqueurs, beuveries du peuple*"–which translates, more modestly than the text implies, as "taverns, off-licenses [and] popular drinking-dens."

[88] Féval *fils* gives this title in English (although he inserts an unnecessary hyphen) and adds a French translation, "*bar des amoureux.*"

[89] The English version in the text reads: "Hand's down here, is subdner Rama," which Féval *fils* gives in translation as "*Bas les mains, c'est le dompteur Rama.*" *Subdner* is presumably a mistranscription of "subduer," but that word is rarely, if ever, used in English as a substitute for the admittedly-clumsy animal-tamer. (The most common English equivalent of the French *dompteur* is, of course, lion-tamer, but as Felifax specializes in tigers that would sound odd.)

[90] This is one of the younger Féval's attempts to replicate his father's fondness for puns; it has to strain for effect, but its macabre quality makes up for its awkwardness.

[91] Féval *fils* has "old wishfully," given in parenthetical translation as *vieille passionée*; "old flame" is the conventional English equivalent of the French phrase.

[92] Newgate Prison–a setting used to great effect by the elder Féval in *John Devil*–had been demolished in 1902 and the Central Criminal Court built on the site, so its use here is blatantly anachronistic.

[93] Alain Gerbault (1893-1941) was the first person to circumnavigate the globe single-handed, in the sloop *Firecrest*, in an unhurried journey that lasted from 1923 until 1929.

[94] *Roupie*–the French version of *rupee*–has a double meaning; it is also used as a slang term for snot.

[95] Féval *fils* adds his own footnote at this point to explain that this sentence refers to one of his earlier works, the four-volume novel *D'Artagnan contre Cyrano de Bergerac* (1925).

[96] Boar hunting had died out in England under the Stuarts, there being precious few wild boar left after 1600. There were certainly none in the late 1920s, and it would have been illegal to hunt them if there had been. Since their subsequent reintro-duction, however, there has been much talk of reinstituting the sport in the 21st century.

[97] I have retained Féval *fils*' *whoop*, although his parenthetical explanation of the term's alleged meaning would be a better definition of the English huntsman's *halloo*, sounded when the prey is sighted rather than when it is killed.

[98] The Essex Union and the Duke of Buccleuch's Foxhounds were, and still are, among the largest and most prestigious hunts in Britain–the latter is based in the Scottish borders. Both have been targeted in recent decades by anti-hunting protesters; the Essex Union was recently involved in an inci-dent which might be held to constitute the allegedly-accidental reintroduction of boar-hunting to England.

[99] *Cobs* and *drag* are given in English in the text; I have left them unaltered although the latter may convey a slightly mis-leading impression now that "drag-hunting" has come to mean hunting without live prey.

[100] Féval *fils* renders this exclamation in English as "Real business, seriously!"

[101] Although Exhibition Road does extend as far as the south-ern edge of Hyde Park and Kensington Gardens, its terminus is a long way from Kensington Palace, which is situated on the Western side of the complex.

[102] The Trimurti is the Hindu trinity comprised by Brahma (the creative principle), Vishnu (the preservative principle) and Shiva (the destructive principle).

[103] Féval *fils* has "very excentric" (*sic*).

[104] Marguerite de Bourgogne is a character in Alexandre Dumas' famous play *La Tour de Nesle*, based on a legendary mass-murderess. The elder Paul Féval was fascinated by her, continually citing her as a key exemplar in his works. It is highly unlikely that a British journalist would make such a comparison, and even more unlikely that a subeditor on the *Daily Herald* would have let it stand.

[105] The Gemonies were a flight of steps in Rome from which criminals were flung into the river Tiber.

[106] Féval *fils* has "Most fantastical!", but translates it parenthetically as "*Très bizarre!*"

[107] Féval *fils* has "dead-house," which he translates parenthetically as "*morgue.*"

[108] This is almost exactly as Féval *fils* renders it, although I have reversed the order of "Old" and "stubborn" and contracted his "I will."

[109] See Note 12.

[110] Féval *fils* has "Red military Cross," which is meaningless in itself but might be intended to refer to the Victoria Cross, which has a red ribbon; Palmer would not have been eligible for that award–nor, in all probability, for the Military Cross, although the text takes care to provide an excuse for that.

[111] This is even less plausible than a policeman receiving the Military Cross. Frenchmen often kiss one another on the cheeks on ceremonial occasions, but Englishmen never do, under any circumstances whatsoever.

[112] Antinous was a page and favorite of the Roman Emperor Hadrian, who became a popular subject for sculptors after drowning himself in the Nile, presumably driven by melancholy. The comparison is slightly odd, but might be intended to re-emphasize Lady Deborah's perversity.